Contrariwise

A Tale of Twins

LM Foster

This is a work of fiction. Names, characters, places and incidents are products of the author's imagination. Any resemblance to actual events, locales, organizations, or persons, either living or dead, is entirely coincidental.

Cover Photos by Marie Gammage

9th Street Press
www.9thstreetpress.com

"I know what you're thinking about," said Tweedledum: "but it isn't so, nohow."

"Contrariwise," continued Tweedledee, "if it was so, it might be; and if it were so, it would be; but as it isn't, it ain't. That's logic."

– *Through the Looking Glass* – Lewis Carroll

MARY

When my sister Madeline and I were twelve years old, my parents went through a messy divorce. When I say messy, I don't mean that there were domestic scenes and cops, lawyerly coups d'état, or anything else that might seem to scar my sister and me in later life. But the separation of twins cannot help but leave some marks. Twins belong together.

Madeline and I are what they call mirror twins – she's left-handed and I'm right-handed. They say the lefty is always the evil twin. But that remains to be seen, as I tend to be a little evil myself.

Anyway, back to Mom and Dad's divorce. They had been married for fifteen years when the axe fell, and I can't imagine what *that* must be like. Maddie and I are almost twenty-six now, and a fifteen *month* relationship is a year more than either of us have ever lasted. By the time Mom and Dad were our age, we were already a year old – I can't imagine having a little baby right now any more than I can imagine fifteen years with the same person, so . . . I dunno.

Dad was bored, I guess. He hooked up with a fresher version of Mom, a little younger, a lot dumber. Maybe it was one of those mid-life crisis things – do men have mid-life crises in their mid-thirties? I dunno. All I know is that he had moved on to greener pastures by the time he was thirty-seven.

Dad would've stayed married to Mom. You know how men are; they're never anxious to change the status quo. He liked the big house we lived in, the luxuries that two established incomes provided. His little-on-the-side, Erica – she didn't care. She was ten years younger than Dad, and probably had a little-on-the-side of her own.

But Mom was betrayed and devastated, unforgiving and sure. Dad's indiscretion was the last straw. Maddie and I were not aware that there had been other straws, but apparently there had been, or perhaps infidelity was the one unforgivable sin to Mom. Regardless, she wanted a divorce, and Dad, caught red-handed, did not fight it. He just shrugged, signed the papers, and looked forward to the next stage of his life, one that didn't involve monogamy.

Dad was never one of those men that needed a woman to take care of him, anyway. He knew how to feed himself, knew how to keep the house clean, pay the bills on time. Dad loves women, don't get me wrong – he just never needed one to take care of him. So I think he relished the new freedoms more than anyone would have guessed.

Mom, on the other hand, was done. She'd never shared old-boyfriend stories with us – I dunno, is that something moms do? So I don't know if Dad was her first and only – maybe he was. Maybe that's why she took his stepping out on her so hard, with so little sense of humor. But as far as I know, she hasn't had a boyfriend in all of the years that she's been divorced.

Maybe I'm the only one that thought their divorce was messy. There wasn't any discussion on who would go with whom. No one asked us if we wanted to stay together – that always struck me as shoddy, breaking up the set, a sure sign of failure. It was like Dad's winding up with not a single plate or bowl that matched. Everything just got thrown into a box when we moved out, helter-skelter, pell-mell. Messy. For the first year or so, everything about Dad just screamed divorcee. He was so obviously the loser in the fight. We moved into a tiny apartment; we were broke while he bought furniture and household goods to re-establish himself as an individual; the dishes didn't match.

There was no reason that Mom couldn't have kept both of us, except that I think somewhere in there, there was the idea of a *burden*. It would be unfair, a burden, for Mom to raise us all by herself. It would be unfair for Dad to not get to watch at least one of his little girls grow up, and it would certainly be unfair for him to get off scot-free in the burden department – why should Dad get to be all on his own again, footloose and fancy free, while Mom was saddled with two kids?

There was no discussion about who would go with whom, either, because I had always been daddy's girl, whereas Maddie had always taken more to Mom. If there had only been one of us, we would have no doubt experienced that glory that only children encompass – the unshakable love of both parents. But I guess when you have two at the same time, and there are two diapers to change and two bottles to warm, one parent just picks a favorite, and gravitates toward that one. I was Dad's favorite, so when the divorce happened, I moved out with Dad, and Maddie stayed in the big house with Mom. There was no discussion.

It wasn't like we were moving across the world apart from each other, anyway. Just across town. We wouldn't go to the same school anymore, but that was okay. I went to the fenced-in public school down the street from our tiny, crummy apartment, and Maddie continued on at the sleek little split-level middle school that I had once looked forward to attending, surrounded by a park and sitting on a grassy hill in our old neighborhood. It was all okay, though. No one would stare at us for being twins anymore; each September wouldn't bring the same dumb questions from new peers; teachers would not comment on our similarities.

And the custody arrangements allowed us to see more than enough of each other anyway, allowed us to never get stale. Mom had us both one weekend, Dad had us both one weekend, then Mom and Dad switched off with the opposite twin. This all lasted until we were sixteen and old enough to drive. Maddie of course went to the rich kids' high school, and I attended the more rough and tumble one closer to our apartment. By the time we were sixteen, our structured visitations slacked off a bit. By that time, we both had other things to do besides see our parents on the weekends.

MADELINE

The change that was the most noticeable in my life when Dad and Mary left was that the silliness was gone. They were always giggling and making jokes. Someone has to be the jokester, and someone has to laugh – Mom and I were always the audience. It wasn't that Mom was stern or overly serious – she was just not funny or giggly like Dad and Mary. And I missed that for a while. Mom was what one might call stand-offish. She always considered herself to be a realist – *if you suspect the worst about people, you'll seldom be disappointed* was more or less her philosophy on life.

But I guess Dad disappointed her – she'd never dreamt the worst about Dad, that he was a *philanderer.* I remember hearing my mom say that word to someone on the phone – *We are getting divorced because Larry is a philanderer* – and I remember having to go look it up. It was one of those words that you cannot even guess what it means by just its sound alone. I suppose, had we been religious, she would've used *adulterer,* instead.

At twelve years old, I of course didn't understand the pain that cheating can cause, the actual physical sickness it can bring on, nor even at twelve could I understand the emotional damage. But even as I got older, it always seemed to me that it was not the physical betrayal or even the emotional havoc of promises broken that led Mom to divorce Dad. I always got the impression more of disgust than anything else. Mom didn't cry in front of us, she didn't scream at him. The attitude I always got from Mom about Dad's infidelity was as if the much beloved and much pampered family dog had done his business, smelly and messy, in the middle of the living room rug, and then Mom had accidently stepped in it, perhaps barefoot. Mom didn't blame the other woman – but Dad was apparently too unconcerned to know better than to shit where he ate, and that was just too disgusting for Mom. So he had to go.

And just so it didn't seem that she was that upset about it, she let him take Mary with him. Mom wasn't cruel or vindictive over Dad's betrayal. She would never even attempt to punish him by not allowing him to see his daughters. Our custody trades were always cordial and pleasant – no screaming hostility, no hatred openly displayed in the driveway for the neighbors to witness. Just a matter-of-fact *Hi, how ya doin', here's your other daughter, see ya on Sunday evening.* Neat, orderly, efficient. Mom wouldn't have had it any other way, and Dad just went along with the flow, as he always did.

I missed Mary terribly for the first few months, and Dad, too. The house just seemed too quiet. Mom would go over my homework with me, and we would have dinner and watch whatever was on TV, but when it came time to go to sleep, I missed my sister. They say that the bond between twins is special. I don't know if it's any different than between any other sisters, or even between close friends. I didn't miss our *bond* – I missed *her*, herself, someone to talk to before I drifted off to sleep.

But there was the phone, and the internet, so I never really missed her. We spoke every day, even if we didn't see each other every day. On the weekends, our favorite game was to try to dress as alike as possible, just by describing what we wanted to wear beforehand. Since we had always favored identical clothes, it was not really that difficult – I would pick the outfits one weekend, and Mary would pick them the next. We enjoyed dressing alike, wearing out hair the same way. We enjoyed looking at each other and it being like looking in a mirror. My sister was beautiful: petite, blonde and blue-eyed, with a pixie smile that could melt stone. So was I.

Mom and Dad were always proud and indulgent of this aspect of our personalities – no matter our individual differences in outlook and temperament, behavior and handedness, when we were kids, my sister and I always dressed exactly the same, at least when we were scheduled to be together.

Erica, Dad's first girlfriend, was freaked out by the fact that Larry's little girl had a twin sister. I've heard that some people are unusually fascinated by twins, and some people are just as unusually freaked out, and Erica was one of the latter. I heard her mention something about *The Shining*, once. Maybe it was the circumstances – there were only two of us *sometimes*.

Erica couldn't tell us apart any more than anyone else could when Mary and I were together, but when I was there to visit Dad by myself, and Mary was with Mom, it would only take Erica a few words to know it was me. I was more subdued than Mary, she said, more respectful. Maybe she found me more subdued, because, whenever my sister and I were at Dad's house, dressed identically, as always, it never failed to amuse Mary to say, "Come play with us, Erica. Forever and ever and ever."

Erica and Dad's marriage-ending relationship didn't last more than six months after Mom threw him out. On the other hand, I don't know how long it had been going on before my mother discovered the damning evidence of their affair, a hotel receipt in his pocket. Just as sordid and clichéd as that. I overheard the expression *biological clock* one Saturday afternoon, and then I saw Erica no more.

During the lull between Erica and the next one, Dad called Mom one Sunday afternoon and asked if he might come in and say a few words to her when he dropped me off and picked Mary up. Mom, ever cordial, said, "But of course." Mary and I sat on the patio and pretended to be talking, but we were really watching our parents. The driveway exchanges had always been pleasant, but Dad never came into the house, so this was an oddity to us. They were sitting across from each other at the kitchen table, near enough that we could hear what they were saying if it wasn't for the sliding glass door.

Dad leaned forward and smiled. He tilted his head at Mom a little, and asked her something.

"He's asking to come back!" I said to Mary. "He wants to get back together."

Mary studied Dad's smile. Whatever he had asked Mom hung in the air for a moment. Dad raised his eyebrow a little, smiled wider, waiting patiently for her answer.

"I don't think that's what he asked," Mary said. "I'm not sure what it is, but I don't think it's that."

Mom hesitated another heartbeat and then threw back her head and laughed.

Dad's smile didn't dim. He just shrugged and looked out the window at us. He nodded toward the front door and Mary arose. She gave me a hug. "I don't think he asked to come back," she repeated.

"Maybe it was just a joke," I suggested.

Mary and I would witness this same exchange on two other occasions. Once when we were fifteen, right after Dad had broken up with Kelly, and once, a few days before our sixteenth birthday, right after he'd broken up with Marcia.

Again we were sitting on the patio, on the other side of the glass door from them, pretending not to watch. Mary studied Dad's expression through the glass – it was the same as it had been on the two previous occasions – a little playful smile, a raised eyebrow, a question lingering in the air.

Realization dawned on Mary and her eyes widened. "Oh, my God, Maddie!" she whispered to me in awe. "He's asking her if she wants to get a little!"

"Get a little . . .?" And then I realized what she was talking about. "Oh, my God, Mary, no!" I looked in at Dad, and it hit me, too. His face held no seriousness, like it would if he was asking for

6

reconciliation. Just a sly, smug little grin. While I watched, he winked at Mom.

"Go for it, Dad!" Mary said, *sotto voce*.

But as she had on the previous occasions, Mom just laughed. Apparently that shit stain on the living room rug would not leave her memory long enough for her to even pet her once beloved pooch.

Good for you, Mom, I thought to myself. *Stick to your guns.*

MARY

For our sixteenth birthday, Mom and Dad, each the custodial parent of one twin, gave us their cast off cars, and each bought themselves a fresh one. Mom's was actually new, in addition to being fresh – it was a Lexus – things were good in the real estate biz that year. Dad's was a used Chevy, nicer and fresher than the beater he gave to me, but still used. Dad was a civil engineer for Caltrans, and it was a position that didn't lend itself to feast or famine, like real estate. Just a steady income. It wasn't like I wanted for anything, that I had to get an after-school job to help Dad make ends meet, or anything Dickensian like that. We were comfortable, in our little postage-stamp-sized apartment. But not new Lexus comfortable.

Maddie got Mom's Buick. Not really the kind of sporty car that a teenage girl dreams of, I told her. But I did like it. It was still shiny, unlike my Chevy, and it was all plushy and soft inside, whereas mine was all plastic. But a car was a car, and we were glad for our parents' largesse, unequal as it was.

In one of those incidents of serendipity and coincidence, one of those simple things that in and of itself makes no lasting impression, but in the big picture turns your life in an entirely different direction, my sister and I were invited to the same high school dance, then, in our sixteenth year. I had met my suitor one afternoon while getting gas, and my sister had met hers when a girlfriend from her school had introduced them at a football game. The kid was the friend's cousin from across town.

So in conversation, it was discovered that Maddie and I had both agreed to go to the same dance, and that neither of us were really looking forward to it that much, as neither of us was that impressed with these guys that had asked us. We wanted to get dressed up, we wanted to go to the dance, but our dates were just . . . *meh*.

For the first time ever, the most obvious of all twin clichés occurred to us. We decided to once again dress identically, and if we discovered that the other's date seemed more promising, we decided to switch on them. Just to see if we could pull it off.

Like Marty McFly in *Back to The Future*, we had to make sure that we didn't run into each other at the dance. The plan was simple – it would become effortless later, once we had cellphones – I would be sure to arrive at the dance a few minutes late, and Madeline would already be there, waiting in the ladies' room. She would point out her date to me, and I would point out my date to her, and if we agreed, we would switch. The dupes were unaware that there were any twins, and they didn't know either of us well enough to notice any subtle difference between who they brought and who came out of the bathroom, anyway. The trick would be in getting one of them to agree to leave the dance almost as soon as he'd arrived, lest he see his date with another date, and realize that there were two of us. It probably wouldn't matter, but why expose the secret if it wasn't necessary to do so?

My date's name was Andy. He had dark hair and the most beautiful big brown eyes. He wasn't shy — he had asked me out at the gas station, had he not? But he was quiet, rather bookish, I found, after his initial bravado. Andy just didn't have a whole lot to say. Maddie's date was named Jimmy. He was the opposite of Andy — tall and blonde, a football player. He looked like he could be our brother. Maddie and I favor our dad — blonde and blue-eyed, and that's the kind of guy I've always been drawn to. Jimmy talked a lot, Maddie said. The drive to the dance had been all him talking, she told me. Maddie was never much for big talkers, whereas I liked to listen to them, liked to hear their line, if they were polite about it.

So, as luck would have it, my sister and I did like each other's dates better than our own. We considered it a harmless bit of fun to switch on them. We even came up with the perfect trick for our names. When I came out of the bathroom, and Jimmy called me Madeline, I casually mentioned that my good friends really called me Mary, which I told him was my middle name, and didn't he want to be my good friend? Maddie did the same thing, telling my date that her name was Mary Madeline, and she actually preferred to be called by her middle name, and even liked that shortened from Madeline to Maddie.

So Andy and Jimmy, two young men that attended the same high school but didn't know each other, dated twin sisters without ever knowing the scam. It didn't last for either of us — Andy and Jimmy were not the ones. But the switching idea was now in place. We worked it throughout high school, and for a long time after that. Until Maddie thought she was in love . . . but I'll get to all that in a minute. Guys that would better like me — the sharp dressers, the talkers — always seemed to ask Maddie out, and the rough, outdoorsy types were always asking me. How's that for a twin conundrum?

When we graduated from high school at eighteen, my twin and I were finally reunited. It seemed like it would be permanently, but if you want to hear God laugh, tell Him your plans. Maddie and I got a little two-bedroom apartment together. She went to work at the *ReMax* office with Mom. Mom had offered me a position there, too – it was all to be some kind of intern/gofer/receptionist-type position until Maddie and I got our real estate licenses – but the idea of selling real estate never appealed to me. There was always a level of phoniness to it. Mom had taken us along on a few Saturday afternoon open houses, and she was not the same person that she usually was, when she was showing a house. There was always something grating to me, something unnatural to her sweetness when she would say, "Okay, now? Bye-bye, then," to prospective buyers. So, I passed on the nepotistic in at Mom's real estate office.

Instead, I got a job at a bar called *Mickey's*, within walking distance of our apartment. At first, I could only be a server, but by the time I was twenty-one, I had worked my way up, through an excellent attitude and flawless work ethic, to be a bartender. And the best part about it was that I could pick my shifts. I'd been there so long that I was the owner's buddy, his go-to girl. By the time I was twenty-two, I was assistant manager. I knew the way the place worked, inside, outside, upside-down.

Mom was never too pleased with my choice of employment. Maybe it didn't have the correct phony cachet to her, I dunno. But I loved it. The people that came into *Mickey's* were mostly cool, and like I say, I was given responsibilities beyond my years. And I loved talking to people, making friends. I'm just an outgoing kind of person, and the work suited me.

I liked working the lunch rush the best. That's when my favorite type of men would come in: all the young professionals that worked in the offices downtown.

I liked dressed-up men. A tuxedo was of course the ultimate – there is not one thing in the world better looking than a tow-headed blondie in a black tuxedo – but of course, we can't dress 'em up like that all the time. So a well-cut suit is my second favorite, a man that wears one effortlessly, who knows how to tie a tie, knows which button on the jacket to fasten, which one to leave undone, knows not to stick his hands in his pockets and ruin the line. It never ceased to amuse Maddie that I had a subscription to *GQ Magazine* – she referred to it as my *suit porn*.

If he had to dress casually, I liked to man to wear a nice button collar shirt over his tee. I wanted to tell all the dudes that came into the bar – wear clothes that fit ya boys – too tight t-shirts? What is this, *A Streetcar Named Desire*? I hated uncovered t-shirts pretty much in general – ones with sayings on them, concert tees, black tees with large pictures. Ed Hardy would close his doors tomorrow if it was up to me.

10

Do you think that I believe you're a badass just because your shirt says you are? Please.

And all the men that wore boldly-colored bowling shirts could keep them, and go talk to another bartender. You are not Don Draper on vacation, it is not 1969. You just look old and stupid.

And wife-beaters? There's a reason they call them *undershirts*, fellas. I'm pretty sure that you're a man, that you've got muscles – why do you think you've got to display them to me and everybody else? Put some clothes on, boy! Put on a nice tailored shirt, a tie, a well-cut jacket – let me wonder what's under there, make me want to strip you down to your undershirt, once we're behind closed doors, just to find out.

So I would go out with any of the downtown professionals that stopped in for lunch, if they were attractive, if I had a yen to find out what they had under that suit. Some of them were very nice, but mostly, I got the impression that they thought I was easy or stupid, simply because I was a bartender. So I was disappointed with the professionals, but I still always thought they were cute.

MADELINE

After we graduated from high school, my sister and I moved into an ancient but adorable apartment building downtown, not far from where she worked. I went to work with Mom and got my real estate license. But it was a busy office, and I quickly discovered that I was not entirely cut out for the cutthroat world of such a place. It was not quite *Glengarry Glen Ross*, but it was close enough. My lack of ambition made me the prime candidate for secretary, and while the pay was not as much as a salesman, neither did I have the stress. Mom said that I could always give sales a whirl, since I had my license, but I never did. All the signs had salesman's names on them anyway – when prospective clients called, they always asked for the name on the sign. Attempting to cage a sale and commission off of one of those would've amounted to theft.

Our office was in the same building as the Inland Empire office of *BF Walker*, a prominent real estate developer, and I liked to watch the field guys come in through the side door. The construction guys, the ones that worked outside with their hands. This was the type that I liked, as opposed to Mary, who always had a little yen for the suits. I had my fill of suits. I dealt with realtors and escrow officers and bankers, and I found them mostly to be smarmy and full of themselves. The construction guys seemed much more down to earth. But they never came into our office, and like I say, they only entered their own office through the side door.

Then one of the project managers from *BF Walker* stopped me in the lobby and asked me out to lunch one day, not long after my twenty-sixth birthday. I knew he was a project manager by the expensiveness of his suit, and if that was not conspicuous consumption enough, it said, *William Proten, Project Manager,* on his card.

He didn't work at the office next door, he told me, but was based in Orange County. He would only be making the drive for a month or so, he said, to get the local boys up to speed on some new project. I stifled a yawn. The only thing in the world more boring than the ins and outs of real estate are the ins and outs of real estate development, at least the design part, the part that's all really just on paper. He was older than me, maybe thirty-three or thirty-five, very suave and very blonde, all characteristics that my sister adored. He didn't do a thing for me, but I was suddenly reminded of the times in high school, when Mary and I had switched dates.

Ol' Bill Proten, confident and impeccably dressed, was just Mary's type. What could it hurt? It wasn't like he was going to be around for very long. I told him that I was not free for lunch today, but if he would call me a little later this afternoon, I was sure we could arrange something for later in the week. I gave him Mary's number and told him that I was looking forward to talking to him.

I went back to my desk and called my sister, told her about the set up. If she wasn't down, I would simply call Bill and tell him that, silly me, I'd given him the wrong number, and I'd have to endure lunch with him. That would only be polite.

But Mary was thrilled at the idea. "A project manager?" she asked, impressed. "And he'll think I'm you, office manager and all, instead of just a bartender."

"I'm not office manager, Mary, for God's sake," I said. "I'm just the secretary. Not any farther up on the *just the* ladder than you."

"You'll be office manager, someday, just like someday I'm going to be running this place," she said, and I could hear the smile in her voice. "And you wear those cute little business suits, and no one snaps their fingers at you when they want something."

"You choose to work there," I told her.

"Oh, it's not so bad. I like working here. It's just that it's not always the best place to find a date." She paused. "Okay, when he calls, I'll tell him that I'm free for dinner. If we hit it off, I'll tell him that he can't come in the office there to talk to me, because Mom freaks. I'll tell him it's a rule or something."

"Whatever works. I'm sure I can avoid him during the day. He says he's only going to be working here for a month."

"Thanks, Maddie," she said. "This is going to be fun."

.

MARY

Things went like clockwork with our little harmless deception. Bill and I hit it off immediately, and I started going out with him almost every night. For our dates, I dressed like Maddie, and wore a little less make-up than usual. It wasn't that he was any less inclined to try to get in my pants because he thought I was my prim-dressing sister instead of a bartender – he just was a little more polite about it. We had a lot of laughs, and when his month's tenure was up in Riverside, he went back to Orange County. I didn't miss him – he was not the one. He still gives me a call if he'll be in town for the weekend. The whole thing was just a little innocent fun.

It never ceases to amaze me how much my sister and I embody the term *mirror twins*. Or maybe a more accurate term would be *opposite twins*. When we dressed identically, even our parents had trouble telling us apart. But when we went to work, Maddie put on a conservative, mid-calf business skirt, and I threw on a pair of jeans and a *Mickey's* tee. All day long, she spoke to realtors and brokers, escrow officers and prospective home buyers. All day long, she talked to *money*. I spoke to beer-truck drivers and liquor salesmen, food vendors and people out to get drunk and have a few laughs.

But when it came to men and our taste in them, Maddie and I became *each other*. Each sister would put on the clothes and mannerisms that the other showed to the world, the persona that had attracted just the kind of man that the other liked. I'm not saying that I never dated men that worked with their hands, and that Maddie never dated businessmen. There was always an occasional one or two of those. But the ones that we really liked – it always seemed that we arrived at them through the old switcheroo. It just seemed that Maddie and I knew at a glance which ones would appeal the most to our sister.

On a few occasions, if there was one that was just all-around, physically attractive, despite what he was – we would even wait for a few dates to pull the scam. There was Mike, for example.

I have always preferred a long, thin, straight-haired blondie. I loved to run my fingers through all those different shades of yellow, dark at the roots then brightening out to that tow-headed platinum glory at the ends. My dad has blue eyes, the same clear powder-blue as Maddie and myself, and a blue-eyed blondie never failed to catch my attention. But the ones with green eyes – dark like emeralds; the eyes of a cat, or pale like the curious, deadly glance of a praying mantis – even a homely, green-eyed blonde would make me stop in my tracks and turn around for a second look.

And I liked men that were shaped like men, the ones with hips as wide as their shoulders, men that needed to wear a belt to keep their pants up. The broad-shouldered, narrow-waist types that my sister preferred always seemed a little too womanly to me.

And lean Mike certainly fit the bill. He was fine, with the most exquisite light-green eyes – even if he did sport two sleeves of way too colorful tattoos, even if he did play video games, even if he was between jobs when he sauntered into the bar and immediately gave me his best line. He wasn't wearing a suit, but I was in a mood that day, and he was very cute, and that weekend, I broke all of Mom's rules.

But his apartment was a mess and I could tell there was friction with his roommate. He was probably late with the rent, what with being unemployed and all. And I couldn't stand the fact that he played those insufferable games if I left the room for a millisecond. But he was cute and he was good, and even though I had tired of him after one or two weekends, the next time he walked into the bar, still out of work, but still as fine and sexy as a summer day, I told him that I had gotten a new phone number, and gave him Maddie's digits.

I told Maddie that Mom's rules were shot, and that Mike would be calling her for Round Two. Maddie giggled and agreed. He was a little thinner than she liked, and blonde, which was not her type – but still she enjoyed him for the weekend, then told him that *Mickey's* management didn't like our boyfriends hanging around, so if he came back to *Mickey's* he had to pretend that we hadn't been intimate. He came back a few times, but since Maddie and I were done with him, I made sure I was always busy, and eventually he gave up and moved on to greener pastures.

And there was Neil, who was dark and clever and single, who had waltzed into *ReMax* one Friday afternoon, looked at a few of their property listings, and then had just swept Maddie off her feet. She called me from the ladies' room at *Paul's*, the most expensive restaurant in town, and said that she'd had a little too much to drink, and asked if I could hide out when she came home, because Neil was making her forget Mom's rules, also.

"He's a little too free with the info on how much money he makes," she told me. "But I'm dying to see if he's as confident and clever in the dark."

Apparently he was, but Maddie just couldn't get past his constant bragging of his well-padded finances. So after a sisterly midnight confab, when the two of them left to take the flyer to Catalina early

Sunday morning, it wasn't the two of them at all, but Neil and Maddie's twin sister. It was a three-day weekend, and I was more than happy to take him off her hands and enjoy a little sun and shopping on Catalina, as well as whatever restaurant and hotel Neil had booked for himself and the secretary from his realtor's office. And I was definitely happy to enjoy *him*.

Maddie and I shared a few other men in the same manner. The lynchpin was breaking Mom's rules: if you were too eager, then they didn't come back. Not only did we know this, we were counting on it. A long weekend was long enough for both of us to get a turn. And when they didn't call back, that was fine with us, no one was the wiser. None of them was the one, anyway, so what did it matter if we had a little harmless fun?

****

Then they leveled an old building downtown, and started building a new one. This brought in the ironworkers for lunch and happy hour. They were a boisterous lot, mostly young, tattooed, arrogant. Many of them asked me out, and while some of them were cute, they were just not my type. I like a man with a little bit of polish to him, like my dad. Men with rough hands and a rough demeanor were more my sister's style.

A dark-haired charmer named Drew bellied up to the bar almost at quitting time one Friday and asked me what I was doing after work. He was just a little too down-to-earth for my tastes, however, even though he was cute. He still had dirt under his fingernails after all that work on the high steel, and, well . . . yuck. Bill the project manager had once asked my sister out, and now I saw the opportunity to return Maddie's favor.

In order to avoid Drew in the future, I gave him the same ridiculous lie that Maddie had given to Mike, that the management frowned on the staff dating customers – if we were gonna go out, I told him, he'd have to keep it on the DL, and pretend he didn't know me when he came in to *Mickey's*. Such an insane stricture in the modern world didn't seem to faze him, and besides, he told me, he wouldn't be in town too much longer anyway. The skeleton of the building was almost completed. The ironwork was almost done. How serendipitous, I thought. The easiest way to keep the twin thing a secret was if they weren't going to be around too long.

It had worked so well with Bill. I gave Maddie's number to Drew.

16

MADELINE

My sister had pretended to be me for her date with the project manager. She'd borrowed my clothes, did her make-up as if she was going to the office instead of the bar. I did the same for my date with Drew – I *became* Mary. I wore one of her tight, short skirts, and a pair of her stiletto heels. I did the whole smoky eye-make-up thing. I could tell that Drew was impressed, but then I reflected that he was perhaps not any more impressed than when he'd met Mary at *Mickey's*. This was more or less how Mary dressed every day, and Drew was the kind of man that she attracted.

And Drew certainly was attractive, at least to me. He was swarthy, with a perennial five o'clock shadow, and collar-length, straight black hair. He wore boots and tight pants and what is commonly referred to as vintage tees. He had a tattoo of a goldfish on his forearm, and when I asked about it, he seemed a little surprised that I didn't know about the symbolism. Apparently bartenders were usually versed in such things. It wasn't a goldfish at all, I learned, but a koi, and it was supposed to demonstrate that Drew had a lot of drive and perseverance, because in mythology, the koi was supposed to have swum up a waterfall to reach his goal. The fish symbol also meant good luck, he told me. I thought that my own luck had certainly changed when he'd tried to pick up my sister.

On our first date, we went to *Dave and Buster's* for dinner, which was nice enough, if a trifle noisy. Then we went to see the latest super-hero movie at the multiplex, which was a lot of fun. Drew was funny and silly and sexy, and when he put his arm around my shoulder in the theater, I again thanked my sister for knowing what I liked.

But when he put his hand on my bare knee, I gently pushed it away. On the rare occasions that my mother would get in her cups after she divorced Dad, she never failed to hold forth to us on the evils that men do. All clichés was Mom: *give them an inch and they'll take a mile, there's a lot of dog in a man. Make them wait, girls,* she'd tell us. *Never give in too soon. If you give in too soon, they don't come back.*

So I playfully pushed Drew's hand off my knee, even though it was hot and calloused and I liked it there very much. When the movie was over, I let him put his arm around my waist as we left the theater. He asked me if I wanted to get a drink, and I told him that I had an early shift tomorrow. I didn't invite him into our apartment, but I did allow him to push me up against the wall next to our door and kiss me like he meant it. I kissed him back and he smiled and asked if I was sure that I didn't want to invite him in.

I smiled back, wiped a little lipstick off of his mouth with my thumb. I told him that I'd love to invite him in, but I did have that early shift. Drew grinned in defeat and asked me if I'd like to go to the ballgame with him on Friday. I smiled coquettishly and told him that I'd have to check my schedule – I thought that was very bartender-y of me – but that I'd love to go to the game with him if I wasn't working.

I let him kiss me deeply again, allowed him to press his body against me, and it was great. He was just as sexy as he wanted to be, and it was only my mother's admonitions in my mind that made me bid him a swift good-night. I didn't want to let Drew know that I was willing to give in too soon. I wanted him to come back.

Drew said goodnight, said he'd call me tomorrow about going to the game, and left. When his footsteps had faded down the steps, I unlocked the door to our apartment. Mary was sitting on the couch, watching TV. She knew that I wouldn't let Drew in after only one date, so she hadn't felt it necessary to hide in her bedroom, or just be absent all together. She looked expectantly at me and said, "Well?"

"He's a cute one," I said. "He's got a goldfish tattoo."

Mary shook her head. "It's a koi, for God's sake, Maddie. It's supposed to mean that he's strong and brave and lucky." She eyed me a trifle darkly. "Is he lucky, Maddie?"

I grinned. "I would say that his luck remains to be seen. We're going to the Angels game on Friday."

Mary rolled her eyes. "How romantic. No candlelight dinner at *Paul's?*" *Paul's* was Mary's favorite place to begin a night out, but I found their cuisine over-rated and their servers to be snooty and condescending. Bill the project manager always took Mary there for dinner when he was up from behind the Orange curtain, before she brought him home and no doubt quickly divested him of his expensive suit.

"I think a ballgame *is* romantic," I said.

Mary shook her head. "Whatever floats your boat. Dad always says, 'Make 'em spend a little money.'"

"And Mom always says, 'Make 'em wait.'"

Mary grinned at me. "Are you gonna make Drew wait?"

"At least till after the game," I said flippantly. "He's only gonna be in town for a little while."

****

18

The Angels game was a lot of fun. I'm not really what you'd call a huge sports fan, but I do understand the rules to these things that seem to fascinate men so utterly. We had a few beers at the game, and this time I allowed Drew's hand to linger on my knee. He was cute, and just like his tattoo proclaimed, he seemed strong and brave. I decided enough time had passed for him to find out how lucky he could get, too. He wasn't going to be in town much longer, and if he didn't call me back after tonight, that was okay.

The Angels lost, which bummed Drew out a little bit. He asked me if I'd like to go back to his apartment and watch a movie. I said okay, thinking that it was a silly euphemism — we were both grown-ups, for God's sake, and we both knew that there was going to be very little movie watching once we were alone. But I guess I would've had to feign shock and outrage on behalf of women everywhere, would've had to trot out *What kind of a girl do you think I am?* if he would've just said, "Hey, Maddie, let's go back to my place and get it on." Even though that was precisely what we were going to do, and we both knew it. *Watching a movie* had simply taken the place of *Seeing my etchings* in the battle of the sexes' parlance.

Drew's apartment was fairly neat for a place occupied by two men — he said he had a roommate, who was, of course, conveniently absent. Drew went through all the innocent motions, picking out some other super-hero movie on Netflix, and even making popcorn. But after he dimmed the lights and we settled in on the couch, after the credits rolled on the *Spiderman/Avengers/Whatever* movie he'd chosen, the popcorn sat forgotten on the coffee table and we started making out.

I liked the feel of his calloused hands on my face and body, his masculine smell, so different, so *other*. Mary likes them to wear a lot of cologne, but not me. I like men that smell like men. My response let him know that I wasn't going to say no this time, and he was ardent, tangling his hands in my hair and kissing me fiercely. It was awesome. After several minutes, there was an unspoken signal as old as time — Drew stopped kissing me. He stood up and took me by the hand, and we went to his room.

The best thing about a first time is all that anticipation. You are so wound up: he is just so damn cute, so sexy — that's why you picked him — and you just know it's going to be great. He's going to be everything you have imagined such a cute, sexy thing *could* be, and therefore, barring some unanticipated physical letdown, it usually *is* great. It's only later on, after you already know about whatever foibles or inadequacies he has, if there are any, that it can become tiresome.

19

Drew was great. He was not as awesome as his kisses had indicated, but he was still great. I was more than willing to take advantage of him at every opportunity for the time that he was going to be in town, until the ironworking game took him to the next project, hopefully in some other city.

****

On Drew's last Saturday night in Riverside, we had our regular little date: out to dinner then back to his place to not watch movies. It was fun as always, and there were a few promises that he'd call me, once he got to Las Vegas, where the next job was. He just had a few more boxes to put into his truck and then he'd be nothing but a charming memory. He invited me to come up for the weekend sometime, once he got settled in. Perhaps. He had been a lot of fun.

The following morning, I helped Drew carry down the rest of his boxes. We were standing on the curb, stretching out our good-byes, when a motorcycle rumbled up and parked behind Drew's truck.

"This would be Wes," Drew told me. "Good. I can give him his key back."

Drew hadn't mentioned his roommate much, certainly not that he was a biker. I'd never dated any bikers – you don't run into a lot of them in a real estate office, although a biker named Clyde had tried to pick Mary up at the bar once. She'd taken a picture of the Harley he rode, just to show me, but he was too old and too scary to fix me up with, in her estimation. She'd told him to kick rocks and had not given him my number.

Wes took off his helmet, and smiled at us. He had black, curly hair and dark blue eyes. I imagined that he was probably an ironworker like Drew. He was wearing old, faded jeans and motorcycle boots, a ratty looking red flannel with the sleeves rolled up. But despite the casual, worn attire, he was just as sexy as he wanted to be. *No wonder Drew didn't talk about him,* I thought. Drew was my age, but this one was a little bit older than me – and he was the kind of man that women look at twice.

Drew was working at getting the key to their apartment off of his keyring, so Wes introduced himself. I started to do the same, but he interrupted me. "You're Maddie. I know." He smiled again and looked at his roommate. "Drew told me about you."

And whatever could Drew have told you about little ol' me? Wes had one of those devious, killer smiles – he might not have meant that Drew had been describing our sexual exploits when he said *Drew told me about you,* but it sure seemed that way from his smile.

20

"He hasn't said much about you, Wes," I said. "Do you guys work together?"

At last, Drew succeeded in removing the key. "No," he said. "We don't work together. He's afraid of heights."

"I work for *BF Walker.*"

"No way!" I exclaimed. "I . . . that is, my sister . . . my mother works at the *ReMax* office next door."

"All three of you?" Wes said curiously. "I thought you worked at *Mickey's.*"

What difference did it make now? Drew was leaving for Las Vegas, scant minutes from now. "I sometimes work at the *ReMax* part time," I said. To avoid further discussion on *all that,* I asked him, "What do you do for *BF Walker?*"

"I'm construction supervisor for a project called *Hidden Palms.* Is that the most ridiculous name or what?"

"No way!" I repeated in astonishment. "Do you know Bill Proten?"

Wes's eyebrows went up in surprise. "As a matter of fact, I do. He's an asshole, in my humble opinion."

"I agree," I said and grinned at him. "My sister . . ." was it really the time to bring up my sister? Drew didn't even know I had a sister. But Drew was leaving. "My sister goes out with him, sometimes."

Wes shook his head. "I hope you have better taste in men." He looked at his friend. "Although, I don't know about this guy . . ."

"This guy is outta here." Drew handed the key to Wes. I watched a little unreadable expression pass between them, then he said, "You'll look after Maddie for me, won't you Wes?"

It was a slight blow to my ego to realize that I'd meant no more to Drew than he'd meant to me. Just like the little twin switcheroo my sister and I pulled off on our unknowing suitors, Drew was passing the torch. He was letting Wes know that it was okay for him to just move right on in, if he was game, since Drew was about to be a memory. I might have been insulted, if it wasn't for the fact that Wes was a thousand times more attractive than Drew.

"I most certainly will," Wes said. "In fact, how does breakfast sound?"

He grinned at me and I felt myself grin back. His smile was infectious. "Breakfast sounds great." We both looked at Drew.

"None for me, thanks," he said. "I've gotta hit the road." He gave me a hug and a kiss, then hugged his friend. "Thanks for letting me stay with you, Wes. Keep building those overpriced houses."

"Anytime. And you keep building those high-rise firetraps."

They slapped each other on the back again. Then Drew got into his truck, waved. Then he was gone.

"Is it okay if we take your car to breakfast?" Wes asked. "I've only got one helmet."

I smiled at him. "What kind of a biker are you?"

"I'm only a biker temporarily. I had a little accident. This lady in a Caddy hit me coming out of the jobsite. My truck is in the shop."

"Were you hurt?" I asked.

Wes shook his head. "No. But the truck was a little wounded."

"I bet it's fun to ride a motorcycle," I said.

"Not when it's cold," Wes said and smiled at me again. "I prefer it strictly for . . . recreation."

I thought that he must not have a girlfriend, or he'd have two helmets. For recreation. Lucky me.

"My car's over here," I said. Wes locked his one helmet onto the bike and we walked to my car.

We decided on the local *Denny's,* and after the waitress took our order, Wes said to me, "So you and your sister both work at the *ReMax?* Is business that good?"

I looked at him and decided that he was a keeper, if he was interested. So I thought it was best to get my secret out in the open immediately. Honesty is always the best policy, if you want to interest someone, right? Besides, it was too much trouble to remember that I was supposed to be a bartender/part-time realtor. And there was not going to be any trading off with Mary with this one.

"I have a little confession for you, Wes."

"Do tell," he said in surprise, and smiled again. "I'm all ears."

"My mother's a realtor at the *ReMax,* and I'm a secretary there. Full-time. It's my twin sister Mary that works at *Mickey's.* Drew came in there one day and asked her out. Mary is . . ." I thought quickly – how do I make this sound as innocent as possible? "Mary was already seeing someone," I lied. "I was not. Mary said she'd go out with Drew, anyway, then called me."

He blinked in surprise. "So Drew thought he was dating the girl from the bar? But it was really you?"

I nodded, and waited for his further reaction. It was a harmless thing we did, but I was glad that I let him know about it from the start. I was already getting lost in his blue eyes, and I knew that I didn't want him to discover our little game on his own, later. Far better to let him know about it immediately. It was not like we did it all that often, anyway.

Amused, he asked, "Do you do this all the time?" as if he read my mind.

It was a good reaction. He wasn't shocked or dismayed. "A few times. Your buddy Bill Proten thought he was going out with me. He asked me out to lunch one day at work. He's not really my type. But I knew Mary would like him, so she just pretended to be me."

The waitress brought our plates, and we tucked in. After a few minutes of eating in silence, Wes said, "Well, that's a different kind of game. I'd always suspected twins could do that kind of thing." He studied me for a second. "I'm glad to hear that you didn't care too much for Bill, though. He is truly a jerk."

"Seriously," I said around a mouthful of eggs. "He is definitely not my type."

Wes squinted at me. "What exactly is your type?"

You are exactly *my type*, I thought, with your tricky smile and your willingness to immediately accept the stewardship of your roomie's . . . what had I been, Drew's girlfriend? If I was, all parties involved, including Wes, seemed to know that it had only been temporary. His willingness to pick up what Drew had left behind didn't seem that much different than my sister and me switching off on the men that asked us out. How could Wes be offended?

"Well . . ." I smiled at my plate. "I'm not sure what my type is," I said, though I was completely sure, and he was definitely it. "But I know Bill Proten doesn't qualify."

"Maybe I'll stop by the office some time and see you," Wes said and grinned again. "I reckon you'll be all lonely since Drew's gone. I actually have to be in tomorrow for a meeting. How about lunch?"

I marveled at his nerve. The thought crossed my mind that I'd be offended and angered at his gall, and Drew's, if he was some little ugly thing. I guess good looks give a guy confidence.

I thought that it would great to have lunch with him - but he'd soon discover that I was a little bit harder to get than any of Drew's stories might've led him to believe. Wes lived here; he was not just some ship I was going to hop on as it passed in the night. I would make him wait, if for no other reason than he was so good-looking and confident.

"I would enjoy that," I told him. "I rarely go out to lunch."

We ate breakfast, and he asked curious questions about how Mary and I switched off on our dates. I told him about that first dance in high school, and I stressed that we only did this thing when someone would *initially* ask us out. I didn't tell him that not only did we switch on people we had just met, but sometimes we switched on men we'd already *known,* like in the Biblical sense. That was just too slutty a secret to be revealed on a first not-even date. That was too slutty a secret to *ever* be revealed.

MARY

Maddie came home just as I was walking out the door to go to work. I asked her how the farewell with Drew went, and with a thoughtful little smile on her face, she told me that it had gone well, that he'd said that he'd call and invite her to Vegas some weekend. She said that she didn't think that he actually would, but that was all okay with her. Maybe she was glad to be rid of him and his dirty fingernails.

I didn't talk to my sister much at all that week. I'd taken a bunch of afternoon shifts for one of the girls, so I was gone when Maddie arrived home from work, and she was already asleep when I got off.

Then on Friday evening, a sharp-dressed, dark-haired guy came into the bar. He was wearing a flawlessly cut black suit, and I figured him for some lawyer from one of the firms nearby, or maybe an accountant or engineer. I thought he could use a haircut, but his slightly shaggy look was in nice contrast with the suit. I thought he had to be some kind of professional, out to start the weekend with a few drinks and a little pleasant conversation with the bartender. He was cute, and I smiled at him when he sat at the bar.

He ordered a shot of rum with a ginger ale chaser, and just sat there studying me while he drank it, smiling. "Isn't your name Maddie?" he asked after a moment.

Ah, so this was a little surprise from my sister! I wondered if she'd tried this one out already – I hadn't seen her all week – he was black-haired and blue-eyed, after all, which is her type. And fairly attractive on top of all that – his best feature was his somewhat devious smile. Or maybe Maddie had just sent him my way untried, because she was out looking for another ironworker.

I pointed at my nametag. "My middle name's Maddie. Some of my friends call me by my middle name." I smiled back at him. "But you can call me anything you want, honey." I was in a mood, and he did look good in that suit.

"I understand you used to go out with my friend Drew," he said slyly. "Since he was leaving anyway, he suggested that I come over here and check you out."

My smile faltered. *Check me out?* Is that how things went with the dirty-fingernail crowd? Drew was gone, so he'd given the okay for his buddy to just waltz in here and *check me out?* And this guy was nervy enough to lay it out for me, just like that. No pretense, no flattery. He was here because Drew had given a thumbs-up report on my sister (who he thought was me) and he'd just decided to see if he could have the next turn.

If I had any doubt that this was exactly what he was saying, he confirmed it for me with the next words out of his mouth. "In fact," quoth he, "Drew said that if I came over here and asked you, you might be down to come back to my place after your shift. Have a little fun."

I cannot tell a lie: my mouth dropped open. Did he really think that such a line would work on me? Just what kind of things had my sister been getting up to, what kind of man had her little plaything Drew been, that his buddy would think that she would be amenable to a little fun with him, just so inelegantly requested? My hand itched to slap him, but that would just get me fired.

I said, "I don't know what kind of a girl Drew said I was, pal, but—"

"Oh, I think you know exactly what kind of a girl Drew said you were," he said, and actually *leered* at me. "You're the kind of girl that likes to have fun. With guys just like me."

I didn't think I could be more insulted, but I was. "You're dreaming, pal," I said evenly. "You're just a little bit too lippy to be my type."

"Just what is your type, Mary? I have it on good authority that I'm just your type."

And then the rude bastard looked toward the door. I followed his gaze, and saw my sister standing there, grinning from ear to ear. She approached and actually embraced this asshole, gave him a big fat kiss. Then she looked at me, still grinning.

"Mary, I'd like you to meet my friend, Wes." She looked at him appraisingly for a minute, then damned if she didn't kiss him again. "My *good friend*, Wes. Wes, this is my sister, Mary."

"We've met," he had the nerve to say.

I just stood there and looked at them in disbelief, dumbfounded, still angry. Maddie had settled onto a barstool beside him; he had his arm around her. They were both grinning at me.

"I thought you were going to smack him," Maddie said to me, then looked at him. "What did you say, anyway?"

"Just what you told me to say," he replied. "That Drew sent me over here for a good time." Wes looked at me blankly, the leer gone. As if he hadn't just propositioned me as if I was a streetwalker. "It's nice to meet you, Mary." *Oh, yeah, now he thought he'd be polite.* He noticed that I was not smiling, and looked at my sister again. "I don't think that she thinks our little joke is very funny, Maddie."

"Joke?" I managed to say.

26

"I thought it would be funny to send Wes in here to try to pick you up. Based on what Drew told him." Maddie wiggled her eyebrows at Wes and kissed him for a third time. "I told Wes that Drew thought I was you all along."

You told Wes that Drew thought I was a slut all along, I thought. *You thought it would be funny to send your very good new friend in here to proposition me in the most vulgar way possible, like I was some kind of a whore. As a joke. You thought it would be* funny.

Wes stood up and threw a ten on the bar. He said, "I'm going to go get out of this monkey suit and get the bike. I'll be back in a little while." He kissed Maddie yet again, and told me again that it was nice meeting me. Then he left.

Maddie watched him walk out of the bar then turned back to me. "Isn't he just something?" she asked, grinning eagerly. "Isn't he just something *else?*"

I blinked rapidly at her, furious. "So let me get this straight. You thought it would be funny to have some strange dude just walk in here and insult me?"

Maddie's grin faltered. "Insult you?"

"Did you not tell him to say that Drew said I was an easy party girl, and that he was here to give it all a try?"

Maddie's grin bloomed again. "Well, yeah. Something like that. And you don't think that's funny?"

"What would I find even remotely funny about that?" He was attractive, and I'd believed that she'd sent him to me, and I'd responded to that. And then he'd turned immediately into a discourteous son of a bitch. It was like seeing a big, flaky jelly donut, then picking it up and biting into it, only to discover that it was full of dirt. I supposed Maddie would think *that* was funny, too.

She shrugged. "I thought you'd think it was funny because if Drew sent him, then you'd know that he had to be saying all those nasty things about me and not you."

What an ego she has! I thought in amazement. Some good-looking, sharp-dressed dude starts talking me up – it started out pleasantly enough – and I'm not supposed to be thinking that he's talking to *me.* Things start to get insulting, and I'm just naturally supposed to realize that he thinks he's talking to *her.* I'm not to be insulted when some guy walks in here and says he's heard all about me, and then just propositions me like a whore. I'm supposed to be thinking about her, understanding all along that he's talking about *her.*

"Whatever," I said. We might look alike, but I'd always known that we didn't think alike. I was still pissed that she'd think getting some stranger to speak to me like that would be funny. "Who is this guy?"

"This guy is Wesley Francis Thomerville, and he is something *else.*"

"Why would you tell him that I – that you – why would you tell him anything about Drew?"

"He already knew all about Drew. They were roommates. That's how I met him. He says Drew didn't say much about me, but I don't think that I believe him." Maddie smirked, then shrugged again. "What difference does it make? Drew's gone, and now Wes and I . . . now Wes and I are together."

"Together? *How together?* Didn't Drew just leave on Sunday? *Five days ago?*" I was appalled. "For Christ's sake, Maddie, didn't you listen to anything Mom ever said?"

"We're not *that* together," she said. "Not yet. And I listened to everything Mom ever said, Mary. I heard it a lot more often than you did, remember? We've had dinner every night this week, and lunch a couple times, and he's very . . . affectionate. I like to kiss him. He's funny and intelligent . . . he's awesome."

"I think he's an asshole," I said, before I knew the words came out of my mouth. "What did you tell him about us? What did you tell him about Drew and Bill and Mike and Neil?"

"I glossed over it all a bit. I didn't mention Mike and Neil at all. I told him that Drew thought I was you and that Bill Proten . . . he knows Bill, by the way."

"What?" Bill had called me just that afternoon, saying something about coming to see me the following weekend.

Maddie said, "Yeah. That might get a little sticky. Bill thinks you're me . . . Well, we're just gonna have to tell Bill that you used to be me, that you used to work at *ReMax,* but now you work here. Or something like that."

"Are you insane?" I asked her. "I used to be you, but now I'm me? *What the fuck, Maddie?*"

"Is Bill the one?" she asked, using my own expression. She knew that I had an image in my mind of the man that I would someday meet, someone who would be perfect for me, that I could settle down with. *The one.*

"No," I said truthfully. Bill was just a fun date every now and then. He had plenty of money and was not averse to spending it on expensive dinners. But he was not *the one.*

"Then we're gonna have to just think up some explanation for how he is not actually dating the girl from the *ReMax* office. Because

Wes is dating the girl from the *ReMax* office, and . . ." Maddie looked at me solemnly. "Wes just might be *the one* for me."

She has got to be kidding, I thought. Maddie had never spoken of *the one* before. They had all been pretty much interchangeable to her. And this guy – sure, he was cute enough, with just the hair and eye color that she favored – but *pretty is as pretty does,* our mother always said, and anyone that would participate in such an off-color joke . . .

And he'd pulled it off so easily. I'd been convinced that Wes had sincerely been trying to pick me up, that he completely believed that what Drew said was true, that I would just take off with him for the asking. He didn't stammer or giggle or give himself away. I could tell that he really did have that kind of nerve. I could tell that in the right situation, Wes was capable of not being a nice guy. In the right situation, he would be perfectly willing to take up with some tramp based on his buddy's recommendation. How could Maddie think that such a person could be the one?

"I like him very much, Mary. I don't know if I can hold out much longer. He just went to get his bike–"

"He's a biker?" What had she done, dress him up in that suit, because she knew I would be attracted to that? Maddie knew that I wouldn't look twice at a biker, no matter how blue his eyes were. But that suit . . . oh, yeah, ha, ha, dress up the biker in nice threads, and that'll be sure to get my attention, so he can then turn around and insult me. Ha, ha. Hi-larious.

"He's not a biker," Maddie was saying. "He works for *BF Walker,* just like Bill. He's a construction supervisor. Out in the field, at the jobsite. He was only dressed up today because he had to go to some meeting, so I thought it would be funny to send him in here . . ."

So he wasn't a biker, but she had known that the suit would catch my eye.

"But he has a bike. A big ol' black Yamaha. I begged him to take me for a ride on it, and he went out and bought another helmet, just for me. He should be back soon. I like him a lot," she repeated. "I don't know if I'll be able to hold out much longer."

"Stop acting like a schoolgirl," I snapped. "Have some self-control." But then I softened. "You're a grown woman, Maddie. If you think it's time already . . . go for it." I paused, took in her shining eyes, her happy smile. "So I guess we won't be sharing this one?"

A bright, hot flash of jealousy and hatred transformed her features. It was only there for a split second, but it was intense enough that I took a step back in surprise. "No. We won't be sharing this one."

Then the scary look was gone and her smile returned. "This one is all mine."

And I guess that must've made it doubly funny for you, I thought. *You send some good-looking, well dressed guy in here* — because she had sent him, even if it was not for the usual reason, to set me up with him — *you knew I'd take the bait. And then he starts in on all this filthy talk. What if I had gone for it, Maddie? What if I had really liked him, just like you do? Then it would've been really funny, huh? Because I'd bet dollars to donuts that he would've gone with me. You send some guy in here to turn me on, then you snatch him away to keep for yourself? Ha, ha.*

What would you have done if I would've taken him up on it, Maddie? How funny would it have been to see your new beloved walk out the back door with me, after you sent him in here to play your little joke? I can tell by his evil little grin that he would've left with me. He just met you, and you told him that I'd be down for a little fun, right now, just like that. I'm sure he wouldn't have passed that up. Now that would've been funny!

"He's all yours," I said. "Construction supervising bikers aren't really my type." *No matter how good they look in a black suit,* I thought. *Especially not ones so willing to participate in a mean-spirited joke.*

Maddie stood up. I noticed for the first time that she'd already changed out of her work clothes: she was wearing jeans, all ready for her bike ride. This really had been a set-up, not some off the cuff thing. She'd put some thought into it. Hardy-har-har.

A rumble came through the open door to *Mickey's,* and she cocked her hand to her ear theatrically. "There's my ride. Don't wait up."

"Have fun," I told her. "Don't do anything I wouldn't do." *Don't do anything he might* think *I wouldn't do, after God-only-knows what you've told him about me,* I thought with a touch of bitterness. How *could* she think all of that would be funny?

MADELINE

Wes and I went back to his apartment after our bike ride, and didn't watch movies, just like Drew and I used to do. Wes didn't seem to think it was too soon, didn't seem to hold it against me, didn't seem to think less of me for it; but then that wasn't something he was going to verbalize to me, now was it? Whatever. It is the modern day. I liked him very much and that was sufficient reason for my hasty surrender, at least to me.

And Wes was so much better than Drew, just like I knew he would be. He was more affectionate; I took that as a sign that he liked me almost as much as I already liked him. I know that sounds completely adolescent, but it's true, nonetheless. Sex is great and all, but every girl is looking for someone who also likes her for herself, too – it's just that you gotta get that sex part out of the way, sooner or later. Because if that part isn't worth it, then all the affection in the world isn't going to make up for it.

But this wasn't something I had to worry about with Wes. He pushed all the right buttons in just the right order. It looked like I had finally found one that I could stand to keep around for a while.

.

MARY

It seemed that Maddie had indeed found *the one*. She and Wes became inseparable. Not to mention *so damned cute together*. She was hardly ever at home, and I expected to hear at any moment that she was going to move in with him.

This fairytale romance had been going on for about six weeks when Wes showed up at the bar one evening to meet Maddie and myself for dinner. My shift was over, and I'd changed out of my bar clothes to a nicer outfit. It wasn't every night that I got to go out with my sister and her boyfriend, after all. *Whoopee.* So I was sitting at a table, not standing behind the bar when he walked in.

He smiled at me, and there was something about the quality of his smile that alerted me to the fact that he thought I was Maddie. I decided to go with it – they liked jokes, right? I picked my drink up with my left hand and smiled back at him. I arose and watched him approach, waited for him to realize I was not my sister. He didn't, but just went right ahead and put his arms around me. He started to kiss me, and I just went right ahead and kissed him back. It was nice – not nearly as wonderful as Maddie had gone on and on about – but nice. In the middle of it, his phone rang. He froze, then immediately broke the kiss. He glanced at me curiously, then answered his phone.

"Hello, darlin'," he said. "I was just talking to your sister." I realized that he had a special ring assigned just for her, and that was the only reason he'd stopped kissing me. He hadn't known I wasn't my sister till just that moment, when his phone rang. I grinned at him while he talked to her.

At last he hung up. "Why did you do that, Mary?" he asked. He didn't seem upset or flustered in any way, not embarrassed at his mistake. Just curious.

"Why did I do what, Wes?"

"Why did you kiss me?"

"You kissed me, honey," I told him.

He grinned. "But you didn't stop me. You didn't point out my mistake." He plopped down onto the chair and considered me. "Did you want me to kiss you?"

I also sat, shrugged. "Like you said, it was your mistake."

"But you didn't stop me," he repeated.

Again I shrugged. "Just consider yourself the victim of a twin joke."

His eyebrows went up. "Oh, I see. This is to make up for that other twin joke. For Maddie sending me in here to pick you up."

"To try to pick me up," I corrected him.

"You didn't think all of that was very funny, did you?"

"It might've worked, had you not been so vulgar." He smiled at the compliment. And it *was* a compliment. He really wasn't all that.

"I think that was mostly the point, Mary. The crudeness was supposed to be funny. Maddie thought you would wonder what kind of a guy you'd fixed her up with."

"That's exactly what I thought. What *did* Drew say about her?"

Wes shrugged noncommittally, changed the subject. "You know, you kiss just like her. I never would've known that you weren't her." He tilted his head and considered me again. "You didn't answer my question, though. Did you want me to kiss you?"

"It was just a little twin joke, like I said."

Now he grinned that devious smile. "I don't think Maddie would think it was funny, Mary. Just like you didn't about the other thing. She's kind of–"

"Possessive?" Maddie had never been so before, but she'd never thought she'd found *the one* before. There was a basic, *He's all mine* tone to her voice when she talked about him that had never been there about anyone else. It fascinated me. I couldn't see what was so special about him. Seriously. He was cute, but so what? Maybe it was because I prefer blondes, but ol' Wes didn't seem that much to me. Certainly not *the one*.

He grinned wider. "Yeah, I guess you could put it that way. She's possessive." It didn't bother him. I could tell he rather liked it.

"And already," I said. "Don't fret, Wes. I won't tell her you kissed me by mistake. It can be our little secret." I leaned across the table closer to him, lowered my voice. "Here's another little secret. The easiest way to tell us apart – I'm right-handed. The evil twin – she's left-handed."

"I'm not so sure which one of you is the evil twin," he said.

.

MADELINE

Wes told me later that evening how he'd walked in to *Mickey's*, thought it was me sitting there waiting for him. He told me that Mary had let him kiss her. He told me that she'd said it was another twin joke.

I reflected on this silently for a minute. *Okay, Sis,* I thought. *We're even now. I don't find it funny this time, but you didn't find my joke funny, either, I guess. The next time won't be even* remotely *funny, however. You need to entirely leave off ever again attempting to make Wes think you're me.* I found it odd that she hadn't been the one to mention her little joke.

It wasn't like she was trying to get a little kiss because she found Wes irresistible, like she was dying to find out what he was like. I might've found that amusing. But she didn't even *like* Wes. With a little exasperated tone to her voice, she was always telling me that she just couldn't see what I found so wonderful about Wes.

Just what was so wonderful about Wes? What wasn't wonderful about him? He was four years older than me, and that gave him a confidence that the *boys* my own age hadn't seemed to have achieved yet. He was tall, not overly so, about six one, just tall enough that I had to stand on tippy-toe to kiss him. He had broad shoulders and narrow hips, a swimmer's body – which had always been my favorite.

When the swimming and diving events were broadcast during the Olympics, I became mesmerized. Mary would shake her head and try to take the remote from me, threaten to change the channel. I would slip the remote under my leg where she couldn't get at it, and then she'd give in and watch the events with me. She'd try to bait me: "They say they're all gay, you know." I would not take my eyes from the screen – the Olympics only happened once every four years, and I didn't want to miss a single occurrence of one of them shaking the wet hair out of his eyes, or maybe making a little quick bathing suit adjustment. "They're not *all* gay," I'd reply, "but they're *all* sexy."

Wes had a swimmer's body, just like all those Olympians I never missed every four years, and he had inky black, curly hair, and dark, porcelain-blue eyes. In this, he was like I'd conjured him out of my most enduring visions of what looked best on a man – as far as I was concerned, there was nothing to compare to blue eyes and black hair. Mary used to say that I'd climb over a roomful of blonde models to talk to the janitor if he was dark-haired and blue-eyed. She could keep the blondies, most of the time. Usually, they reminded me too much of our dad.

But it was probably Wes's smile that made him the most attractive to me. It was rarely one of those big, toothy things, although he would flash one of those if he was really pleased about something. Mostly it was just a little *I'm glad to see ya* kind of thing, or a wily, *I'm exceptionally glad to see ya* grin, which never failed to make me give in to my own devious thoughts. Wes's smile lit up his whole face, lit up the whole room – I could absolutely not help but smile back at him, no matter what little problems or annoyances I might be feeling at the moment.

And Wes had a sly sense of humor to go with his sly smile. He was generally just an all-around nice guy, but sometimes he'd quietly say things that seemed innocent at first, but after a moment's reflection would prove themselves to be quite dirty, or completely ironic, or just plain hilarious. He'd make fun of people or situations, but he was never mean or small about it.

He was smart: he was the youngest construction supervisor they had at *BF Walker,* a job that usually went to wizened old guys that had weathered the ups and downs of the industry. But Wes was cool and calm and could always think up a solution for unprotected OSB in a freak rain storm, road construction delays caused by faulty inter-governmental relations at the office. The suits in charge of design and the paper pushers in charge of permits were never far from a derisive comment from Wes when things went wrong at the jobsite, but he always had a stop-gap or a temporary way around them. I loved to hear him talk about his job.

Wes was kind and generous. He was affectionate. He said he loved me, and I loved him right back. He was sexy. When I was alone, I thought about him, and when I was with him, I thought about being alone with him.

It looked like maybe I had found the vaunted *one,* the man that I could grow old with. When I imagined what it might be like to go the rest of my life and be with no other man but him, the thought was plausible. He was everything that I thought I needed.

When I didn't make any response to his confession about kissing my sister, Wes said, "I knew after a second it wasn't you, though, so I stopped."

I smiled fondly at him. "I'm sorry, Wes. That was kind of a sneaky thing for her to do. I guess she's still mad about the other thing."

"It's definitely a new experience, dealing with twins," he said. "I think I can tell you apart, though, if I concentrate for a minute. I promise I won't kiss your sister again by accident. Or otherwise."

Would that he would've kept his promise.

MARY

What a smug bastard Maddie's boyfriend is! I thought, after they dropped me off at home and the two of them went back to his place. *Did you want me to kiss you?* He had as big of an ego as Maddie did.

No, I should've told him, *I didn't want you to kiss me. I just wanted to show my sister that mean jokes are a two-way street, that I could make her stupid boyfriend feel just as stupid as she had made me feel, when she sent you into my bar to make get me all hopeful, then completely insult me.*

Or, I could've said, *Yes, I wanted you to kiss me, because I wanted to see what it was that so impresses my sister. Unfortunately, even after kissing you, I still can't see what all the fuss is about.* That would've taken his conceited ass down a couple pegs.

Bill and I went out to dinner the following night. Bill, smooth and blonde and free with his money, was no less smug than Wes, but he was infinitely more attractive. He asked me how things were at *ReMax*, and dutifully, like I'd promised Maddie I would, I told him that I'd gotten into an argument with my mother, and that I was now working at *Mickey's*.

He seemed a little surprised to hear that, and I cursed Maddie and her demands. I cursed my loyalty to her. "That kind of stuff happens sometimes, when you work for relatives," Bill said.

"I like my new job better anyway," I told him. "Like you say – it's good to get out from under my mother's thumb."

Bill told me that he wouldn't be seeing me for a while, because *Walker* was transferring him to Northern California to oversee some project in Sacramento. I must've looked sadder than I felt, because he added, "I'll be back eventually, though. Six months, probably. Eight at the most."

I realized that I was sad, a little bit. Now I wouldn't even have Bill to amuse me. "I met one of your co-workers," I told him. "Wes Thomerville."

Bill snorted. "He is not hardly my co-worker, Mary. Subordinate is more like it. He told you he was my co-worker? That's quite a promotion for a stick-building supervisor." He paused, marveling at his underling's gall. "Where did you have the unfortunate pleasure to meet Wes Thomerville, anyway? The gutter, perhaps?" Bill smiled at his own wit.

"I don't spend time in the gutter," I said, offended. "He came into the bar."

"Did he try to pick you up?" Bill asked immediately.

How annoying men are, I thought. Bill and I only saw each other maybe once a month, if that, and here he was, giving me a tone, as if I was his fiancée, as if he owned me. It was none of his business who tried to pick me up, or who succeeded. But he was fun, and I didn't want to argue with him, especially since he was leaving anyway, so I chose not to be actively offended.

"No," I said. "He didn't try to pick me up. He said I looked familiar, asked if I used to work at *ReMax.* I said yes, and he said he'd seen me there, because he worked for *Walker,* and I asked him if he knew you." How easy it was for me to lie, I marveled, especially to someone who was being annoying.

"What did he say about me?" Bill asked, with a little bit too much interest. Maybe he had more reluctant respect for Wes than he was letting on, seeing how he was suddenly so keen to hear his opinion.

"He said he worked with you on some project." It had actually been Maddie who'd told me this, and that Wes didn't care for Bill, apparently not any more than Bill cared for him. "*Secret Trees* or something?"

"*Hidden Palms.* I actually thought up that name. The main road leads into the subdivision from around a hill, so it *is* hidden, and I thought it would be a clever name . . ." Bill looked at me and realized that I could not possibly care less about his inspiration for the name of some housing development. He said, "But Thomerville didn't work *with* me, he worked *for* me. He's still out there building it. I'm going to Sacramento."

"So, it's his project now?" I grinned at my little dig. Naming was important, but wasn't building more important? The name would eventually be forgotten, but the construction would stand.

Bill tossed off the rest of his drink. "I guess you can put it that way. Once actual production starts, it's up to the construction guys. I move on to the next big thing."

Bill grinned and asked me if I wanted to go back to my place, so I could show him how much I was going to miss him. He promised to show me how much he was gonna miss me, and I reflected that it didn't matter if you were a waitress or a secretary, some men just didn't show a lot of respect. Whatever. He wasn't the one.

****

So, Bill was gone, and my prospects were bleak. He texted – but one of the reasons that Bill was not the one was that he talked about his job entirely too much – and his texts were mostly what he perceived to be clever quips about his new associates in Sacramento, about how naïve they were, compared to someone such as himself, who had weathered the last couple years of a dire development scene here in SoCal, where the land was still there, but the buyers had evaporated. He'd only avoided the axe because of his skills, he often told me; even though he was young, his savvy was so valuable to *Walker,* that they hadn't even cut his pay. Or at least not much. Now things had started to look up, and he was in Sacramento to spread a little bit of that inestimable acumen around. Or at least that was Bill's story. As if I cared.

So Bill sent me texts about himself and his job. Yawn. And he sent me nasty little texts about the things we used to do together. Don't get me wrong, I wasn't ashamed of them. I'm a grown woman after all, and these things we did were not even remotely shameful. I'd enjoyed them very much.

But Bill's harping on them was annoying. He was not the one, and I could not, of course, expect him to be texting me about our plans for the future. We had no plans for the future. But neither did I ever get just a nice, how-are-you-my-friend text from him. *What's up in your life? What did you do today? I miss you.*

No, nothing like that. It was always, *Royson is such a tool,* or *The rental that Walker put me in has a great view,* or *I miss having sex with you.* His texts were always about him. The only mention of me was when he talked about how much he had liked what I had done *for him.*

Yawn.

Contrast all that to my sister and her boyfriend, and their adorable little relationship. I wondered what I'd missed here – Maddie had not behaved like our mother's good girl. She'd taken up with some pick-up's roommate, for God's sake. Not to put too fine a point on it, but if you wanted to call a spade a shovel, Drew's sheets hadn't even had a chance to cool off before Maddie had climbed between Wes's sheets with *him.* Surely, the man couldn't have much respect for her. Surely, he couldn't trust her very much.

Mom had always gone on and on about the importance of making them wait. *They'll take whatever you give them,* she'd always said, *and there is very little value placed on something easily obtained. You girls don't have anything that every other girl doesn't have. But if you put a value on it – this man wants what you have, and if you make him wait, make him jump through a few hoops to get it – then he'll put a value on it, too.*

39

Men like those hoops. If you make him jump through enough of them, maybe set a few of them on fire along the way, then he'll come to believe that what you have is special. It must be better than what all the other girls have. It must be special, because you've made it so difficult for him to obtain it.

It was all so ridiculous. This was the twenty-first century, and women have come a long way, baby, and such game-playing should not have a place in the modern world. We are liberated, free, masters of our own minds, bodies, actions. If we are attracted to some man, as attracted as he is to us, and we want to do him on the first date, then there are no moral strictures upon us. It was too ridiculous to even suggest such a thing to a modern woman.

It was so ridiculous, so ridiculously true. If you think that you might want some man for more than just a one-night stand, then you make sure that you make him wait. The moral strictures may have been removed from the concept of the one-night stand – the men were certainly down, and you found that when you did such a thing, your girlfriends and your sister were not judgmental. But if you wanted that guy to come back for more than just maybe one more go, then *you just didn't do it.*

But this universal truth, something I'd never seen to *not* occur, had not occurred with Maddie and Wes. She had nailed him within a week of meeting him, not to mention being fresh and hot from his roommate's bed. It should not have turned into the loving, trusting relationship that it had indeed become.

I was fascinated. What was I missing here? Why was this working? Why did Wes trust Maddie? Why did he seem to value her for more than the tramp that she'd demonstrated herself to be?

Maddie was all in love. Apparently everyone in the building where she worked knew she was Wes's girl – even our mom approved – so there were no more *Walker* project managers coming in there and asking her out anymore, so she didn't send any prospects my way. It was as if that little convenient aspect of our lives as twins had never even existed.

Maddie had eyes for no one but Wes – she'd become unreadable to me. She'd become almost like Bill: her texts were only about herself and about the next wonderful, adorable thing that Wes had done. She never asked me about what had happened at the bar that day anymore, never asked me if I had spied any cuties. It was all about her and Wes and their happiness.

So I studied him. He still didn't seem all that to me. I've heard stories – sometimes, when your friend is in love, sometimes you, eager to be in love, too – somehow you decide that it is the *man* and not the *love* that you want. You decide that you, too, are in love with your friend's boyfriend. You decide that you would be as happy as your friend or sister, not if you could also find love, a love of your own. You decide that you would be as happy as your sister, if only you could have *her* love, *her* man.

But it wasn't so with me. Wes was . . . *meh*. There was absolutely nothing special about him to me. He was cute enough, but no cuter than any of the others guys I saw day after day. He was not especially funny or witty. He had an okay job. What was it about him that had so ensorcelled my sister?

And why had he taken up with her so completely? He had spoken the L-word within the first week, Maddie told me, a mere day after she had spoken it to me. *I love him!* she'd told me gleefully, almost immediately after their first roll in the hay, followed by another litany of his wonderfulness, all those endearing qualities about him that she saw and felt so keenly. None of which I could see. Maddie had not said, *I think I love him*, or, *I could love him*. She had simply fallen completely for him, *in love* for the first time in her life, and Wes, ever perfect, had told her that he loved her, too, right on cue.

But does he love her? I wondered. Love is such an overused word. I love ice cream. *My love is like a red, red rose, that's newly sprung in June.* You are my love. *I love thee to the depth and breadth and height my soul can reach . . . and, if God choose, I shall but love thee better after death.* And of course, Bill's frequent comment, his take on the phenomenon that supposedly drives the world: *I love how you do that thing with your tongue.*

So I wondered, what kind of a love was it that Wes had for my sister? I wondered and wondered and wondered. It shouldn't be working out, not based on the way it started, and the fact that it was indeed working out, made me wonder. Why? Did Wes just love Maddie for her body, for that thing she probably also did with her tongue? Did he love her because she so obviously loved him? Did he love her for her serious, somewhat austere personality, so much like our mother, so unlike my own joking silliness? If that cruel joke she played had been Maddie's foray into joking silliness, I thought it best that she stay serious.

Did Wes love her at all? Or was he just going along for the ride? Just like my dad – he never would've changed the status quo with Mom, had he not been found out. If he'd ever felt that monumental love for Mom, it had long dissipated – else why had he taken up with Erica? But neither had he felt a monumental love for her, either, apparently. Dad had always been willing to just go along with the flow, like a leaf in the stream, bumping up against this woman or the next, as the current willed. If this one didn't work out, there would be another one along soon enough. It was all okey-dokey with Dad.

Maybe Wes was the same way. Maybe he was just going along with Maddie and her love. Maybe he had other women on the side, just like Dad did. I couldn't imagine that he did – Maddie was with him all the time. But then, Mom hadn't imagined that Dad had women on the side, either – and they'd lived together. Yet Dad had managed.

Wes met Maddie frequently at the bar. He would smile and wave at me, order a shot of rum with a ginger ale chaser, and sit at a table and wait for my sister to show up. So I had the opportunity to study him. Wes looked at other women the way a diner at a fancy restaurant might look at the fabulous dishes other patrons had ordered, as the servers carried them to other tables. *Wow, that looks good,* the diner might think as the lobster was carried over to Table 6. But the diner would never dream of getting up and going over to Table 6 and sampling the lobster, and Wes never seemed to wish he'd ordered something else when his own plate, my sister, was delivered to his table.

But did he love her, really? I wondered what it would take to evaporate that love – I wondered what it would take to make it disappear as immediately as it had appeared. I wondered what simple events might occur, what coincidences, what misunderstandings, things that happen every day – what events would need to fall in line, harmless in themselves, but when viewed together – what could happen that would make Wes stop trusting Maddie? And if he was so superficial, hadn't I better take steps to protect her? If Wes was so fickle that he could get angry with Maddie over anything – hadn't I better start looking out for her? And if he was so fickle, wasn't she better off without him?

MADELINE

In addition to being cute and smart and sexy, in addition to having a great job where he got to work outside, in addition to being the love of my life, Wes also played the guitar, and sang lead for a band called Rolling Blackout. The other guitar, the bass player, and the drummer were all pals of his from *BF Walker,* other construction guys.

I thought they were awesome, but Rolling Blackout didn't have a lot of ambition, I must say. They played mostly in the drummer's garage, and would do weddings and birthdays, bar mitzvahs and parties, but I don't think that they'd ever played to a paying crowd that was just there to listen to their music.

All that would have to change. I thought that they should share their talent with a larger audience. I thought the name was a little ponderous – it made you think of death metal or something like that, and that's not what they were at all. Their sound was kind of a poppy, rock-country amalgam. Catchy, upbeat tunes.

I read somewhere that it's the music more than the lyrics that set the mood of a song. Some notes are just sadder, no matter what is being sung about. This was true of my favorite Rolling Blackout ditty, a little number called *My Disgrace.* The tune was bouncy and danceable, and if you weren't paying attention to the lyrics, it might escape you that the song was entirely dark. Wes might dance around and look sexy while he played his guitar, but he was actually whining about how some woman had ruined him, without ever specifying exactly what she had done. Each chorus was a warning about the possibility of a fall – down the steps, over a cliff, from a boat, from a tall building. A bridge frequented by suicides. It was a song about revenge, really, but you only got that if you paid close attention to the lyrics.

As luck would have it, *Mickey's* owner decided to expand. He knocked down a couple of walls that had housed a long storage room, and voila! there was now enough space for a decent-sized stage and, if they pushed some of the tables back against the wall, a large dance floor. *Mickey's* owner started to think of his bar in terms of a club or even a venue, at least for a few nights a week.

The first foray into entertaining the masses was a poetry slam, contestants awarded by the applause of the crowd. In this, *Mickey's* was attempting a little competition with the hipster coffee house down the street. But apparently, the hipsters stayed down the street, for while there were six very eager poets, the audience more or less ignored them. Other than from each poet's own partisans in the crowd, there was only a smattering of applause or interest from the rest of the patrons.

I found most of their stuff a little difficult to follow, but then I've always felt that most poetry goes right over my head – especially if it doesn't rhyme. Wes sat in the back with me and giggled uncontrollably, until tears of mirth literally ran down his face. He thought that all the poets were just too preciously pretentious; try as he might, he couldn't help but laugh at them. I glanced over behind the bar at Mary occasionally, and she, too, rolled her eyes. For once she was in agreement with Wes. Poetry slam night was not repeated.

The comedians that showed up for Comedy Open Mike Night didn't fare much better. Some of them were quite funny, or at least I thought so, but they didn't make Wes laugh nearly as much as the affected poets had inadvertently done, and again, Mary rolled her eyes. The crowd again only applauded thinly.

And then I got an idea. Mary was standing behind the bar with Jon, *Mickey's* owner. I watched them survey the several empty tables, the crowd – it was rather small for a Friday night. I watched Jon frown. I told Wes that I'd be back in a minute.

I greeted Jon and he smiled at me, then looked from me to my sister, then back again, the way he always did. Jon was one of those people who was fascinated with twins. He shook his head. "I swear," he said to me, "I just can't tell you guys apart. Are you sure you won't come to work for me, Maddie? It would be quite the shtick to have twins working here together. We could have contests to see who was best at telling you guys apart."

"We're not dancing bears, for Christ's sake, Jon," Mary replied in annoyance.

Jon shrugged. If it would make him a buck, Jon was more than willing to turn us into dancing bears. "It would bring in more of a crowd than this," he said and gestured at the young lady bombing on *Mickey's* brand new stage.

"I've got a better idea," I said. "You need a band, Jon."

"Oh, no," Jon replied, shaking his head firmly. "No open mike nights for bands. Those metal guys are too damn loud, and the people they bring in are all underage. They almost shut down *The House of Ale* over too many minors being in there to see the bands."

The House of Ale was Jon's competitor a few blocks over, and Mary had told me the scuttlebutt – the only reason that they hadn't been shut down for serving liquor to minors was that the bartender's brother was a cop, and the guy had warned him that they were under surveillance.

At this news, the owner had scrapped his fairly lucrative Battle of the Bands night immediately, and had installed a bouncer to check ID's at the door. For a month, getting into *The House of Ale* was almost as tiresome as getting into the dance club across town. People turned away in droves, and the owner took it in the shorts. But it still was better than losing his license over something as stupid as serving minors. After a while, things went back to how they had been at *The House of Ale:* no bouncer, no minors. But no bands, either.

"I'm not talking about an open mike for bands," I told Jon. "I'm thinking of one group in particular. They could be your house band. They're not metal in the least." I dug around in my purse and handed him a copy of Rolling Blackout's demo CD, which Wes and the boys had recorded in the drummer's garage one drunken, rainy afternoon. The quality wasn't great, but it was good enough to show Jon that he wouldn't be hiring Megadeth.

"Okay, Maddie, anything for you," Jon said and smiled at me. He again looked from me to my sister and shook his head. "You guys are amazing," he said again.

"And we're not even Siamese twins," Mary said. "You are easily amazed, Boss."

"I'll give 'em a listen," Jon said to me. "Anything'll be better than this." He again gestured at the stage.

MARY

I was standing behind the bar next to Jon the following Friday when he told Maddie that he would book *her* band. She and Wes had been spending most Friday nights at the bar – it was winter, and too cold for motorcycle rides. The two of them were happy and comfortable together, so the need to *go out* every Friday, like on dates, had waned. They just hung out at the bar and listened to the bad comedians that Jon was still allowing to appear, had a few drinks, smiled and waved at me. Then they'd go on back to Wes's place, and I would go on home to our lonely apartment.

Jon told Maddie to have her band show up before we opened the next morning and they'd hammer out the details. Maddie said thanks and Jon went off to do boss things in the office.

Wes, standing beside her, blinked stupidly. "Your band?"

Maddie squealed and hugged him. "Not my band, silly! *Your band!* I talked Jon into letting you guys play! You're gonna be a rock star!"

Wes grinned uncertainly. "I build houses, Maddie. I don't wanna be a—"

"God hates a coward, Wes," I opined. "Maddie wanted to surprise you." I looked at her eager, expectant face, and thought he *was* a coward, and an ungrateful son of a bitch, too, if he didn't appreciate the favor she'd done for him. It had taken more than a little ass-kissing on Maddie's part to talk Jon into booking a band. The almost disaster at *The House of Ale* had sworn him off of the idea of live music in his place. The bands they'd booked over there had just too many minors for fans.

"I dunno, Maddie," the scaredy-cat was saying. "I wish you would've said something. I don't know if the rest of the guys . . ."

"Why not?" Maddie asked in astonishment, as if he'd turned down the opportunity to open for the Rolling Stones, instead of a first gig at a little bar. "Why wouldn't they want to play here?"

"I dunno, Maddie," Wes repeated. "We've never played anything but parties."

Maddie pouted in disappointment. He wasn't taking her big surprise the way she'd expected, and again I thought he was a cowardly, thankless bastard. What *did* she see in him? I said, "Why don't you call them and ask? If they don't want to do it, I'll tell Jon myself." I looked at my sister. "I'll save you the embarrassment."

Wes took this as an insult, a challenge, which is exactly how I'd intended it. Really, why wouldn't they want to do it? They'd make a little money, get a little publicity. They weren't ever going to be rock stars like Maddie had suggested – that had more to do with talent, I thought, than exposure. I'd heard their amateur-grade CD. A gig at the Hollywood Bowl wouldn't make Rolling Blackout into rock stars. But why not play a little Riverside bar?

"Okay," Wes said, looking at me defiantly. "I'll call them." He went out onto the patio where he could have his conversation in private.

Maddie looked at me in bewilderment, and I assured her, "I'm sure the rest of them aren't as chickenshit as he is." Maddie grinned despite the slight to her beloved. Even she, blind to Wes's overall nothing-specialness, had to admit that he was being a little chicken on this one. After a few minutes, Wes returned, all smiles, and told us that the other members of Rolling Blackout were completely stoked about Maddie's little surprise. I gave her an *I told you so* wink.

He hugged her and said, "Will you be our manager? Book our venues, make sure we get paid?"

Maddie shook her head. "That's all up to you. I just gave you a little push. But I'll tell you what I will do. I'll make all the arrangements for your first video." She smiled at me. "We'll ask Jason about it."

Jason lived in the apartment below ours. I think he was in college – whatever he did, we always saw him lugging video equipment around.

****

The following morning, while Wes and the other members of the unfortunately named Rolling Blackout were discussing their budding career as *Mickey's* house band, Maddie and I visited our neighbor. It turned out that he *was* a film student, but was not so much an aspiring auteur as he was a would-be documentarian.

"I'm not really into making music videos," he said. Maddie frowned. I'd always thought that Jason was a little sweet on her, and seeing that frown, he quickly added, "But I'm sure I could do it. It's actually rather formulaic. You just film them lip-syncing to the song, then intercut with other footage . . ." Jason sensed he was losing Maddie with even this most basic technical description. "I'm sure I could do it, Maddie," he repeated. "But I'd also like to follow them around for a little while."

"Like reality TV?" I asked.

47

Jason glared at me. He was definitely not sweet on me, and it was odd and somehow refreshing to know someone who differentiated so easily between us, despite the fact that we looked exactly alike. "There is nothing whatsoever real about reality TV," he claimed. "Every obstacle is scripted." He looked back at Maddie, and again he smiled. "I've been looking for a band to film, actually. A-week-in-the-life kind of thing. Do you think they'd go for that?"

Maddie frowned again and Jason mirrored her frown. It was obvious that he wanted to please her. *Why couldn't she pick a nice guy like him?* I thought.

"I'm not sure, Jason," Maddie said. "Wes is—"

"Wes is chickenshit," I supplied.

"I don't think they'd want you to come to the jobsite or anything like that," Maddie said, ignoring me.

"Nothing that in-depth," Jason said, and smiled again. "Nothing about their day jobs. People don't really care about stuff like that. Just rehearsals, live performances. Maybe a few interviews."

"*Rolling Blackout's Hometown Debut,*" I suggested, holding my hands up like a movie director, and now Jason smiled at me, also. "I'm sure you can interview Jon all day long. Call him the man who's giving them their big break. He'll see it as publicity for the bar."

"What do you think, Maddie?" Jason asked. "Tell 'em that if they let me do the documentary part, I'll do the music video part for free."

"That sounds great, Jason!" Maddie enthused. "I'll run it by the lead, and see what he says." She always called Wes *the lead* when she was talking about him in the context of the band, and I found that to be just as annoying as when she referred to him as *the front* or *the rock star.*

Wes would never be a rock star, not even if he was backed by real rock stars. He had a nice enough voice, and he could play guitar well enough. But I thought he was no songwriter. I was appalled by *My Disgrace,* the one that Maddie liked so much, the one that sounded like a little upbeat pop tune until you listened to the words to it.

When I look into your eyes,
All I can see is evil
And if you're Death then I will die
My soul's beyond retrieval

Step back from the edge there, honey
That cliff is mighty steep
The fall will give you time to think
Damn, this canyon's deep

Met you in a parking lot
It would become our garden
You caused my sin and my disgrace
And I still beg your pardon

Watch out for that railing, baby
There's not one thing to see
The drop makes people look like ants
Too far down for me

You corrupted what I've been
But I can't forget your touch
I'm not sure but if this is love
I must thank you very much

Don't go out on the deck right now
It's not a place to dance
One slip and you'd be gone for good
Not one single chance

You're the witch that stole my will
Always miss my will the most
I have become your spineless slave
Your private transparent ghost

Sorry these old stairs are so dark
The bulb blew out today
Just go on down ahead of me
You can lead the way

My sky's always black like night
Yet you remain my sun
Your light is the demonic kind
You are my only one

The jumpers really like this bridge
Once here they seldom fail
Only one step into the air
Past this fateful rail

Hope they catch you when you fall
It will be from my shove
How can I endure all this pain
And believe that you're my love?

Once I'd realized that it was really about some guy's desire to push his girlfriend off the nearest high place, I'd asked Wes, "What did this girl do to you that you hate her so much?"

"What girl?"

"The girl. From *My Disgrace. You corrupted what I've been/But I can't forget your touch* and all that. How did she corrupt you?"

"Where did she touch you?" Maddie asked, and hugged him.

Wes grinned at me. "I'm flattered that you know the lyrics to my song, Mary."

I rolled my eyes. My intention had certainly not been to flatter him. Not in this lifetime. "Maddie plays it all the time. On the rare occasions that she's home. I can't help but know the words, because I've heard it like a million times. I'd just like to know what horrible thing this girl did to you to make you want to kill her."

"Is that what you get out of it?" he asked, still grinning.

"Hope they catch you when you fall/It will be from my shove. That kinda spells it out, doesn't it?" I said.

Wes shrugged. "Artistic license and all that. Maybe he's just thinking about pushing her."

"He?" Maddie asked. "It's not you?"

Wes laughed. "I build houses, Maddie. I'm not a wounded poet. I kinda just manufactured all those emotions one day – what if some guy loved some woman, but felt that she'd mistreated him in some way–"

"In what way?" I insisted.

"That's just the point, Mary. I don't know in what way. In some terrible way. And he loves her, but he also hates her, and thinks about pushing her off a cliff. But I've never actually felt that way about anyone. I just made it up." He looked back at Maddie. "No one's ever hurt me like that."

Not yet, I thought.

****

Jason followed Rolling Blackout around for about three months, culminating in his three camera recording of their big gig at *Mickey's* annual New Year's Eve shindig. He arranged for some buddy of his to record their song properly in a studio, then he got the music video portion out of the way. He brought the band together with his girlfriend, Carmen, who was some kind of design student, and she helped them pick out clothes and flashy instruments to project the proper rock star image.

She didn't have a whole lot to work with. Phil, the drummer, was a little bitty guy. He was muscular and sported two sleeves of way too colorful tattoos, just like Mike, the unemployed cutie that I'd once shared with my sister. Phil reminded me of a tiny peacock. Carmen put him in a wife beater, which brought out all those blue sparrows and orange fish. She had Jason rent or borrow a beautiful set of black, sparkly Zildjian drums, and sat him behind them on a stool so tall that he could barely reach the bass drum pedal. But it didn't really matter – the sound wasn't going to be important, just the look.

Angelo, the bass player, was a giant bear of a man; his white bass looked like a toy in his big hands. Carmen dressed him in a black duster, and stood him as far away from little Phil as possible. Cody, the second guitar, who also sang – I thought he was a much better singer than Wes – was a skinny blondie, whose face seemed to be almost entirely made up of his nose. He had the most beautiful green eyes, though. There wasn't a whole lot that Carmen could do with poor Cody. He was just as ugly as homemade sin, but he had to be right up there with Wes, because of course, they decided to do the video of *My Disgrace*, and Cody did a lot of harmonizing with Wes on that one. Carmen tried to hide him behind a big acoustic guitar, but it couldn't hide his face.

Wes, not so much by virtue of his own attractiveness, I thought, but because of the overall homeliness of the rest of his band, got the most camera time. Carmen dressed him in tight black jeans and had him wear a pair of snakeskin cowboy boots. She had him wear a leather jacket and a dark blue t-shirt. She wanted him to wear a pair of Blues Brothers' style Ray-bans – I thought they complimented his black hair – but Maddie vetoed the idea. She told Carmen that she loved the color of the shirt she'd picked out so much because it brought out the color of Wes's eyes – she said it would be a shame to cover them up with sunglasses. Whatever.

Jon let them film the video in the bar – it took almost an entire Sunday. People stood outside on the sidewalk, wondering why we weren't open for brunch as we usually were, and Jason went out there and filmed them also. He said something about the illusion that they were lined up to see the band. This was the first time he set up the three cameras, and like I say, he took six hours to film a three minute song. I thought it was the hokiest, corniest thing ever – Wes looked like a caricature of a schoolgirl's dream of a bad boy, all dressed in tight black denim and leather – Carmen even had him play a black guitar. Even if he did occasionally ride a motorcycle on a nice, sunny day, there was absolutely nothing bad boy about Wes. And the snakeskin boots were just entirely too much.

The rest of the footage Jason shot was of the band rehearsing and playing Friday nights at *Mickey's*. Wes usually wore a ratty flannel, faded jeans and Converse – how had I ever thought that he was a sharp dresser? It was just from that one black suit, that one time. I never saw him dressed up again, all the time that he and Maddie were going together. Maddie said he only wore a suit once or twice a month, when he had to go into the office at *Walker* for production meetings. She said he enjoyed it very much, but I didn't believe it. If he liked to dress up so much, why didn't he do it more often? It sure made him better looking.

Jason shot hours and hours of live footage of Rolling Blackout at the bar. They played every weekend for the three months that he followed them, and he filmed every performance, sometimes with more than one camera, finally using three again for the big New Year's Eve party. I had to admit that they were popular – *Mickey's* would be packed when Rolling Blackout performed, and Jon smiled from ear to ear, like the greedy shark he was. *There is absolutely no accounting for taste,* I thought. They were okay, but I didn't think they'd ever get out of *Mickey's*.

MADELINE

As circumstances would turn out, I only got to see the completed video for *My Disgrace* once. I don't know if Wes ever got to see it. A few days before Thanksgiving, Jason brought the DVD upstairs and proudly played it for Mary and me. It was his first attempt at something *so commercial*, he told us, and he said he thought he'd outdone himself.

I thought it was *brilliant*. Wes was so sexy as to be mesmerizing – Jason had caught the blue of his eyes, the little Elvis-like curl to his lip as he sang about the evilness of this woman he'd made up. I wanted to send it immediately to record companies and MTV, which sent Mary into gales of laughter. Jason smiled indulgently at me and said that the video still needed a little polishing before it was ready for MTV. He said that he also wanted to include it in with the rest of his documentary. He wasn't even done shooting all the footage for that – there was still another month of gigs to film, so he didn't leave a copy of the *My Disgrace* video for us. I would see the raw footage he'd talked about sometime later, but by then, a lot of things had changed. Between me and Wes. Between me and Mary. Between Mary and Wes.

MARY

The broken Rearden family – twin girls raised separately by a divorced Mom and Dad – had a somewhat bizarre Thanksgiving tradition. The word *tradition* is not even really accurate, as a tradition is something that you actively re-enact, something you plan out ahead of time, is it not? Our Thanksgiving *routine,* to use a better word, was simple. If Dad had a girlfriend, we went to his house, and Mom went to her friend Frieda's house in San Diego. If Dad was between women in the autumn, he took us out to dinner, and Mom went to her friend's house. I remember only three or four of those dinners out, growing up. Dad almost always had a woman.

After we left home, Mom still went to Frieda's – neither the holiday itself nor the cooking of the meal for it had ever been much of a big deal to Mom. Maddie and I still went to Dad's if he had a girlfriend, and if he didn't, Maddie and I would cook.

The year Maddie was dating Wes, Dad invited her to bring him along. Joanna, Dad's current girlfriend, cooked the largest dinner I'd ever seen, and she was delighted to fete both Larry's daughters and one daughter's boyfriend. I could tell that Joanna was very fond of my dad. She was somewhat younger than him, and not as pretty as most of the ones he'd dated, and I could tell that she wanted very much to impress us with her dinner. He seemed to like her very much, also, and I thought that perhaps the leaf had finally brushed up against something he would cling to.

Wes and Dad hit it off immediately, drinking rum and ginger ales and yelling at the television and high-fiving each other throughout the Lions' and Cowboys' games. I got way more than my share of the Lions and the Cowboys at the bar, not to mention grown men screaming at them. I spent a lot of time with Joanna in the kitchen. She was kind and sweet and just a little bit nervous about the meal, and she kept thanking me for helping. She didn't have to keep thanking me. I enjoyed helping – it was nice to hang out with a woman who knew how to cook, a homely, down-to-earth woman, someone whose biggest ambition on that day was to please my dad and his daughters. It was a desire I could never remember my mother ever expressing on Thanksgiving. Mom had always made it seem like a chore. Cooking Thanksgiving dinner was one thing she was glad to be freed from when she divorced Dad.

Dad discovered something else that he and Wes had in common besides football, and it cemented their new buddyship. Men seldom cared about each other's personalities, I'd often noted, if they had some commonality. One of them could be an axe murderer, but if they were both mechanics, they were immediately pals.

My dad was a civil engineer, a road builder. Once he found out that Wes was a homebuilder, Dad was just as pleased as punch with Maddie's boyfriend. Together with his daughter, the home seller – or at least a secretary in a home seller's office – they talked at length about real estate and real estate development and the roads that served them. I was mostly ignored. But it didn't bother me too much. Like I say, I enjoyed hanging out with Joanna, whom, I realized, wanted simply to be a *homemaker* with my dad.

After he carved the turkey and everyone was served, Dad even trotted out his favorite story about the Van Buren Bridge. This bridge was actually two bridges, side by side, with a gap between them. Two lanes heading out of Riverside to the north, and two lanes heading back in, to the south. To Maddie and me, and to probably everyone else who wasn't in the public works field, the Van Buren Bridge was nothing more than a commonplace structure, put there so one wouldn't get one's tires wet crossing the Santa Ana River. Nothing to even notice, and certainly nothing to hold forth about at Thanksgiving dinner. But the bridge meant something to Dad, and so by extension, I guess, it meant something to his daughters as well. Dad worked for Caltrans, so he hadn't had anything to do with the latest reconstruction of the spans, but all the people involved were his colleagues, and he'd followed the project with interest and a type of glee known only to civil engineers.

One of the iterations of the bridge – there had been many in the long history of Riverside – had collapsed in 1969. It had been Dad's witnessing of this event that had inspired him to become a civil engineer in the first place, and now he meant to regale Wes with the whole story. I'd heard him tell the tale a few more times than Maddie had, and I sighed. He had a new victim now – Wes might actually have an interest, being in the construction biz and all – so Dad began with obvious relish.

"It was 1969, and I was only a little kid, but Dad wanted me to see what was gonna happen. It had been raining for days, and the water had just kept getting higher and higher. We stood on the shoulder and Dad said, 'Watch Larry. It won't be long now.'

"The old bridge had slender concrete pilings, Wes. You would've thought that they could handle it, but the water was hammering at them. The river was not that high up, not all the way to the road bed, but it was swift." Dad grinned, seeing it all over again. "One minute the guardrail was a flat, straight line . . . and then a few of the pilings started to give way. The guardrail began to twist and bend like it was made of spaghetti. Then it dipped, lower and lower like a smile. And then the entire span collapsed." Dad smiled like the guardrail, and Wes smiled back. I rolled my eyes at Maddie, and she gave me a *don't be mean* look.

"Did you know that during construction of the new bridge, they dug up the remains of the parts that had collapsed in 1969, Wes?"

"I heard something about that," Wes replied. "Heard it was somewhat of a surprise."

Dad nodded. "There wasn't the kind of environmental watch dogs then that we have now, so the old team just buried the collapsed parts in the riverbed."

"That environmental stuff nowadays–" Wes began.

"Don't get me started," Dad said, around a mouthful of turkey. "Butterflies and birds and Kangaroo rats, holding up construction. And people wonder why the freeways are so congested."

"And why new houses are so expensive," Wes agreed.

What do you know about the prices of the houses you build? I thought. He didn't have anything to do with selling them. He was nothing but somebody who ordered a bunch of carpenters and plumbers around. Or at least that's what Bill had said about him.

"It *was* a surprise to find the old spans," Dad continued, "so they didn't remove them at the time – it would've caused a delay and would've cost too much. There was a redesign, and they built the false work around the unearthed corpse of the old bridge. Eventually, they got rid of it, after construction was completed.

"There was a lot of rain during the first phase of construction, more flood damage."

"I remember that. Traffic was a mess for a while," Wes said.

"Traffic is always a mess out there, still, new bridge or not," I opined. Maddie smiled and looked down at her plate when the men ignored me.

"After the rains, they repaired the damage and worked around the clock to get back on schedule, remember?"

"Yeah." Wes grinned. "I remember envying their overtime."

"Have you been out there to see it, Wes? Enough room for three travel lanes in each direction. Big fat pilings. They even put in big pretty raincross street lights."

"It's nice," Wes said.

Dad went on to tell Wes that seeing the bridge fall into the water when he was a kid had made him marvel at the frailties of the things man constructed, made him wonder if he could design things that lasted better. He'd wanted to be an architect at first, but hadn't got very far in that ambition, decided in college to be a civil engineer instead, and blah, blah, blah. I'd heard this story *so many times,* so I got up and went to the kitchen to get the other bowl of mashed potatoes.

I could hear Wes's voice, telling a story similar to Dad's, about how he'd watched an apartment complex go up next to his high school, or something, and that had led him into construction management. Or something like that. I cared neither for Wes, nor what had inspired him to his mundane job. Nor did I care for his sucking up to my dad with his similar story. I puttered around in the kitchen until he stopped blabbing, then brought out the potatoes.

MADELINE

Wes told me how much he'd enjoyed Thanksgiving dinner, how much he liked my dad. He'd already met my mom at the office, and said he liked her, too. He liked Mary, he always told me, even though he said he thought that she didn't like him too much. "I think she feels like I'm stealing you away from her," he told me.

I guess all the familial bliss of Thanksgiving dinner decided him, even if he imagined that my twin didn't care for him, because barely a week later, Wes asked me to marry him. Jason caught it all on video, because Wes made it into a public event – maybe he thought I wouldn't say no if he did it in front of a giant crowd of people. As if I would ever say no.

He popped the question after Rolling Blackout's regular Friday night gig at *Mickey's*. Jason told me that he'd captured the utterly flabbergasted look on Mary's face: at some signal from Wes, he had one of his assistants train a camera on her.

The band finished their set, and while the crowd was still cheering wildly, my favorite rock star called me up on stage. I walked up the two steps, and before I knew what was happening, Wes dropped to his knees and held up a little black velvet jewelry box. Inside was a ring, crowned with the largest diamond I'd ever seen. It would shrink back to the size it actually was, just a nice little engagement ring – but when Wes opened the box, the rock looked as big as an ice cube to me.

The crowd fell silent – Wes didn't even need a microphone for the people in the back to hear him ask me to marry him. Of course I said yes, and the cheers were deafening.

MARY

I thought that it was one more example of Wes's basically cowardly nature that he chose a crowded bar in which to asked my sister to marry him. Not only had he chosen a crowded bar, but he'd asked her onstage, with all his "fans" as witnesses, and with Jason filming the whole thing. Of course, Maddie had no choice but to say yes. Maddie was the sweetest person – she wouldn't dream of turning him down, embarrassing him by saying no in front of all those people.

After the shock wore off, I walked over to the stage and gave her a big hug and kiss. I made over the little chip of a diamond that Wes had given her. Apparently, he was a cheapskate as well as a coward. I even gave him a little kiss on the cheek and said congratulations.

I smiled and told Maddie how happy I was for her. But I wasn't really happy at all. I thought she was making the biggest mistake of her life. How *could* she really want to marry this loser? She would move out immediately, of course, I was sure of it. Then I would hardly get to see her any more, even less than I did now. And for what? Wes was nothing but a mildly attractive, no-talent construction worker. How *could* my sister be so happily willing to throw away her life on someone like him?

They didn't talk about setting a date that night – just some vague mention of *maybe in the spring*. I hoped that Maddie would come to her senses by then. I just couldn't believe that she really thought she had found *the one*, that she really intended to marry Wes Thomerville. It was just impossible, ridiculous. She could do so much better than him. I desperately hoped that she would see this before it was too late.

Maddie didn't move in to Wes's apartment – she said that she wanted to spend as much time with me as possible before she and Wes . . . *got married!* Every time she said the phrase, she would squeal in delight, like a schoolgirl. Wes had actually asked her to marry him, they were actually going to get *married* and live happily ever after! Maddie really believed all that fairytale bullshit. She loved him more each day, she told me. I realized that she wasn't going to come around. She was totally blind to Wes's completely average ordinariness. I was sure she'd be sorry if she married him.

They had not been engaged for an entire month yet when Rolling Blackout performed at *Mickey's* always-rollicking New Year's Eve party. Jason was there to film the whole thing – he promised that it was the last time he'd be in my bar filming. After tonight's performance, he said, he planned to compile everything and release his documentary. *On an unsuspecting, entirely uninterested world*, I thought.

My shift was over at eight, but there I was, still sitting in the place where I spent most of my waking hours, because my sister was there, waiting for Rolling Blackout to finish their set. Then we were all supposed to go to Benny's house for the real party. Benny worked at the tobacco lounge next door.

At nine-thirty, their interminable set finally ended. Just like me, Wes didn't want to work on New Year's Eve, and he'd told Jon that they weren't going to play past ten. Jon didn't press them – they were bringing in quite the crowd of a Friday night, and Jon thought he was being generous in letting them go early on New Year's Eve. Jon thought of Rolling Blackout as employees, people that depended on his moods for a living, like his bartenders and wait staff did. I don't think he ever realized that the gig was just a fun way to spend Friday nights to Wes and his band.

But Wes's real job called to him as he and his bandmates were loading out their instruments. Something about a fire at the jobsite, at *Hidden Palms*. Apparently, someone had set one of the barely constructed homes ablaze, and while it had been contained and put out, and had not spread to any other structures, Wes's boss wondered if it wouldn't be too much trouble for him to run out there and take a quick look-see, even if it was New Year's Eve.

Wes, loyal company man that he was, said it would be no trouble at all. He told the boss that Phil would even go with him. They tied the tarp over their instruments, and bid farewell to Angelo and Cody, who, being family men, were going home to their families. He hugged Maddie and told her that he shouldn't be too long, that he would catch up with her at Benny's party as soon as he could. Then he waved goodbye to us, and he and Phil got into his truck and drove off.

MADELINE

New Year's Day saw me sleeping 'til noon, and still feeling like something the cat dragged in when I at last opened my sleep-clotted eyes. I awoke in my own bed, fully clothed. I felt a little surprised at that. Where was Wes? I thought back to Benny's party. I remembered drinking and laughing with Mary and a bunch of her friends from the bar, waiting for Wes to show up.

I sat up in bed and my head pounded. I didn't remember Wes showing up, I didn't remember a countdown at midnight. I didn't remember coming home to my own bed. I didn't remember anything.

I looked on the bedside table for my phone. There was my purse – I never brought my purse into my room. I always left it on the coffee table in the living room. Someone had brought it in here and set it down. Had it been Wes? Where was he, anyway?

I dug around in my purse and extracted my phone. There were two missed calls from the night before, from Wes. Nothing since about eleven-thirty. Where the hell was he?

My phone lit up in my hand and I jumped. It didn't ring – it was on silent. A feeling of unreality began to creep over me. I never brought my purse into my room, and I never put my phone on silent. I frequently set it down sometimes when I was at home or at Wes's place, and would forget where I'd left it – I was always having to have Mary or Wes call it for me. If it was on silent, I'd never find it.

It was Mary. She said, "Are you okay, Maddie?"

"I'm not sure," I said slowly, truthfully. "Where are you?"

"I'm in the living room. Are you sure everything is all right?"

Everything is most assuredly not *all right*, I thought. "Where's Wes?" I asked her.

"I have no idea where Wes is, Maddie. What happened last night?" she asked with a tone of embarrassed curiosity.

"What are you talking about?" I asked. Then feeling ridiculous for speaking to my sister on the phone when she was standing in the other room, I said, "I'll be right out."

I hung up and got dressed unsteadily, my head feeling like it was trapped inside a bass drum. Mary was sitting on the couch, looking none the worse for a New Year's Eve party that I found with dawning amazement that I could not remember at all. Her big round eyes and sober, mortified expression made me feel all the more unreal.

"There's coffee," she said.

I made myself a cup, and was disconcerted to discover that my hands were shaking. A fear was stealing over me. I'd gone to a party with my sister, expected to meet my boyfriend there later, after he got back from checking out whatever had burned at *Hidden Palms*. I'd expected to wake up in his arms after a delightful late night together, ready for the two of us to embrace all the good things that the new year would bring, not the least of which would be planning for our wedding.

Instead, I awakened at noon in my own bed, with a raging headache, no Wes to be seen, and my sister looking at me in embarrassment. I had no memory past walking into a party and having a few drinks.

I took my coffee back out to the living room. I sunk onto the couch and looked at Mary. "What happened?"

Her eyebrows went up in surprise. "You're gonna have to tell me, Maddie. The last time I saw you, you were talking to some guy. Then you were gone. Next thing I knew, Felicia told me that she'd found you passed out in Benny's back bedroom." Felicia was a waitress at *Mickey's*, Mary's best friend at work. "I couldn't get you to wake up all the way, Maddie!" Mary said with concern. "What were you drinking?"

"I don't remember," I said, not for the first time. "You found me passed out? Then what happened?"

"Felicia called us a cab and helped me get you into it. She even rode over here with me, and helped me get you upstairs and into bed."

If Felicia had helped to drag me into my room, that would explain why my purse was on the bed side table. Maybe she put my phone on silent, too, thinking that I needed to sleep it off without interruption. I didn't remember drinking that much, didn't remember talking to any guys. I'd never blacked out in my entire life, but I've heard that these things happen sometimes. Whatever I'd been drinking must've gone straight to my head. It was a little embarrassing, but lots of people passed out at New Year's Eve parties, didn't they?

"Where's Wes?" I asked again.

"I haven't seen Wes," Mary said. "All this happened before eleven o'clock. I didn't go back to the party. I was worried about you, and . . . besides, I didn't have anybody to kiss at midnight, anyway. So I just went to sleep."

"He didn't come over here looking for me?"

Mary shrugged. "I don't know, Maddie. I'd been drinking, too, and I just went to sleep. If he knocked, I probably didn't hear him, and you . . . you were out cold."

"He's probably worried." I went to call Wes and tell him I was okay, but Mary held up her hand.

"Wait, Maddie," she said, that embarrassment plain on her face again. "You don't remember anything that happened last night?"

"No. I remember walking into Benny's place with you, taking a red cup that someone handed to me. I thought they said it was champagne, but I'm not sure. I remember standing there with you, drinking. Then I woke up here." I went to call Wes again.

"Don't," Mary said. "There's something else." She pushed a few buttons on her phone, then handed it to me. "Someone sent these pictures to me right after we left the party, according to the time on them. I didn't see them until this morning. I don't recognize the number."

There I was, passed out, close to the edge of a bed. My hand was partially hidden beneath my cheek, but the engagement ring was visible on my finger. My mouth was agape in a snore. Less than an inch from my open mouth, a man was holding his penis. There was a bright yellow smiley face tattooed on the back of his hand. I looked at Mary, unable to speak.

"There's another one," she said.

The next picture was from a little wider angle. Now it showed me, and Mister Smiley Face with his dick next to my mouth. But now there was another penis, coming in from the top of the frame, casting a shadow across my forehead.

I looked at Mary, stunned. "Who?" was all I could say, like an owl.

Mary shrugged, took her phone back. "I don't know, Maddie. You disappeared on me. I don't recognize the tattoo, and I don't really have an eidetic dick memory." She dared to grin at me. "But I don't think I know either of them."

"Let me see it again."

"Ah, Maddie, it's disgusting. Just a sick joke. You don't have to—"

"*Let me see it again!*" I screamed. My own voice reverberated painfully inside my skull. Mary dutifully handed me the phone. I looked at the number that had sent the pictures: it was unfamiliar, with an LA area code. Then I looked at the group of recipients, about twenty in all. There was Benny himself, and Felicia, and Jon, and oh, my God! *Wes!*

"The bastard sent them to Wes," I said flatly.

"Surely he can see that it's a joke," Mary said immediately. She knew Wes had seen the awful pictures; she could see his name there in the list, just like I could. "It's obvious that you're passed out. It's not like you're participating . . ."

I pressed the button and Mary's phone dialed the number that had sent the horrible pictures to her, to Jon, *to Wes*. A man's voice answered. I didn't recognize it.

"Who is this?" I demanded.

"Hold on there a second, honey," he said mildly. "You called me. Who is this?"

"This is Maddie Rearden," I told him. "You sent two obscene photos of me to all my friends last night. Who are you? How did you do that? Why did you do that?"

The man laughed. "You must be the girl that passed out at Benny's party. Not a smart thing to do."

"Why would you do such an awful thing? Those pictures are disgusting!"

"It wasn't me, honey, honest. I'm not even from around there. I don't know you – I didn't even know anybody at the party, except for Benny. Some chick asked to borrow my phone for a second. She said she wanted to take a picture, said her camera was on the fritz. She was gone for a few minutes. When she came back, the pictures were already on there, and she'd already sent them out to a bunch of numbers. I even said that it was a pretty fucked up thing to do, but she said you'd think it was funny. I deleted the pictures. I didn't forward them to anyone."

"Who was this chick?" I asked.

I could hear the shrug in his voice. "Some girl at Benny's party. Like I say, I didn't know anyone there but him."

"What did she look like?"

"I don't remember, honey. I'd been drinking, just like everybody else. Just like *you*, apparently. I don't remember what she looked like, and I deleted the pictures as soon as she gave me my phone back. I'm sorry, but I can't help you." He hung up.

I dialed the number again, but it went straight to voicemail. *I'll get to the bottom of this somehow*, I thought. *Maybe I'll even prosecute. There has to be some law against wagging your dick in some sleeping woman's face and taking pictures of it and sending it to the world. There just has to be. Somebody has to recognize that stupid smiley face tattoo. The guy on the phone's got to be lying. He knows some of the people that Mary knows. He knows Wes, for God's sake.*

There was a knock on the door and both of us jumped. Mary arose and opened it. Wes glanced at her, and she looked at her feet. Then he strode into the living room, and stood there eyeing me furiously. After what seemed like a long time, he said, *"What the fuck, Maddie?"*

"I don't remember anything. Mary just now showed me the pictures."

He glanced over his shoulder at my sister, who nodded.

I expected him to sit down beside me then, to take me in his arms and comfort me, to vow, like I had done in my own mind, that we would track down whoever it was that had done this terrible, disgusting act. But Wes did none of those things. He just stood there, looking angry and betrayed.

It occurred to me and Mary at the same time that he believed that these pictures were some kind of record of a wild New Year's Eve bacchanal in which I had been a willing participant, while he was out looking at a burnt out, half-built house. He interpreted the shame on my face now not as chagrin that I'd been so horribly pranked. He interpreted it as shame that I'd been found out.

Mary found her voice before I found mine. "Jesus Christ, Wes! Surely you don't think that Maddie–"

"I don't know what I think!" he shouted. "You fucking twins – you always have come off as a little shady to me. Maybe those guys . . . maybe they were twins, too, and the four of you all decided–"

"You're out of your fucking mind, Wes!" Mary was angry now. "Somebody did this to her! She doesn't remember anything. I lost her at the party, and then–"

"Or maybe she lost you," he sneered. "Maybe she found something better to do."

I couldn't believe his reaction, would not have guessed in a million years that he'd behave this way. "The last thing I remember was taking a drink somebody handed me," I said calmly. "Maybe I was drugged."

"Oh, yeah, that's convenient. That's very *CSI*," Wes said.

"Whatever happened, nothing else . . . happened," Mary said. "Felicia found her passed out in the back bedroom. She had all her clothes on. It's just a mean joke, Wes."

Wes glared at her. "Yeah, you twins are all into the mean jokes." Mary also glared and Wes turned back to me again. "Here's what I came over here to tell you. I got a call last week. Proten's got all the permits approved for the project in Sacramento. They wanted to know if I wanted to go up there and supervise construction. Phil can finish *Hidden Palms*. There's only six units left, including the one that burned. I wasn't going to go, but now . . . I'm leaving in the morning.

"You've got a key. You can go get your stuff anytime you need to. Drew's supposed to be coming back in a week or so for his sister's wedding – I told him he could stay there. Maybe you guys can renew your friendship."

Mary looked helplessly at me, but I didn't feel helpless. My anger rose up, clearing the pounding from my head, clearing my feelings of disgust and betrayal. "How dare you, Wes?" I said, evenly enough. "Just who the fuck do you think you are, talking to me like this?"

"I know exactly who I am, Maddie," he said, his anger not diminishing, not at all. "I'm just not sure who you are." He looked at Mary. "Either of you." Then he softened, just the tiniest bit. "Look. I have to think about all this. You can keep the ring. I'll be in touch." And then he turned around and left.

Mary ran after him and called his name from the door. He kept going. She turned around and looked at me in amazement. "He's *the one*, Maddie! You're supposed to be getting married! Aren't you going after him?"

But I was still angry, awash in furious disbelief at his actions. "Fuck him," I said. "He must not be the one, if he can believe that I'd . . . that I'd . . ." and then I burst into tears.

Mary shut the door and sat down on the couch beside me. She gathered me up in her arms and rocked me, stroked my hair, told me everything would be okay, just as I'd expected Wes to do. She told me that he'd realize it had all been some kind of cruel joke. She told me he would come to his senses. He would come back to me.

I just kept repeating, "Why would anyone do such a terrible thing to me, Mary? Who could hate me so much?"

.

MARY

A week later, Maddie was sitting at the bar, nursing a rum and ginger ale. She didn't order them separately, like that heartless bastard Wes used to, but still, it was what *he* always drank, and I wished she'd go back to gin and tonics, like she'd always preferred before she met him.

All the people that worked at *Mickey's*, all the staff and regulars that had received those pictures, had more or less stopped whispering behind their hands and giggling at each other whenever Maddie showed up at the bar. The first time it happened, she'd felt their eyes on her, and had immediately left. Felicia then walked up onto the little stage, flipped on the mike, and announced that whatever people thought, it had all been just a cruel joke.

"You people are acting like a bunch of high school kids," she'd said stridently, "and I am ashamed of you." She turned off the mike and went back to waiting tables. I considered that it was no doubt a good thing that Jon was not there at the time. He thought the whole thing was hilarious, and I didn't think he would've appreciated Felicia shaming customers and staff alike over it.

But Felicia's words seemed to work, and Maddie more or less felt comfortable enough to again come in to *Mickey's*. She was sitting at the bar, drinking Wes's drink when Drew walked in and stood beside her. Maddie didn't see him, and I just stood there, open-mouthed. He glanced at her, then back at me. To both of us, he said, "Maddie?"

Maddie looked over at him. "I'm Maddie, Drew," she said.

He smiled and gave her a hug, before she could react. "Wes told me that you and your sister . . ." he looked at me, grinned a little awkwardly. "I'm sorry . . . but I asked you out, right?"

I opened my mouth to speak, but Maddie cut me off. "You're not her type, Drew." She smiled faintly at him. "So she fixed you up with me."

I at last found my voice. "Just a little harmless fun."

He smiled at me. "Sure, I understand. No harm done." Then his expression sobered, and he looked closely at my sister. "Wes told me about the other thing, Maddie. He sent me the pictures. . ." Drew realized that perhaps that was not the best thing to mention, and continued quickly, "I told him that it had to be some kind of trick. You're obviously passed out, and I know that you'd never do anything like that."

"We think she was drugged," I said.

Drew looked at me curiously. "I'm sorry," he repeated. "I forgot your name." I pointed at my name tag. "That's right. Your name is Mary, but your friends call you Maddie . . ." Drew shook his head, realizing now that all that was bullshit. He looked at Maddie again. "Yeah, someone drugged you. I told him that it couldn't be real.

"Wes told me that he's asked you to marry him." He glanced down at Maddie's hand. In her resentment over Wes's childish reaction, she'd taken off his ring and had not put it back on. Drew seemed a little bit disconcerted at its absence. "Look, Maddie, he's a hothead. It was all kind of a shock to him . . . but I'm sure he'll see it for what it was. I'm sure he'll come around eventually." Drew took one of Maddie's hands off the bar and held it. "He loves you. He won't be up there in Sacramento forever. He thinks the people are snooty, and this is his home. He'll be back when the job's finished and you guys can just take up where you left off." He squeezed Maddie's hand and released it. "In the meantime, would you like to go to my sister's wedding with me? It's on Sunday. I know it's short notice."

I could tell from the look on Drew's face that it was an entirely innocent, entirely friendly suggestion. He was not trying to pick Maddie up on the rebound, not trying to *renew their friendship* as that asshole Wes had so callously put it.

But when she glanced at me, I shook my head, almost imperceptibly. I thought it was the worst thing she could do. Her beloved Wes, jerk that he was, would not see her going with Drew to his sister's wedding as the innocent thing that it was. He would no doubt see it as validation of all the bad things that he thought about her. Wes would see it as another sign that she was just a slut, that she would go right on back to Drew's bed, there in his own apartment, even if it was just for the weekend.

Maddie caught my little head shake, even if Drew did not; we are twins after all. But she chose to ignore it, and told him that she'd be delighted to go to the wedding with him. Drew asked if she was hungry, and before I had a chance to say anything, she was standing up and putting on her coat.

"It was nice seeing you again, Mary," he said to me, with that little confused look in his eye. I'd seen it enough in my life. It was often there when people saw my sister and me together for the first time. Some people had a little trouble believing that there were two of us, when they had only known about one before. We are, after all, identical twins, and that just amazes some people.

Maddie told me goodbye, ignoring all the signals that I was sending her about how this was not a good idea. I didn't think that she would sleep with Drew – she was still furious with Wes and his immaturity, but I knew that she still loved him, even if she claimed that she didn't. The love that Maddie had for Wes, that belief that he was *the one,* her willingness to marry him – I knew that a girl didn't forget all of that just because of some stupid argument.

I hoped that Maddie *would* forget about Wes eventually, however. He was no good for her. I knew all along that his love had not been as strong as hers, and his freaking out and running away, his apparent inability to perceive that the whole sordid business had been nothing but a cruel joke – that just proved to me that he wasn't the one for my sister. She was better off without him. And she seemed to be getting along well; she didn't cry or tell me that she missed him. But I knew she wasn't over it yet.

MADELINE

Drew was a perfect gentleman. He made nary a pass, spoke nary an innuendo. We went out to dinner, then went back to Wes's apartment and finally, actually, did watch movies. He took me home, saw me to my door, didn't ask to come in. Mary was there waiting for me, and she immediately started in on how she thought it was all a bad idea, that Wes might think–

"Fuck what Wes might think," I told her, and she shut up. It had only been a week since these horrible events had occurred, the pictures, Wes leaving town. My mind had not wrapped itself completely around the fact that I had gone from engaged to be married to dumped and abandoned in so short a period of time, not to mention being the victim of a disgusting practical joke.

I could not think of romance – old romance, new romance. I couldn't think of romance if Ryan Gosling had breezed in from the Great White North and asked me out. I was just numb, with an overall glazing of anger. If Wes believed that I could be thinking about jumping back into bed with Drew after the two of us had been on the brink of marriage, then he was even more irrational than I'd first believed.

I still could not understand his reaction, couldn't yet fathom that I'd lost him over some incredibly mean prank. I could not yet accept that I'd lost Wes through no fault of my own. I could not yet believe that I'd really lost Wes.

I accompanied Drew to his sister's wedding. She was a lovely bride, and I only looked down at my naked left hand once, only thought once how I, too, would've been a lovely bride. Drew, whom I discovered to possess an undreamt of depth of compassion, caught me looking at my hand, and assured me again that it would all turn out all right. Wes loved me, he said. Wes would be back.

After the wedding reception, Drew told me that he had to be getting back to Vegas. He gave me an entirely brotherly kiss on the cheek. I told him that I had a few things to pick up from Wes's apartment, so he left me standing there in front of it.

I went upstairs and crawled into Wes's bed. It still smelled like him, and I wrapped myself in his sheets and cried. I cried at our lost future, I cried at the cruelty of some complete stranger – the guy on the other end of the phone had said *some chick* had taken the awful pictures, but somehow that idea never settled in my mind. No woman could do something so cruel to another woman. I believed that the man's voice on the other end of the phone had been the culprit.

I cried for my underestimation of Wes. I could not believe that I'd so misjudged him, that he could ever have even *entertained the idea* that I'd participated in some pornographic act with two men and had allowed those pictures to be taken of it – I couldn't believe he could *entertain the thought,* nonetheless leave me over it. I cried for the love that I'd had for him. I cried.

I thought about how smug I'd been in my happiness, how much I figured that I'd have Wes forever. We were in love, we we're going to get married. We were going to live happily ever after, grow old together. Then just like that, in the clichéd blink of an eye, the snap of a finger, the click of a cellphone camera, the bark of a few angry words, he was gone.

It was all so sad, yet so ridiculous. Such melodrama. Did women really allow themselves to get caught *in flagrante delicto,* allow themselves to be photographed cheating on their boyfriends like that? Did most boyfriends just flat out believe that their girlfriends would so allow themselves to get caught? Not only must Wes think me a bitch, he must think me a really stupid bitch. I'd just promised to marry him – if I was so anxious to do two guys at once, wouldn't I have taken better plans to hide it, if I still wanted to marry him? Just how stupid did he think I was?

****

When I went to work on Monday, I thought I caught a couple of the construction guys peering in at me as they walked by the office doors on their way to the side entrance of *BF Walker.* I had to be imagining it. Surely, Wes wouldn't have told any of the guys he worked with – it looked as shameful on him as it did on me. Maybe I was imagining it. Or maybe one of them had received a copy of the pictures, too.

My mother picked up on my doleful mood, and when I at last told her what happened, she expressed disbelief that *the nice blue-eyed boy* could be so childish, that he couldn't see that I'd never do such a filthy thing. I told her that I was becoming a little paranoid, that I was beginning to think the guys from *BF Walker* were peering in at me and laughing, just like the people at *Mickey's* had done at first.

"Well, your boyfriend got to run away," Mom said. "Why don't you run away, too?" When I looked at her in confusion, she said, "I'm serious, Madeline. I know how hard it can be to endure this kind of embarrassment. When I divorced your father . . . it wasn't quite the same thing, but I could still feel people looking at me, snickering into their fists. I had to put up with it, because I had you to raise, and there was no place for me to go. But why should you put up with it? You don't have any kids – you're as free as a bird."

"Where is it that you suggest I go, Mom?"

She sat down in front of her computer. "Where did you say *he* went?"

"He went to Sacramento."

She typed. "Okay. You don't want to go there, then." She brought up a list of job opportunities at *ReMax* offices, nationwide. Hell, it might have been *worldwide*, for all I know. Mom studied it intently for a few minutes, then smiled gloriously at me. "How does San Diego sound? There's a secretary/receptionist opening at the Rancho Bernardo office, and as the gods frequently smile upon your mother, I just happen to know the office manager." Mom grinned. "What d'ya think, Madeline? We'll get you a little apartment – I'll help with the first and last and all that. Rancho Bernardo is very nice."

The awful thought suddenly occurred to me that Mom was ashamed of me. Somehow, she'd seen the pictures, and she thought I was a tramp, just like Wes did. "Are you trying to get rid of me, Mom?" I asked, tears welling up in my eyes.

"Of course not, Madeline." And the look on her face said it was true. She didn't believe any of it, any more than Mary did, or Felicia. "It's just like I say. I remember when I divorced your father. I wished I could've run away. It doesn't have to be forever. Just a little time to get over from the memories, to get away from here, and *BF Walker*, and that horrible dive where your sister works."

I had to admit, when she put it that way . . . "It sounds great, Mom."

"I shall make it so," she said in her poetic way.

And damned if she didn't. Before I had a chance to cry and mope through Valentine's Day, I had a little U-Haul trailer and a rented U-Haul trailer hitch attached to my old Buick. Mom and Mary helped me pick out a nice little apartment, not far from my new office, and Mom lent me the money for the first and last and the security deposit. My new boss was Mom's old friend Frieda, whose house she had been going to for Thanksgiving dinner since we were kids. Frieda even hired a couple guys to help me take my stuff out of the trailer and move it into the second floor apartment.

Mary cried when I said goodbye, petulantly telling me that I was as big a coward as that son of a bitch Wes for leaving her.

"It's not forever," I promised her. "I'll always have my old job waiting for me. Mom's right, Mary, can't you see that? I need to get away for a little while. I promise I'll come back."

Mary sobbed harder and hugged me tightly. "And you can visit on the weekends!"

I nodded, and got in the car and drove away. I knew I'd miss Mary and Mom and Dad, too, but my heart felt lighter than it had since before the axe fell on New Year's Day. My heart felt almost as light as it had the night Wes had asked me to marry him. *But leave all that*, I thought. I had a clean slate now, and it would not do to dwell on any of that.

.

MARY

I was devastated when Maddie moved to San Diego. It was just like our mom to help her to the cushiest possible escape from the whole ugly mess, and it was just like Maddie to devour the ice cream sundae, instead of staying here with me and swallowing the bitter pill. I never would've believed that she'd leave me behind, just to escape the memories of one failed love affair. What had it been, anyway? How long had they been together, six months? Seven? Whatever.

I thought that Mom's way out had not helped heal whatever wound Maddie had suffered. Running away never cured anything. I thought that Maddie should've stayed here with me, and faced the familiar, painful things. She should've looked at the little stage where the cowardly bastard had proposed; she should've driven by his apartment; she should've looked at the construction guys from *Walker* when they walked by. All the painful things – she should've endured them, until they were painful no longer. It wasn't as if they'd been married for twenty years, for God's sake.

But Maddie left, almost without a backward glance. She started a new life, and seemed very happy in it. We talked nearly every day, but visits were few and far between. I wanted to go down to see her, but it was quite the drive, and I didn't have much of a car. Maddie promised that she'd make the trip up to Riverside to visit me, but somehow, she never managed to come through.

I was left to muddle through, alone. All because my sister's one time one and only couldn't take a joke. I thought about Wes sometimes, still marveling that Maddie could've ever thought that he was *the one*. I'd known all along – all it took was a simple misunderstanding, a cruel joke – and all of Wes's vaunted love had evaporated like a mist. I could never understand what Maddie had seen in him – but I'd been able to see what a bastard he was from the day he'd walked into my bar and played his own cruel joke on me.

MADELINE

Moving to Rancho Bernardo was like the godsend of myth, the just what the doctor ordered of popular cliché. The office was nice, with no developer located next door, with no accompanying construction worker types parading by. The work was easy and fun, and Frieda was a barrel of laughs, again, just like the cliché.

I received a small package in the mail about a week after I'd settled in, and when I saw Jason's name and my old address on it, I realized that it must be a copy of his completed documentary on Rolling Blackout. I wanted to watch it, for Jason's sake – I knew how much time and effort he'd put into the thing. I wanted to watch it for Jason – but I just couldn't. I threw it into an open box, half full of sweaters. I would later toss the box into the back of a closet. I never bothered to unpack it. I'd never been much of a sweater wearer.

The very best thing of all about my new life in Rancho Bernardo occurred when Evan Michaels walked into the office one delightful spring afternoon. Evan could've been Wes's older brother, and I am embarrassed to say, that's probably the only reason I noticed him in the first place.

Romance had not re-entered my mind – several of the guys from the escrow and title companies had asked me out, and even one or two of Frieda's clients – but I turned them all down. I didn't know why I was suddenly so popular – couldn't they see that I was sad and depressed, despite the great job and cheery surroundings?

Frieda recognized my confusion, and answered my unspoken question. "They sense that you're wounded, Madeline." She always called me *Madeline,* just like Mom did. "They think you'd be an easy kill." Also like Mom, Frieda didn't care too much for what she believed was the core motivation of all men: to see what they could get.

But when Evan walked into the office, I must have stared at him, because he smiled at me a little self-consciously, as a person will when someone is staring at him. He introduced himself, and told me that he was there to meet Frieda: she was showing him a house that afternoon.

I stammered that I would go get her. But Frieda had been watching through the glass wall of her office and came out when I stood up. She looked curiously at me, then greeted her client. "Ah, Mr. Michaels, so nice to see you again."

"Please, Frieda. Call me Evan."

Frieda nodded, then snapped her fingers at me. Apparently, I was staring at him again. "I have some bad news, Evan," she said. "I won't be able to show you that property today. Something pressing has come up. Can we reschedule for tomorrow? Unless . . . Madeline? Would you like to show the house to Mr. Michaels?"

I looked from Frieda to Mr. Michaels, then back to Frieda. I'd never shown a house in my life, but I'd been to enough open houses with my mother when I was a kid, that I knew how such a thing went. And here in Rancho Bernardo, the houses practically sold themselves. And he was very attractive. Frieda was doing me a solid.

"I would love to," I said, regaining my composure. He was just a man after all, no matter how much he reminded me of Wes, and I've never been much of one to stammer and act silly around men. He wasn't Wes, after all – Wes was gone. He was just a prospective home buyer, and Frieda saw that I thought he was cute. She was offering me a pleasant way to finish up the work week, spending a nice afternoon showing a house to her good-looking client.

"I'll get the file," she said, and returned to the office.

"I'm Madeline Rearden," I told him, and thought that once upon a time, I might've sent him and his expensive suit Mary's way. But maybe not. He did have black hair and blue eyes, which I still favored, even after Wes. He smiled at me and I realized that he didn't really look like Wes at all, past the similar coloring. Wes was gone. He'd abandoned me. And Evan Michaels was cute in his own right. He shook my hand and said he was glad to meet me, and I forgot all about Wes.

The house that I showed to Mr. Michaels – *please, call me Evan* – was a cheery two bedroom with a huge living room, comfortable kitchen, and a small, cozy, well maintained lot. He didn't seem overly interested in the amenities: the flawless wooden floor and lovely fireplace in the living room, the fact that the place had two full bathrooms. He asked about schools, and I consulted Frieda's file. Yes, there was a grade school within walking distance.

This pleased Evan more than the granite countertops in the kitchen. He had a little girl: Emmaline, age six. He was a widower, he told me, and little Emmy an orphan. His wife had died in a car accident in San Francisco less than a year before, and he was relocating here to get a fresh start for himself and his daughter.

It was the saddest story I'd ever heard, and I felt an overwhelming desire to hug him and comfort him. His tale of losing his young wife made me feel foolish for all the agonized soul-searching and feeling sorry for myself in which I'd wallowed about losing Wes. Wes was gone, as surely as Evan's poor wife, but he wasn't *dead.*

Evan said simply that he would take the house. Then he asked if I'd like to meet Emmy. I smiled and said that I'd be delighted. Evan directed me to a little day care facility across town, and I waited in the parking lot while he went inside and retrieved his little girl. I didn't even primp in the rearview mirror. Not too much.

Emmy was dark haired like her father, with his enormous blue eyes. She looked at me solemnly when Evan introduced us, then dropped a totally unexpected curtsey, and said, "So nice to meet you, Miss Madeline." She said it *Mad-uh-LINE,* like the storybook character, and I smiled.

"You can call me Maddie," I told her.

Emmy looked at her father as if for permission. He nodded, and she said, "So nice to meet you, Maddie." She was adorable.

"Would you like to see our new house?" Evan asked her, and at last a smile bloomed on the serious little girl's face. I guessed that I would've been a serious little girl at her age, too, if I'd so tragically lost my mother.

We drove back to the house, and Emmy ran around from room to room. She grabbed my hand and pulled me outside with her, while she inspected the back yard. "Can I have a playhouse here, Daddy? You said that I could!"

"Of course you can have a playhouse," Evan told her. He looked uncertainly at me. "Do you know any carpenters?"

I was so delighted with him and his little girl that I didn't even think of Wes, who could've slapped together a fairy playhouse for little Emmy in a weekend. Instead, I said, "Frieda will know someone."

Emmy ran up and hugged me tightly around the waist. "Thank you for our pretty new house, Maddie!" she cried.

"Oh, honey," I explained, "your daddy picked it out. I just brought him over to see it." But Emmy continued to hug me, and Evan smiled. Finally, I just said, "You're very welcome, Emmy. I'm glad you like it."

Evan asked if I'd like to have an early dinner with them, and I said I would. We went back to the office; Frieda looked curiously at me again, and smiled a big grandmotherly smile at Emmy, although Frieda was no grandmother. She was a lifelong bachelorette – her only family, she often told me, was my mom, and now me. Evan repeated that he would take the house, and Frieda said she'd have the escrow papers ready for his signature in the morning.

Evan drove a slick black Audi. He was not completely unfamiliar with the area, he told me, and quickly found a nice, quiet, expensive restaurant. I would discover that Evan preferred nice, quiet, expensive things.

After dinner, the three of us went back to their townhouse. It was his cousin's timeshare, he told me with a small moue of distaste, and he'd be glad to leave it as soon as possible. Well-appointed as it was, he didn't like the neighborhood, and there was no place outside for Emmy to play.

I met Mrs. Franklin, their live-in nanny. She was about fifty, genuinely grandmotherly. Evan told me that she would not be moving to the new house with them, because her own daughter was about to have a baby, and she'd promised to return to San Francisco to help out. I saw tears well up in Emmy's eyes when Evan told me this news. *The poor little thing!* I thought. She just lost her mother, and now her nanny was leaving, too. It was all so sad.

Mrs. Franklin told Emmy that it was time to take her bath and start getting ready for bed. She gave me another adorable hug, and again thanked me for getting them the new house.

Evan and I sat in the ugly living room of the time share, and he asked me if I'd like a glass of wine. I nodded and he smiled at me. No. Evan didn't really look anything like Wes.

He asked me how long the escrow would last, how soon before he could move into the house. I told him that Frieda could close an escrow faster than anyone in the business – it shouldn't take too long at all. We made small talk. He told me that he was some kind of junior vice president in charge of something for some bank. I really didn't pay much attention. What he did for a living wasn't important to me. Details about men's jobs and how much money they made always bored me.

Evan had just offered to drive me back to the office when Emmy ran out into the living room, wearing a pair of Little Mermaid footy pajamas. She gave her daddy a hug, then jumped on the couch next to me, and gave me a hug, too. "Will you tell me a story before I go to bed, Maddie?"

I looked at Evan and he smiled doubtfully. "If you know any stories," he said. "She's kind of picky."

It was definitely a challenge for me. What kind of stories did I know that were suitable for a little girl? I knew stories about unreasonable boyfriends and cruel practical jokes, and dads that cheated on moms, and the definitely-not-for-the-ears-of-little-girls deals that sometimes went on between twin sisters. I now knew stories of the tragic loss of wives and mothers.

Off the top of my head, I concocted a brief tale about a beautiful, blue-eyed princess. She had a pet unicorn named Chas. The beautiful princess's name was Emmaline. Her father, who also had blue eyes – I smiled at Evan – her father, the king, had searched the entire kingdom for a new castle, just so that Emmaline would be warm and happy and have a nice place to play with Chas. He had at last discovered such a castle, and soon he and the princess would move, and Emmaline would have her very own playhouse, and she and her daddy would live there, happily ever after.

Emmy approved of my story, even though she told me that she didn't have a pet unicorn named Chas. Mrs. Franklin told her that it was time for bed, and Emmy gave me a big hug and kiss and ran happily off to bed.

On the ride back to the office, Evan told me in words of pleased surprise that Emmy had not been so effusively happy and affectionate with one single person since her mother's death.

"Oh," I said, flustered, flattered. "She's just excited about the prospect of her playhouse."

"No," Evan said resolutely. "She liked you." We had pulled into the office parking lot. He stopped the car and looked at me, solemnly, just as Emmy had done. "It was so nice meeting you, Miss Madeline," he said, repeating Emmy's words. "Thanks for everything." Then he smiled. "I'll see you in the morning."

I smiled back at him, got out of the car, watched him drive away. I saw that there was a light on in the office, so I went back inside. Frieda was standing next to the printer, watching it slowly spit out the paperwork for Evan's home purchase.

"You know what that's printing?" I asked, repeating Frieda's favorite question. She turned and smiled at me, and we said in unison, "Money."

"I think I'll give you the commission on this one, Madeline," Frieda said. "I didn't think he'd go for it. It's a little homey for a banker. What did you say to him about it?"

I shrugged. "He has a little girl. She liked the backyard. She sold it to him more than I did."

Frieda looked curiously at me. "The paperwork says there is no Mrs. Michaels. Is he divorced?"

I wondered why she thought I'd know such details about someone who was no one to me but a prospective client. But I did know. "He's a widower."

Frieda clapped her hands together. "How nice for you, Madeline! And he's so attractive!"

"Ah, Frieda, I don't know . . ." But I did know. I liked Evan very much, after only one afternoon together. I liked him and his adorable little girl, and the obvious love between them.

"Let's just see how it plays out, shall we?" Frieda said. "I saw how you two looked at each other."

I smiled, and Frieda hugged me. Just like Emmy, I felt happy and affectionate for the first time in quite a while.

MARY

I would hear updated reports of Maddie's whirlwind courtship with the rich banker from Frisco on a nightly basis. And whirlwind it was. The ink hadn't even dried on the papers for the house and they were dating. He hadn't but barely finished generously tipping the guys from *Bekins* before she was moving in with him. It was barely the end of August before he was asking her to marry him.

All of this, I had to see. So on the first Saturday in September, I rented a car and drove down to Rancho Bernardo to meet the man and child that were destined to someday be my in-laws.

I arrived early. I wanted as much time as possible with my sister, who it seemed I hadn't seen in a million years. She was waiting for me in the driveway when I pulled in, and we had many hugs. I looked closely at her. I always expected the differences in our lives to make differences in our faces. I was still slogging it out at *Mickey's,* fighting off passes from bar flies, going home to the same lonely little second floor walk-up from which Maddie had escaped. Jon had promoted me to manager, but Maddie was living the high life in a ritzy community with a wealthy banker. She was going to get married. She had it made.

But still we looked exactly alike.

The house was lovely. The child was lovely. I watched her slide gleefully across the polished wood floor in the living room in her footy pjs, then climb up into Maddie's lap like it was the most natural place in the world for her to be. She looked solemnly at me, then curiously at Maddie, then back at me. "Can I have a twin sister, too, Maddie?" she asked.

Why, you already have mine, little girl, I thought. *How greedy of you to want another one.* "Maybe after Maddie and your daddy get married, maybe you might have a little brother or sister," I told the kid. "But they won't be your twin."

"Am I really going to have a brother or sister, Maddie?" Emmy asked in delight.

Maddie glared at me. "Maybe someday, Emmy," she said to the little girl. "Right now, go wake up your daddy, so he can meet Mary, too." The child complied, sliding across the floor again, then bounding down the hall.

Maddie showed me a notebook – it was filled with page after page of her weird, left-handed script. These were the stories that she told to Emmy. Emmy loved them so much, and requested that her new mommy regale her with them so often, that Maddie had taken to writing them down.

"That way, I don't repeat myself in the same story," Maddie told me. "Emmy corrects me if I tell the same detail twice."

What a pushy brat, I thought. I read a few pages of Maddie's fairy tales – legends of the blue-eyed princess, and her blue-eyed father, the king. He saved her when she was endangered by fiery dragons and marauding trolls. She and Chas the unicorn had adventures. I thought the stories were quite clever, and asked Maddie to scan them and email them to me so I could read them all. She was completely complimented by my praise, blushed even, and said she would send them to me immediately.

"Although eventually, you're going to have to invent a blue-eyed prince to start saving the princess," I told her. "Little girls grow up, and sooner or later, Emmy's going to want someone besides her daddy to save her. She'll want to be bestowing true love's first kiss and all that."

Maddie was appalled that I could suggest that she start making up love stories for Emmy, appalled at the idea that Emmy would ever be interested in such things. "By then she won't need me to read stories to her," Maddie said.

Whatever.

Maddie closed the notebook and leaned forward. She whispered conspiratorially to me, "Tell me if Evan reminds you of Wes at all."

Now it was my turn to be appalled. *Wes who?* Here she was, in the catbird seat, with money and family and a wedding on the horizon, and all she could think of was to ask me if I thought her new man reminded her of that cowardly loser? *Seriously?*

I'd already seen pictures of Evan, of course. Maddie had never taken to Facebook, but still she sent me pictures. Here she was with Evan on Catalina. Here she was with Evan and Emmy at the San Diego Zoo. At Disneyland. Here was a picture of the giant rock that Evan had given her for an engagement ring.

I knew that Wes and Evan were about the same height. Wes had dark blue eyes and Evan had light blue eyes, and they both had black hair, because Maddie was something of a one trick pony as far as the type of men she liked. But there the resemblance ended. Wes dressed like a slob, and was always shaggy-looking, always in need of a haircut. Wes had a boring, only marginally well-paying job. It was his unfortunate lot to work outside in the heat, and he used to frequently come into the bar dusty and sweaty after one of his harder days. He was neither witty nor funny. He was a coward, and could not take a joke.

On the other hand, when Evan came out to greet me, he looked like he could've stepped out of a Land's End catalog. He was wearing a dark blue sweater over a white, collared shirt, a pair of jeans and deck shoes. No ratty flannel. No battered Converse. His black hair was cut stylishly short; no riot of unkempt curls and waves. I offered my hand, and his grip was firm, his hands soft – no callouses from slinging lumber around all day, or whatever it was Wes had done to make his hands so rough. I didn't know this personally of course – I don't think I ever shook hands with Wes – but Maddie had commented on it. Evan's voice was as smooth as his hands – no dropping his g's and calling Maddie *darlin'*.

I looked at her in amazement. Except for their coloring, I saw absolutely no resemblance whatsoever between Wes and Evan. Maddie was nuts. Evan was a sophisticated, successful, wealthy businessman. Compared to him, Wes was nothing more than a dull, stupid, outdoorsy, country bumpkin. There was no similarity, no comparison to be made. *It's just like her,* I thought, *not to realize how good she's got it.*

Later, I asked her if she really thought that Evan looked like Wes – did she really still think about stupid Wes, when she had all this wonderfulness? She admitted that no, she didn't really think that Evan looked like her ex-boyfriend, and no, she didn't think of him very often.

"I just wanted to hear what you thought," she said to me.

I told her that there was no resemblance, unequivocally none, and she dropped the whole discussion, speaking instead about how happy she was, how much in love with Evan, how blessed she felt to be mothering his little girl.

But I couldn't get over her initial question. My sister had hit the jackpot, for God's sake, and all she could do was ask me if I thought he looked like Wes. *Wes who?*

****

Not a week later, the hillbilly himself showed up on my doorstep. To say that I was gobsmacked into speechlessness would be no exaggeration. It was a Friday night. I was off, and hadn't had even the prospect of a date for several months. So I'd decided to just stay in, watch a few movies on Netflix, eat some ice cream, and feel sorry for myself in my loneliness.

I answered the door in my bathrobe. I looked at Wes in surprise and he looked back at me for a moment. Then he said softly, "I'm so sorry, Maddie!" and launched himself into my arms.

Well, I'll be goddamned! I thought. Here was ol' Wes, breezed back into town, repentant, thinking that he could just waltz back into my sister's life with an itty-bitty *I'm sorry* to make up for all his unreasonable mistakes. And here he was, making at least one of the same mistakes, thinking I was Maddie.

He stopped hugging me, looked at me, and I waited for him to figure it out. But just like the first time, he didn't. He hugged me again, said he was sorry again, and burst into tears, just like the gutless adolescent I'd always suspected him to be. I closed the front door and led him over to the couch. He sat next to me and alternately begged my forgiveness and cried on my shoulder.

When he finally seemed to get a hold of himself, I told him that I forgave him, because it's what I thought Maddie, with her new, bright, shiny, successful life in ritzy Rancho Bernardo would've done. And in the middle of thanking me for forgiving him, Wes started to kiss me, and I should've stopped him then, I should've told him.

But one part of me thought that he deserved to be duped, he deserved to be made the fool, just like he'd made Maddie love him so much, and then made her the fool by abandoning her, all over a stupid joke. One part of me wanted to hurt Wes because he'd hurt Maddie. His actions had led Maddie to hurt me, to abandon me. I figured that allowing him to make this mistake, again, would surely hurt him.

But another part of me liked his kisses. It'd been many months – Bill never had come back from Sacramento, at least not that I'd ever heard, and I hadn't had a date worth taking home in some time. And Wes was safe, familiar enough – I was pretty sure he wasn't going to murder me, even after he found out that I wasn't Maddie. *And besides,* another small voice piped up in my head, *now I'll get to finally find out what all the fuss was about.*

So I let Wes kiss me, and I kissed him back. I listened to his murmured apologies and his whispered gratitude, and told him it was all okay, and one thing led to another, and Wes made love to someone he thought was my twin sister, right there on the couch. And then on the floor. And then on the couch again. I hesitated to take him to my room – I couldn't recall, no matter how hard I tried, if he'd ever stayed here with Maddie, if he'd know which room had been hers. Surely he'd been in there with her – sometime when I wasn't home, maybe? So I hesitated.

But Wes never sought softer, more private accommodations, and eventually, we fell asleep together on the couch. Wes slept soundly, sated, secure that he'd been forgiven. I also slept soundly, sated enough

– he wasn't the ravening be-all and end-all lover that Maddie had often made him out to be, but he was all right, and it had been a long time.

But I was completely sated in my revenge – I'd pulled a cruel joke on Wes, just like he'd once pulled a cruel joke on me. And I'd gotten even with him for not believing that someone had also pulled a cruel joke on Maddie. She might've forgiven him for all that, now that he'd seen the error of his rush to judgment – but I doubted that she would forgive him for *this*.

Besides, Maddie had moved on. Who in the fuck did he think he was, that she would just be waiting here for him, to grant him forgiveness and all else he'd asked for, the moment he showed up?

****

Even if Wes wasn't all that, all the unaccustomed lovemaking must've taken it out of me more than I would've realized. I must've slept for quite some time, because when I finally opened my eyes, I found myself covered in a sheet. Wes was sitting in a chair across from me. He had a watchful, unreadable expression on his face, but when I smiled at him, he smiled back.

He waited for me to sit up, and then said, "Hungry?" He showed me a Cutie – one of those little tangerines – I loved them and always kept a bag of them in the fridge. Before I could respond, he said, "Catch!" and tossed it to me. I caught it in my right hand, as a righty will do, and just like that, the gig was up.

"You are a bitch, Mary," he said evenly.

"And you are a son of a bitch, Wes," I replied. "When did you figure it out?"

I realized that he hadn't figured it out. Maybe when he woke up, he came to the conclusion that his forgiveness had been just a little too quietly, a little too eagerly given, so he decided to test me. He hadn't figured out that I wasn't Maddie until he saw that the woman that had forgiven him so demonstratively was right-handed.

"Is this how it's been all along?" he asked. "Have you always been standoffish to me because you were jealous of your sister? Have you wanted me to fuck you all along?"

Ah, there was that vulgarity again, something that I'd always suspected was right below the surface of his personality. I laughed. "You flatter yourself, Wes." And he did. He'd been all right, but nothing to write home to mother about, even if my mother had been amenable to hearing about such things.

"Where's Maddie?" he asked, and I was reminded of that fateful New Year's Day, now nine months gone, when Maddie had kept saying *Where's Wes?* until he'd finally shown up and broken her heart.

"Maddie doesn't live here anymore," I told him. "Maddie has moved on."

The dejected look on his face made me almost forget my righteousness, my desire to hurt him. Tears welled up his eyes again, and I thought that maybe my little joke had been a little too mean this time. He'd thought I was her, the only one that could forgive him. He'd thought that he'd been forgiven, that everything was going to be all right again. Maybe I'd crossed the line, allowing him to feel that kind of hope.

"Where?" he said.

"You were just so sad," I said, ignoring his question. "I knew she was gone, and you . . . you were so sad, Wes. You needed someone to forgive you. And . . . I've been lonely. Maddie's gone, Wes, and I . . . I liked kissing you," I lied, at least partially. Kissing him had been okay, but it wasn't something that I couldn't have stopped, had I chosen to stop it. But telling him this little half-lie might soften the blow of what I had to tell him next.

"Where's Maddie?" he said again.

"My mom got Maddie a job in San Diego, not long after you left. She said it would help Maddie to forget . . ." I watched him wince, and a little bit of my old vengefulness returned. *Damn right you should wince*, I thought. *Look at the mess you made!* But I continued gently. "Maddie works at the *ReMax* office in Rancho Bernardo. She lives in a big airy house with a man named Evan and his little girl. They're engaged." The tears spilled down his cheeks. "I'm sorry, Wes."

He rose to leave and I also rose. I blocked his path and hugged him, intending it as a sisterly show of condolence. But the only thing between us was the thin sheet with which he'd covered me (probably when he still believed I was Maddie), and he felt me shudder when his hand touched my bare back.

He looked at me curiously, and I wiped some of the tears from his face with my thumb. Still he looked at me, immobile, unspeaking, and I thought, *what the hell, why not?* I put my arms around his neck and kissed him, and slowly, hesitantly – as if he was thinking it over – Wes kissed me back. It had been a long time, and my sister's cast-off was better than nothing. Besides, if he was here with me, it would keep him from running off and ruining her happy little life in San Diego.

****

After our weekend of forbidden passion – it lasted the whole weekend – I didn't really expect to see Wes again. He'd only asked me to explain Maddie's situation one more time – I told him that she lived in a beautiful house, had a great job, was engaged to a brilliant banker, and was playing mother to an adorable little girl. He didn't bring it up again.

But he stayed there with me, and made love to me many more times. He left Sunday night, saying he had to attend a production meeting bright and early the next morning. He kissed me goodbye.

But I wasn't Maddie, and I'd broken all my mother's rules. I'd known all along that I wasn't Maddie, even if Wes had not, and my behavior had not been very ladylike, by any means. So I didn't expect to see him again. He'd come back to town to beg forgiveness of his ex-fiancée, someone who might be expected to forgive him body and soul, someone who could be forgiven *herself* for surrendering to his tearful pleas in a Detroit minute. They'd once been engaged to be married, after all – and theirs would have been a joyous reconciliation. No one would've looked askance at Maddie for nailing Wes three times in the living room, then all over the apartment, all weekend long.

But I was not Maddie, and after the first three times, Wes had known that there wasn't going to be any joyous reconciliation with the fiancée he'd wronged so completely. He knew it, and I knew it. Yet he stayed, and I let him stay. His style grew on me, and after a while, I moved him up the ladder from okay to not bad. I hadn't had a sex weekend like that since lean, blonde Mike, and I figured, what the hell, I might as well enjoy myself while it lasted. I was sure I'd never see Wes again.

But to my surprise, there was Wes, walking into my bar when he got off of work on Monday, resplendent in a dark blue suit. He'd said he had a meeting that day, but still the thought crept into my mind – had he left his suit on because he knew I'd like it? He sat at the bar and ordered a shot of rum with a ginger ale back. I brought it to him, and just kind of stood there, waiting to see what he would say next.

"Isn't your name Mary?" he asked, and smiled openly at me. Not slyly, not deviously.

I pointed at my nametag. "That's what it says." I wondered what game he was playing. The thought crossed my mind that perhaps Wes was not as sensitive to slutty behavior as some of his peers might be. He'd taken up with Maddie, fresh from Drew's dirty-fingernailed embrace, had he not? And they had been all set to live happily ever after, until . . .

Yes, perhaps Wes didn't hold slutty behavior against a girl too much. *Unless there were pictures,* I thought, a little evilly.

I smiled back at him. "But you can call me anything you want, honey." He'd been a lot of fun, and he did look good in that suit. And Maddie had found a new happily ever after in Rancho Bernardo.

"I understand that your sister used to go out with my friend Drew," he said. "Drew didn't have much nice to say about her, but he told me that you were the sweetest, prettiest girl in town."

Still, the open, friendly smile. Was Wes trying to pick me up? Was he trying to do it right this time? Was he trying to be charming and gentlemanly? Was he trying to make up for the time that he'd walked in here (at Maddie's urging) and treated me like a whore, the one act that had made me hate him all along?

"In fact," quoth he, "Drew said that if I came over here and asked you politely, you might be kind enough to go out to dinner with me sometime." He paused, then said, "Hi. I'm Wes Thomerville." He extended his hand and I shook it, feeling the rough callouses. They were quite familiar to me now, as he had run his hands all over me for the better part of the weekend.

I just stared dumbly at him. It was indeed the nicest pick-up line I'd ever heard in this bar, and if it wasn't for the lifetime of history that had gone before, if he'd just walked in here for the first time and asked me out to dinner like that, if he hadn't been engaged to my sister at one time, then I most certainly would have –

"Would you?" he said, and I blinked as if slapped, because it seemed like he was reading my mind.

"Would I what?"

"Would you go out to dinner with me sometime?" And the look on his face said it all: he was lonely, and he knew I was lonely, and we'd known each other for a long time, and we'd been great together, and Maddie was gone, and oh, *why the hell not?*

"I know I'm probably not your type," he said. He glanced down as his well-cut suit, and grinned innocently at me, knowing that he looked exactly my type right at that moment.

"Yes," I said. "I would go out to dinner with you sometime."

Now he let that devious smile peek out, but just a little bit. "How about tonight?" When I hesitated, he said quickly, "If that's too soon . . ."

I felt a genuine fondness for him, then, for the first time ever. "No, that's not too soon, Wes. I get off at eight."

****

And so began my love affair with my sister's ex.

Thanksgiving was a little different that year, but it was the same as the previous year in a lot of ways. Mom went to see Frieda in San Diego, as she always did. But Maddie cooked them dinner and they shared a happy little family time with Evan and Emmy. Maddie invited me to come, too, but I said that Joanna would be heartbroken if I didn't go over to Dad's.

What neither Maddie nor Mom knew, of course, was that Wes went with me.

I told Dad ahead of time that a little switcheroo had taken place on the boyfriend scene. I didn't go into all the gory details about the pictures and all. I just told Dad that Maddie and Wes had broken up in January – he said he knew that they had – and Wes had left town. Dad knew all about Evan – Maddie had sent him the pictures of that rock, too. I told Dad that when Wes had returned to town and discovered that Maddie wasn't here waiting for him, one thing had led to another, and now . . . we'd just moved into a new apartment together.

Yeah, that happened, just before rent came due in November. One could say that memories of Maddie haunted my place and his place, too, and that we saw her ghost whenever we were at either place together. Or one could just say it was time for a nicer place for both of us, and with our combined incomes, we could afford a nicer place. One could say that it was just the natural thing for us to do, what with our long history and all.

If Dad was surprised, he didn't say so on the phone, and he simply greeted Wes as his long-time-no-see buddy. The fact that he was now living with his other daughter didn't bother Dad at all.

****

Wes and I never talked about Maddie, but after we moved in together, she remained the 800 pound gorilla in the room. It was unspoken, but we knew that we were going to have to tell her about us some day. I knew it, he knew it.

As Christmas loomed, the look became plain on his face. The time had come. Maddie had to be told. It would be a nasty surprise if she showed up here for the holiday, just knocked on the door to my new place, and Wes opened the door. That would be awkward indeed. I smiled and told him that I would do it, by myself, and his look of grateful relief made me unwillingly remember what a coward he could be.

But it was really no big deal to me. I was fine with telling Maddie about us by that time. Whatever it was that Wes and I had – I don't know what you'd call it, I certainly didn't love him – whatever it was we had, we had it by then. Wes and I were together, and I was confident in our togetherness. He'd forgotten all about my sister, and whatever they'd once shared.

And whatever Maddie would have to say about it . . . what could she possibly have to say about it? It was not as if I had stolen Wes from her. Theirs had just been one of those things that hadn't worked out. It wasn't like it was my fault that they'd broken up. And besides, she had her own man and her own life in Rancho Bernardo – a much better man and a much better life than I had. So what could she possibly have to say about me and Wes?

If I had any doubts that Maddie had moved on, she cleared my conscience when I pulled up in her driveway in Wes's truck and she failed to even recognize it. She just asked me why I'd rented a truck this time instead of a little car. "Doesn't it get terrible gas mileage?" she asked.

I thought the truck was as good a segue into the news I had for her as any. "It's Wes's truck, Maddie," I said softly.

Her mouth dropped opened like the legendary fish out of water, and she blinked rapidly. "Wes came back?"

Oh, no, don't let your little tiny mind run off in that direction, sister mine. There's not going to be any changing your mind now, no going back. You've got your big house and your charming fiancé and your darling little girl, and I have . . . not much, but what I do have is mine.

"He's been back since September," I told her. *And he's with me now,* I thought. "I told him that you're getting married." She still blinked, her mouth still hung open. "You're still getting married, aren't you, Maddie?" I looked over my shoulder at her lovely house.

Now her mouth snapped shut. She stopped blinking. "Of course I'm still getting married."

"You're still in love with Evan, you still love his little girl?"

"Of course I do, Mary."

"I know you do, Maddie." I smiled. "That's why I know you won't have any problem with the fact that I've been dating Wes." She started to blink again, but immediately got a hold of herself. She just looked at me silently, until I finally said, "Come on, Maddie. Say something. I gotta know that you're okay with this."

MADELINE

Mary didn't say, *You gotta tell me what you think of this,* or *You gotta tell me whether I'm making a mistake.* Oh, no. She didn't care about my opinion, didn't want my advice. She just wanted me to tell her that I was okay with her *dating Wes.* Because she was obviously okay with it.

There were so many things I wanted to ask her. Had he finally come to his senses? Had he finally realized his mistake? What had he said to her when he came back? Had he said he still loved me? Had he said he was sorry? But none of that mattered anymore, did it? I was going to marry Evan, and Wes was . . . *Wes was dating my sister.*

And then there was the idea of how *all that* had come to be. I couldn't even begin to frame the questions that would touch on the how and the why of Wes and Mary dating. Mary had never even *liked* Wes, how could she be dating him?

And then there was that word, *dating.* A euphemism for the ages was that word. I knew how Mary *dated.* She wasn't dating Wes, she was fucking him, and despite my new happy life, despite my love for Evan and Emmy, I felt a sharp spike of jealousy arc through me, body and soul.

But my mind suppressed it. There was no reason for jealousy. Wes had abandoned me; Wes was an irrational, childish coward, just like Mary had always termed him. *My, but hasn't her mind changed!* But I knew she didn't have to respect some guy to sleep with him.

I fought the jealousy down. I didn't love Wes any more. I hadn't even seen him, hadn't spoken to him in almost a year. I'd never spoken to him again, actually, not one time, after he questioned my morality and ran off to Sacramento. I hadn't but rarely given Wes any thought in all that time, why should I think of him now? Why should I care who he was *dating?*

And Mary. If she wanted to take up with someone whom she'd once termed a *chickenshit,* who was I to say her nay? Wes was her problem now. He'd ceased to be my problem on New Year's Day, of his own free will, at his own volition. Family gatherings in the future might be a little awkward, but our family had never been much on gatherings, and I was sure I could avoid seeing him. Seriously, why the hell should I care?

"I'm okay with it, Mary. I hope you guys'll be—" but Mary hugged me and said thanks, so I didn't have to actually say, *I hope you guys'll be very happy together.*

Because I didn't hope they'd be very happy together. I hoped that Mary would recover the loyalty that I'd believed in for my entire lifetime. I'd once believed that it would always be the two of us against the world, and in the face of that, I hoped that she'd realize that what she was doing was just *icky*.

It didn't matter that Wes and I meant nothing to each other anymore. It was just not right, somehow. Mary had never even *liked* Wes before, and I hoped he'd scratch whatever strange itch she'd suddenly discovered for him, and then she'd cut him loose just as soon as possible. I hoped that she'd come to her senses and realize that her being with Wes was wrong, that it made me uncomfortable. I didn't want to see Wes ever again. I certainly didn't want him at my wedding, and she, of course, my twin sister – she had to be there.

"I brought you a surprise, Maddie," Mary said, and I didn't dare to imagine what kind of additional surprise she could have. I wasn't sure I could take any more surprises right at that moment.

Mary reached into her purse and brought out a little spiral-bound book. The cover read, *Princess Emmaline, by Madeline Rearden.*

"Felicia did the illustrations," Mary told me.

Mary had typed up all my stories and printed them in some little curlicued font. Felicia had drawn very good pictures of dragons and castles – there was Chas, the unicorn! Then Mary had bound it all up in with a little spiral spine. I recognized it from a machine for binding reports at Mom's office.

I looked at her, touched. It was one of the nicest things she'd ever done for me. Finally, I found my voice. "It's beautiful, Mary! Thank you so much!"

"I told you I thought that they were clever. I made up about a dozen of them. Thought they'd make great Christmas presents for some of the girls at the bar who have little kids."

"It's beautiful," I said again. "The pictures . . ."

"I told Felicia she needed to get out of the bar and go to art school."

"Thank you so much, Mary!" I repeated, and hugged her.

Mary said I was welcome. Then she looked at me awkwardly, and stammered something about having to get back to Riverside. The weight of her *other surprise* had returned. It seemed that she'd just wanted to pop all the way down to Rancho Bernardo, give me her thoughtful little gift, and oh, yeah, drop that other bomb on me.

She'd heard Mom say – when did she ever talk to Mom? – she'd heard Mom say that I might be bringing my little family up to Riverside for Christmas so that she and Dad could finally meet them, and Mary hadn't wanted me to find out that she was seeing Wes from anyone but her. Mary said that she was so happy that I was okay with it, and she was glad that I liked the little book. But she had to be getting back now.

She had to be getting back to Wes.

Of course, she didn't actually say that, but it was there, nonetheless. She didn't want to embarrass me, hadn't wanted me to embarrass myself, by discovering the new status quo on my own. She'd just thought it best to let me know about it, but now she had to go. She was glad I liked the book, told me to keep writing those fairy tales, and we'd come out with a second volume. But she didn't have anything else to talk to me about. What were we supposed to do, compare notes?

I walked Mary back down the driveway to Wes's truck – she hadn't even made it into the house. I recognized it now – there was the blue fender that just didn't quite match the rest of the paint, from where he'd been in an accident before we'd even met. When Mary opened the door, I tried to tell myself that I couldn't smell him. But I was lying to myself.

All the old memories came back with his scent, and I missed him, and I ached for him, and I thought, *Ah, Wes, I loved you so much! Why'd ya have to be such a son of a bitch?*

MARY

I gave Maddie a hug and told her thanks. I knew she'd be flattered by my compilation of Emmy's stories, but then I realized that there really wasn't much else to say. So I got back into the truck, waved, and drove slowly away from her big, expensive house. But I pulled over when I got to the bottom of the hill, because my hands were shaking. It took me a minute to get a grip on myself.

Why had I felt the need to tell her thanks? She was engaged to be married to Mr. Rich, Blue-Eyed Banker Boy, so why had I felt it necessary to tell her thanks for being okay with me seeing her cast-off? I certainly hadn't felt the need to ask her permission beforehand, and Wes certainly hadn't, either. We'd been together since he'd tossed me that tangerine; we'd agreed to move in together, and he had not bothered to stop and wonder what Maddie would think then. If he had, he'd never mentioned it to me.

And why had I neglected to tell her that little detail, that we were living together, that we were so much more than *dating?* I felt a little cowardly at the omission, but then I thought, *That just would've too much, all at once.* She'd find it all out soon enough, if she brought her little family to town for Christmas.

But it would turn out that even that little awkwardness was to be avoided. Whatever plans Maddie had made with Mom and Dad for visits at Christmastime – separately, of course: there was no bringing Mom and Dad together, not even for holidays, not since Maddie and I had left home – whatever plans Maddie had made to return in triumph to Riverside were scrapped before the week was out. She and Evan and Emmy would be spending the holidays in San Francisco with Evan's parents, she told Mom. They missed their granddaughter, and they wanted to meet their son's intended.

Look what you've done, my Mother's expression said when she actually lowered herself to come in to *Mickey's* to tell me the news. *You've made it so your sister won't even come home for Christmas.*

I wondered if Maddie thought that I'd believe that this sudden change of plans had nothing whatsoever to do with her not wanting to run into Wes over the holidays. Mom certainly didn't believe it. Did Maddie want me to buy that her sudden desire to accompany Evan to Frisco had nothing to do with the prospect of introducing her once-betrothed to her now-betrothed?

Sure I could buy that, if she wanted to sell it to me. It was just the way things went, the orderly progression of her new life. Just like me and Wes moving in together was the orderly progression of my new life, how things should be, now that my sister had abandoned me so she could live the good life. It was time for her to meet the people that would soon be her in-laws. She wasn't avoiding any unpleasantness in her hometown. It wasn't like that at all.

****

Mickey's former house band reunited for a gala performance on New Year's Eve. The line-up was a little different: Phil was supervising construction on a *Walker* project outside of Monterey, so they had scared up a different drummer. They played through to midnight this time, swinging into a fair rendition of *Auld Lang Syne* as the crowd counted down the death of the old year. Wes pulled me up onstage and kissed me as the clock struck twelve, and not one person in the crowd turned to anyone else and made note of the fact that it had been Maddie with him the year before.

I thought it a little odd, but then none of us had actually been present at the bar for the joyous cries of *Happy New Year*, now had we? But still . . . not even Jon, from whom I'd expected a snarky comment, made a mention of what a difference a year makes. Perhaps Felicia had made an announcement again.

95

MADELINE

Evan's parents were sweet and welcomed me into their home and lives with open arms. Their house was done up like something out of the North Pole: wreaths and garlands, lights and ornaments and an enormous Christmas tree, stockings hung by the chimney with care, even one with my name on it. We had a huge dinner on Christmas Eve, and Evan and I and Grandma and Grandpa helped Emmy to set out milk and cookies for Santa Claus.

Evan's parents bought me a lovely angora sweater and I only thought for a moment about that box of sweaters, moved unopened and unpacked from my apartment to Evan's house. It was now in a closet off the living room, beside a box of toys that Emmy had outgrown. I only thought once of Jason's movie, *Jason's movie of Wes*, never watched, which I remembered tossing into that box. So long ago, when I was still sad and depressed.

But I wasn't sad and depressed now, was I? I was about to marry into this wonderful family, and who knew, maybe someday, Evan and I might have a child of our own. I would've never really considered all that, but Evan's mother had mentioned it a few times. How nice would a little brother or sister for Emmy be?

We stayed for the whole week between Christmas and New Year's. Evan left Emmy with her grandparents, and we attended the San Francisco Symphony's New Year's Eve Masquerade Ball. I wore a black velvet dress and a mask made of peacock feathers, and we danced on the stage of the Davies Symphony Hall. Evan told me how much he loved me and kissed me at midnight, and the thought of *Mickey's* little rickety stage never crossed my mind. The memory of Wes asking me to marry him there, the idea that, if not for the cruelty of strangers, it would be me there kissing *him* at midnight instead of my sister – these ideas didn't occur to me at all. Not at all.

I hadn't really thought about Wes much since he'd left town. It was only my sister, making a special trip south to let me know that she was *dating* him, that had even brought him back to my mind. And it wasn't like he'd stayed there in my thoughts since, him and all the memories of the things that we'd shared in our brief time together. It wasn't like that at all.

****

As the new year progressed, so did the plans for the wedding. On Valentine's Day, Evan gave me a lovely diamond pendant, just like you see on the jewelry store commercials. He drove me out to the Maderas Golf Club, and like he'd just thought of it, he suggested that it would be the perfect place to hold our wedding and the reception. Quiet and expensive. I gleefully agreed. The place was beautiful, with the hills as a backdrop, and they had a huge ballroom, too.

It was a lovely, romantic day. There weren't even any memories of Valentine's Day with Wes to mar it, because I'd never spent a Valentine's Day with Wes. The lover's holiday had already passed when we met, and by the time it rolled around again, I'd already moved to Rancho Bernardo, had already begun my new life. And by the time it rolled around again . . . I would be Mrs. Evan Michaels.

****

The wedding was scheduled for the last weekend in June. By mid-April, everything was more or less set: the invitations had been sent out, the band and the caterers and the ballroom at Maderas booked. I even had my dress all picked out, altered and tailored, ready to go.

The only thing that I didn't have yet were any bridesmaids. Frieda had agreed to be my matron of honor – she'd already helped with all the details, including picking out my dress – all the things that Mom should've done. But Mom was in Riverside, and it was a long drive, and she'd confided in me that it would just tickle Frieda to death if I'd allow her to help with all the planning. She didn't have any family of her own, Mom said, and it would just be the nicest thing if I'd let Frieda pretend to be my mom in preparation for the big day. It was all right with me. Frieda was not at all as critical as my mom would've been, anyway.

But I still didn't have any bridesmaids. My twin sister had of course agreed, and Felicia, but somehow, I'd never been able to get them to come down to pick out dresses. I began to believe that the time would just get away from me, dresses would never get picked out, and I'd wind up with no bridesmaids at all. Evan was spending a king's ransom on this wedding. It would not do for me to be without attendants, just because the only close girlfriend I'd ever had in my life had always been my twin sister, and she'd somehow been too busy to come down and pick out a dress.

So on a sunny Tuesday in mid-April, I called Mary and told her that I would be coming to Riverside on Thursday, because I'd gotten a few days off. I told her to gather Felicia up – I told her that I had

Evan's credit card, and that we would be going shopping for bridesmaids' dresses, and that I wasn't going to take no for an answer.

I expected her to demur, to make some excuse, but she was enthusiastic. "That sounds great, Maddie! They're . . . they're . . . painting my apartment, so you'll have to stay at Mom's . . . hell, we'll both stay at Mom's! You picked the perfect time! I have Thursday through Sunday off, and Wes'll be at some builder's conference in LA, so you don't even have to worry about running into *him!* Come on up, Maddie! I can't wait to see you!"

And just like that, my only worry was swept away. It was true that Mary had been distant – she'd not seemed too keen on the bridesmaid deal, had not been able to make it down to any wedding planning sessions. But I guessed that I'd been a little distant, too. I hadn't called her too often, had not visited once. I had not *insisted* that she come down and help me with the wedding preparations. And it had all been because of Wes, because of her and *Wes.* I hadn't wanted to hear about how all of that was going, although I knew it was still going, because my mother had reluctantly told me that it was.

"Yeah, they're still seeing each other," was all Mom would say, with a sigh. She felt the same way about it that I did. Sure, there was absolutely nothing wrong with it, really – Wes and I had broken up a long time ago, I was getting married, why shouldn't Mary go out with him? But Mom also thought that it was just not right, somehow, and she didn't even like to talk about it.

But Wes was going to be out of town, and Mary said she couldn't wait to see me. I found that I couldn't wait to see her, either. I realized that I missed her, and deeply, like I'd missed her when she and Dad had first moved out. I realized that I shouldn't be letting my feelings of awkwardness over who she was dating get in the way of seeing her. He was going to be out of town, anyway, so there wouldn't even *have to be* any feelings of awkwardness.

I joyfully told Evan that I was leaving early Thursday morning and spending the entire weekend with my sister. He was happy for me; he knew that we were close, but that we didn't talk much. He thought it was just the geographical distance. Evan had no idea that Mary was dating my ex-fiancé. Evan had no idea I even had an ex-fiancé. I'd never told him about the whole Wes chapter of my life – the horrible pictures, the ridiculous break-up. He never asked much about my life before we'd met, and the whole thing had just been too awful to tell him about. It was none his business, anyway, and it was all over.

He said that he would take Emmy to the zoo and stay in a hotel down there with her, visit the animals a few days. It was only thirty miles away, but he said that Emmy would think it was exciting to stay in a hotel, just like she had when we'd gone to Catalina.

"Be sure to call me if you decide to come home early," he said. "So I can come up and get you. If you decide to come home early, Emmy would want you to be at the zoo with us."

I nodded, but said, "I don't think I'll come home early. My sister and I have a lot of catching up to do." *And Wes will be out of town.*

Evan gave me a quick kiss and said, "Let me know, either way. I wouldn't want you to miss the zoo."

****

Bright and early on Thursday morning, I arrived at my mom's house. Mary was waiting for me, and so was Felicia. We hugged and jumped up and down like schoolgirls, then we drove all over the Inland Empire looking at bridesmaids' dresses. Mom even came along. We finally decided on some floor-length, ruched, mermaidy-looking things. Mom thought they were horrible – she said something about Morticia Addams – but she didn't have to wear one, now did she?

My wedding colors were blue and white – "Light blue, like Evan's eyes," Mary told Felicia and giggled – and the dresses were the perfect shade of powder blue, and they fit both girls without needing any alterations. So it was decided. Mom threw up her hands, Mary told the sales girl to wrap 'em up, I paid, and the four of us went back to Mom's house, exhausted but satisfied.

Mary and I cooked dinner, and it was almost like old times. There didn't even seem to be any of the old friction between Mom and Mary. There was only one little rough patch, when Mary made some snide remark about Mom's taste in clothes, because she had pooh-poohed the dresses that we'd picked out.

Mom looked at her haughtily and said, "How nice to have you home again, Mary. When did you say you were leaving? When did you say that they'd be done . . . painting your apartment?"

I thought I detected a little glare at Mom when Mary replied, "They should be done on Sunday, Mom. Just about the time that Maddie's going back home."

Whatever embers of mother-daughter enmity had flared up at that moment quickly died back down and the four of us sat around and had a glass of wine together after dinner. Then Mom excused herself, saying she was worn out from all the shopping. She said she'd let us talk about the things that young women talk about, and bid us good-night.

After she left, Mary and Felicia and I opened another bottle of wine and cavorted down Memory Lane. We recalled every boyfriend we'd ever dated, and wowed Felicia with some of our switcheroo stories. The three of us got drunk. We got drunk and talked about men, but even through our drunkenness, there were two men none of us mentioned. We didn't talk about Drew, because talking about Drew would've led to talking about Wes. And none of us wanted to talk about Wes.

We poured Felicia into a cab about midnight, then Mary and I went up to the room we'd shared until we were twelve years old. We talked in the dark, just like when we were kids, mostly reminiscing about those days, before Mom and Dad divorced. We talked about Dad and his poetic appreciation for that stupid bridge. We talked until it started to get light outside, and then we finally drifted off to sleep.

It was so nice to see her again, I thought. It was a shame that circumstances — *her choice of circumstances* — made it impossible for us to do this more often. Perhaps I'd be able to coax her down to Rancho Bernardo sometime, after Evan and I were married.

MARY

It was so much fun seeing Maddie again, going shopping with her. The dresses we finally decided on were horrible – for a change, Mom was right – but even all the fun shopping had been getting tiresome by then, so I just went along with what Felicia and Maddie picked out. It was a bridesmaid's dress, what did I care? I was only gonna wear it once, and Evan was paying for it, so the ruched all the way up the back and all the way up the front mermaid look was just going to have to be in for stylish weddings at the country club this June. When no one was looking, I sent Wes a picture of it. He replied with a smiley face and agreed that it was hideous.

The only dark moment of the day was when Mom made the remark about my apartment being painted. She knew that Wes and I lived together, and had let me know that she didn't approve. It was okay that Maddie was shacking up in ritzy Rancho Bernardo with some rich banker, but her daughter the bartender was just giving away the milk for free. And there was also the fact that I was giving the milk away for free to Wes, whom she had once called *that nice blue-eyed boy*. But not anymore. Wes was in the doghouse, right there next to me, as far as my mother was concerned.

The whole painting-the-apartment scam had been my idea, and Mom had reluctantly agreed that there was no reason to tell Maddie that Wes and I were living together yet. *It might ruin her big shopping day*, Mom had said. Whatever.

Wes really was out of town. I hadn't made that part up. He really was at some construction management seminar in LA, just like I'd said. But if Maddie had come to our apartment, she would've known that I was living with some guy, and she would've known exactly who it was. There weren't too many guys that had as extensive a collection of ratty flannel shirts, and who else would I be living with, if she knew I was dating Wes? So I thought it was best to just stay at Mom's with Maddie. It was just a little harmless deception, and I'd tell her eventually. No sense ruining her big shopping day.

And everything went perfectly until Friday afternoon. The whole ruse held: they were painting my apartment, Wes was out of town – we hadn't even mentioned him – I was going to stay there with Mom and Maddie two more nights. Then on Sunday morning, Maddie would go home to her happy little family, and with Mom's disapproval hanging over my head, I would meet Wes back at our sinful love-nest for brunch, and we could all get on with our lives.

****

The glory and the evil of texting is that while one is with one group of people, one can be talking to someone else, and the group of people one is with is none the wiser. I noticed that Maddie was careful not to mention Wes at all. But Wes was bored at the conference, and I texted him, on and off, for most of the afternoon on Thursday, while we shopped.

He understood that Maddie didn't want to see him, and I think he was secretly grateful about that, seeing as he'd been the one that had ruined everything between them. But he didn't have any trouble talking about her wedding and her husband-to-be. Wes was with me now, and he was happy with me – whatever he'd felt for Maddie was gone, and he had no trouble at all with the fact that I was helping his once-betrothed pick out bridesmaids' dresses.

Our secret conversation lasted right up until Mom bid us good-night – the conference was over for the evening, and Wes and the rest of them were going out to the bar or whatever guys did when they were stuck in LA overnight. I told him to have fun and told him *Luv u 2*, when he texted *Luv u*. It was something that he'd started saying and texting to me about the time we moved in together, so I said it back. I didn't really love him, but he was nice to have around. Having Wes to come home to was certainly better than all the lonely days I'd spent after Maddie left.

Friday afternoon found me and Maddie playing gin rummy. Mom had gone to work, and playing cards was another throwback to childhood, something we'd done for endless hours as kids, something we'd both enjoyed. As I dealt, I noted that Maddie didn't even take her phone out of her purse – she wasn't much on modern conveniences. Maybe it had something to do with the fact that a cellphone had been the instrument of her embarrassment.

She wasn't much of a texter, had never even made a Facebook page. So while I answered the things people texted to me – Felicia said that she thought she'd spied my old buddy Mike leaving the bar when she came in for her shift, and Jon whined to me that he was short-handed, could I maybe come in? – Maddie just sat there and looked at her cards.

She didn't even send any messages to her betrothed. I asked her why not, and she said that Evan was at the zoo and was probably busy, and he'd just bought her a new phone, and she wasn't very good at working it yet. That was Maddie: technologically uninterested.

I didn't even hear from Wes until he texted me about two o'clock: *This thing is 2 boring 4 words. I'm not staying here another night. I've had enough.*

I replied: *I'm staying at my mom's with Maddie til Sunday.*

Ok. I'll see u when u get home. Im outta here after the next lecture.

And then I didn't hear anything more from him. I figured he was probably driving, or just didn't have anything else to say. Maddie and I played cards for the rest of the afternoon. We had a great time.

About five-thirty, I lost a hand, and that meant I had to go out to the kitchen and find us something to eat. I made a couple of ham sandwiches, and when I got back out to the table, I noticed that Maddie looked a little flushed. When I asked her if she was feeling okay, she said, "I don't know, Mary. I think I might be getting sick." She looked up at me, and now she went from flushed to pale. "Would you be too mad if I went home?"

"Now?" I said in disbelief. "But we're having such a good time!" I set her sandwich down on the table. "Maybe you'll feel better if you eat something."

Maddie took one look at the sandwich and got up and ran into the bathroom. She was in there for a minute, so I looked at my phone. Wes had texted: *I'm back. I thot 4 a minute that u forgot to pay the Netflix bill, but it turned out that it just needed 2 b reset. What r these movies u put in our queue? Im gonna erase them all. ☺ There wont b one horror movie left on there when u get home.*

U leave my movies alone! I texted back.

Maddie came out of the bathroom. She looked at me with my phone in my hand, as if I was holding a rattlesnake. When I set it down on the table, she told me again that she was sorry, but she was sick, and she had to go. I gave her a hug, told her I hoped she'd feel better soon. I told her I'd say good-bye to Mom for her, told her I'd missed her. I walked out to the car with her, told her to drive carefully. I waved good-bye as she squealed away, as if the legions of hell were after her.

It wasn't until I went back in the house to text Wes that I'd be home after all, and in just a few minutes, that I realized what had happened. My phone was sitting next to Maddie's untouched ham sandwich, just a little closer to her chair, just a little closer than where it had been earlier, when I'd been out of the room. My dumb-ass had left it lying next to the deck of cards, right across the table from where my sister had been sitting. Hiding who I was texting was a new thing for me, and I hadn't even thought to take my phone out to the kitchen with me when I went to make sandwiches.

Maddie had read Wes's text. She couldn't help but read it, because I'd left my phone lying right there, out in the open. And she'd ran off, not because Wes had been saying how much he loved me, not because Wes had been talking dirty to me, describing the things he liked to do, things that he had undoubtedly once done with her. Wes's text had been nothing like that; Wes never texted anything even *remotely* like that. But his innocent words were still damning: *u forgot to pay the Netflix bill,* and *our queue,* and *when u get home.*

It was obvious from his little domestic text that Wes and I were so much more than dating, and it had come as just as much of a shock to Maddie as Mom had predicted it would. It wasn't like I left my phone there on purpose for her to find. It wasn't like I'd *just* been talking to him. He hadn't said anything for three and a half hours. My phone had just been sitting there, more or less dormant, all that time. It made a little noise, after being silent nearly all damn day, and she had just naturally looked over at it.

Oh, well, I thought. *I tried to shield her, but she was going to have to find out sooner or later, anyway. At least it didn't ruin her shopping day.*

MADELINE

The wall to wall traffic on the way home helped to calm me down a little bit. If I hadn't had to concentrate on not running into the car in front of me, I might've just cranked the old Buick up as fast as she would go, and no doubt crashed and burned. I was just that pissed.

It was not so much that Wes and Mary were obviously living together, all cuddly in their easy, domestic bliss – *I'm gonna delete all your horror movies from* our *Netflix queue*☺. Hardy-har-har.

Alone in the car with only myself and my rage, I admitted that their relationship, its continuation, did bother me. I let the immature part of me have its say – *Why does she get to be so happy with Wes? What's wrong with me, what's right with her, that she should get to be so fucking happy with Wes?*

But then my rational mind stepped in. It wasn't their togetherness, their domesticity, their co-habitation that was really bothering me. It wasn't even their happiness. I was on the brink of my own happiness, already ensconced in my own domesticity – why, how, could I possibly care about Wes and Mary, shacked up in some little Riverside walk-up?

I was going to be married soon, be a member of the country club, all those things that Mary had always dreamed about. I was going to be living the life that she'd always wanted. Why should I care that she was living the life that I'd almost had? The life that she was living, the life that I could've had, had been ruined by the very man she was living it with, so how could I possibly care?

No, it wasn't their living together that pissed me off so much, made me so angry that I held the wheel in a white-knuckled death grip. It was that Mary had lied to me about it. She had lied, and she had gotten my own mother to collude with her in her lie. Mom knew that they weren't painting Mary's apartment.

What a coward my sister is! I marveled. She'd always called Wes a coward – maybe it was rubbing off on her. Why hadn't she had the guts to tell me? If they were all in love and living together, why had she felt the need to hide it? *Could it be that she's ashamed of it?* Did she really think that I gave a rat's ass about what she and Wes were doing, when I had my whole life ahead of me?

A new thought struck me. *Did she think she was protecting my feelings?* That one was hilarious. I laughed, and the sound was shrill and hysterical in the car. If Mary had ever even *considered* my feelings, if she'd ever thought about me for *one second*, then she would never have started up with Wes in the first place. If she'd ever cared about me, she would've told him that I'd forgotten about him, and then showed him the door.

But no. Mary had been hard up, and Wes had been convenient. He had the requisite equipment, was good-looking – even if she hadn't *ever even fucking liked him before*, for God's sake – he would do on a dark and stormy night. Her undeniable *needs* had been all that had mattered to Mary. My feelings hadn't entered into any discussion that she had undertaken with herself about whether or not it was a good idea to fuck Wes, to move in with Wes.

Wes was cute and he was good, and that had been Mary's entire motivation. The fact that I would be appalled by the whole thing, that our mother would be appalled, didn't bother her at all. I realized suddenly that Dad probably knew, too. Dad wouldn't care – Dad had lived his own brand of ickyness for years, and he liked Wes, anyway. What difference did it make which daughter his buddy was seeing? Wes had just switched directions on the bridge.

MARY

When I texted Wes and told him that I would be coming home after all, he wrote back, *That's great! I have a little surprise for you.*

My mind was on the Netflix queue, but Wes's little surprise was much better than anything on TV. Drew had called and invited us to come up to Vegas for a visit. Wes had begged off, saying I was busy all weekend. But when I'd texted to say that I was not going to be busy after all, he'd called Drew back and it was on again.

It was Friday night, after all, and neither of us had one other thing to do all weekend. He was supposed to still be in LA and I was supposed to still be entertaining my sister. But all that had fallen apart, so I quickly packed a small suitcase and we jumped in the truck and headed for Sin City.

We laughed and joked and talked about gambling, and I admitted to myself again that I was glad to have Wes. I certainly wouldn't be going to Vegas by myself, and I'd never have been able to coax Maddie into such an impulsive, devil-may-care thing anymore. She had responsibilities, a child. She would soon be an upstanding married woman. I still couldn't say that I loved Wes, but he was sometimes a lot of fun, and he was mine, which is something that I really could no longer say about my sister.

I speculated about what Wes had said to Drew about which sister it was that would be showing up in Vegas with him. Then I ceased to wonder about it. They talked on the phone all the time, and Wes had probably told him about us right from the beginning. Whatever Drew thought or said – that was all between them. I doubted that he would be all uptight about it like my mother was – it was just one of those things and Drew no doubt couldn't care less which sister his friend was dating, any more than our dad did.

MADELINE

When I pulled into the driveway at home, there was a light on in our bedroom, and I realized that I'd forgotten to call and let Evan know that I had indeed decided to come home early, as he'd asked me to do. I was surprised that he was home, and I wondered if Emmy had taken sick. But then I saw a shadow moving on the ceiling – Emmy was jumping on the bed. Maybe the zoo had just not been to her interest that day.

I unlocked the door, put my purse on the table next to it – all the routine things one does when one comes home after a long drive. I walked up the steps, and down the hall, paused in the open doorway to our bedroom. I expected for Emmy to see me and come running over and give me a hug. Emmy's joy whenever she saw me was the part of the routine of my life in sunny Rancho Bernardo that I enjoyed the most. But Emmy was not there, thank God, and the routine of my life in sunny Rancho Bernardo ended in the blinking of an astonished, disbelieving eye.

Evan hadn't gone to the zoo. He'd called and had the zoo delivered, a very special kind of grown-up zoo, with a very special kind of female animal.

Evan was naked, handcuffed to the headboard. A young woman, also naked, was standing on the bed over him, jumping and laughing – it was her shadow that I'd seen on the ceiling. Another woman, wearing thigh-high, black leather boots, a black corset, and nothing else was standing beside the bed, grinning at them.

What followed was like something out of a bad rom-com, but there was nothing whatsoever either rom or com about it. Evan stopped smiling gleefully up at the young nude woman when he saw me standing in the doorway. His mouth fell open in shocked surprise, mirroring my own expression, and I could see his mind trying to think up some way to explain. The girl in the boots followed his gaze, and she, too, stared at me in disbelief. At last the naked girl, wondering why the party had suddenly stopped, confused as to why all the grins had suddenly evaporated, stopped jumping on my bed, and also turned and looked at me.

We stood there staring at each other in stunned silence for what seemed like a long time, then both women, as one, turned and looked back at Evan. He swallowed several times. He tried to speak, found that he could not, then tried again. At last he croaked out, "Maddie . . . I . . ."

"Maddie, you *what?*" I screamed. But it was all so ridiculous. My reacting with hysterical, jealous anger would just be too pat. Insanely, my mind flew back to that New Year's Day, when I had wondered if women really allowed themselves to get caught cheating on their boyfriends in the manner that Wes believed I'd allowed myself to be caught cheating on him. Did successful bankers, community-minded members of the country club, really allow themselves to get caught, handcuffed to the bed, with two . . .

They turned from considering Evan, and looked at me again.

I lowered my voice and said to the naked girl, "You, get off my bed. Put some clothes on. Then both of you – get out of my house."

The girls didn't move, didn't run out of the room in shame, as I expected them to immediately do. They just looked back at Evan.

"Did you hear me?" I said, my voice rising again. *"Get out of my house!"*

Still they didn't move. Evan said, "They won't leave until they get paid." The women looked back at me; the naked one stepped off the bed. "My wallet . . ." Evan gestured with his head at the dresser. "Go on, Sparkle." *What the hell kind of a name was Sparkle?* I thought. "Gala, it's all in there. Just take it and please . . . just go."

Gala was the one in the boots, apparently. She swiftly crossed the room and took a wad of cash from Evan's wallet. The wallet was of imported calfskin, with his initials monogrammed on it, a present that I'd given him for his birthday. While Sparkle picked up a lacy black robe from the floor and quickly threw it on, I watched Gala toss the money into a medium-sized valise on the floor beside the dresser. I just had time to have the image of all manner of sex toys burned forever into my brain before she squatted – gracefully, I must admit, what with the boots and all – and snapped the little suitcase shut. She arose, looked briefly at Evan, then walked out of the room.

Sparkle hesitated. She looked over her shoulder at Evan, then looked back at me. She met my eyes, and there was maybe a little bit of pity there. Whether it was for me or for Evan, I'm not sure. Then she pressed the handcuff key into my hand and quickly followed her partner out of the room.

I heard the front door slam, and wondered absently what the neighbors would think if they happened to look out their windows and see two half-clad women scurrying off into the night. Then I again looked at Evan, spread-eagle, handcuffed to the very brass headboard that I'd picked out, and realized that what the neighbors thought certainly didn't matter to me anymore, because they would soon be my neighbors no longer.

Evan blinked his enormous, powder blue eyes at me and again stammered, "Maddie . . . I . . . ."

"If you say another word, I'm going to tape your mouth shut," I told him. Another blue-eyed man had once ignored my explanations about a sick joke. I surely wasn't going to listen to this one try to explain *this*. "You just stay right there and keep quiet."

I took a suitcase out of the closet and started throwing clothes into it. I by-passed all the expensive dresses that Evan had bought for me, by-passed my wedding dress in its large bag. I wouldn't be needing *that*. I went over to the dresser and swept all my underwear into the suitcase, all my neatly folded shirts and jeans. When I couldn't fit another thing into it, I snapped it shut, and turned again to look at my just about to be ex-fiancé.

He opened his mouth, and I said, "I swear to *Christ*, Evan, if you say, *Maddie, I,* again, I will gag you." He abruptly closed his mouth. I took off my engagement ring, showed it to him, then went into the bathroom and flushed it down the toilet.

I went back into the bedroom and set the handcuff key on the top of the dresser. "I'll call someone to come over here and unhook you." He opened his mouth and I shook my head. "If you say one word, it'll be Child Protective Services that I call, and they're not open until Monday." He closed his mouth again. I sighed. "Don't call me, Evan. Don't ever even *call me.*" I turned and walked out.

The closet off the living room was standing open, the light on. I wondered if the . . . *hookers* . . . had stolen something. I looked into the closet, thinking there wasn't much of anything in there to steal. Maybe they had hung their street clothes in there or something. What did I know about how hookers operated?

I saw that old box of sweaters, next to Emmy's outgrown toys. The thought struck me that there were clothes in it that were *mine,* from before I'd known Evan. The clothes in there were something that he hadn't purchased for me. This thought made me feel a little sentimental for them, even though I'd never been much of a sweater wearer, so I picked up the box, carried it outside, and put it into the backseat of the car. Then I went back into the house to get my suitcase.

I slammed the front door as hard as I could, thinking that if the neighbors hadn't seen the whores scuttling off, they surely had heard the rifle-shot noise of the door. As if in answer to my thought, a porch light came on across the street. I didn't lock the front door. Someone would still have to go back and release Evan, and I thought that if I had one shred of luck left, perhaps someone might walk in and rob the place in the meantime. I got into my car, backed it out into the street with a companionable squeal, then roared off down the street. I made sure that everyone on the block knew that *something* had gone on that night at the Michaels's house. They would soon know that what had happened was an *ending*, because they wouldn't be seeing me anymore.

I drove out of the neighborhood, then pulled over and called Frieda. I wasn't crying, wasn't shaking. My anger and disgust laid a cool layer of calm over me. So calm was I that I could've returned and slit Evan's throat as nonchalantly as a ninja assassin, had I been so disposed. But his crime was not capital – it was far too sad and commonplace to arouse my ire enough that I wanted to kill him. I just wanted to get as far away from him as I could, as quickly as possible. Besides, poor Emmy was going to need a father, because she had just lost another mother.

I told Frieda what had happened, using small, quiet words. I waited through the silence of her disbelief. Finally, she said, "What are you going to do?"

"I'm going to go back home, Frieda. I have to get away from here."

"Of course you do, dear," she said. "I meant . . . what are you going to do about Evan? Who are you going to call to . . . cut him loose?"

I thought about it, thought about whose numbers were in my phone. There was his golfing buddy, Alan. His boss. But they were just other men – they'd probably think the whole incident was funny. Who knows, maybe they did the same kinds of things when their wives were out of town. "I don't know who I'm gonna call," I told Frieda.

She laughed, and it was like a wind chime tinkling in an icy breeze. "You go on back to Riverside, Madeline. I'll go over there and uncuff him."

And picturing that made me laugh, too – Evan's utter embarrassment when his matronly real estate agent showed up to release him from his self-imposed – oh, here was a good word – *bondage*. "I love you, Frieda!"

"I love you, too, Madeline. I'm sorry about all this, but I can't help but say that it's better you found out sooner, than later. Give me a call next week and tell me your plans."

As soon as I figure out what my plans are gonna be, I thought. "I will, Frieda, and I owe you one."

"Think nothing of it," she said, and told me goodbye.

Then I called my sister. All of a sudden, all the things that I'd been so angry about on my ill-timed flight from Riverside faded into the background. She and Wes, living together, hiding it from me – all my fury about that seemed laughable now. Now I truly had something to be furious about. But Mary didn't pick up, and all these revelations were not something you explained in a voicemail. They were probably all cuddled up, watching horror movies on Netflix. Still, my anger at their deception was but a mouse when compared to the elephant of my utter disgust and disbelief at what I'd almost married. Just like Frieda had said – I was too relieved that I'd found out about Evan's little peccadillo in the nick of time. I couldn't concern myself with Mary and Wes at the moment.

So I called my mother, and told her that something had come up, and that I'd be coming back to Riverside tonight. I told her I'd give her all the details when I arrived.

On the long drive back, I considered my relationship with Evan – I tried to recall any actions on his part that should've hepped me to the fact that he was a deviant. Evan was sophisticated, witty, funny. He was generous, affectionate, loving. Thinking over our relationship, the whirlwind courtship, the quick proposal, I realized that all of his charming qualities had made up for the fact that he was also a somewhat meagerly-endowed, never more than adequate lover.

I wondered if his desire for two women at once, if his need for them to bring along an entire *suitcase* full of accoutrements somehow made him feel better about his overall shortcomings – I actually guffawed out loud at *that* word – in the lovemaking department. It was sad – I'd loved Evan, even if he hadn't been much in bed. My love for him and Emmy and our little family life had made up for what he lacked on that score. He was adequate, after all, and there should be more to a relationship than just sex, anyway, I'd told myself.

But apparently what he lacked was something that my love alone couldn't overcome. Apparently he possessed the need to prove to himself that he could please two women – ha, that was such a laugh, he couldn't even please one, one that loved him. It was clear to me that Evan was willing to pay to have two whores pretend that they were impressed.

When I got home, I told Mom everything. I thought that if I didn't, Frieda surely would. Then she made me some hot chocolate just like when I was sad as a kid, and told me that I was more than welcome to come home, to run away from this debacle, just like I'd run away from the other one. Then she gave me a couple of Valiums and tucked me into my old childhood bed again.

Mary returned my call the next morning, and I asked her to come over to Mom's. "Why are you back at Mom's?" she asked, genuine concern in her voice. It made me think once again that whatever was going on with her and Wes was not really the biggest problem in my life.

"If you come over here, I'll tell you," I said. "It's not really something that I want to discuss on the phone."

"I can't come over to Mom's right now, Maddie. I'm . . . I'm in Vegas."

Sure, I thought, *things didn't work out for our happy weekend together, so you just ran off to Las Vegas with Wes. No use wasting a weekend off. I left out of Mom's house sick, and were you concerned about that?* But again, I couldn't be worried about all that. She was on the phone with me now, she sounded concerned now.

"It's nothing that can't wait, Mary," I told her. "Just come over here whenever you can."

****

I stayed in bed all day Saturday, and Sunday, too, hiding from the world. Evan didn't call, thank God, but Mom said that Frieda called to check on me. Mom brought me trays of food and murmured soothing words, as if I was physically sick, instead of just heartsick, disgusted and embarrassed. Again.

On Sunday night, Mary burst into our childhood bedroom, her face a picture of the same concern that had been in her voice on the phone. It hadn't caused her to make a beeline back from Las Vegas, but how could I complain? She was here now. Just like I had to Frieda, I calmly explained what had happened.

"Oh, my God, Maddie!" Mary said in disbelief, then repeated it about three times. She wore the same expression of disgust and embarrassment that Mom had encompassed, and I thought that it was one of the few times in our lives that the three of us were in perfect agreement. The next words out of Mary's mouth were an apology that she hadn't been honest with me about her living arrangements.

"You and Wes are the least of my worries right now," I told her.

MARY

Oh my God, had life turned into one surprise after another, *or what?* First, there was that nasty practical joke on Maddie on New Year's Eve. Then Wes had overreacted and bolted. Then my mother had given my sister the golden ticket to the good life. Then Maddie left me. She'd met, moved in with, and planned to marry her blue-eyed Prince Charming. Then Wes had come back to town, and maybe somebody else was going to get to live the good life for a change, because Maddie's good life had just gone down the drain with the click of a pair of handcuffs, now hadn't it?

It just goes to show ya, I thought, *just when you think you know somebody . . .* Maddie had never shared behind-closed-doors stories with me about Evan, as she had about Wes and previous boyfriends. We weren't that close anymore, hadn't had a chance to have too many face-to-face girl talks, like in the old days, when we shared an apartment, and maybe a few other things, too. So I didn't know if she should've been able to see the handwriting on the wall that Evan was a pervert. But either way, I felt sorry for her.

She'd blown through two fiancés in a very short time. Two almost marriages, two futures decapitated by one stroke each. I thought it was just awful. My sisterly pity and protectiveness reasserted itself. I'd always felt that I was the stronger of the two of us, anyway. Hadn't I been the one that had left the big house and lived with Dad in a tiny apartment for all my teen years?

Dad was the best Dad ever, don't get me wrong, but I didn't get a gently used, late model Buick for my sixteenth birthday. Hell, Maddie still had that car, more than ten years later, whilst my Chevy had long ago been consigned to the scrap yard. I didn't get a great job handed to me, just because my mother ran the office. I didn't get an immediate escape hatch to sunny Rancho Bernardo, almost the very second that something went awry in my life.

And even with all these advantages, Maddie's world was still in shambles. So I figured that it was time for me to take an active interest in my sister's life again. I knew that Mom would welcome Maddie back home with open arms, give her that swell old job back. Mom would once again make it just as easy and cushy as possible for Maddie to flee all her little problems and embarrassments in San Diego. Anyone else would've had to stay where they were and just deal with it, find a new place to live, muddle through. Most people didn't have a Get-Out-of-

This-Painful-Situation-Free card. But Mom would make it all better for Maddie, just as she always had, at least as far as a job and a home were concerned.

But I knew that there would still be some months of emotional healing before Maddie was over what had happened with the banker. I thought she'd moved in with him entirely too quickly, anyway. Maybe that's why she'd missed the signals that Evan was not *the one*, any more than Wes had been. Wes couldn't take a joke; Evan obviously had *all kinds* of issues.

Maddie needed to take it easy on the romance front. Someone needed to make sure that she didn't rush off pell-mell into another disastrous relationship. And there wasn't anyone else to look after her but me. One more failed love affair, one more horrendous surprise, might just put her around the bend, I thought. It had been a sincerely rough time for her – no matter where she'd looked for love, it had been in all the wrong places.

I left Maddie at Mom's house with Mom's love and a half-gallon of ice cream. I went home to my . . . whatever Wes was, he was going to have to be a part of this now. He was eventually going to have to face Maddie and start interacting with her. I told him what happened.

"Two hookers?" he said in amazement, and I wondered if he was thinking back to those horrible pictures of Maddie and two men. I wondered if he thought that maybe Maddie had somehow gotten what she deserved. We'd never spoken of that cruel practical joke – he'd come back looking for Maddie's forgiveness, so I'd figured that he'd realized his mistake, had at last recognized it for what it had been, just a horrible prank. And since Maddie had not been here to accept his apology, since she had a brand new happy life, since Wes and I had . . . gotten together, we'd never discussed what had happened on that New Year's Eve. But maybe he still thought Maddie had some complicity in the whole thing.

"I'm going to have to look out for her," I said. *"We're* going to have to look out for her. You're going to have to finally clear the air with her, so we can all get on with our lives."

Wes frowned at all that, but finally agreed. What else could he do?

MADELINE

I stayed in bed at Mom's for a week feeling embarrassed, feeling sorry for myself. Mary came to see me every day, and it was her inability to hide her pity that finally got me up. She hadn't pitied me too much for the end of a relationship wherein I'd deserved her pity, I thought. She hadn't thought that I was too weak not to be able to handle The Mary and Wes Show – and my breaking up with Wes, her taking up with Wes, had wounded me more than this Evan thing.

Wes had been *the one* in my mind – and then he'd left me like a whore. But he'd come back, and I'd never gotten the chance to hear his apology, because Mary told him I'd moved on. And then she'd comforted him in his . . . whatever it had been.

While I hid out in my narrow childhood bed for a week, I thought about Evan . . . *ah, Evan was just icky.* I supposed that I'd been in love with Evan. But it had been a rebound love, truly – Evan had just swooped in and saved me from my shock and loneliness, and I'd loved him for that. And I'd been willing to marry him and live happily ever after with him and Emmy, because it had been such a relief to have all my sadness so immediately removed.

But I realized that it *had* been more relief than love that had made me agree to marry Evan so easily. Simply put, I'd been willing to overlook his inadequacies because I was grateful for his company. Discovering his propensity for hookers had underlined these inadequacies for me, and I thought that he'd really done me a favor. Breaking up with Evan had saved me from a lifetime of behind-closed-doors dissatisfaction. And while I'd once believed that giving up great sex had been a small price to pay for a happy, un-lonely life, now that I'd been spared all that, I wasn't so sure. So I didn't mourn so much for whatever feelings I'd had for Evan – it was all for the best.

But it was Mary's pity that really roused me from my immobility. She was so secure in her new life, her love with Wes, that she came off as just the tiniest bit condescending, just the tiniest bit superior. So finally, on the Friday after the Friday-of-the-Whores, I surprised Mom by cooking dinner, and told her I'd be ready to go back to work on Monday. She smiled and hugged me, reminded me to never forget that there was a lot of dog in a man. She told me that there were good ones out there – *there had to be,* she said with a little giggle, *because I've heard stories about them* – I just had to be a little bit more careful with the next one I chose.

I thought that it would be a while before I chose another one, before I had anything to do with any men at all. Just as I'd been after Wes left me, I was in dumb, numb, disbelieving shock. The only difference was that there was no heartbreak involved this time. Regardless, the idea of romance was still as far from my mind as plans for taking the next rocket to Mars.

Mom thanked me for dinner, and then about eight o'clock, she retired to her room. I'd been in bed for a week; I was not sleepy, was a ball of energy. I called Mary – as with a lot of Friday nights, she was working. So was Felicia. Out of the blue, Mary said, "Do you want to see Wes?"

"Why would I want to see Wes?"

"You're going to have to see him sooner or later, Maddie," she said, with that air of superiority again. "He's my . . . we're . . . he's a part of my life. You haven't been enough of a part of my life lately, and it's because of him. I want that to come to an end, Maddie. I want us to all be friends."

Friends, I thought. *We'd never* all *been friends*. I'd loved Wes, and my sister had put up with him because of me. But she'd never liked him, had always called him a coward. *They were never friends*. Then we'd broken up and my sister had taken up with my ex-fiancé. Now she wanted us *all* to be *friends*.

"Sure," I told Mary. "I'll see Wes." *Send him right on over*, I thought, *since I'm not quite sure where you live*. "Is he at the bar?"

She told me that he was, but that she'd send him over – like she read my mind. We are identical twins, after all. *And now*, I thought, *after all these years, we even like the same type of men. But leave all that*. He was hers now.

****

I've never dreaded yet at the same time also looked forward to anything so much in my life. I was amazed to discover that I couldn't remember exactly what Wes looked like, nor could I recall the sound of his voice. In the first days and weeks after he'd left, I'd missed him like a limb. There was an ache at his non-presence, an empty space beside me, behind me, in front of me that should've been occupied by him. There was always an invisible hole just on the periphery.

That invisible hole in my life had eventually, slowly filled up with the dust and detritus of everyday life, like leaves drifting into some animal's discarded burrow. The hole left by Wes's absence had been filled in by time and distance, the move, the new job, Evan. Even the best memories fade. Try as I might, I couldn't clearly picture Wes's face. Where once the memories of him were like breathing to me, real and alive – in thinking back, I realized that after a while, they'd become like an old-fashioned home movie with no sound, then like a clear photo. Then they'd become like an old photo, then like some old photo of a stranger that I vaguely remembered seeing once, a long time ago.

But even though I couldn't remember his face, I admitted to myself that I missed him, that maybe, despite everything that had happened, I might still have feelings for him.

I puttered around in Mom's immaculate living room, straightening things that didn't need to be straightened, dusting non-existent dust. I waited. I wondered. I tried to remember him.

The doorbell rang and I took a deep breath, exhaled. I paused and did it again behind the door. I thought that the look on his face would tell me everything. I opened the door.

Wes said my name, and the familiarity of it cut me to the bone. He stepped across the threshold and embraced me, and I was enveloped in his scent. Evan had always worn expensive cologne; it was a pleasant smell, but it was all there was to him – newly showered, I could never identify any individual male-scent to him at all. Wes was wearing something now – that was no doubt Mary's influence, because Wes had never been a big cologne wearer before – but still I could smell him, that old, familiar, Wes-fragrance, musky, maybe a little dusty. It made me light-headed. Maybe I couldn't remember his face, but I knew I'd missed a lot of things about Wes. With that one hug, I realized that maybe I'd missed the way he smelled most of all.

With his smell, his hug, all the old memories were brought into sharp focus again. I could remember his face now, could remember everything about him. It was as if I'd been looking through a frosted over window, the memories on the other side indistinct, the colors pale, milky. It was like Wes had wiped his hand across that glass, and with that one swipe everything was real and vibrant and alive and present again, as if not a moment had passed since I'd seen him last.

Thus with imagined wing our swift scene flies
In motion of no less celerity
Than that of thought.

All that I thought I'd forgotten was immediately, clearly, achingly remembered. *God, how I love you, Wes!*

Now came the apology. "I'm sorry I doubted you, Maddie," he said softly, still holding me lightly by the elbows. "It took me too long to realize that it was all true, that it was just some kind of horrible prank."

There was repentance in his eyes — but that was all. There was no longing, no desire to renew old ties, and I was glad of that, because after all, he was with Mary now. If I'd seen longing in his dark-blue eyes, I might've betrayed my sister. Wes was *the one*, would always be *the one*.

But I wasn't the one for him — his expression confirmed it. He was utterly sorry for his mistake, but he was someone else's man now.

I veiled my own longing and said that it was all okay. "Sometimes things just don't work out," I told him, dismissing the prank, encompassing the situation in which we found ourselves now.

He nodded, acknowledging the present. "Mary told me about . . . what was his name?"

"Evan," I supplied.

Again Wes nodded. I noticed that he was wearing his hair a lot shorter than he had in the old days — all the curls and waves were under control. Another sign of Mary's influence, I thought. She'd always said he looked too shaggy. I thought the new haircut made him look older, took away some of the native cuteness of him, replaced it with a strait-laced look that just didn't fit him.

"I'm sorry about . . . I'm sorry that you and Evan broke up," he said. Then he smiled, that same old glorious Wes smile, and again I felt cut to the heart. "But I'm glad you're back home, Maddie. I missed you." And he hugged me again.

"I missed you, too, Wes," I said, but I didn't let my voice betray how completely I'd missed him. I hadn't realized it until just that moment, and I was enough in control of myself to not let it show.

Damn him for being so adorable, damn him for not coming down to see me and apologize in person. Damn him for believing Mary when she told him I'd moved on. Who knows what I would've done had Wes shown up on my doorstep, with his smell and his blue eyes and his glorious smile? Who knows what might've happened had he come down and told me how sorry he was in person?

Wes released me and crossed the room. He sat on the couch, and while there was plenty of room for me to sit next to my sister's boyfriend — we were all *friends*, after all, and no one would ever look askance at me sitting a discreet distance from my sister's boyfriend in my mother's living room — I sat across from him in a chair instead. I could no longer smell him from there, and I could look at him, discover what other changes Mary had wrought.

"What are you gonna do now?" he asked me gently.

119

I shrugged. "I have the best mother in the world. She saves me every time." He looked away at that remark, and I thought that it was right that he should – it was his fault that I'd needed to be saved the first time.

It was all his fault, him and that terrible asshole with the stupid smiley face tattoo. Between the two of them, my life had been ruined. *But leave all that.* My life was not ruined completely, was it? I'd dodged a bullet in Rancho Bernardo, and while I'd certainly miss poor little Emmy, I wouldn't miss Evan. And here was Wes. He wasn't mine anymore, but I'd get to see him again, and maybe give him a hug sometimes, get to smell him. We would be *friends*. My life wasn't utterly ruined. Just stunted.

"I'm going to go back to work with Mom on Monday." I smiled at Wes then, to let him know that I wasn't heartbroken over Evan, that it was really funny in a disgusting kind of way. He smiled back. Like we were friends. "Eventually, I'll have to get another apartment. How are things at BF *Walker?*"

"The new project is called *Wandering Springs.*" Wes rolled his eyes. "The geo study showed something about a waterway. *An ancient waterway,* dried up about the time of the dinosaurs, for crying out loud. But that was wet enough for Proten's imagination, so he called it *Wandering Springs.*

"There's gonna be a big fountain at the entrance. Half-acre lots, luxury homes. A property owners' association to maintain that big waste of water. The ground-breaking was last week. I managed to avoid that – it was all Proten's show. Construction starts next week. I'm kinda at loose ends until then."

I wondered if Mary knew that her old boyfriend Bill was back in town. I wondered if Wes knew any of the details of his girlfriend's one-time *relationship* (for lack of a better word), with his nemesis.

Wes and I made small talk – the weather, the idea that development was perhaps finally looking up again in SoCal. We carefully avoided the topic of his and Mary's happy little life together.

I said, "How's Angelo and Cody and Phil? Is Rolling Blackout still packing *Mickey's* every Friday night?" Then I realized that it was Friday night, and apparently they weren't, because here he was, talking to me.

Wes smiled regretfully, shook his head. "We play there maybe once a month. Phil is overseeing a project in Monterey, and our new drummer is not as good as he was." Wes shook his head again. "You'll always be able to see your sister on the nights we play, though. She hates the band. She tells me that it's a dumb thing for a grown man to be doing. She always makes sure she's off the nights we play."

120

I looked at Wes again. It was too warm for one of the soft old flannels that he preferred, but I noticed that his Converse were also gone, replaced by some kind of expensive running shoes. Wes didn't run.

A bright bolt of anger shot through me. It was bad enough that Mary had changed how he dressed, made him cut off all his adorable curly hair, but it was tragic that she'd made him feel self-conscious about playing music, too. Mary hated his band, and had the nerve to tell him that she did? Wes loved to play music, even if he'd never had any ambition to be a star. And Rolling Blackout was great. *A dumb thing for a grown man to be doing?* Had she really said that to him?

On a hunch, I asked, "You still have that big Yamaha?" How I had loved riding that bike with him, all snuggled up close against his back, my hands around his waist.

Again Wes shook his head. "I sold it to Angelo. It doesn't look so big when he's on it."

Damn Mary anyway, I thought. I knew she'd made him sell the Yamaha. She was trying to change everything that Wes was, just to suit herself. He'd been perfect the way he was, and if she didn't like it, why didn't she just let him go and find herself a young lawyer, or . . . a banker, or something? If she didn't like Wes the way he was, why did she keep him? Why didn't she just cut him loose and let him find someone who appreciated him for himself? Someone like me?

But leave all that, I cautioned myself. Obviously Wes didn't mind Mary's trying to change him.

"Well, I love the band," I said. "I'll come see you guys' play."

Wes smiled at me again, and I caught a small swelling of gratitude in his eye. *I'd never try to change you, Wes*, I thought. *I like you just the way you are. Even though I'm not allowed to anymore.*

"I'd like that very much, Maddie," he said.

We made further small talk. Wes told me again that he was glad that I was back, and I said that I was glad to be back. I realized it was true – I couldn't believe that I'd dreaded seeing him again. He was just as beautiful as he'd always been, despite the short haircut and the ridiculous running shoes. I was glad that we were friends.

Then his phone rang. He didn't answer it right away, and I got the impression that he didn't really want to get it, but after the forth ring, he took it out of his pocket and said hello. After a moment, he said to me, "Mary wants to know if you want to come back to *Mickey's* with me. She's off in a little while, and says that you haven't seen . . . our place yet."

Had he really hesitated before saying *our place?* Or had I just imagined it? Regardless, Wes was leaving now. His master had summoned him, and if I wanted to hang out with him any more that evening, I'd have to hang out with my sister, too.

Usually, I would've demurred – it was going on nine o'clock, and everybody at *Mickey's* would be several drinks ahead of me. Being sober around a bunch of drinkies was never my cup of tea. The hours that Mary worked had always been kind of a pain, as far as our socializing together was concerned. But I'd been in bed for a week, feeling sorry for myself. I had plenty of energy. It wasn't really that late. And I liked seeing Wes, talking to him.

And I'd discovered an overwhelming curiosity, maybe born of that little hesitation when he said *our place*. I found that I was curious to see them together, see them interact. I was curious to see just exactly what their relationship was like, how much in love they really were.

I nodded at Wes, and he told Mary we'd be there. I took my own car – I didn't want anyone to have to drive me home later – and followed him to *Mickey's*. I parked in front of the place, and Wes pulled up next to me. He said something about having to go pick up a gallon of milk, but said he'd be right back. *How domestic*, I thought.

Mickey's was busy, but not as busy as it had been in the old days, when Rolling Blackout played there on Friday nights. I couldn't believe that Jon had allowed them to curtail their gigs: the band had always been a cash cow for him. But I knew that Mary was manager now, and perhaps she had a little more say as to who played Jon's bar than she had in the old days. I was again appalled at Mary's telling Wes that she hated his band, his friends. How *could* she say something like that to him?

Mary smiled at me from behind the bar, and I couldn't help but smile back. She was my sister, after all, and besides Mom and Dad, the only person in the world that loved me. And I loved her, would always love her – even if she had turned the only *man* I'd ever loved into an uptight, short-haired, wearer of name-brand running shoes. Even if she'd made him stop being a musician, something he loved. Even if he was now hers.

I sat at the bar, which was mostly deserted, except for a few guys at the other end. Mary said, "Catch this, Maddie," then nodded at a young girl behind the bar with her. The girl slid a mug of beer down the bar to me.

I caught it and she gleefully clapped her hands together. "My protégé, Debbie," Mary said. "She loves doing that." Debbie came down to our end of the bar, and Mary introduced us.

"You guys look exactly alike!" Debbie marveled, and Mary rolled her eyes.

"That's because we're twins," she said. "Now, do you think you can handle things for twenty minutes? Darrin will be here to take over then." Debbie nodded solemnly. She was tall, dark-haired, a little gangly. She wore bright red lipstick, but still looked like she was about fifteen. She had to be at least twenty-one to be working behind the bar, but she surely didn't look it. "I'm counting on you, Debbie," Mary said and winked at me. "I'll see you tomorrow."

Mary took her purse from beneath the bar, and came around the end of it. I told Debbie it was nice meeting her, and Mary and I headed for the door. We met Wes coming in, a grocery sack in his hand. Mary said, "Why'd you bring the milk in?"

"I thought you could put it in the fridge behind the bar."

"I told you I was getting off," she replied. There was no edge to her voice, no rebuke, but still I found her tone a little parental. I noticed that they didn't embrace. No kisses. Maybe it was for my benefit. Or maybe they were so comfortable together that PDA's were not necessary.

Or maybe the honeymoon was over.

Wes was parked right outside the door, behind my car, and he opened the door for Mary. She got in and he handed the milk to her. He walked up to my window. "We're at the Windemere," he told me. "Up the hill. By Raceway Ford."

I smiled to think that only someone like Wes, in the building industry, familiar with the names of housing developments, would actually know the name of the apartment complex where he lived. I doubted that Mary knew what they were called. Then another thought struck me. "By Raceway Ford? *In Moreno Valley?*"

Raceway Ford, Moreno Valley – the confluence of the 215 and 60 Freeways. Always under construction, the traffic always a nightmare. Wes had always hated that area because of the killer traffic, no matter how nice the apartments were.

He shrugged, grinned. "It's still Riverside, actually . . . Just follow me," he said.

Wes avoided the tail lights on the freeway, skirting UC Riverside and taking instead a frontage road. *He must love her,* I thought, *for her to be able to get him to live up here.* There was absolutely nothing wrong with the area, but still I could picture Wes sitting in traffic in the morning. Wes hated traffic. Their little love nest was on the wrong side of the hill from where he worked.

Their apartment was huge. The place Mary and I had shared downtown had two tiny bedrooms, a microscopic bathroom, a kitchenette-living room combo. Wes's old place had been similarly small. But the apartment that they shared had a giant living room, a full kitchen, an amazing bathroom. A balcony that overlooked the light bulb-shaped pool. Even without the extra bedrooms and bathrooms, even without the manicured lot and the location, location, location, it was easily as nice as Evan's house in Rancho Bernardo.

And Mary was house proud. She took me on a grand tour, pointing out all their lavish furnishings, including a big leather couch on which Wes had carelessly flopped when we walked in. I thought that I caught my sister glare at him – I almost thought she was going to chide him for bouncing on the furniture, like our mother used to do. They had a big screen television, an enormous bed – I tried not to think too much about that. The master bedroom had a walk-in closet.

The place was all Mary as far as decorating went. She favored dark colors – maroons and forest greens – and heavy, dark Mediterranean style furniture. Wes's apartment had been all baby blues and sunny yellows. He'd had a dusty surfboard above the couch, and a big stuffed marlin that had taken up almost the other whole wall.

After the tour, we went back out into the living room. I asked the man of the house, "Where's the fish, Wes?"

Before he could reply, Mary said, "Storage. Along with that stupid surfboard. When did you ever surf?" Wes shrugged. "And most of his furniture. Nothing matched."

"*All* of my furniture," Wes said. He looked at me. "Nothing matched."

Well, I thought, *you signed up for this.* He was apparently okay with the fact that my sister had changed his appearance to suit herself, that she'd put most of what he was in storage. He didn't seem to care that maybe the only reason she was with him was because his income allowed her to live in this giant apartment. I would've bet that the name on the credit card receipts for all this dark, heavy, brand-new furniture wasn't *Mary Rearden.*

But leave all that. It wasn't any of my business. He was my friend. She was my sister. I should be happy for them.

We talked for a little while, and then Mary gave a theatrical yawn and reminded me that she had an early shift in the morning. She invited me to stop by and see her at the bar then, told me that she was glad I was back. The two of them showed me to the door, and it was only then that I noticed her touch Wes for the first time. I turned around outside the front door to say goodbye again, and as I did so, Mary draped her arm most possessively around Wes's waist and said, "We've missed you so much, Maddie."

The plural was not lost on me, the ownership inherent in that *we*, telling me that *he is mine and I'm not even worried about anything that was between you two in the past.* Mary was so secure in their relationship that she again came off as superior. She'd always possessed a streak of it – she'd always thought of herself as the smarter of the two of us, the savvier one. The one more hip to the ways of a cruel world. Her smile showed all of that to me – *I know what I'm doing*, it said. *I'm sorry that you can't seem to get your life together as well as I can.*

Wes just smiled blankly at me. *If you want to be her pet paycheck, groomed and directed, what difference could it possibly make to me?* I thought. *You are not the man I thought you were, Wes Thomerville, if you're willing to allow my sister to run your life for you like this. Maybe I dodged a bullet with you, also.*

But on the drive home, I again let the immature part of me have its say. It was the part of me that missed Wes the most. It made me admit to myself that he *was* still the man I thought he was, the man for whom I'd once been willing and eager to forsake all others. I admitted to myself that I had an unsisterly desire for my twin's boyfriend, and when my immaturity started to whine that it was only because he had been mine first, my rational, adult mind tamped all that down.

It didn't matter what I wanted. He was happy with Mary. He didn't want me. And besides, how trampy and disloyal would it be of me to just sweep back into town and steal my boyfriend back? And worst of all, what if I tried, and he turned me down?

MARY

Maddie was impressed with my apartment. That came as no surprise, because it was impressive. I'm the only one with any design sense in the family – Mom always favored that ultramodern look, all smooth lines, plastic and stainless steel. Dad let his women decorate his place, and therefore it was a mishmash of tastes, as one departed, leaving her stamp behind, and another one arrived with new ideas. Maddie had never expressed much of an interest in making her surroundings her own – she'd always gone along with my tastes. It was another characteristic that always showed me that I was the stronger personality – I made the decisions and Maddie just went along with the flow.

She showed up at the bar about ten o'clock. We weren't open yet, and it gave me a moment to talk to her. She told me it was great to see Wes again, and I detected just the tiniest bit of – what would you call it? Envy, maybe? It could tell that it wasn't that she wanted Wes back. She envied me because she'd just lost somebody, and I had somebody. Wes wasn't really her type anymore, anyway – he was more sophisticated than he'd been in the old days, not as rough and tumble as she liked.

And it didn't matter what Maddie wanted anyway. Wes and I were . . . well, she'd find out soon enough. And it was not in the manner that I would've wished for, but I really didn't have a plan on all that anyway.

Maddie was sitting at the bar, drinking her now trademark ginger ale, and I was taking a quick inventory before we opened. Debbie, that skittish fluff-head, came running up from the back somewhere. Hysterically, she cried, "Miz Thomerville! Miz Thomerville! There's a giant spider in the ladies' room! Jon said to tell you, and you'd get rid of it!"

Maddie blinked as if someone had thrown her ginger ale in her face. She looked at my left hand. There was no ring there, but when she looked back at me, I'm sure that the guilty look was plain on my face. I'm sure it was only there for a split-second – what did I have to be guilty about? But I'm sure it was there, and I'm sure she saw it nonetheless.

I told Debbie that I would kill the spider in a second. I told her to go get a few more bottles of Jack Daniels from the storeroom. We had plenty of Jack, but I wanted to get rid of her. Maddie stared at me, her eyes bulging in her face. I opened my mouth to say something, closed it again. I tried a second time, but before I could speak, Jon walked up.

"Miz Thomerville!" he said, mimicking Debbie. "There's a big ol' hairy spider in the bathroom! Your baby bartender has a fear." Then he noticed Maddie, saw the look on her face, and realized his faux pas. He didn't feel bad about it – the embarrassment of others was never a concern of Jon's – but he did realize that perhaps he'd let a cat out of its bag that was not his to release. He tried to recover, saying, "Oh, my God, Maddie! How great to see you again!" He gave her a big hug.

Maddie allowed herself to be hugged, still staring at me with those big eyes. She was speechless, and when Jon stopped hugging her, he looked from her to me and just stammered something about getting back to the books. Then he fled.

It had happened when we were in Vegas, barely a week ago. On that Friday when Maddie had read Wes's text, realized we were living together, and fled back to find disaster waiting for her in San Diego.

Friday night had really already passed. It was actually early Saturday morning. One of Drew's favorite bars was about a block away from one of those little all-night wedding chapels. We were reeling past it, Wes, Drew and myself, on our way to some other bar that Drew wanted to show to his old pal. We'd been drinking a little bit already, were really quite half in the bag. I nodded at the chapel, and said, "I was first born. It's not right that my sister should get married before I do." I'd been kidding, really. I didn't want to marry Wes. I didn't even love Wes. I was just kidding. Really.

But Wes was drunk, and who knows what thoughts lurk in a drunk man's mind that he might not act on sober? He just said, "Okay," grabbed my hand, and dragged me into the chapel. Drew looked dumbfounded, and suddenly sobered up a little bit. But he didn't object, and even lent us the chased silver ring that he always wore, for the length of the brief ceremony.

And just like that, with one borrowed ring and Drew acting as a silent witness, drunken Wes and my drunken self had gotten hitched in Vegas. Dad knew, but not Mom. She'd been all excited about the prospect of Maddie's wedding at the moment, anyway, what with our picking out those horrible bridesmaids' dresses the very day before. I was going to tell her, and Maddie, too, after Maddie's triumphant return from her honeymoon.

The minute I got back from Vegas on Sunday, before I'd even seen Maddie, before I'd heard the horrible news of Evan's little party, I had to stop by *Mickey's*. Jon wanted me to interview the little girl that had applied to be the new bartender. "She seems a little shy to me," Jon said. "A little dumb, a lot naïve. You're the one who's gonna have to train her, work with her. You decide if she's right for the job."

So Jon sat in on the interview, and Debbie was okay. She was a little shy, but she was almost painfully respectful, and when I told her that she could start the next day, she'd effused, "Oh, thank you so much, Mrs. –?"

Jon, of course, had failed to introduce us at the onset of the interview, because he was about as unprofessional as a business owner could be – his making me come in on a Sunday to interview a prospective bartender was just the least of it. I don't know why Debbie just assumed I was married, but I was, little more than twenty-four hours before, so I said, "Thomerville. Mrs. Thomerville." I liked Debbie's respectfulness, and if she wanted to call me Missus, if she wanted to call me by my brand new name, it was okay by me. It was surely better than *Miss Mary,* which I suspected it would've been otherwise. She was just that young.

Jon's eyebrows went up in surprise, and I said one word in explanation: *Vegas.* That was enough for him, and he welcomed Debbie into the *Mickey's* family, then once again fled to his office, which was his M.O. But it never failed to tickle him that Debbie called me *Miz Thomerville,* as if I was someone twice her age, instead of just a few years older.

Now Maddie just stared at me, her expression not unlike Drew's when Wes had dragged me into the wedding chapel. I said, "I was gonna tell you, Maddie. You were all happy and picking out bridesmaids' dresses. You were going to get married yourself, and we were happy for you, and we were in Vegas . . . We've barely been married a week." I would not say I was sorry. I wasn't sorry. It wasn't my fault that her glorious country club wedding had fallen through. It wasn't my fault that the banker had turned out to be something that she hadn't imagined.

"Congratulations, Mrs. Thomerville," Maddie said at last. She reached across the bar and gave me a hug, and again I thought, *she was going to have to find out sooner or later.*

I told her thanks, but it was thanks for the congratulations. It wasn't thanks for being okay with me being married to Wes, like it had been thanks for her being okay with me *dating* Wes. I didn't need to acknowledge her okayness with it – what was she going to do about it, one way or another?

"Next comes Mary with a baby carriage, I suppose," she said, reciting the end of the old children's rhyme.

I laughed out loud at that one. "Oh, no, Maddie. I haven't even got around to a ring yet. It was just a spur of the moment thing. A Vegas thing. No babies for me. You got all the mommy urges when the

128

egg divided," I said, referring to our twin-ness. "I have no desire for any of that." Have a baby with Wes? Tie myself to him forever? Was she nuts?

Maddie blinked again, and I realized that maybe it hadn't been the nicest thing to say. She had been a mommy for a little while, and I knew that she'd loved Evan's little girl very much. I lowered my eyes to show her that I was sorry I'd made such a thoughtless remark. I added, "You don't have to worry about being an aunt anytime soon, Maddie. I'm surely not ready."

And Wes? We had not even discussed such things. We'd just gotten married on the spur of the moment, probably entirely because Maddie was already getting married. I hadn't thought about a future with Wes. I didn't even love him. He was just nice to have around, and I'd gone into the whole marriage thing, even drunkenly, with the idea in the back of my mind that I could always divorce Wes, and I would, on the very day that I couldn't stand him anymore. Divorce had worked out well enough for my mom and dad.

If *the one* ever walked into my bar, Wes would be my ex-husband so fast – I would drop him like third period French. But in the meantime, he was great to have around. He wasn't too much of a slob, and he did what he was told. Marrying him had just seemed to be the thing to do at the time.

MADELINE

I was afraid to get up off of the barstool. I wanted to flee, to go and have a good cry with the immature part of myself, the part that had cried out *Now we'll never get him back!* the moment that that country twit Debbie had called my sister *Miz Thomerville.*

The immature part of me wanted Wes back, had never stopped wanting Wes, and I frequently let it out and indulged it when I was alone. I allowed myself to picture a world where maybe Wes might realize his mistake – he might realize *all* his mistakes – and then he'd break up with my sister and come back to me. Stranger things had happened – the whole phenomenon of the two of them together in the first place was a stranger thing, right there.

But now my immature self was destitute, and I wanted to cry. Wes had made his choice. But I couldn't move yet. I had to wait until the strength returned to my legs.

Jon unlocked the front doors to *Mickey's* a whole half an hour ahead of time. I watched Mary glare at him. Jon had always struck me as a conscientious business owner – there were people on the sidewalk waiting to make him money, and he wasn't going to let a little thing like hours of operation stop them. I was glad of the people coming in. *Mickey's* didn't seem silent like the grave anymore, and I wouldn't have to talk to Mary – I wouldn't have to talk to *Mrs. Thomerville* – anymore, right at that moment.

A man came up and stood next to me at the bar. He looked from Mary to me in confusion, just like Drew had once done. He said, "Mary?" to both of us, and I realized that it was blonde Mike, whom Mary had once picked up, whom we had once shared. I pretended that I didn't know him and pointed at my sister.

Mary smiled at Mike with undisguised delight. I had not once seen her look at her *husband* like that. "This is my sister Maddie, Mike," she said. "She's just . . . moved up here from San Diego." She looked at him appraisingly for another moment. "How the hell have you been?"

Mike smiled at me for a second, then turned his attention to my sister. He believed we'd never met before, after all – he didn't know that I knew he had a tattoo of the sun around his navel, and that he frequently exclaimed *Oh, Mama!* during intercourse.

I said to Mary, "I've gotta go. Mom wants to take me shopping." I told Mike, my one-time paramour, all unbeknownst to him, that it had been nice meeting him. He smiled again and said likewise. I said to Mary, "See you soon, *Mrs. Thomerville.*"

Mary nodded and I walked away. At the door, I turned and looked back. Mike had a surprised look on his face, and I imagined that he was asking if she was really married. I watched Mary shake her head dismissively, then lean a little closer to him and smile. It was way too friendly a smile for a married woman, I thought, but she was a bartender, she was in the being-friendly-to-the-customers profession. Whatever. It was none of my business.

****

Mom hadn't actually mentioned anything about going shopping, but it would have to be done. I couldn't go back to work in the jeans and t-shirts that I had swept into a suitcase at Evan's house. I had a few outfits suitable for the office, so it didn't have to be today, but it would have to be soon.

I found Mom wearing her lime green gloves, working in the little garden she kept in the backyard. I was suddenly struck with the idea that I was going to wind up just like her. I was going to wind up an old, lonely, bitter, unloved man-hater, just like my mother. I wouldn't even have any children to comfort me in my old age like she did. The only man I'd ever loved was married to my sister – it would be a long time before I'd look for another one, if ever. My heart was just too fragile. So I saw myself, just like Mom, with nothing to do on a Saturday morning but tie up the tomatoes.

I stood next to her and said, "Mom." She told me good morning, but didn't glance up from the gardening. "Mom. I need you to look at me."

It was going to come as another blow, another shock of disloyalty, if Mom knew that Wes and Mary were married. She'd just being protecting my feelings, had been ashamed of her other daughter's behavior – that's why she hadn't told me about Wes and Mary living together. She'd been disgusted by it. *Living together* was the modern expression, but when I thought of them, I always heard my mother's ugly, pejorative term: *shacking up*. It was something Mom didn't want to discuss with anyone, me least of all.

But for a whole week now, Mary had been an honest woman. She was *Mrs. Thomerville*, and I got the idea that maybe Mom was ashamed of *me* now, with my inability to keep a good man, my inability to recognize a bad one. Maybe Mom was too ashamed of the romantic

131

shortcomings of the daughter she had raised to even acknowledge the successes of the daughter raised by her philandering ex-husband.

Mom looked up at me and I said, "Did you know that Mary and Wes got married?"

She said, *"What?"* and dropped her little gardening trowel. She stood up and stared at me, open-mouthed. "When? *What?* She doesn't even like him!"

It was some kind of wonderful revelation to hear my mother say the one thing that I'd believed all along. *Mary didn't even like Wes.* I thought it had been my immaturity always pointing the fact out to me, but here was Mom, a pretty much uninterested third party, saying the same thing.

"When they were in Las Vegas," I told her. "The day after we bought bridesmaids' dresses. Before . . ."

"It won't last," my mother opined. Then she repeated, "She doesn't even like him. She orders him around . . . I've never actually seen this, of course. Your sister doesn't come over here very often, and this is one more reason why. She obviously doesn't want to hear what I have to say.

"But when she does lower herself to talk to me, and she mentions him . . . she never has one nice thing to say. *Wes dresses like a slob. Wes needs a haircut again. Wes needs to get a better job, show a little ambition.* Why would she marry him?"

"It was a drunken, off the cuff thing, I guess."

Mom was angry now, ashamed of my sister. "Off the cuff. Getting married, off the cuff. She is your father's daughter, Maddie. Always doing thoughtless things, with no plan for the future. And who could expect anything but drunken, dumb things from someone who's never had any more ambition in life than to be a bartender?"

My first instinct was to defend Mary, as I'd always done when Mom bad-mouthed her. But I found that the words died before they made it to my mouth. Mary was a grown-up, a married woman, for God's sake. She didn't need me to defend her. Besides, Mom was right. Why had she married Wes, when she didn't even like him?

"I'm sorry, Maddie," Mom said, and I caught a little understanding there, something I'd never before seen: Mom knew that I still loved Wes. "It won't last," she said again.

I smiled in gratitude. Maybe I wasn't so immature after all. He'd been mine first, and even though he was now lost irrevocably, maybe it was all right that I still loved him. It was certainly all right with Mom. "Can I help with the tomatoes?" I asked.

MARY

Mike laughed at me when I told him that yes, it was true, I was married, for a whole week now. "How could you have married anyone but me, Mary?" he said. "We were so good together."

And I had to admit that it was true. Tatted-up Mike had done things for me that no other man had done. But it was only physical – he was just tatted-up Mike, unemployed, slovenly, a gamer. He hadn't been the one, any more than Wes was. But he had sure been an awesome way to spend the weekend.

I felt a little thrill of excitement, just talking to him. I had not felt a little thrill of excitement like that in a while. Sure, Wes was all right. I'd married him, hadn't I? But Mike . . . it was fun just talking to him, looking at him and his blonde hair and his light-green eyes. Remembering the things that we'd done – the twinkle in those eyes told me that he remembered, too.

"I am devastated to find you wed," Mike said, and threw back the Bloody Mary he'd ordered in one gulp. "But it's too early to drown my sorrows. I can't be sitting around here crying in my beer all day." He was not devastated, just amused. "When do you work again? Maybe I'll come back then and admire you from across the room." He winked and I shivered. "Wallow in my unrequited . . . *love* for you."

Mike had never loved me, nor I him. And when he said the word, the connotation certainly wasn't about pink hearts and roses and chocolate-covered cherries, not about proclamations of undying devotion. When Mike said *love*, the suggestion was just that, *suggestive* – alluding to activities dark and wet and hard, peaks and valleys and giggles and screams.

It was just the fact that he'd said it so nicely that made me shiver. Mike had never been vulgar. He didn't have to be. He didn't have to draw me a crude picture. He was too cute, and he just let his tone say it all.

I told him when my next shift was going to be, and he said he'd come back in then, and worship me from afar. Then he paid for his drink, gave me a big tip, and left. I thought it might be fun to let Mike smile and wink and worship me from afar. It would be fun to be lusted after a little bit. Just a little harmless fun.

MADELINE

My phone rang as Mom and I finished with the gardening. It was Wes, asking me if I wanted to take a bike ride with him. Surprised on about fifteen levels, I said, "I thought you sold your bike?"

"Not a motorcycle ride, Maddie. Bicycles. Mary's working all day – you could ride her bike. I don't have a damn thing to do today, but sit around this . . . place, and it's such a nice day."

"I'm not sure if your wife would want you spending the day with anyone but her," I said gaily.

Suddenly, Wes's marriage to my sister offered me a kind of barrier, behind which my immaturity and I could peep out at him. He was never coming back, but we were friends. I could kid him. I could bury my wishes – they were already buried – *he* had buried them. So what was the sense in being upset about it? *Carrying a torch burns,* my mother always said. We would be friends, and I could kid him about the innocence of taking a bike ride together on a sunny afternoon.

"About all that, Maddie," he said, and then he hesitated. I waited. I wasn't going to help him out. Finally, he said, "It was just one of those things. I was drunk. Maybe I should've waited . . ."

Waited for what, Wes, you son of a bitch? the immature part of me screamed in my head.

"All water under the bridge, Wes," I said, again brightly. "Come on down. I'd love to go on a bike ride with you. If you're sure it's okay with your wife."

I could hear the smile in his voice. "I'm sure it's okay."

We rode the bike trail that paralleled the Santa Ana River, and Wes decided that he wanted to stop and eat the lunch he'd packed beneath the Van Buren Bridge, Dad's favorite. Wes had always been one to remember useful little details like that, bringing food along and all. I told him that it was probably not the safest place to stop. The river bottom was known to be full of undesirables, I said. I pointed out the masses of graffiti that lined the bridge pilings.

Wes laughed at me, telling me that the freaks only came out at night, and that he would protect me if we were suddenly beset by a band of marauding bums. He didn't seem to notice the ugly graffiti - I watched him look up at all that concrete, saw the admiration for the accomplishment of the sturdy new construction. Wes liked the stupid bridge as much as my dad did.

It was almost May, and the water was low, but not as low as it would be in the heat of summer. It had rained just a few days before – the last gasp of rain we'd have until fall, I thought – and Wes pointed out the bent over vegetation. "That was all under water for a little while," he observed.

"When we were kids, Dad would drive us over the bridge every time there was a good hard rain," I told him. "I think he was looking to witness a collapse again."

"Now there's a sidewalk. There wasn't one on the old bridge."

I grinned at him. "I know. Dad parked in the Sizzler and made us walk across it with him, right after it opened. Across the north side, then down the rip-rap – Mary broke a heel. Then under the bridge, back up the rip-rap on the other side, and across the sidewalk on the south side. We thought he was just taking us to Sizzler."

Wes laughed. "Why does your dad like his bridge so much?"

"He watched the old one collapse when he was a kid, like he told you. And it made him want to be an engineer and blah, blah, blah. And then the family saga goes that he met Mom right up there by Central Avenue. Her car was broken down and he stopped to help her. The first ride they took together was when he drove her across the bridge to call a tow for her car. Then I guess there was a traffic jam on the bridge when Mom was in labor with us. Dad always likes to say that we were almost born on this bridge." I looked up at the masses of concrete above us, and still continued to be unimpressed.

"When I was in high school, a friend of mine fell off the railroad bridge up the road."

"Did he . . .?"

"Drown?" Wes shook his head. "There wasn't enough water to drown, and he was lucky enough not to hit any of the rocks. He broke his leg pretty bad, though." He paused, looked at the water. "I don't think I've ever heard of anyone drowning in Riverside."

I also looked at the river. It had several channels, spread over its wide, weed-choked bed, all running efficiently along, none more than a few feet deep. My mother, who was from Pittsburgh, always said that the Santa Ana wasn't a river at all, just a damp place in the road. She came from where there were real rivers. Boats. Water-skiing. The Coast Guard. Navigable waterways. People drowned in Pittsburgh all the time.

I thought that you might be able to hold someone under and drown them in the Santa Ana, but they probably wouldn't drown if they fell in on their own, even if they couldn't swim. There just wasn't enough water. I agreed with Wes. No one would ever drown here.

"Unless it's been raining for a few days." He pointed at the bent over vegetation again. "When it rains, the water rises, sometimes very quickly. It gets deep and swift," he reminded me, just like Dad always did.

Just like a real river, I thought.

"And if you somehow fell into it then, you might just be swept away." Wes walked down to the edge of the water. After a minute, he exclaimed, "There's a fish! Right here!" That was the Wes I remembered. As enthusiastic about life as a little kid. He took out his phone, bent over and tried to take a picture of the fish.

"Please don't fall in," I said. "I'd be laughing too hard to save you."

Wes grinned. "I'd just worry about saving my phone."

We had a pleasant afternoon together. The fact that he was married to my sister, that he was now my *brother-in-law* had indeed laid a warm blanket of safety over the feelings that I still had for him. We were comfortable, family. He'd made his choice, and I was happy to just be in his company. The possibilities that had gnawed at me, the idea that I might someday get him back – they were all silent now, didn't tear and pull at my mind. Sometimes, a person can be happier, I found, once such a hope has been extinguished.

When we were getting ready to leave, I said, "Speaking of people falling off of things – do you still play *My Disgrace* when you guys perform? That one was always my favorite."

Wes rolled up the little plastic lunch bag in which he'd packed our sandwiches, and tied it under the back of his bicycle seat. He smiled at me. "Sometimes," he said. "The new drummer, Randy, features himself a songwriter. We do a lot of songs he's written. Cody loves his stuff."

"Sing *My Disgrace* for me, Wes," I asked him. "It was always my favorite."

"Now?" he asked, grinning. "Here?" He was flattered.

"Why not? I'll do Cody's parts."

"Okay."

The two of us harmonized on *My Disgrace* as we rode along the bike trail, side by side. I enjoyed the sound of his voice, and his weird, sad, vengeful song, comprised of made-up feelings. My favorite song, the one that didn't sound vengeful at all, unless you listened to what was really being said.

Hope they catch you when you fall
It will be from my shove
How can I endure all this pain
And believe that you're my love?

His music was something that my sister didn't share with her husband. They might be united in domestic bliss, two hearts beating as one and all that. But he didn't sing for her, because she didn't like it.

But he would sing for me, if I just asked him. He liked to sing, and anyone that told him it was a dumb thing for a grown man to want to do just didn't understand him. I could tell that he liked having me for an audience, and I thought that sharing this one thing with him was better than nothing. Wes might be my sister's husband, but he'd always be my rock star.

****

The year marched on. The day in June when I was supposed to have married Evan passed without my even realizing its significance until the following morning. Everything in life was as best as could be expected. Mom promoted me to office manager when the previous office manager took a transfer. She gave me a raise, and with the bump in pay, I bought a new car. I took a nice apartment near the job. Mom said she was sad to see me move out, but I knew she was just being kind. She'd become set in her ways in the years since I'd left home, and having her adult daughter there all the time disturbed her serenity. Her middle-aged years were full enough with selling houses and tending her garden. I was just in the way.

There were no more earth-shattering, mind blowing surprises, at least not for a while. Then all sorts of insanity would occur. But up until mid-August, there were no more shocks. Mom didn't join the circus. Dad didn't become a monk. Mr. and Mrs. Thomerville didn't announce that they were expecting.

One morning, at the height of the dog days of summer, I looked up from typing a letter to Appian Escrow to see Drew standing on the other side of the counter. He smiled and I ran around and gave him a big hug. He asked me if I could go to lunch, and I said that I most certainly could.

We went to the same *Denny's* where Wes and I had enjoyed our first breakfast together, a million years before. We ordered, then Drew took out his phone and showed me a picture of a lovely redhead. "That's Connie," he said. And then he showed me another picture, of

137

an adorable little girl – she was about five years old. "And that little bundle of energy is Allison. Connie and I are getting married next week. That's why I'm home, Maddie. Wes is my best man. Will you come to my wedding?"

I told Drew that I'd be honored to come to his wedding. I got up and gave him a big hug, almost knocking the waitress over as she brought our food. As we ate, Drew told me the fairy tale story: it had been love at first sight. So he could be near her, he didn't travel anymore, but instead found a job with one of *BF Walker's* competitors there in Vegas. "Building the same kind of overpriced houses that Wes does."

He told me that Connie's little girl was an angel, and he planned to adopt her as soon as they were married and the paperwork could be ordered. "She already calls me Daddy," he said and grinned with pride, as surely as if the little girl was his by blood.

"Which reminds me," he said, and told me he'd be right back. I watched through the window as he went out to his truck, rummaged around in the glove compartment, then returned. "I want you to autograph this for me," he said and handed me a copy of *Princess Emmaline*.

When I looked at him in utter surprise, he said, "Mary sent it to me. When I told Wes about Connie and Allison. The kid loves it."

I blinked, amazed at how stories written for a little girl I'd once loved had gotten all the way to Las Vegas, amazed that another little girl enjoyed them.

Drew continued. "We just got into town last night, and we stopped into the bar for a minute to see Wes. Allie was clutching her copy and I asked Mary if she had another one, one I could get you to autograph for me. She found one in the storage room."

I was amazed most of all that there were copies of *Princess Emmaline* lying around in the store room at *Mickey's*. I took the pen that Drew held out to me and wrote, *To Allison – May all your days be as happy as Princess Emmaline's. Your friend, Madeline.*

Drew said thanks, took back the book and flipped through it. "This one – *Chas Meets a Leprechaun* – I think that has to be Allie's favorite." Drew smiled at me, then his expression grew curious. "They really are clever, Maddie. Although I never thought you'd write any heroic stories about Wes, even if they are just fairy tales."

I almost choked on my coffee. *"About Wes?"*

His curiosity intensified. "Sure. That's what Mary told me. That you were living down there in San Diego, that you must've been reminiscing about the old days . . ."

"Mary didn't tell you about Evan?"

Drew shook his head. "Mary told me that you were gonna get married, when they came up to visit me, when they . . ." Drew looked a little alarmed at that train of thought, so he quickly added, "Then the next thing I know, Wes is saying it didn't work out. I didn't hear any details." He sipped his coffee, deflected the subject back to my book of fairy tales. "When Wes told Mary that Connie had a little girl, she sent me a copy of *Princess Emmaline* for Allie."

"And she told you that the hero was supposed to be Wes."

It was a statement now, because I could picture her doing it. Wes had considered it unnecessary to regale Drew with the sordid tale of The Evan and Sparkle and Gala Show. That had been nice of him; he was protecting me from undue embarrassment on that score — and why make Drew feel sorry for me, too? Wes and his loving wife and my own mom and dad already felt sorry for me, why bring Drew in on the pity party as well?

But *Mary* wanted Drew to feel sorry for me. Mary was up there in her luxury apartment with her adorable, blue-eyed husband, who had once been mine. Drew knew all this, and in her superiority, Mary had wanted him to pity me. She wanted to make herself look good, to cast herself in the role of beneficent, trusting sister. *Look, Drew, how kind I am, to let my husband keep my lonely sister company, take the occasional bike ride with her of a sunny afternoon, while I work at my meaningless, menial job. Look how trusting I am, how secure in my marriage and in Maddie's pitifulness, that I would let Wes be alone with her after she, in her loneliness and wistfulness, wrote fairy tales casting him as the king and hero!*

Drew held up the book and pointed to a picture, like a kindergarten teacher reading to his charges. He was going to be a great daddy. "Is that not Wes? Right there?"

I looked at the drawing. It could be Wes. Felicia had never met Evan, after all, and I could see how Drew might think the brave king wrestling the dragon could be Wes, especially if Mary had told him that it *was* Wes.

"I didn't draw the illustrations, Drew. A friend of Mary's from the bar did them, and she knows Wes, so maybe the pictures *are* of him. I don't know. But the stories surely aren't about him.

"Just like you, my ex had a little girl, and I wrote these stories for her. The mighty, heroic king was her daddy." I smiled at Drew. "We were going to get married, the king and I, until I discovered that he wasn't heroic in the least."

I was still furious with Mary and her smug condescension. I was so sprung over Wes that I wrote fairy tales about him, almost a year after he'd left me. I so yearned for my lost love that I created a mythology about him. Gee, Drew, isn't it cute? Isn't it sad? But that part of Mary's story wasn't even the worst: the kicker was that she wanted Drew to believe that, in her pity for me, she was all okay with my yearning for her husband.

That was bullshit, fresh from the farm. If Mary for one second even *suspected* that I still had feelings for Wes, she would most certainly not be okay with it. But she wanted to make Drew believe that she was all okay with my pathetic feelings, because there was no possibility of my requiting them. Wes was hers and it was just sad that I still wanted him so much that I wrote kids' stories about him. But she was not jealous about it. *Right.*

There was some mythology for you. If Mary really believed the fantasy that she'd told Drew, she'd be jealous, all right. If she got down off of her condescending high horse long enough to contemplate that yeah, maybe I might want Wes back – then she wouldn't let him out of her sight.

But I kept my fury at my sister in check and grinned at Drew. "You don't really believe–"

"I thought it was a little screwy, to tell you the truth." Drew grinned back, a look of relief on his face. "I never did figure you for much of the pining away sort, Maddie, and while I love Wes like a brother, he's no dragon-slayer. Especially not after the way he treated you."

"I forgave him for all that a long time ago, Drew," I said immediately.

"But that doesn't make it any less of a dumb-ass mistake on his part."

"Does Wes think I wrote *Princess Emmaline* about him?"

"If he does, he didn't hear it from me." Drew smiled again. "Little girls' stories are not something we discuss a lot. Mary sent the book to me, for Allie, and when I called to thank her for it, she flat out told me you wrote them about Wes, because you still weren't over him. I don't know if he was standing right there, if he heard her or not." Again, Drew looked curiously at me, but now his interest was colored with a large portion of that compassion that I knew him for. "Are you over him, Maddie?" When I didn't answer right away, he said, "Personally, I'd like to hear that you're not.

"I don't like to say anything bad about your sister, but . . . you and me . . . we used to go together, Maddie. I'll always think of you first, be on your side. Back in the day, I travelled around a lot. You lived here, it never would've worked out. But I liked you, and if I couldn't have you, well . . . what better man to look out for you than my best friend?

"But Wes made an ass of himself. He messed everything up. He should've gone after you, but he said that Mary said you'd moved on. He said that Mary was willing to . . . to take your place. I guess that's kinda how he thought about it at first. I don't know how he feels about it now, Maddie. We don't talk about that kind of thing a lot."

Drew leaned closer to me across the table. "Here's all I'm going to say, and I hope it's not too mean, but . . . I don't really care for Mary too much. The whole thing with them just comes off as wrong to me. In other words, I think Wes married the wrong sister. And that's why I say that I hope you're not over him, because I still hope that he realizes his mistake." Drew leaned back, sipped his coffee and looked solemnly at me. "He's not happy with her – he doesn't complain, but he doesn't say anything nice, either. He doesn't talk about how great she is and how much fun she is, like he used to say about you." He added darkly, "Marriage, divorce . . . sometimes they're just pieces of paper."

"Thanks, Drew. I really appreciate your support. I don't pine over Wes, and I certainly don't make up fairy tales about him." I nodded at *Princess Emmaline*. "But if he ever did change his mind . . . just between you and me . . . I'd take him back in a heartbeat."

Drew grinned, grabbed my face across the table in both rough hands, and kissed me on the forehead. "Life is long, Maddie, and we're still young. Ya never know what could happen."

****

Connie was a lovely bride – maybe all brides are lovely. Allison was a delightful, well-behaved child, and watching her skip down the aisle strewing rose petals made me think of Emmy. I wondered if she missed me, or if her father had already found another mom for her. Perhaps someone who remembered to call if she was going to be coming home early.

Drew looked great, like something out of a bridal magazine; he even managed to keep that five o'clock shadow at bay. He and his bride and the delightful child he intended to adopt as his own appeared to be a happy little family with a bright future. The most part of my mind reflected on their happiness-to-be, and wished them well. The most part of my mind was itself happy and joyous and optimistic, as befitted a wedding. I smiled at my sister and danced with her husband, had a few drinks, laughed with the newlyweds, read *Chas Meets a Leprechaun* to

Allie. Overall, it was a very nice, refreshing day, a celebration to renew one's faith in the future.

The other part of my mind, however – the immature part – scowled out at Mary from behind my cheerful, smiling eyes. How dare she tell such lies about me to Drew? How dare she incite others to pity me? Sure, maybe I *was* still hung up on Wes, but Mary certainly didn't know it. Wes himself didn't know it. I was cool and in control. I was so cool that ice cubes wouldn't melt in my pockets. Because if I let anyone see that I was still hung up on Wes, then I would deserve all their pity.

I considered this fiction that Mary had created – *Oh, my poor sister! She can't get over my husband, but I'm not sweating it.* That was such a laugh. If she even ever *dreamt* that I still coveted her husband, she'd have a fit. She'd have a small litter of carnivorous kitties, as my dad used to say.

Mary and I had shared all our playthings up until we were twelve years old, except for those things that we *didn't* share, those things that Mary had considered to be all hers. I remembered a certain adorable Raggedy Ann and Andy set we received from some distant relative one Christmas. At first I liked Ann, but when I expressed an interest in Andy, Mary freaked out and hid him under her pillow. She told me I was not to play with Raggedy Andy. I was not to even *look* at Raggedy Andy. Raggedy Andy was hers, and she threatened me with bodily harm if she should catch me as much as peeking at him.

Now Wes is hers, but her pillow certainly isn't large enough to hide him, I thought. And Mary would certainly want to hide him, to remove him from my sight, to keep a wary eye on him, if she even *suspected* that this longing that she had so cavalierly described to Drew actually existed.

Mary didn't think I still had a thing for her husband, because I hadn't told her that I did. Since the day she'd told me that she was *dating* Wes, my desire to confide my feelings to her – my feelings about anything, but most especially my feelings about him – had completely evaporated. Since Mary and Wes took up together, I discovered that the trust in my sister that I'd valued for as long I could remember was compromised. I kept all my feelings to myself now.

And it was a good thing I hadn't confessed that I still loved Wes. Why, if I had, then she might've gone around telling people how pitiful I was, still holding onto an impossible dream, writing fairy tales about her blue-eyed husband, casting him as hero and dragon-slayer.

Oh, wait . . .

The immature part of my mind was only immature emotionally, perhaps, because it was certainly not immature in its appreciation for an attractive man – it led me to check out Wes looking absolutely good enough to eat in his tux. I was so pluperfectly angry with Mary right then, so furious that she'd tried to make me look like some kind of idiot to Drew, to make herself look like some sort of kind, indulgent sister, that I didn't even stop myself from thinking impure thoughts about Wes, resplendent in his best-man tuxedo. For a change, I didn't tell myself that it was wrong to imagine such things about him because he was my brother-in-law. I didn't admonish myself that such thoughts were disloyal to my sister.

How disloyal had she been to me, and repeatedly? This tale of pitifulness that she'd fed to Drew – which was an out and out lie – was just the latest in a string of disloyalties. Her entire relationship with Wes was just one big disloyalty.

Maybe it was the champagne, but I realized that it didn't matter, that it had *never mattered* that he was married to her High and Mightiness – I could think anything I wanted. So I just sat right there next to my perfect sister, and imagined divesting her husband of his tux, throwing those shiny patent leather shoes across the room, the two of us giggling and talking dirty to each other, just like we used to do.

I shifted in my chair, crossed my legs, and imagined what I would do to my sister's husband once he was undressed, and I discovered that thinking about seducing him made me feel guilty not at all. I discovered that I quite enjoyed fantasizing about Wes with Wes standing right there. What harm was there in it? It pleased me, made me feel all warm and squishy, and not one person was harmed. Not one person knew anything about it but me.

When the minister said, "By the power vested in me by God and the State of California, I now pronounce you husband and wife," I looked over at my sister and an entirely new and wonderful idea struck me. I thought, *You want to tell people that I write stories about Wes?*

The minister said, "You may now kiss your bride!" And everyone cheered.

My sister liked to tell people that I wrote stories about her husband? By God and the power vested in me by a fertile imagination, then I would write stories about her husband!

And they won't be stories for little girls, either, I thought. Mary had once said that I'd someday have to write love stories to keep Emmy amused. No more fairy tales. I'd have to make up a prince, a lover, someone with whom a now more mature Emmy might share true love's first kiss.

I smiled to myself. Mary had made the perfect suggestion – I'd write love stories, all right. But they wouldn't be for Emmy or anyone Emmy's age, not even for the innocent teen Emmy would someday become. They'd be just for me, for my own amusement, for my own indulgence.

143

Mary wanted to tell people that her poor, love-sick sister wrote kids' stories and starred her husband in them? I'd write stories that starred her husband, all right, but they wouldn't be for kids. They'd be along the same lines of the things I'd been thinking while I watched the wedding.

Maybe I'd even send them to her someday.

It was a silly notion, but it stuck in my head. All through the reception, the idea kept returning. I'd write down all my fantasies about Wes. Doing so would allow me to keep the details straight, keep me from repeating myself. That was the reason I'd written down Emmy's stories. *To keep the details straight.* I giggled, and Mary asked me if I was drunk.

Maybe I was, but the idea remained in my mind. I'd lost Wes in reality, but how much fun would it be to write little stories about having him? Then I could have him any time the mood struck me.

I commenced that very evening, when I got home after Drew and Connie's charming nuptials. I poured myself a glass of wine – why lose that champagne buzz? – and sat on my little couch (it was neither maroon nor forest green). I called up the word processing program on my laptop. No need to write them out long hand. I wouldn't need to have a notebook in my hand, to page through to find just the right bedtime story. I created a folder on the desktop, put his name on it.

The first one was a sword and sorcery legend, about a mistreated princess and her lost knight. I thought, why not start off in that same fairy tale vein? A cruel witch had separated the lovers with a wicked spell, but a white magic sorcerer restored them in the end. The scenes in the beginning showed that the kingdom was not entirely of a patriarchal bent, because the princess had quite the unladylike romp with her blue-eyed knight before the curse fell. And of course, the ultimate reunion was decidedly blue.

****

There was another bar across town from *Mickey's* – right around the corner from my apartment complex, oh, so coincidentally – called *The Beachcomber.* The owner's name was Gordy. He was in his mid-forties, and also acted as bartender. He took a shine to me right away, after I asked him why he'd given his bar a beachy name when there wasn't a beach around for fifty miles. It was the name on the business license, he told me. He'd relocated from Newport.

I stopped in there sometimes after work, had a beer, and talked to Gordy. He was nice, and only made perfunctory, oblique passes at me.

As one does with bartenders, I wound up more or less telling him my life story. Not a lot of details, not too many names: I was engaged to be married once, but that one had hit the ramp, and then when he finally came back, he wound up married to my sister. I'd been engaged to be married again, but that one had turned out to be a pervert. Gordy was sympathetic, as the best bartenders always are. We became friends.

One Friday night, we got to talking about music and bands. One thing led to another, and before I knew it, I was having the same conversation with Gordy that I'd had with Jon, a lifetime ago: why didn't he book a band, bring in some custom? *The Beachcomber* had a little raised area, now filled with tables – it could be a stage. I told him that I even knew of a band that might be willing to gig there. They were pretty good, I told him, and I was sure that they'd play for cheap. Just like Jon had done, Gordy said he'd give 'em a listen.

I called Wes that very night. Rolling Blackout wasn't playing *Mickey's,* so I knew Mary was working. There was absolutely nothing untoward about me calling my brother-in-law, of course, but I liked it better when I knew she wasn't there. "Do you have any kind of a contract with Jon?" I asked.

Wes laughed. "Not hardly. We only play there maybe once a month now, if that much. He's been talking about bringing back Comedy Night."

Yeah, that had been a moneymaker, I thought derisively. *The sound of no laughter had pulled the dollars right in off the sidewalk.*

"I found you another gig, Wes," I told him. "It's a little place, smaller than *Mickey's.* But they've got a stage, and the owner's been looking to start having live music. He says he's willing to give you guys a listen."

Wes hesitated, and again I thought of all the times that Mary had called him a coward. But it turned out that his hesitation was not from reluctance, but from his being touched by my effort. "That's so nice of you, Maddie!" he said softly. "Wow. I'll call the guys right away. They've been kind of bummed out that we haven't been playing too much anymore."

They've been bummed out because your wife is such a bitch, my immature mind said.

****

145

So it came to pass that fall: Gordy booked Rolling Blackout to play the tiny stage at *The Beachcomber* on Friday nights, and sometimes Saturdays, too. Mary came in to watch them on her first Friday night off, saying to me that she didn't think that they could be any worse than they were at *Mickey's*. But after Wes bounced through his usual poppy rendition of *My Disgrace,* she told me that she'd been mistaken. They *were* worse, in her estimation.

"God, how I hate that stupid song!" she told me, with her usual superior tone.

You're nothing but a bartender, *for God's sake,* I thought. *Wes has more talent in his little finger . . . but leave all that.* She sat through their whole set – she was the front's wife, after all. Their set lasted longer than in the old days, and by the time they were finished, Mary couldn't wait to leave. *The Beachcomber* had a large store room, and Mary didn't even wait until they had stashed their instruments before she gathered up her phone and her purse and made ready to depart.

She told Wes that she'd see him at home, and said to me that she still couldn't understand how I could stand their corny, cheesy music. "This new guy – what is he, twelve? The stuff he writes sounds like it's for tweens."

Then she turned on her high and mighty heel and left. I don't know exactly where she went or what she did on her Friday nights off after that, but she never again came back to *The Beachcomber* to watch her talented husband perform.

I, on the other hand, never missed a set. Randy, the new drummer – he'd been with the band for almost as long as Phil had been, but he would always be the *new* drummer – was quite the prolific song writer. There were love songs and ballads and drinking songs, but my favorite was still the one that Wes had written, the one about pushing the imaginary woman that had done him imaginary, unspecified wrongs off the nearest high place.

It didn't take long for the band to garner a small but loyal group of fans. Just like Jon had once feared, they were a cadre of probably ten or twelve just-barely-of-drinking-age girls. But they never missed a performance, standing shoulder to shoulder in front of the tiny stage, their boyfriends behind them. Gordy didn't care that they were young. He could spot a fake ID from a mile away, and if they tried to smuggle in any of their underage friends, he'd just show them the door.

One night in October, when Angelo started in on the bassline to *My Disgrace,* Wes said, "This one goes out to my friend, Maddie." My little immature heart soared. Hot damn, but he was sexy, up there with his guitar.

146

One of his groupies called out, "Is this song about her?"

From the back of the room, a familiar voice yelled, "No! This one's about his wife!"

The crowd laughed, except for the young girl – she didn't like to be reminded that the fine singer for Rolling Blackout was married, any more than I did. I turned around to see Drew and Connie threading their way through the crowd. I gave them a big hug, and we stood behind Wes's smitten fans and listened to Rolling Blackout's set together.

Afterwards, Wes actually had to sign a few autographs and turn down a few eager, stammered propositions before the four of us could sit around one of *The Beachcomber's* little tables and catch up. I wondered how Mary would feel about the little girls looking so keenly at her Raggedy Andy.

I told Drew that I thought it was funny that whenever he and Connie had the chance, they'd pack up Allie and come back to Riverside for a visit. "Most of us like to go *to* Las Vegas, not leave it," I said.

"My mom loves to see Allie," he said. "And besides, my best friends are here."

It seemed to me that Drew also liked to overlook that his best friends were *just* friends. His best friend was married to someone he didn't like, and I was just someone who liked to hear Wes sing, not too much different from the small crowd of young girls that showed up every weekend.

The reality of the current situation became abundantly clear right after Wes, Drew, Connie and I had downed a few rounds. All the little girls had long since left, no doubt to take out their yen for the local rock star on their boyfriends. Wes's phone rang, and he got up from the table and walked a short distance away to answer it. But he didn't walk far enough away. We heard him say tersely, "I don't know when I'll be home. Drew and Connie are here, and I–"

There was a burst of angry words from the phone, and the newlyweds and I exchanged a glance. "Uh, oh," Drew said. "Trouble in paradise."

Wes argued with his wife for a few more minutes, then hung up and sat back down with us. We were all silent, self-conscious. Then Gordy said, "Last call, ladies and gentlemen. You don't have to go home, but you can't stay here." He always said that. I think that it was the best part of being a bartender to him.

Wes sighed. "Can we go over to your place, Maddie? I'm sure Drew's mom doesn't want a bunch of drunks at her house." We were all a little bit drunk. "And Mary's—"

"Of course," I said, thinking *and Mary's a bitch, and I love you.* Why the hell not? My sister's husband and I would be chaperoned, after all.

We sat around and sobered up a little at my place, talked some more. It was a lot of fun, the way I'd always pictured my life would be. Talking with good friends, Wes and I together . . . *but leave all that.* Wes had made his choice. He was my brother-in-law. We were friends, and whatever we had once been, however the future had once looked, friends were all that we'd ever be now.

When the sun started to peep through the windows, Drew said that it was time to go home and collect his daughter. They had promised to take her to Castle Park that day, to let her ride the big merry-go-round, maybe play a round of putt-putt golf. I gave him and his bride a big hug and told them to stop by again before they went home. They went downstairs a little ahead of Wes. He was going with them, though, because he'd left his truck at *The Beachcomber.*

Wes hesitated in the doorway for a minute, like he had something important he wanted to say. Whatever it was, I was down to hear it. But at last he just said, "I wanted to tell you how much I appreciate you setting this gig up for us, Maddie. And how much I enjoy seeing you out there in the crowd. I . . . I can't tell you how much that means to me."

"I'm your biggest fan, Wes," I said happily. Not softly, not longingly. I had my emotions completely in check, even though I wanted to rush into his arms and *squeeze* him. I felt almost a magnetic pull in his direction.

I got the impression that he wanted to hug me, too, but I figured that it would just be a hug of gratitude for my loyalty, a brother-in-law hug, *a friend hug.* Whatever it would be, I thought that I might lose my practiced composure if I hugged him right then. It had been a long, fun night, and I was still a little bit buzzed. But it was over now, he was going back to his wife, and I just couldn't hug him right then.

Wes looked down the hall. Drew and Connie were already outside, waiting for him, anxious to get back to their little girl. He looked back at me, and for a split second, I thought he was going to come back into my apartment and hug me anyway, a big ol' good-smelling Wes hug. I waited. My self-control was enough that he would have to do it. Whatever happened after that – he could call Drew and tell him to go on home without him – whatever happened would happen, but Wes would have to initiate it.

Another heartbeat passed, and the moment with it. "You'll be there tonight?" he asked.

"You know it," I said.

He smiled and said, "I'll talk to you later, Maddie." Then he was gone.

I closed the door and leaned heavily against it. *What a trial our life has become!* the immature part of my mind whined. I just would've had to reach out my hand, and maybe Wes would've . . . but what if he didn't? What if he'd said, "Ah, gee, Maddie, thanks for coming to my shows, but really, you know, I can't . . . I don't want to . . . Mary . . ."

Then what little I had of him would be gone. And I couldn't, anyway. He was married to my sister, and I couldn't betray my own blood, my twin, my other half. *Ah, leave all that,* my immature mind said. *Sometimes ya just gotta do something for yourself, and he was ours first . . .*

My life was sad enough without adding lying to myself to it. I knew that if Wes wanted to, I would, and loyalty and blood be damned. I'd never bitch him out on the phone in front of his friends, for doing something that he loved. But life wasn't always a bed of roses, and apparently Wes was happy with his choice.

He hesitated, though, that little hopeful voice in my head said. *He wanted to say something else, maybe* do *something else. It was plain on his face.*

He was going to have to do it, then. I would not let my guard down. It was holding back too much.

MARY

Goddamn Wes and his goddamned band. On one of the few Friday nights I was off, I was sitting at home like an orphan, while he closed the bar and then saw the sun up with stupid dirty-fingernailed Drew and his devoted bride. Wes had said he'd come home right after they finished their set, but then Drew had breezed in from Vegas, and all the plans had changed. The plans hadn't been much – we were just going to sit around and watch a few movies, spend the evening in together. But they had been *my* plans, and how dare he change them? I didn't like sitting around by myself, when I'd expected my husband home when he'd said he was going to be.

I started in on him when he walked in the door. He'd brought breakfast, but I wasn't hungry. I was pissed off. "Thanks for leaving me all by myself all night."

"You could've come down and hung out with us." He sat at the kitchen table and began unwrapping his food.

"I work in a bar, Wes. I don't want to spend my Friday night off in another one."

I watched him eat, watched him shrug. "I didn't know Drew was gonna show up."

I realized I was being unfair – Drew didn't come to town very often, and Drew was his best friend. I realized that I wasn't really mad at Wes – surely, what difference did it make to me if I missed one night watching movies with him? It was not like I was desperately in need of his company.

I realized that I was angry because Mike had been sitting in my bar last night. He'd asked me if I wanted to go have a drink with him after my shift was over, and what would've been wrong with that? We were old friends, after all. But I'd told him no, I had to be getting right on home after work.

And for what? A boring movie date with my husband? I could've closed some other bar myself, had a few drinks with my old good friend tatted-up Mike. I could've had a little fun, a few laughs, looked at Mike's smiling green eyes and remembered the old days. But no. I had to get home to my husband, and then my husband hadn't even shown up.

"Maybe you can ask Drew to give you a heads-up the next time," I said.

Wes nodded and finished his breakfast. Then he gave me a perfunctory kiss on the cheek and said that he was going to get a few hours' sleep. His stupid band was playing again that night and I thought it was so childish of him to spend the whole weekend at that tiny little dive. What did he think he was, twenty? I had an early shift; I'd be off by nine, and they'd just be ramping up their set by then. Afterwards, he'd want to hang around and chat with Drew again, get drunk and act like a teenager. Pass. Drew wasn't all that, and *The Beachcomber* was a hole. Or worse, he'd want to bring his old buddy home and stay up all night, drinking here. Yawn.

Wes had his weekend all planned out, and it didn't seem to include indulging his wife in anything she wanted to do. I was being unfair – Wes didn't get to see Drew much, and he surely didn't stay out drinking every weekend. He was generally home before midnight on the nights he played *The Beachcomber*, and was never not sitting here waiting for me whenever I got home from work.

But the hell with him. He had his old friend to hang out with for the weekend. I decided that if Mike came back into my bar tonight, I'd go have that drink with him. He was *my* old friend after all, and it would be just a little harmless fun.

MADELINE

I woke up at about two o'clock in the afternoon, refreshed, not feeling at all like I'd stayed up all night drinking like a teenager. I made myself a nice little lunch, then sat down on the couch and wrote another story about Wes.

This was a science fiction epic. Our lovers are trapped on an alien world, refugees from some genocidal conflict elsewhere. But they are happy despite their travails, desperately in love, frequently having the hots for each other – in their humble hut, on the barren heath.

But then the enemy arrives.

The enemy and a brave pilot from home have a dogfight in the purple sky above the lovers. Things don't go well for the pilot, so with only his trusty laser, the blue-eyed refugee on the ground separates from his woman and shoots upward to draw the fire of the enemy, diverting attention from his crippled confrere in the sky. The alien enemy snaps at the bait, firing mercilessly at this puny annoyance on the ground. A massive trench is dug by his flaming weapons. A canyon, really.

The unknown flyer recovers enough to shoot down the distracted enemy, and then he, too, crashes and burns, tragically. With the danger gone, the lovers realize that the immense trench now separates them, he on one side and she on the other. The canyon stretches for untold miles, as far as the eye can see in both directions. It's so wide that they can't even hear each other's anguished cries of despair. But they can still see each other, and through signs and gestures, they decide to climb down to the canyon floor in order to be reunited. The journey is perilous – the rock still smokes in places – but through their determination to be together at all costs, they each manage to climb down. At the bottom, they discover a little river, bursting forth from the shattered rock, and they make love in the deep pool that is the river's source . . .

Seriously.

By that time I'd written probably fifteen of these tales. The male lead didn't always look like Wes – how many different ways can one describe an attractive man with dark blue eyes and curly black hair? So sometimes my hero was a tow-headed blondie with sky blue eyes, or a charming redhead with laughing tan eyes, or a brown-haired, bearded man with soulful brown eyes. But they were all tall and lean, with broad shoulders and a swimmer's body. My male character was sometimes a biker, a surfer, a cowboy. He was a butcher, a baker, a candlestick-maker. But he was always Wes.

I threw in details from all the men I'd even known: one of my characters liked to lick his thumb before he counted his money, like Neil. One of them had a sun tattooed around his navel like Mike. Not a single one of them desired to prove himself to two women at once, however. Not one of them wanted to be handcuffed to the bed, either.

Blondes, brunettes, redheads, black-haired, blue-eyed Adonises. *Rich man, poor man, beggar man, thief; doctor, lawyer, Indian chief.* They were all Wes. They didn't always look like him, but anyone that knew Wes (such as Mary, hee, hee) would know that they were always him.

The heroine was not always a small blonde with blue eyes, either. She was sometimes a willowy gypsy with enormous black eyes, or a zaftig, creamy-skinned ginger with freckles. A cowgirl with sunburned skin and work-roughened hands. Once she was even a statuesque, stately Zulu princess. The woman was always me, just like the man was always Wes. And even though she never had a sister, twin or otherwise, her love, her longing and lust for the hero, her eagerness to satisfy it, over and over, was exactly the same as my own for my sister's husband.

The story was never the same, but the basic plot varied little. There was love and sex, then separation by one cruel fate or another: vengeful witches, alien battles, horrible misunderstandings. Most of the tales were just raunchy, but I felt some of them to be poetic, these records of my impossible dreams. Mark Twain said, *For everything in a dream is more deep and strong and sharp and real than is ever its pale imitation in the unreal life which is ours when we go about awake and clothed with our artificial selves in this vague and dull-tinted artificial world.*

The dream of again possessing Wes was so deep and strong and sharp and real in me that I wrote stories about it, for my own amusement.

But there was little wistful, *unrequited* longing to my tales. I had enough of that *in the unreal life which was mine.* My little smutty stories ended smuttily, with the joyous lovers reunited for another round of breathless, incredible, sweaty sex. Some of the endings were actually quite pornographic, with lengthy descriptions of penetrations and earth-shattering, screaming orgasms. They were descriptions that I'd never have dared to save to electronic record in black and white, if I'd ever intended anyone else to read them. But I knew what I wanted, knew what I liked, and I had no trouble whatsoever recording it for myself.

****

I discovered that these two pastimes – writing dirty stories about Wes and watching his band – made me feel happier and more well-adjusted than I would've ever imagined. These things – which were not actually thrilling in themselves, after all – made me feel like I was living the carefree life with Wes of which I'd always dreamed, the life I'd once expected to live.

But every now and then the thought struck me that I might be becoming just the slightest bit delusional. I was really just a lonely woman with only an insane fantasy about my sister's husband to give me a reason to live. When my mind was traveling along these sad (though rational) lines, I would start to think that the time was past nigh for me to start looking for a man of my own. I could always keep my fantasies about Wes, my stories; I could always go to see him shake his sexy ass on stage, and think about that. But all those things only went so far. A real, live man – that was what I really needed.

I was sitting in *Mickey's* one afternoon, a few days after Halloween, hanging out with my sister for a minute after work. Mary was looking exceptionally pretty and perky that night – she was in a remarkably cheerful mood. I marveled that we still looked exactly alike – she really had Wes, and I just dreamt of him – but that dream was apparently enough to keep me looking just as happy and perky as she did.

Besides, I was going to get to see Wes play that very night, so there was a reason for my festive mood to match hers. I finished my beer and bid Mary adieu and walked out of *Mickey's*. Not four paces down the street, I ran into blonde Mike walking the other way.

"Baby!" he said, and gathered me up into a hug. "I was just coming to see you!"

He was under the impression that I was my cheerful, perky, happily married sister. In a heartbeat, I remembered that long ago weekend, that other time when charming, devil-may-care Mike had also thought I was my sister. I – *we* – had known Mike before I'd ever met Wes, and I remembered that he'd been a whole lot of fun. He wasn't much in the personality department, not much of a conversationalist. He was a gamer, a slob, usually between jobs. In other words, he wasn't an all-around great guy like Wes. But Wes was married to my sister, and I remembered that Mike was something else between the sheets . . .

Yep, Wes was gone, and here was Mike, hugging me, thinking I was Mary. All those personality qualities that I loved about Wes – I still got to experience them whenever we talked. But all those physical things about Wes that I'd also liked so much – I only got to experience those in my mind.

And here was Mike, who was no conversationalist, who didn't even play guitar. But here was Mike, hugging me, smiling at me, thinking I was my sister, with whom he'd had a few bitchin' sex weekends once upon a time. *Why the hell not?* I thought. *What could it hurt?*

I'd have to tell Mary, of course. Then she'd understand why ol' Mike believed that they were cheating on her husband together, the next time he walked into *Mickey's* to say hi. But by that time, I would've already had my fun, and if I had to explain the little deception to Mike, explain that my sister was not indeed an adulteress, well, what of it?

Maybe I'd even go back for seconds, if he was down after I'd explained. Why the hell not? I was single – I could do whomever I wanted. Wes didn't even have to know, and what could Mary say about it? She had Wes, so she couldn't hardly have one single thing to say about my having a little dalliance with her onetime – *our onetime* – entirely funnest way to spend a weekend.

"I got off early," I told Mike. "It must be kismet." I leered at him. "You want to go back to your place?"

Mike's blonde eyebrows went up in pleased surprise. "That sounds like a plan." He grinned, took my hand, and we walked a few paces. Then he stopped, grabbed my chin and kissed me, right there on the sidewalk. *What a philandering tramp he must think my sister is!* I thought, and kissed Mike right back. He wasn't Wes, but I wasn't ever going to kiss Wes again.

And I was amazed at how awesome it was to kiss Mike, how kissing Mike drove Wes right out of my mind. It seemed as if it had been a lifetime since I'd kissed a man, a million years since I'd been wrapped in that delicious, male smell. Yeah, Mike and I would never discuss movies, he'd never make me laugh with his hilarious, clever sense of humor; he'd never sing to me. But on the other hand, Wes would never, ever kiss me again, or anything else. And I knew that Mike was more than capable in the anything else department.

A girl cannot live by fantasies alone.

At ten o'clock, after hours of amazing sex, Mike and I stopped to catch our breath. We were about to get back to it again when both of our phones rang at the same time. His was sitting on the nightstand beside his side of the bed, and mine was in the same place on the other side. We smiled at each other, then turned and answered them.

Mine was a text from Wes: *Do you live? We're holding the set for you.*

Even though I had hardly caught my breath, even though I was yet warmed from Mike's caresses, I still thought, *Ah, Wes, I love you so much.* I would always love Wes, regardless of what underhanded methods I might use to scratch that physical itch that I would never again scratch with him.

I texted back: *I had a little car trouble. I'm getting a jump right now.* I have nothing if not a sense of humor, and it wasn't any of his business what I was doing. He was only my brother-in-law, after all.

But I did love him, and I did want to see him play. Mike had expertly worn the edge right on off, and I now had to get to *The Beachcomber.* I was done with Mike for the moment, and he no doubt wanted to get back to his video games. It wasn't like we were going to talk.

Go ahead and play, I texted to Wes. *I'll be there for the encore.*

I looked over at Mike, only to find him staring at me, open-mouthed. Speechlessly, he held up his phone so I could read it. *Where the fuck are you?* the text said.

"I was going in to see you . . . we were finally going to . . . now you're texting me . . ." He shook his head. "You're Mary's sister, aren't you?" He looked at his phone as if it was some piece of alien technology, as if it had suddenly come alive, sentient, in his hand. "That's the only thing that makes any sense."

I tried to look as ashamed as possible. "I'm sorry, Mike." I wasn't ashamed at all. I was single, hard-up, and I knew that Mike was fantastic, even if he didn't know that I knew it. So what if I'd borrowed Mary's identity for a few hours, had lived her (and secretly my) old wild life for a minute? She was living the life that I should've had, with Wes, 24/7. All that writing of dirty stories had riled me up a bit, and when I saw an outlet, I took it.

"I'm sorry, darlin'," I repeated. "But you're just so damned cute."

Mike's green eyes twinkled. "It's one hundred and twenty-five percent okay with me . . . ?"

"Maddie."

He grinned. "Right. It's okay with me, Maddie. You coulda told me, it would've been okay." He looked at me like I was a stark raving lunatic, but even if I was, that was okay with him, too. I was just his kind of lunatic. "In fact," he said, smiling, reaching across the bed for me, "let me show you how okay I am with it."

I smiled back at Mike. He was real, he was here, he was down. Wes was married to my sister. Whatever I had with Wes was only in my imagination. Wes could wait.

MARY

Mike sat at my bar with a dumb grin on his face. He shrugged. "How was I supposed to know it wasn't you?"

It was eleven-fifteen. My shift had ended at nine-thirty, but Jon was just going to have to pay me for the hours I'd worked while I was waiting for Mike to show up. I'd finally made up my mind to go have that drink with him. It would've just been a little harmless fun.

My husband amused himself every weekend, and while I didn't begrudge him that – it wasn't like I wanted to go over there to that firetrap and listen to his awful band – why shouldn't I amuse myself also? Mike was sexy and I liked his line. I had something he wanted and I liked to listen to him ask me for it.

Wes had moved back down the ladder to *meh*, again. Our love life was routine, almost scheduled: he was only interested on Saturday or Sunday mornings, after he gigged at *The Beachcomber*. I imagined that playing his little juvenile tunes with his buddies made him feel like he was a teenager again. Whatever.

I'm a night owl, a bartender, for God's sake. I like to hear a little suggestion ahead of time. I like to think about it for a while. Anticipate. A little nudge in the morning isn't really my style. And I didn't love Wes, anyway. Don't get me wrong – he was nice to have around during the week – I liked that he was there with me at night when I worked early shifts. But he was just not all that.

Of a Friday or Saturday night, I liked a little excitement. And Mike had started coming into *Mickey's* every weekend, sitting at the bar and keeping me company while I worked. He would grin at me and make cute comments about how good I looked – just little whispered remarks that no one else could hear. I liked it. I looked forward to seeing him and his beautiful green eyes saunter into the bar. I liked how he smiled at me: it made me remember how he *used* to smile at me, those couple of weekends when we were alone. It was all just a game that I enjoyed in my head; it didn't mean a thing to anyone but me. And maybe him.

I sighed now and considered Mike, sitting at the bar with a half-apologetic look on his face. Sometimes men are just so lame, so unobservant. He had absolutely no idea that it wasn't the first time that he'd been with my sister. Maddie hadn't clued him, and I surely wasn't going to, either. Mike wouldn't mind – he didn't mind now. But it was all just a cute, dirty mistake on his part at the moment. He thought that

I was above reproach, and my sister was a devious tramp, unable to help herself in the face of his undeniable potency. If he ever found out that we'd played him in the past . . . well, he just didn't need to know about any of that.

It was definitely an odd, touchy situation, at least to Mike. I could tell that he was curious to see how jealous I was about the idea that my single sister had just swooped in and snatched him up, when we'd been dancing around the idea of a little harmless infidelity for quite some time now.

Men don't care. He didn't know Wes – he didn't have anything against Wes. But if my husband couldn't keep me at home, that wasn't Mike's fault. If my relationship with my husband didn't lead me to be offended by his innuendo, didn't lead me to say, "Look, Blondie, it doesn't matter that you used to make me absolutely climb the walls with some of the things you used to do – I'm a happily married woman now, and your describing it in my ear is just disrespectful," then it wasn't Mike's fault. If I didn't tell him to shut up, he was going to keep talking dirty to me. It amused him, and he could tell that it amused me. He didn't know if it was going to work or not, and that unknowing also amused him.

He was willing to come into my bar and proposition me, just for the hell of it. If I came around eventually, that was all good; if I didn't, he would eventually give up and move on to greener pastures, just like he'd done once upon a time. The fact that I was married now didn't even figure into it – either I would do it or I wouldn't.

But since he was sitting here fresh from nailing my sister, and he knew I knew it, he expected some kind of jealousy from me, some kind of outrage. Men are conditioned to expect women to be jealous. The idea that their woman is going to be inconsolably furious, perhaps even homicidal if they are intimate with someone else – the guilt and shame they are conditioned to feel if they transgress – that's the main way we keep them honest. It's the classic thing, just like the main theme of *The Lord of the Flies* – men don't not sin because it's wrong to do so. They don't sin because they're afraid of getting caught and punished. If the threat of punishment is removed . . . why, they'll just go right ahead and push Piggy off the cliff. Damn near every time.

So Mike expected me to be jealous, to be angry with my sister, to be angry with him. That's why he'd pleaded ignorance. He might've just let the whole thing slide on by, if Maddie hadn't told him that she'd call and explain that she'd been a bad girl.

When Maddie was in a playful mood, *then* she liked to text, and she always sent ones that were written like old-fashioned telegrams:

Caught ur blondie outside the bar. Stop. He thot I was u, so I let him think it. Stop. What a bad girl u r, I am. Stop.

    Did u?

    Went right on home with him. Don't stop ☺

I wasn't angry with Maddie, and I certainly wasn't jealous. Men had always been something that we'd shared in the old days, and nowadays . . . I'd taken that drunken plunge in Vegas, and there wasn't supposed to be any sharing going on any more, anyway, so how could I be mad?

Ah, the old days! Men were fun – why shouldn't my sister and I share them? There had never been any sense of permanence to any of them. None of them had been the one – why shouldn't we share them, just like a big ol' banana split? We'd never hurt anyone, the men least of all. They were all just temporary, just diversions.

And there had never, ever been even the slightest reason for either of us to ever consider something as ridiculous as jealousy. Jealousy over a man? How silly. I'd never seen jealousy from Maddie about anything, ever. We'd shared everything as kids: clothes, toys. Nothing had ever mattered enough to Maddie that she would get jealous if I wanted it, too. She would just share it with me. We're sisters, after all.

I'd never even seen a hint of jealousy from Maddie, for all our lives. Except for that one time, after she'd sent Wes into my bar to humiliate me, and I'd off-handedly asked her if we would be sharing him, like we'd shared some of the other ones. There had been jealousy then, a thunderbolt that transformed her features so suddenly and completely as to make me step back. "No," she'd said then. "We won't be sharing this one. This one is all mine."

Funny how things turn out sometimes. Not only was Wes not *all hers*, they had no connection whatsoever now. I knew he didn't care about Maddie anymore, and I knew she didn't care about him, even though I did know that she liked to watch his stupid band. Wes was mine now, and while I could take or leave him, had in fact been contemplating a little harmless diversion on the side – he was still my husband.

And because he was my husband, it was just as well for Maddie that she didn't feel anything for Wes anymore. Because we couldn't be having that.

I looked at Mike and considered the jealousy that he expected me to feel. Jealousy was such a stupid emotion – it had to do with fear. You're afraid that someone is going to take away someone that you value, that you *love*. You're afraid that someone is going to steal that person from you, and you're afraid that you're helpless to prevent this theft, because that person might just go along with being stolen. That's the main idea behind jealousy to me – that feeling of helplessness, because you feel you're not in control.

I wouldn't feel jealousy if I thought someone was angling for Wes. Wes belonged to me. I was sure in that – I knew him. Wes wasn't a pussy-hound like Mike, so I didn't have to worry that he'd be amenable to some random woman stealing him away from me because he wanted to find out about something that he thought he was missing. So I didn't live in fear, didn't feel helpless that my husband would suddenly decide that he was going to do better with the next woman that made a play for him. So I wasn't jealous. Wes himself was above reproach. Quite a bit boring, maybe, not overly exciting to me anymore, perhaps, if he had ever been. But Wes was mine, and I knew he wasn't going anywhere.

It wasn't that Wes wasn't attractive to me; it wasn't that Wes wasn't attractive. Give him a good haircut, dress him up in a nice dark suit, and Wes was fine all day long and three times on Sunday. So I knew he was attractive to other women, too. Hell, he was once the walking, talking embodiment of scrumptiousness to my sister. It was just that I knew Wes. He was mine.

So I wasn't jealous, not fearful, not helpless. But I was possessive.

Possessiveness, unlike jealousy, doesn't involve fear. Possessiveness is why we lock the doors, why we hide the silver. Possessiveness is about being on the lookout for thieves. I knew Wes wouldn't run off with the next woman that winked at him, but that didn't mean that I was going to stand by and let any women get by with winking at him. You don't knock on my door and tell me you're from the Gas Company so you can case my house, and you don't look too long at my husband, like you might have a mind to try to steal him, either. My husband belongs to me.

That's why it was a good thing for Maddie that she no longer harbored any feelings for Wes. We would've had words about that. That just wouldn't do. I wouldn't want her being too appreciative of my car or my new jacket, and I certainly wouldn't want her to be too appreciative of my husband. I wasn't religious, but there were commandments against coveting. I wasn't concerned about the one about committing adultery – Wes wasn't the type – but I'd be damned if I'd put up with my sister or anyone else coveting something which belonged to me.

So it was a good thing for Maddie that she'd long since forgotten about Wes.

I looked at Mike. What should my reaction be to her little swoop? I couldn't possibly care less – Maddie had perhaps saved me from myself, perhaps prevented me from partaking in a momentary, harmless indiscretion. It wasn't like Wes had anything to worry about – it wasn't like Mike was going to steal *me* away. At least not for more than maybe an hour, and hour and a half. It wasn't even like Maddie had permanently prevented all that, if I decided that I wanted to do it. So I wasn't angry at my sister in the least.

But tatted-up Mike expected some reaction, so I decided to go with mild betrayal, and then put it on him. "Well," I said, "she did break the code."

"Code?" he said doubtfully, over the rim of his beer mug.

"Yeah. You never mess around with someone your sister dated. Not even years later. It's just not done." This was a plot to some sitcom I'd seen once. "But you didn't know about the code, you didn't know it wasn't me, and I'm sure you won't let it happen again."

"Baby," Mike said with that devilish grin, "I thought it was you. I was duped. Used." He batted his beautiful mantis-green eyes at me. "I'm sorry. It'll never happen again. What else can I say?"

"The evil twin is a lefty," I told him, just like I'd told Wes once. Thinking of Wes, I added, "Just toss something to her, preferably before she starts taking her clothes off. If she catches it in her left hand, you know she's not me. It's foolproof."

MADELINE

I went directly from Mike's bed to Rolling Blackout's performance, pausing only to smooth out my hair in the rearview mirror of my car, and reapply my lipstick before hurrying into *The Beachcomber*. They were only playing on Friday this week, and I really wanted to see Wes, to hear him sing. After all that had happened that afternoon, I discovered that I really *just had to see Wes*.

They were running late, no doubt because they had held their set, waiting for me while I finished up pretending to be my sister and screwing our one time paramour eight ways to Sunday. Wes was singing some slow love song that Randy had written; he smiled at me when I walked in. Like Mary's opinion of the whole Rolling Blackout phenomenon in general, I found this particular song to be a trifle cheesy, a whole lot sappy. But it didn't matter. Wes was singing it. And the sound of his voice warmed me through and through, like it always did. I took my place behind the line of his awestruck groupies in front of the stage.

Hot from Mike's embrace, I discovered that I was still just as wound up as when I'd first decided *what the hell* and went on home with him. I would've thought that taking the edge off of months of deprivation would have calmed me down a bit – it sure seemed to have done so on the quick car ride over here. There was no doubt about the fact that I'd been hard-up – I would've thought that taking out all my pent-up frustrations on Mike would've made me able to consider Wes with a calmer, more detached eye. I was physically satisfied, Wes was my sister's husband, off limits everywhere except in my mind. I would've thought I would've been a little bit more in control of myself.

But great sex with one guy is not always the antidote to no sex at all with the guy you really want. I would've thought that just feeding that need would have satisfied it – I would've thought that I could've happily gone back to celibacy again, now that the physical yen had been so thoroughly and gloriously fulfilled. Driving over here, I'd felt like a big, fat house cat sitting by the fire, warm and sated, purring contentedly. I thought that Mike had released the lean and hungry alley cat that I'd become.

Sure, I was feeling great when I walked in the door of *The Beachcomber*, all warm and fuzzy. But when I saw Wes, that need came back, and I was amazed to realize that the fact that I had just enjoyed myself to the fullest only put a finer, keener edge to my desire for Wes.

It was no longer that desperate, hopeless, uncontrollable longing. Being with Mike had calmed the overactive reactions I'd been having – I no longer turned around and looked at every man that passed me, just because I could smell him. But I still wanted Wes.

I reflected that if Mike was my husband, I would've had no reason not to be faithful to him. He was fantastic; his touch had turned me back into a calm, thinking human being again. If I'd been in love with him, I should have no reason at all to even think of another man.

But I wasn't in love with him, wasn't married to him. The man that I loved was onstage, and the moment I saw him, I was flooded with the same kind of desire that I'd felt for Mike – not high-flung and unrequited, not poetic in its tragic impossibility. Mike had brought the sexy back in little Maddie, and I looked at Wes with a devious kind of want, a dirty, almost predatory kind of desire.

I didn't think about how much I loved Wes at that moment, how much I liked his sense of humor, his personality. All I could think of then was how good my body felt, and how it could all be repeated again, if I could just *get at* Wes. Mike's touch had calmed my need for a man, but it had only inflamed my need for *this* man.

Wes sang *My Disgrace,* and some of the unloosed lust I was experiencing must have shown on my face. I watched him glance at his groupies – they felt no need to hide their lust, were perhaps incapable of doing so, being young girls. Then he looked back at me and he recognized the same look on my face. I simply couldn't hide it at that moment, and I probably looked like one of Pavlov's drooling dogs at feeding time. Wes smiled curiously, uncertainly at me, and boldly, I winked at him. He grinned in complete surprise and winked back.

I considered his groupies. The only difference between me and those star-struck little girls was that I didn't have to imagine just how good Wes could be. I could *remember.* They liked to watch Wes play the guitar because he looked sexy doing it, but I remembered that Wes fucked just like he played the guitar – naturally, completely, effortlessly. And that memory, combined with that little yelp in his voice when he sang, sliced right through to the core of me, better than a million whispered *Oh, baby's.* The little girls could speculate, they could imagine, they could fantasize – but I could *remember,* and I found that I was remembering quite clearly at the moment.

Rolling Blackout finished their set, and I waited patiently while the same five or six girls asked Wes to sign autographs on bar napkins and menus. There were fewer groupies than a few months earlier – it wasn't like Rolling Blackout even had a CD available to satisfy the ten or twelve that used to come in to see them, and Wes's undeniable unavailability had sent half of them off to chase other local singers. But these five or six girls would always be there. I wondered how many autographed nothings they had by now. Asking for his autograph was just an excuse for them to talk to him, to have him smile and look them in the eye for a moment.

After this little ritual, Wes ignored the girls, like I imagined a real rock star would, and they eventually dispersed. I had again veiled my lust – it was easy to do so now, because the edge of it had been taken off. I was no longer needy, just contemplative. I was even in control of myself enough to give him a hug and tell him I was sorry I was late. He said he was glad that I was here now, then turned to speak to Gordy.

Barely within earshot, I heard one of the groupies' boyfriends. "Come on, Darlene. You're barking up the wrong tree. He's gay."

I looked over my shoulder at Darlene as she paused on her way out the door. I saw a reflection of my own lust for Wes mirrored in her eyes. *Oh, honey,* I thought, *you're jealous beau is so wrong.* I looked back at Wes, oblivious, laughing at something Gordy was saying. Wes was a lot of things – perhaps most importantly, at least as far as Darlene and I were concerned, he was unattainable – but he was most certainly not gay. Darlene's man shouldn't be so disparaging. If it wasn't for Wes looking so sexy, he might not be getting any tonight.

Wes and I just had time to sit down at one of *The Beachcomber's* round tables, he just had time to offer me that curious, uncertain smile again. He didn't even have enough time to speak to me before his phone rang.

He sighed and answered it. Mary wasn't shouting at him this time: I couldn't even hear her voice. Wes listened silently, and I was only sure that it was his wife on the other end when he said, "I'll be home in forty-five minutes," and hung up. The newly satisfied portion of my mind recognized the response to a proposition in the tone of his voice, and I thought that it had surely been a night for women lusting after my brother-in-law. His diehard fans. Me. Now his own wife.

He started to look apologetic, and I said, "It's okay, Wes. I understand. Your master's voice." I smiled to cover the little jab of that, and continued, "It's about time you spend a night at home instead of closing this bar every Friday." *With me.*

It was just as well, I thought, because I was experiencing the desire to hug him again, maybe just go right ahead and kiss him. Maybe ask him if he wasn't doing anything right that minute, I had an idea for a way to kill that forty-five minutes. My mind was making me think like a filthy slut right then – hell, I hadn't even hit the shower since leaving Mike's – but I didn't care. My dirty little mind would've taken Wes right back there into *The Beachcomber's* ample store room and performed all kinds of unspeakably wonderful things with him, and if he could smell Mike on me, that would've been his problem.

Mercy, I thought. It was just as well that Mary had summoned him. My mind was just running off with all kinds of whorish thoughts, and I was sure that if I acted on even the most innocent of them, Wes would turn me down, anyway. His wife had called him — his wedded wife, whom he had married on a drunken whim in Las Vegas. He wanted to go home to her, and as soon as possible. He was interested in neither me, nor my entirely slutty intentions. It was just as well that his wedded wife had summoned him.

MARY

I cornered Wes almost before he had time to close the door to our apartment. I wrapped my arms around his neck and kissed him. He hesitated, as if he was thinking it over, just like he'd done that first time, so long ago, in my little downtown apartment – the first time I'd kissed him when he knew I wasn't Maddie.

Wes knew that his little hesitation was a turn-on for me. What he didn't know was that it was one of the few that he possessed. Sometimes he would give me a little smile . . . but this one was the best. That little hesitation, like he was thinking it over – then he went on ahead and kissed me back, like he'd made up his mind all over again, just like the first time. He kissed me back hungrily then, just like the first time, after he'd come to the decision that my sister was lost to him forever, and that he was going to be mine now.

It was all in my mind, of course – Wes only knew that if I made the effort to kiss him, and he hesitated a little bit, then it made me want to kiss him all the more. Men are dumb, but they can be taught. He had no idea that the whole little scenario never failed to bring back a sense of triumph to me. He just knew that it was a trigger that made his wife respond, eagerly for a change. Just like I had on that long ago weekend, the first time he'd realized that my sister was gone, and that if he wanted a petite blonde that looked like her, then it was going to have to be me.

And of course Wes couldn't know that the wellspring of my unaccustomed desire tonight was a missed drink with another man. I didn't know if I would've gone ahead and done something more than just drink with Mike that evening. The jury was still out on that. But there was no way I was going to do anything at all, not even have a drink with him, after he'd come in all flushed and apologetic, after Maddie had sent all her cutesy *Don't stop* ☺ texts. Maybe some other time, but certainly not tonight.

But the anticipation of having the opportunity to accept or turn down such an adventure remained, and here was my blue-eyed husband, kissing me, and while he was not ol' green-eyed, tatted-up

Mike, I found that my mood was more than enough to make me want him. Sometimes one's mood is all it takes to throw a little spice onto a well-traveled, oft-seen, same-place, same-thing kind of road. A tryst with Mike may or may not await me in the future, but the consideration of it was enough to make my husband just what the doctor ordered at that moment.

MADELINE

I still felt like that fat, sated house cat when I awoke the next morning. Even the unrequited longing for my brother-in-law had not yet dissipated the physical satisfaction engendered by a good, long romp in the hay with an able and willing partner.

I reflected on Wes's groupies, and wondered if there were a few satisfied boyfriends around town this morning, upon whom the little girls' had exorcised their own lusts for Wes. The thought made me smile, and for once I didn't even begrudge his wife for being the only one that actually got to have him. The way I felt now, wanting him was enough.

My phone rang. It was Gordy. "Hey, my friend, I have a question for you."

I smiled. "I hope I have an answer for you."

"Wes isn't picking up, so I thought you might know. Does Rolling Blackout have any kind of CD? Something we could perhaps sell at the bar? Those girls — they sure do love Wes, and I was thinking that we should give them what they want. At least in musical form."

"At an appropriate mark-up."

"But of course."

"They used to have a demo," I told Gordy. "The sound quality wasn't very good. They recorded it in the old drummer's garage. I don't know if they ever made another one."

"I'm sure even that would sell," Gordy said, and I thought, *Bless your capitalistic little heart.*

And then I remembered Jason's documentary. A clear picture of the package I'd received sprang to my mind. I remembered my little apartment in Rancho Bernardo, before Evan, before Wes and Mary, before Evan's icky betrayal, before my return to Riverside and my taking up the mantle of unrequited love for my brother-in-law. I saw the little package, unopened, unwatched, tossed into a box of sweaters that I would probably never wear again.

"Gordy!" I said. "I don't know if there's a new demo, but there is a movie!" I told him all about its creation, about Jason following the band around for weeks, filming in *Mickey's*, annoying Mary with the constant presence of cameras in her bar. I told him that I didn't think Wes had ever seen it, because he'd left town before Jason compiled it.

There was a pause on the other end of the phone, a moment of silence. Then Gordy said, "Didn't you tell me that your first fiancé left town, Maddie? Then came back and wound up marrying your sister? It was Wes?"

Apparently Wes had never mentioned that his wife was my sister. Gordy knew that we were friends, that I was Rolling Blackout's biggest fan – I'd been the one to get them the gig at his bar, after all. Gordy knew that Wes was married – how many times had the little girls asked the bartender, "Hey, Mister, is that guy singing married?" But apparently, all the ducks had not been set in a row for Gordy until just that moment.

"Yes, Gordy," I told him. "Wes and I were once engaged."

"Well, I'll be damned."

"Don't be," I said with a grin.

"And his wife – your sister doesn't mind you sitting around and mooning over him every weekend?"

I opened my mouth to speak, then snapped it shut again, so shocked was I at Gordy's statement. At last I found my voice. "I most assuredly do not moon over Wes."

"Dude," Gordy said. He always called me *dude* when he was being emphatic. I think it was a carry-over from his days at the beach. "You most assuredly do. You stand out there in the crowd and stare at him, just like all those crazy little girls. Last night, I thought you just might eat him.

"I don't know if he can see you or not. I've been up on that stage a few times, and the lights Terry rigged up are pretty bright. But I can see you from the bar."

"You're nuts, Gordy," I said flatly. I thought that the night before had been the only time that I'd ever let it show. Could I really be that obvious, all the time? Did Wes know? My good mood evaporated.

"Now it all makes sense," Gordy was saying. "You never did seem to me to be the type to be hung up on some local singer. I mean, let's face it – they're okay, but they're never gonna get out of Riverside."

Damn you, Gordy! I thought. *Rolling Blackout is great! Wes has more talent in his little finger than –*

"But now it all makes sense. Wes is the one you were engaged to, the one that ran off. The one that . . ."

"The one that married my sister," I said angrily. "So, yeah, I don't have any feelings for Wes, anymore, Gordy. I just like to hear him sing."

"Look, Maddie, I don't want to offend you. I'm just telling you what I see. You don't moon over him while you're talking to him, but when he's onstage, you've got the same look on your face as those girls."

169

"You're nuts, Gordy," I repeated. "I'll see if I can scare up Jason's video. Like I say, I don't think Wes ever even saw it. If it's any good, maybe we can sell a few copies to the fans. I'm sure Jason wouldn't mind."

"We'll give him a cut," Gordy said, glad that the conversation had removed itself from his faux pas of suggesting that I had a thing for my brother-in-law.

"If we can track him down." I liked to think that maybe Jason was in Hollywood now, or in some far flung land, making documentaries about international problems. But that was what the internet was for. I imagined that it wouldn't really be too hard to locate Jason, especially if money was involved. "I'll see you next week, Gordy. And . . . Gordy?"

"Yes, Maddie?"

"All these crazy things that you think you've seen? You'll keep them to yourself, right?"

"Oh, Maddie," Gordy said, feigning offense. "You wound me. Am I not a bartender? Am I not *your* bartender? Discretion is my middle name."

"Thanks, Gordy. I'll see you on Friday."

I hung up and sighed. Maybe I was more transparent than I realized. Now there were two people that knew I still loved Wes: Drew and Gordy. Three, if you counted my mother. But I was still confident that Wes didn't know. I hid my feelings when I talked to him, never talked to him about feelings of any kind, never talked about the us that once was – and like Gordy said, he probably couldn't see me too clearly when he was onstage. But I vowed then and there to be a little more careful about my expression when I watched him sing.

****

No, Wes couldn't have a clue as to how I really felt about him. I was too cool. So confident was I in this assertion, that I didn't feel guilty at all when I called him, a little later that day. He was my brother-in-law. We were friends. I had news concerning his musical career. Why shouldn't I call him?

When he answered the phone, his voice had that certain lazy quality to it, something I remembered very well, and I knew that he and my sister had indeed been enjoying their marital rights, perhaps had just finished, or were just about to commence again. Well, they were allowed. What possible difference could it make to me?

"Gordy wants to sell your CD at the bar," I said. "I told him I didn't know if you had one, but then I remembered Jason's movie. Did you ever see Jason's movie, Wes?" *Or were you too busy getting out of Dodge, too busy abandoning me over a stupid practical joke?*

"No, I never did get to see it, darlin'," he replied. I heard Mary murmur something in the background and I thought, *Don't call me darlin', you son of a bitch. Your darlin' is right there snuggled up with you.*

"Well, I've got a copy of it, if you want to see it."

"Is it any good?"

Oh, yeah, Wes, I've watched it a thousand times. I sat around and watched it over and over again, mooning *over you, after you left town like a coward.*

"I don't know, Wes. I never watched it either. But I've seen some of Jason's other stuff. He's very professional. I'm sure it's great."

"I'm a little busy right now, Maddie."

I heard my sister giggle, and a bright bolt of hatred for both of them shot through me. I wanted to say, *Hey, Wes, you think you could ask your wife for Mike's number for me? I'm sure she's got it.* But that would just be small and mean, and it hadn't been Mary that had just snatched an old lover off the street, it had been me. Mike and me, Mike and Mary from the old days – it was none of Wes's business, and mentioning anything about it would just open up a whole can of worms that didn't need to be tapped. Ever.

"I've got to dig it out, anyway, Wes. No hurry. I'll talk to you later." I hung up before he even said goodbye. I didn't want to hear that lazy, sex-satisfied drawl to his voice again, thought I would scream if he called me *darlin'* in it again, like he did in the old days.

*****

I figured that perhaps the happy couple was enjoying some kind of second honeymoon, since I didn't hear from either of them for a few days. Maybe Wes had finally gotten his shit together enough to go out and buy my sister a wedding ring. But probably not. She wouldn't wear it, anyway. She'd told me once that wearing a wedding ring cut a bartender's tips in half, and that was the reason that she hadn't pressed Wes to buy her one. Whatever. What could it possibly matter to me?

Mary finally called her only sister on Wednesday morning. "You've gotta come to Vegas with us this weekend, Maddie!"

Ah, yeah, Vegas. With the happy couple. What were they going to do there, renew their vows? With me as dumbfounded witness this time, instead of Drew?

"I don't think so, Mary," I said. "Thanks for asking, but Las Vegas is a couples' kind of place. I would feel like a third wheel. It would be nice to see Drew again, but–"

"Drew?" Then my sister laughed. "I'm sorry, Maddie. You misunderstand me. Let me start over. I don't mean you gotta come to Vegas with us this weekend, like you gotta come to Vegas with me and Wes. That would be a drag, just like seeing Drew again would be a drag." She giggled at the *as if* of all that. "I guess you haven't heard. Felicia is getting married."

I guess I'd been out of the *Mickey's* family loop for a while, what with spending every weekend at *The Beachcomber, mooning* over my sister's husband. Reality and other people's lives had just passed me right on by. "Really?" I said. "Who is Felicia marrying?"

"You remember Tony? The tall, good-looking Budweiser rep?"

"Sure. Yeah. Tony." I remembered Tony not at all. I'd never met a Budweiser rep in my life.

"That's who she's marrying," my sister said. "Jon has given all of us the whole weekend off – me, the bride to be, even Debbie. He booked us a hotel room, is even paying for the strippers. He says it's the least he can do for his girls, for once. So the three of us are going to Vegas to have a bachelorette party for Felicia!"

Oh, yeah, that'll be bitchin', I thought. *What fun!* My happily married sister, and our soon-to-be-happily-married friend, and Debbie, who was just too young and naïve not to be happy. And me, not even *always a bridesmaid,* yet still never a bride. And male strippers. Oh, yeah. A veritable barrelful of monkeys would that be. "I'm sorry, Mary," I told her. "I'm just not feeling a drunken girls' weekend in Las Vegas right now."

"Suit yourself." I could hear the frown in Mary's voice.

Go smile at your husband, I thought. "Wish Felicia well for me, and tell her I'll be at the wedding. Take lots of pictures."

"Whatever." Mary hung up.

****

Wes sauntered into *ReMax* about nine-thirty on Friday morning, all dressed up in his monthly production meeting suit. *If you're thinking I'm going to be impressed,* I thought, *you've got the wrong sister.* I thought he looked a mite strait-laced when he was dressed up. I thought the suit made him look old before his time, and I thought he came off as a little smarmy in it, like his old nemesis Bill Proten. My brother-in-law in a suit did nothing for me.

And that lasted until he smiled. Then he was just ol' Wes again, not trying to impress me as if I was Mary. Just Wes, whom I loved.

"I'm sorry I haven't had a chance to call you all week, Maddie," he said. I had missed talking to him. He called me as often as my sister did, usually at least once every other day, just to say hi, like she did. We were friends, after all. But I hadn't heard from him since I'd called him on Saturday morning, and I'd just figured it had been because of some rekindled fire in their marriage, newly rediscovered since she'd summoned him home on Friday night.

"This job has been just one screw up after another. The office didn't pay some fee, which shut down occupancy on three units. I had nine different people yelling at me over things that I wasn't even responsible for. Heads are gonna roll here in a few minutes." He nodded at the office next door, grinned, letting me know that none of those heads were gonna be his. "I'm here to ask you out to lunch to make up for not talking to you all week."

Damn him for being so thoughtful. Lunch wasn't for hours. A lesser man would've just come in at eleven-thirty, not thinking ahead of time that I might've had other plans. But Wes was asking me ahead of time, so I wouldn't make other plans. He didn't know that I would've canceled other plans to have lunch with him, even if he had come in at eleven-thirty. Damn him.

I told him that lunch would be great.

We went to *Denny's*, because it was close, not because it held any significance to Wes as the place where we'd first had breakfast together. I told him that I'd found Jason's movie. "It took me a minute to remember where it was," I lied. I'd known exactly where it was, unopened, unwatched yet unforgotten, sitting in a box on top of all those unworn sweaters.

"I haven't had a chance to watch it yet." Another lie. It wasn't that I hadn't had a chance to watch it. What else did I have to do? It wasn't like I had a life. The truth was that I couldn't *bear* to watch it. The footage was from those lost days when Wes and I were together, and I knew that somewhere on there, Jason had no doubt included Wes's marriage proposal. I couldn't bear to watch it. Let him watch it by himself, or with his wife. Let her laugh at me when her husband proposed.

"Can you get out of work this afternoon?" Wes asked. "It's amazing what one meeting can do. The underlings are scurrying so efficiently after a few scowling threats from the bosses, that I feel like taking the rest of the day off. They always laugh at me at the jobsite when I show up in this suit anyway. We'll watch this epic together."

"I'm sorry, Wes," I told him. I didn't want to sit there next to him, to see him be unmoved by our old times together. "I've got an open house with Mom this afternoon. Two houses for sale on the same block. I'm supposed to help with refreshments." I reached into my purse and took out my keys. I slipped my door key off of the ring and held it out to him. "Go on over there and check it out. It's sitting on top of the TV. If it's any good, we'll make some copies and you can tell Gordy he can sell them at the bar." I grinned. "Discuss relieving your groupies of their money."

Wes grinned sheepishly. "They're not groupies, Maddie, for God's sake. They're just little girls."

"Whatever they are, Gordy knows that their money's green." I gestured at him with the key, and he finally took it. "Just drop the key in my mailbox, and you can tell me what you think of your film debut at *The Beachcomber* tonight."

****

When I got home from work that evening, I was surprised to see Jason's movie sitting untouched on top of the television, right where I'd left it after I'd dug it from its hiding place and unwrapped it. I knew Wes had been there, because the key was in the mailbox. Maybe something had come up. Maybe he'd just dropped off the key. Maybe he hadn't come upstairs at all.

My phone rang. "You're still coming to the show tonight, right?" Wes asked me cheerfully. "No car trouble or anything this time?"

There was a trace of that little devious Wes grin in his voice, and I wondered if Mary had told him that my car trouble last Friday had really been no trouble at all getting off with tatted-up Mike. Somehow, I didn't think that Mary had told him, or if she had, there hadn't been any specifics. Maybe she'd just told her husband that her sister had met up with an old boyfriend, if she'd mentioned it at all. Whatever.

"No car trouble. I'll be there soon." I asked him why he hadn't taken Jason's movie with him.

Wes laughed, a trifle nervously, it seemed. "Funny thing about that. I'd just opened the door to your place when Angelo called. Something about a leaky water main. I had to run back out to the job."

"Did you shut it off?"

"What?"

"The water main. Did you shut it off?"

"Oh, yeah." He laughed nervously again. "Water company's going to come out and fix it on Monday." Wes paused for perhaps the span of two heartbeats, then he said, "I was thinking that we could maybe watch Jason's movie after the set tonight . . ."

174

"Is everything okay, Wes?" I asked. He just seemed jumpy for some reason.

"Everything's fine, Maddie," he assured me. "Couldn't be better, as a matter of fact. I'll see you when you get here." He said goodbye and hung up.

I looked around my apartment, wondering why he sounded so strange on the phone. Everything was in order: my laptop was sitting on the coffee table, the remote to the TV and DVD player sitting neatly beside it. Jason's movie was sitting on top of the television, where I'd left it. The kitchen was the same, a coffee cup in the sink from before work that morning. I peeked in the bedroom. The bed was even made. If Mary had even told him about it, I wondered if Wes thought I'd had Mike over here.

Whatever.

I shrugged. If Wes was nervous about coming over to watch Jason's movie with me after his set tonight, then he shouldn't have asked. If he wanted me to keep him company while his own beloved bride was drinking up Las Vegas with the happy bride-to-be, then he shouldn't be nervous about it.

MARY

I've always loved Vegas. The lights, the noise, the non-stop party. Jon, in his uncharacteristic magnanimity, had booked us three rooms at *The Wynn* of all incredibly expensive places. We had many drinks in the bar, and then I received a text from the service that told me it was time to go up to Felicia's room: the entertainment was due to arrive any moment.

I hadn't invited Connie – I didn't think a Vegas native would be amused by male strippers. I didn't know what Connie did for a living, if she was part of the business of Vegas, if she worked in a casino, or a bar, or if she had some other nine-to-five like my sister. Regardless, I figured that maybe her husband wouldn't want her at a bachelorette party, complete with half naked men. Even if she would've liked it, I didn't think I would appreciate her reporting all my drunken behaviors back to her husband, and then her husband reporting them back to mine. What happens in Vegas, and all that. I wouldn't touch a male stripper with a ten foot pole, but still I didn't want to have to watch what I said, watch what I did, watch how drunk I got, because Connie might be apt to tell tales on me. So I hadn't invited her.

I'd invited Maddie, but I was just as glad that she hadn't tagged along, either. Felicia was my road dog; she had my back in all situations, and Debbie, as the crude saying goes, wouldn't say shit if she had a mouth full of it. She was just happy to be in the company of the big girls. So I felt a lot freer, a lot more in the anonymity of the Vegas groove without my sister or Drew's wife, either of whom might carry tales about my drunken partying away from Vegas. I didn't get to cut loose very often, now did I, and Felicia's upcoming nuptials were certainly cause for binge-drinking and ogling the strippers.

Actually, ogling the strippers was a new thing for me. I'd been invited to a few bachelorette parties where they'd been the main attraction, but I'd never attended. What was the point, I'd always thought, of looking at men you couldn't have? No matter how cute they were, seriously, what was the point of ogling men that you probably wouldn't really want to have, anyway? Why tease yourself?

So I watched the strippers for a little while. Jon had hired us a fake cop and a fake construction worker – oh, for crying out loud, how much was that not hardly a turn-on – didn't I have a real construction worker at home? Yawn. After a few minutes, I told Debbie that I was going to get more ice, and I slipped out of Felicia's room and headed on down the hall to my own.

I hadn't invited Connie, and Maddie had turned me down. But I had invited Mike, and he hadn't turned me down. I'd decided to finally have that drink with him, and he'd been more than willing to travel all the way to Vegas to share it with me. My girlfriends would not miss me for a little while, and when they called looking for me, I'd just tell them that I'd had too much to drink and had decided to lie down for a minute. We had a whole nother night of partying to accomplish tomorrow, so they certainly wouldn't mind if I wimped out on the rest of this one.

Besides, why should I tease myself with unreal men, when I had a real one waiting for me just down the hall?

MADELINE

The first thing I noticed when I showed up at *The Beachcomber* was that Wes had found a black leather jacket somewhere. It was the type of thing that I'd not seen him sport since he'd married my sister. Curiously, I asked him where he got it.

"I stopped by my storage place today," he said. "I blew a transistor in my amp, and I had a box of them in there. I found my old jacket." He looked down at his feet. "And my boots." I followed his gaze and saw that he was wearing the same pair of motorcycle boots that he used to wear before Mary made him get rid of his bike. "What do ya think? Do I look more like a rock star now?"

I heard a gasp, and turned to see Darlene standing several feet behind me, staring at Wes.

"She certainly thinks so," I whispered to him.

Wes rolled his eyes. Then he grabbed my hand and pulled me across the room toward *The Beachcomber's* little stage. "No pre-gig autographs," he said. "Her boyfriend looks like he wants to punch me, anyway."

I giggled. "The price of fame."

Darlene's fellow groupies had arrived and they all stood in a little half-circle by the door, giggling and staring at Wes. "What are they, fifteen?" he said.

"They've gotta be at least twenty-one to get in here, Wes," I said, amused. "There's a sign on the door."

"I'm old enough to be their—"

"Their big brother," I said. "Or maybe their uncle. Maybe their mom's baby brother." It tickled the hell out of me to see Wes so discomfited by the attention of his young fans. He must be the only singer in the history of rock 'n roll to be uncomfortable about the adoration of young girls.

"Either way, I'm too old for them."

I glanced at Darlene and her friends again. "Well, they definitely approve of the wardrobe change."

"What do you think?" He smiled that old smug Wes smile at me. Whatever his position on the appreciation of young women, Wes was always down for a little admiration from a woman he considered of his peer group. He was not unaware of his effect on us. *On me.* "What do you think of the new old me, Maddie?"

"You look great, Wes," I told him sincerely. *Good enough to eat*, the immature part of my mind said. It had been that part that had felt the same way about Mike the week before. It had been that part of my mind feeding me all those lustful, slutty thoughts when I'd arrived late last week to see my favorite band, and most especially its singer.

"When I saw this stuff in storage, I thought of you." Angelo started tuning up, and Wes turned around and hopped up on the stage. There was a smattering of cheers from the girls in the back. Wes leaned over and said, "You might say that you're my inspiration tonight." He winked at me, and then picked up his guitar and counted off. Randy started to drum, and Rolling Blackout began their set. The little girls ran up in front of the stage and pushed me out of the way, just like I knew they would.

I was dumbstruck at Wes's wink, at his tiny little flirt. I stood there open-mouthed for fully half of their first song, until Betty, *The Beachcomber's* only waitress, came up and handed me a tall drink, a drink that I hadn't ordered. "It's from the singer," she told me. "Gordy says he was instructed to keep 'em coming. Wes wants you to have a good time tonight."

Betty threaded her way through the crowd, and I turned and looked at Gordy, behind the bar. He smiled, shrugged at me. I looked back at Wes, and he winked at me again.

Just what was going on here? Wes was winking at me, buying me drinks, telling Gordy that he wanted me to have a good time? I figured that it was just gratitude for my continuing support of his musical career, just thanks for my scaring up Jason's movie so Gordy could sell it in the bar, maybe make them a few bucks. If it was any good.

Whatever. Wes could show me all the gratitude he liked, buy me all the drinks he wanted, get me falling-down drunk, if it pleased him. He was supposed to be coming over to watch this epic with me after his set tonight – he could drive. I'd go right on ahead and get drunk, admire the new-old him, that him that I'd once liked so much. How bizarre all this was, all of a sudden – I was his *inspiration tonight*. Whatever that meant. *Keep smiling at me, Wes*, I thought. *I'll be your inspiration. I'll be whatever you want me to be.*

And the evening just wore better and better. Betty kept feeding me rum and ginger ales, and Wes never took his eyes off of me for the entire set. He sang to me, just like he used to in the old days, and I quickly got drunk enough to almost pretend it *was* the old days.

The immature part of my mind, surprisingly impervious to alcohol, kept saying, *His wife isn't going to summon him home tonight. She's in Las Vegas.* Perhaps that was why Wes was being so flirty, singing to me, showing me how much he appreciated my support. Maybe he felt a little freer to do so, since his wife was out of town. *Maybe we should be feeling our own kind of gratitude for all that,* my mind said.

When their set was over, Wes quickly, dutifully signed autographs, then extricated himself from his small circle of fans and escaped to the bar, where I was waiting for him. Gordy had two shots of rum and a ginger ale chaser all set up. Wes downed his drinks, and then wrapped me in his arms and gave me a big hug, before I even knew it was happening, before I had the chance to put up my defenses. I melted against him, adrift in his smell, the lost familiarity of his embrace.

Oh, God, I love you, Wes! I thought helplessly, and I just stood there, holding him, letting him hold me. But after a moment, I came back to myself, felt a little self-conscious at my weakness. I looked up at him and said, "What's gotten into you?"

"I told you," he whispered. "I'm inspired. You wanna get out of here?" I blinked stupidly at him. "Come on, Maddie. Let's blow this pop stand."

Wes took my hand and I decided that I had to be dreaming. Wes never said, *let's blow this pop stand* anymore. Wes never wore the kind of clothes I liked anymore. He never winked at me, never sang to me, never hugged me. He never took me by the hand and practically dragged me out of *The Beachcomber.*

And once outside in the chill, damp November air, once outside in the deserted parking lot, Wes never, ever took my face in his rough hands and said, "Kiss me, Maddie!" And he never, ever kissed me, no matter how many times I'd wanted him to, no matter how many stories I'd written about it, no matter how many times I'd dreamt of it.

So I decided that's just what this had to be. A dream. And since it was a dream, I didn't have to think about what it all meant, didn't have to wonder why he'd chosen tonight to do exactly what I had, in other dreams, always hoped he'd do. I didn't have to remember that he was married to my sister. I didn't have to think at all. So I just stood up on my toes and molded myself against him and kissed him back.

At last he broke the incredible dream-kiss and grinned. "That's the Maddie I remember," he said. He grabbed my hand again and we ran to his truck, like teenagers. He opened the door for me, then walked around the front of the truck and climbed in the driver's side. He said, "Come sit over here by me."

"Wes . . . the seatbelt . . . the cops . . ." This dream was so real that I was worrying about getting a ticket for not wearing a seatbelt.

Wes started the truck. "Maybe you better stay over there. Or else we might never get out of this parking lot." He put his own seatbelt on and put the truck in gear. Wes was being playful, like he used to be when he was mine, and I just had time to think again that this was the most realistic, most wonderful dream ever, and we were pulling up to the curb in front of my apartment building.

I climbed slowly out of the truck, thinking that I didn't want to make any jarring dream motions, anything that might wake me from the wonder of all this. But Wes was in a hurry, and he grabbed my hand again and practically dragged me up the steps to my apartment.

I fumbled for the key, couldn't find the right one for a second, and I thought that this was going to be one of *those* dreams, wherein you were stymied from achieving the thing you wanted most by some stupid thing like not having the right key or being faced with a long hallway lined with locked doors.

But then the right key slid into the lock, and we were in my dark apartment, and the hallway wasn't long at all, and my bedroom door wasn't locked, and we were tearing off each other's clothes. And when we fell onto the bed and I felt Wes's naked skin against mine, I cried out, just like Rosemary, *"This is no dream! This is really happening!"*

Wes paused, smiled. "No dream, darlin'."

Wes was really there with me again, at last, after all the months and months that I had wished so entirely for it to be so. At last it wasn't a dream, and it wasn't two characters that I'd made up in my mind. It was him, and it was me, and it was glorious. His smell, his touch, his mouth, his body. There was no other thought in my mind but him, and how much I'd missed him, how much I wanted this to never end.

But end such things must. At last he collapsed, buried his face in my shoulder. I clung to him for another moment, but when I felt an entirely non-apropos tear well up in my eye – how could I feel like crying when Wes was finally here with me? I asked, "Why, Wes?"

He tenderly gazed into my eyes, brushed a stray hair from my forehead. "I could ask you the same thing, Maddie. Why?"

The tear that had threatened rolled down and settled wetly in my ear. I don't think that he noticed it. "What are you talking about?"

"After lunch today, I came up here to get that movie. I remembered that I wanted to check the point spread for the game on Sunday; I bet Angelo fifty bucks, because he said he'd give me the points. My phone was almost dead, and I saw your laptop sitting on the coffee table. When I went to get on the internet to check the points, I saw my name on a little file folder on your desktop." He grinned. "Whatever could be in a file with my name on it on your computer, I wondered? So I clicked it."

I covered my face with the sheet.

181

Wes gently pulled the sheet away. "So I'm asking you why, Maddie. Why did you never tell me that you still had feelings for me? Why did you never tell me that you still thought about me, that you still thought about . . . this? Why did you never give me the chance to tell you that I feel the same way?"

"Oh my, God, Wes, you have got to be kidding me!" I said, gobsmacked, ignoring the implication of his words, *that he felt the same way*. "You leave me like a whore, then the next thing I know, you're shacked up with my sister! The next blink after that, the two of you are married! If you still loved me, why didn't you come looking for me? Why didn't you tell me?"

"Your sister told me that you'd moved on, that you were getting married to someone else. What was I supposed to do, object at the wedding, like something out of a romantic comedy? That kind of shit never happens in real life, Maddie. Your husband would've had me arrested."

"There never was a wedding, was there? Why didn't you just call me, when you first came back to town? When Mary first told you I was gone?"

"She said that you were happy with that other guy, Maddie, that you had a little family." I noticed that he didn't speak Mary's name. He just kept saying *your sister* or *she*. "She told me that you'd forgotten all about me. She told me that she was sure that you'd forgiven me, and maybe I thought that was all I deserved, Maddie. Maybe I thought that was all I was going to get. You'd forgiven me, but I thought that I didn't deserve to have you back."

"Who sounds like a romantic comedy now, Wes, for God's sake?" I wanted to be angry with him, was doing a pretty good job of it. "All you would've had to do was call me. Why didn't you just call?"

"I accepted my fate, I guess. Your sister said you were gone, and I didn't think I deserved any better. I fucked up, and now I was being punished for it. You'd moved on – what good could it possibly do to beg you? You had a new man in your life, and . . . your sister was there, so I just—"

"My sister has a name, Wes!" And the tears started to fall then. He cradled me in his arms and soothed me while I sobbed, mourning all the time we'd lost together. Mourning the loss of my sister, which was surely to come.

"We're just going to have to tell her, Maddie," he said at last. "It was all just a big mistake. I can't . . . I want . . ."

Why were blue-eyed men always stammering at me? "You can't what, Wes? You want *what?* This is all too sudden. You can't just dump

my sister because you suddenly decide you have a warm for me again."
I discovered that I couldn't say her name, either.

Wes sat up, swung his long legs over the side of the bed. He
buried his face in his hands. "I was *so angry*. Those pictures. Those two
guys. It was all so . . . *disgusting*. I never really believed that you would . .
. but how does such a thing happen? I had to get away, had to *think*.

"And then when I came back, and she said you were gone . . . I
thought then that maybe you'd *never* loved me. If you'd really loved me,
then you would've waited for me . . ."

"Are you out of your fucking, mind, Wes?" I shoved him with my
foot. "You left me! Over some ridiculous thing! I don't know how it
happened! I must've been drugged! I've never to this day seen that
asshole with that tattoo on his hand! You left me, and I was supposed
to wait for you?"

"And then when I saw you again," he went on. "The *very first* time
I saw you again, I said I was sorry, and you just shrugged, said some
things don't work out."

I shoved him again. "You looked at me like you didn't know me,
the first time I saw you again, Wes." *You son of a bitch!* "You said you
were sorry, but that's all you said. Why didn't you tell me that it was all
a mistake, that you still loved me, then?"

He looked over his shoulder at me. "I thought I could tell by the
look on your face, Maddie. I thought, if there was still something there,
I'd be able to see it. But you've never given me anything but a blank
look since I've seen you again." He smiled at me. "Except for last
Friday. I thought there was a little twinkle in your eyes then."

You have no idea, I thought.

Quick as a cat, Wes rolled back into bed, back on top of me. "But
I know how you feel now, Maddie. Everything else is water under the
bridge. I've made mistakes – opened my fat mouth when I should've
kept it shut. I kept quiet when I should've said something, should've
told you how I felt, should've begged for your forgiveness to your face.

"But you've made mistakes, too – smiling politely at me,
pretending that you didn't love me anymore. But I know better now. I
read what you wrote, and now I want to hear you say it."

I didn't hesitate. "I love you, Wes. I'll always love you."

"And I love you, Maddie. I've always loved you."

He kissed me then, and nothing more needed to be said.

****

We stayed in my apartment for the entire weekend, like hermits, like we were the only two people in the world. We laughed and joked and made love. He sat on my couch, consulted my laptop, and made gentle fun of my dirty stories about him, asking me if I thought he'd look better as a redhead, asking me if he should get the sun tattooed around his navel.

"That's all artistic license," I told him. "I think you're perfect just the way you are."

"Obviously," he said smugly, and I threw a couch pillow at him. "Although I never knew you thought so highly of my—"

"Shut up!" I said, mortified. "You were never supposed to read any of that. No one was!"

He smiled tenderly at me. "Aren't you glad I did?"

I took the computer from him, put it back on the coffee table and curled up in his lap. "I've never been gladder about anything in my life."

He grinned gleefully. "I've got an idea that'll make you glad. What was it we did in that cowboy one? What did you call it? *Back in the Saddle Again?"* I punched him playfully in the arm. The horrible, pornographic things didn't have titles. "Come on, Maddie. Let's pretend we're in the barn at the old McMurphy place!" He tossed me out of his lap, then stood up and scooped me off the couch. "You got a Stetson I can wear?"

****

But all good things must come to an end – even the best fantasies must draw to a close eventually. Wes was in the shower on Sunday afternoon – the first shower he'd taken alone all weekend – when his phone rang. I peered at it, sitting there on the coffee table. Looking at the picture that popped up was like looking in a mirror.

I wondered if we still looked identical, or if, like the picture of Dorian Gray after his first sin – would there be a difference that showed on my face? I'd betrayed my sister, my twin, my other half – would there now be a shadow on my features, a little cruel twist to my lip, perhaps? Would Mary look at me and no longer see herself? Would she know I had stabbed her in the back?

Wes came out into the living room, wrapped only in a towel, like he lived there. Like he wasn't my sister's husband. "Mary called," I told him, enunciating her name carefully. It was the first time those two syllables had been spoken all weekend.

He looked at me, not guilty, not ashamed. "I'm gonna tell her, Maddie. I'm gonna go home – oh, my God, that horrible red and green apartment was never my home! I'm gonna tell her that it's over. I want a divorce. I'm gonna tell her . . ."

I stood up and put my arms around his neck, laid my head on his chest. "You're gonna tell her what, Wes? That you're going to divorce her because you spent one weekend with her sister?"

I felt guilty, even if he didn't. I pictured Mary, experiencing all the things my mother had gone through after she'd found out about Dad. I pictured her hating Wes, hating me, just like Mom hated Dad.

Wes wanted to change sisters again. His decision was going to tear the sisters apart. I wanted him back, but I didn't want Mary to hate me. If Wes was going to do this thing, he had to be sure. There would be no switching back a second time.

"I love you, Maddie," he said.

Leave all that, I thought. "I think you should give it 'til the end of the year. So you're sure. The holidays are coming, and–"

"No," Wes said firmly. "I'm not going to fake my way through the holidays."

I was relieved at that, actually. I didn't want to be casting furtive glances at him over Joanna's turkey, didn't want to hear what Mary was going to get him for Christmas, didn't want to pretend to give him a sisterly kiss on New Year's Eve. But I couldn't allow him to end my sister's marriage just like that. Not after just one weekend together. I couldn't be the agent of that.

"I want you to go home, Wes. I want you to give it two weeks. I want you to go home and look at your wife and think of all the things that made you want to marry her."

Wes shook his head. "When I look at my wife, all I see if you, Maddie. I only married her because you were gone . . . and she looked just like you."

"That's cruel, Wes," I told him. "There had to be more to it than that." *You weren't thinking of me when you trotted home to her like an eager pony last weekend, now were you?* I thought.

There's a lot of dog in a man, Maddie, my mother's voice said in my head.

"She's gonna know," Wes said.

"She's not gonna know. I didn't even know. I thought I was dreaming." I smiled at him. "I want you to give it two weeks. Go home and look at the woman you married, really look at her – and after two weeks, if you still love me . . . we'll think of some way to tell her."

185

"I know you feel bad, Maddie, but . . ." The resolute look on my face stopped him. "Okay. Two weeks. But I can tell you now, that my feelings aren't gonna change. I'm sorry, and I feel bad, too. It was all my mistake, all my dumb fault. But I love you. Not someone that just looks like you."

I told him that I loved him, too, but it had to be this way. "It's only fair," I said.

MARY

I thought that Wes was acting a little odd when he walked in the door on Sunday night. He gave me this big long explanation about how there had been a water main break at the jobsite, how he and Angelo had to find a big wrench or something and shut the pipe down, because the water was breaking up the pavement and threatening two unfinished units, and it didn't look like the water company was going to get out there and do their job before the houses were flooded. Which was all well and good, except that I hadn't even asked him where he'd been.

We went out to dinner because neither of us felt like cooking. He asked me about Vegas, and I told him that the three of us had gotten smashed in the hotel bar the first night. I told him that we had to convince Debbie that she was not indeed in love with the fake-cop stripper that Jon had hired, and that it wouldn't be a good idea for her to even tell him that she loved him. I told Wes that we slept it off 'til noon the next day, partied a little bit lighter on Saturday night, checked out at check-out time, then had a nice, pleasant drive home.

Wes told me that he and the band played *The Beachcomber* on Friday night like they always did. He, too had slept in on Saturday, kicked around the apartment, watched three movies. Then he hit the sack early, and had just finished another movie when Angelo called him out to the jobsite to stop the flood. "All in all, a pretty nothing weekend," he said. I had to agree with him, which was why it seemed strange that he felt compelled to recite every detail of it to me. Whatever.

We went home and went to bed. I certainly wasn't in the mood, and I was relieved that he wasn't either. He drifted off, but I couldn't sleep. I stared at the ceiling for a long time, thinking about the things I'd done in Vegas. I felt bad about them on an intellectual level – on another occasion in Vegas, I'd sworn before a witness that I'd never do such things again with anyone else but this man sleeping beside me. But I didn't love him, and maybe I shouldn't have married him. But he asked me, and he was mine, so I went ahead and made the promise. Now I had broken that promise.

But on a physical level, I felt awesome. Ah, Mike . . . what a man was Mike, good for exactly what men were supposed to be good for. Even though he really wasn't my type when he was dressed – he dressed like he was eighteen – Mike knew exactly how to turn the key, when and where to push on the gas to get my motor running. It wasn't like I loved Mike, any more than I loved Wes. He wasn't going to suggest that I run away with him, break up my marriage, cause me to become another disgrace in my mother's eyes – my father's daughter. It was just a meaningless little diversion – no one would ever know about it. What happens in Vegas, stays in Vegas.

And if Mike came back into my bar and asked me again, and I discovered that I was willing again . . . well, I'm a bartender, and discretion is a bartender's middle name. Wes would never know that any drunkenly pledged promises had ever been broken. No one would ever know. It was all just harmless fun.

MADELINE

Wes's two weeks didn't even last one week. His promise to consider his marriage to my sister didn't even last a day, I would later find out.

On Friday afternoon, he called and told me that the regular Friday night gig at *The Beachcomber* had been canceled, and if it was all right with me, he'd be over to my apartment about six that night. I hadn't talked to him all week – that had been part of his thinking about his marriage – and I discovered that I missed him very much. "I'll see you then," I said.

I opened the door and he came in, took off his coat, shook the rain out of his hair – it had been raining non-stop all week – and he sat down on the couch. He looked at me like a kid that had been caught with his hand in the cookie jar, and told me what a tangled web he'd woven. On Monday, he'd called Gordy and cancelled their gig. Something about Angelo having to be out of town. He called Angelo and told him that their gig was cancelled – something about Gordy painting the bar. *A recycled lie.* He told Mary that he was going to another construction conference in LA for the weekend, and here he was.

"Look, Maddie. I might've planned it all out ahead of time, but I still did what you asked. I lived with her all week, looked at her, thought about her. We didn't . . . I couldn't . . . but I still did what you asked. Your sister's a bitch, Maddie. A pushy, controlling bitch. I looked at her, just like you asked, and I came to the realization that I never loved her, and I know she never loved me. She was never anything but a substitute for you. It's over. I'm gonna tell her. I want a divorce."

I pushed the rain-slicked hair out of his eyes. "When are you gonna tell her?"

"I'm supposed to be home from this mythical conference on Sunday night. I'll tell her then. I want one more weekend alone with you before the shit hits the fan."

I smiled ruefully. If that was how it was going to be, then that was how it was going to be. Wes didn't love my sister, and I could never imagine how she ever could've loved him. Once upon a time, she hadn't even *liked him*. Even my mother had noticed that.

Maybe it wouldn't be so bad after all. Some things just didn't work out. Now she'd have a chance to find someone else, someone she did love. Now maybe she could find *the one*, and I could have my one back.

****

We made love, made dinner together. It was so odd having him there, just like he was mine, just like I'd always imagined it would be. Sweet, domestic happiness. He helped me load the dishes, then we went out into the living room, sat on the couch, turned on the TV. Just like folks.

It was so strange, and I thought if he suggested watching something on Netflix, I just might scream. But I got a hold of myself. If he wanted to watch something on Netflix, it would be from my queue. Not his. Not *theirs*. There was not one single horror movie on my Netflix queue.

Wes didn't say anything about Netflix. He flipped through the channels for a minute, then asked, "Do you wanna watch Jason's movie?"

Jason's movie. That had been Wes's excuse for coming over here last weekend – he'd wanted to watch Jason's movie. But instead, he ravished me, and I let him, enjoying every single second of it. It had seemed so impossible, so incredible, that I thought I was dreaming it. Then he'd confessed his undying devotion to me, a confession precipitated by his discovery of my undying devotion to him, typed up neatly and filed away in all its pornographic glory on my computer. We had betrayed my sister, committed adultery, began a torrid affair. But somehow, we'd never gotten around to watching Jason's movie.

I got up from the couch and tossed the still-never-opened DVD box to him. "I'll go make popcorn."

A few moments later, Wes called to me from the living room. I looked out at him from the kitchen doorway. "There are two disks in here. One says *Raw Footage.*" He grinned. "I like the sound of that. I'm gonna put that one in first."

"I'm gonna make popcorn," I repeated, and ducked back into the kitchen.

I was just dumping the contents of the hot bag into a bowl when I looked up to see Wes standing in the doorway to the kitchen, glowering, his blue eyes ablaze. He still had the remote control to the DVD player clutched in his hand, and he was obviously furious.

"What's wrong?"

190

"Look, Maddie, I made a mistake one time. I ran off like an idiot. I'm not going to make another mistake until I hear the whole explanation for this."

"What are you talking about?"

He crooked his finger at me. "There's something you need to see. Something you need to explain." We went back out into the living room and he rather authoritatively indicated for me to sit. I sat and he sat next to me, then pointed the remote at the TV. "Tell me who your boyfriend is."

The point of view was from above the little stage at *Mickey's*. I remembered Jason climbing up on a ladder and attaching the camera to a length of exposed pipe – it was remote controlled, he told me. It would run by itself, taping crowd footage, like a security camera. The date stamp said *November 30, 7:20 pm. Mickey's* was packed: all the little tables in front of the stage were full. The film quality was so-so, but the audio was good: I could hear Rolling Blackout tuning up, directly beneath the camera's position.

We watched the people for a minute, just anonymous faces, no one I recognized. Then Wes yelled, "There!" so loudly and angrily that it made me jump. *"Right there!"* He hit the pause button, and then zoomed in on a couple sitting toward the back of the crowd. The man was making some gesture, and Wes zoomed in on the back of his hand. Clearly visible was a smiley face tattoo.

"So he did come into the bar!" I said in amazement.

"Oh, for Christ's sake, Maddie!" Wes yelled. "You're sitting with him!" He backed the zoom out a little bit, and sure enough, it appeared to be me sitting across from that evil man.

"It's not me, Wes," I said immediately.

"Oh, for Christ's sake, Maddie!" Wes repeated. "You want me to not believe my own eyes? You know him!"

"Oh, for Christ's sake, Wes," I mimicked him. "I have a twin sister." I took the remote from him, backed the zoom out a little bit more, then rewound the video until the man was sitting at the table by himself. Then I pushed play, so that we could observe their interaction.

We watched the man with the smiley face tattoo look around the bar for a minute. He wasn't a bad looking guy, a little chubby, with sandy-blonde hair. He looked up and smiled as someone that Wes thought was me approached with two drinks in her hand. She set them down on the table, then sat down across from him.

"Now watch carefully," I told Wes. The woman smiled, said a few words, then picked up her drink. I hit the pause button and looked at him. "What do you see?"

"I dunno, Maddie." Wes was still incensed. "I see you talking to the guy who took your picture with his dick next to your mouth. What do *you* see?"

I ignored his vulgarity. "I see a right-handed woman that looks just like me. I see Mary."

Wes blinked, and his righteous anger faltered a little bit. "Well . . . that doesn't prove . . ."

"That doesn't prove what?" I waved the remote under his nose. "I'm left-handed, Wes!" I was getting a little angry myself. He was just being dumb now. "The woman on the screen is right-handed! It's Mary!"

I hit play again, and we watched the woman on the screen laugh and talk with the man with the smiley face tattoo. She picked up her drink with her right hand. She reached across the table and touched his arm with her right hand. "It's Mary, Wes," I whispered. "She knows him."

Wes took the remote from me and hit the fast forward button. The couple's laughing conversation speeded up; after a moment, the woman arose. She touched her companion's shoulder, again with her right hand, then fast walked out of frame. The man downed the rest of his drink, then got up and quickly strode out of the bar. Wes stopped the video.

"I'm sorry, Maddie," he said, all hangdog. "I'm a hothead, and when I saw that guy . . ."

"That's what Drew said about you." I smiled. I couldn't be mad at him. He wasn't just a hothead, he was an idiot, sometimes. But I loved him, and I couldn't be mad at him.

"Drew says hi, by the way," he said. "I told him about . . . us, and—"

"Oh my God, Wes, if you told him about my stories, I will kill you."

He blinked those baby blues innocently at me. "Oh, no, of course not." Then he grinned. "Maybe just the alien one. And maybe the Serengeti one."

"I can never look him in the eye again," I said, but I also grinned. If anybody would understand, it would be Drew.

Wes looked at the television, now showing a freeze-frame of an empty table at *Mickey's*. The implications settled around us like darkness. "Maybe—"

"Maybe she just forgot," I offered. "I'm sure Mary has – had – use to have – drinks with a lot of customers." I thought of Mike. "Maybe she just forgot. Maybe she never noticed the tattoo."

Wes looked doubtfully at me. That stupid tattoo was something you noticed.

He pushed play, fast-forwarded through the rest of the clip. We saw Mary deliver a couple drinks to a couple tables, always setting them down, always collecting the money with her right hand. We saw Felicia come in, obviously late for work, and then it was only Felicia delivering drinks to the patrons at the tables. Felicia was also right-handed, I noticed, just like my sister, just like Wes, just like Jon. Just like about ninety percent of the population.

I'd never felt myself to be special – after all, there was another person in the world that looked just like me – and being left-handed had sometimes been a burden. But right now, I was grateful for it. Wes knew me, and he knew my sister, and while sometimes *that* might be a little hard to take, I was thankful for that at the moment, too. Wes and I had bumped elbows at dinner enough times if he sat on my left. He knew my oddly-leaning handwriting, noticed that I make my check-marks backwards, had marveled at the weird way I tied my shoes. He had noticed nothing different about Mary in these things, because she was right-handed, just like he was.

The next clip was from the opposite angle. It showcased the stage. There was Wes, and it warmed my heart to see Phil back there behind the drums. I missed Phil. Rolling Blackout hadn't started to play yet. Angelo came up with a piece of paper in his hand, handed it to Wes. There was another piece of paper taped to the amp in front of him, and Wes tore it off, and replaced it with the one that Angelo had given him. It was a revised set-list.

Wes balled the old one up, then looked around, saw a woman standing in front of the stage that looked like me. He smiled, and even though I couldn't hear him on the video, I could tell he said, "Catch." The woman that looked like me caught the ball of paper in her left hand.

I looked at him.

"I know," he said, still hangdog. "That's you. I can see the difference now."

Wes fast-forwarded through the next four or five clips, footage of the band on stage. We weren't going to see Mary in any of those – she was behind the bar.

We discovered that Jason had shot a lot of video, and on this disk, it was indeed *raw footage*. Hours and hours and hours of raw footage. People sitting at tables, standing in front of the stage, lined up outside the bar. Wes fast forwarded through it all, and we watched the television in silence, looking for the blonde guy with the smiley face tattoo.

We didn't see him again until we got to the footage shot across from, a little to the right of, and a little above the bar. It was another remote controlled, surveillance-type camera, but unlike the first clips of the crowd, the video quality was flawless.

Jason's camera damned Mary. Utterly. The first time the blonde man came in, it was daytime. He came on-camera from the right, so I knew the bar wasn't even open yet. Patrons came in from the left – that was where the doors were. Vendors and Budweiser reps and employees and Mary's friends with bad tattoos came in through the back way, *from the right*, when the bar wasn't open. That was the way Wes or I came in if we wanted to see her before hours.

Mary's back was turned when he approached. He said something to her and she turned. She smiled broadly at him, leaned across the bar. He leaned forward also, and she put her arms lightly around his neck and kissed him on the cheek. He grasped her by the shoulders and his tattoo was clearly visible. She made him a drink, and stood there chatting with him, smiling and laughing.

Wes went to hit the fast forward button, and I said, "Wait. I want to see something. Just let 'em talk." We couldn't hear what they were saying – the camera was too far away, and the only audio was the scratchy, echoey sound of an empty bar. Occasionally a muffled car horn from the street could be discerned.

Mary and the tattooed blondie's conversation continued. Wes said, "What do you want to see?"

"Just hold on," I told him, my eyes glued to the TV. "Go get the popcorn."

Wes handed me the remote and went out to the kitchen. Mary was still talking to the man when he came back with the cold bowl. Wes set it down on the coffee table, untouched, and we watched as my sister frequently leaned over the bar to closely speak to this guy, patted his arm. He even took her hand for a minute. Yeah, she knew him, all right.

"What are you looking for?" Wes asked again.

Mary made the man another drink, and he sipped it. He was also right-handed, and that horrible tattoo flashed every time he raised the glass to his mouth. They talked some more.

"Maddie?"

"Hold on!" I insisted.

Finally the man finished his drink and stood up. He leaned over the bar and this time he kissed Mary lightly on the mouth. Then he walked off-camera, to the right again.

I stopped the disk and looked at Wes. He shook his head. "What?"

"*He didn't pay,*" I said.

"So?"

"I'm her twin sister. You're her *husband,* for God's sake. Did you ever not pay for a single drink you got in *Mickey's?*" I answered my own question. "No, you didn't. Not when they were closed, not when they were open. I've been going into Mary's bar since I was eighteen, Wes, and not once have I caged a free drink. Jon frowns on that kind of thing." I pointed at the screen. "That right there? Giving away the product? That would get her fired, manager or not, if Jon saw it." I handed the remote back to him. "This guy is her buddy. Her good buddy."

Wes fast forwarded through probably two weeks of footage shot from the camera above the bar. We saw ourselves, talking to Mary. We saw days when Mary wasn't working, when Darrin, the other bartender, was on duty. The guy with the smiley face tattoo came in three more times. Twice more when the bar was open, crowded. Mary always paused to greet him warmly, set him up with a couple of free drinks.

The last time he came in, it was daytime again. He came in from the right; again, *Mickey's* wasn't open for business yet. Mary again greeted her friend with a hug and a light kiss on the cheek. I couldn't gauge just how friendly she really was with him – she might be giving him free drinks, which was a definite no-no, but I knew that Mary was at least professional enough not to be making out with some guy across the bar. They again talked for a while and then the guy reached into his back-pocket with his tattooed right hand. He extracted a Baggie and laid it on the bar. Mary held it up to the light and peered at it.

Wes hit pause and zoomed in on the bag. It contained three olive green tablets, one with 542 stamped on it.

"What is that?" I said, and reached for my laptop, sitting on the coffee table, so I could Google it. Wes stopped me.

"It's Roofies," he said.

I looked at him in stunned amazement. "How do you know what Roofies looks like?"

He sighed. "It's a long story."

"I most certainly want to hear it."

Wes sighed again. "You met Drew's sister, right? Melody?"

"I went to her wedding. With Drew."

"I heard." Wes smiled. "Anyway, a few years ago, Melody is out at this bar. She's waiting for her girlfriends, but they never showed up. She starts talking to some guy. He buys her a couple of drinks. Suddenly, she starts to feel light-headed. It scares her, and when the guy gets up to use the john, Melody calls Drew. Luckily, he and I were just down the street."

"At a different bar."

Wes grinned, shrugged. "We walk in the place. Melody is sitting at a table with this guy. She's propping her head up with both hands; she can barely keep her eyes open. The guy sees us and bolts out the back door, but we chase him, tackle him in the alley.

"Drew wanted to beat the shit out of him. He kept yelling, 'What did you give to my sister?' But the guy just stood there, cornered between us, up against the wall, looking for an opportunity to run. Drew told him to go ahead and try it, and we'd make a citizen's arrest by curb stomping him right there in the alley." Wes grinned.

"I called the cops. They showed up and handcuffed the guy. The cop took a baggie full of pills off of him, showed them to us. He told us they were Roofies."

"Did Melody press charges?"

Wes shrugged. "I dunno. I never heard anything more about it." He gestured at the TV with the remote. "But that's what's in the little baggie there."

"Look at the date, Wes." The time stamp in the corner of the screen read *December 30, 9:46 am.*

Wes pushed the play button. The blonde looked around nervously, indicated for Mary to stop holding the contraband up the light. She grinned at him and stuck in into her pocket. She asked him something. With an imaginary razor blade, he chopped up an imaginary pill on his bar napkin, then picked it up and pretended to pour it into his glass. He set the napkin back down on the bar, threw his fingers up in a little voila! gesture, then put both hands on one side of his head and mimicked sleep. Mary laughed.

Wes hit the power button and the television went black. I looked at him in surprise.

"I've seen enough," he said, and stood up.

"Where are you going?"

"I'm going home. I'm gonna pack my shit, and then I'll be back. It's not like I've got any furniture there. Everything that belongs to me there'll fit in a couple of suitcases."

"It's dark, Wes. It's raining." I put my hand on his arm. "Stay with me until Sunday, like you planned. One more nice weekend before the shit hits the fan."

"She set you up, Maddie! I want to be done with her. Tonight!"

"There's no sense running off in the dark, in the rain." I looked up at him. "You need to calm down–"

"Calm down? Jesus Christ, Maddie, *she did this to you!*"

"I'm sure she just meant it as I joke. I'm sure she didn't think that you'd–"

"A joke?" Wes roared. "She drugged you, put you in a room with two guys, let them wag their dicks in your face! *She took pictures of it!*"

I stood up and put my arms around him. My own anger bubbled to the surface. "And she sent them to all my friends. She sent them to *you."* He tried to move to the door, but I hugged him tighter. "We'll tell her, Wes. We'll tell her that we know what a despicable, disgusting thing she did. To her own sister. But not now. I have to get my head around all this. I want to be calm. I want to ask her why. I don't want you running up there, furious–"

"You're right." Wes sat down on the couch abruptly, his anger draining away. "If I go up there now, I might hit her. I never thought I'd ever want to hit a woman, but if I go up there now, I might just smack her." An expression of hurt wonder crossed his face, and he took both my hands. "Why would she do this to you, Maddie? *Why?"*

Why would she do this to us? I thought. "I don't know, Wes. But we'll go up there and find out on Sunday."

"We don't have one single thing to feel guilty about, anymore," he said. "Not after this."

MARY

On Friday night after my shift, I came home, took a nice hot bubble bath. I stretched out on my big bed. Wes was at another builder's conference in LA, and I didn't miss him, because I loved having the California King all to myself.

I thought about Mike. Sexy, tatted-up, absolutely-worthless-except-for-the-one-thing-he-wasn't-worthless-for Mike. He hadn't come into the bar all week, but he'd sent a few texts. It was all just as well – it wasn't like I wanted him in there all the time. People might notice his attention to me. He might run into Wes sometime, or even Maddie again. I wasn't worried about Wes – they didn't know each other – Wes wouldn't even notice him, probably. But Maddie might.

If she saw him, Maddie might want to avail herself of his definite charms again, and Mike might be down. That would be okay, I guess; it wasn't like he was mine. I was married to what was mine, unsatisfying as he usually was. If Maddie decided that she had a yen for Mike again, he would fade back into the mists as far as talking to me was concerned. He wouldn't dare to play us both at the same time, even though he had not a clue that we had once both played him at the same time.

So it was not like I missed him. I didn't want to get tangled up in some kind of obvious affair. That would be an embarrassment; my mother would flip out. As long as Mike kept in touch, that was good enough. If I wanted to . . . *see* him again, I'm sure he would come if I called, and then I could maintain my discretion.

And I didn't miss Wes, either. He'd been weird and silent all week – every time I had occasion to look over at him, it seemed like he was staring at me. It was odd.

And I liked having the big bed all to myself. So Friday night was just one big alone self-fest. It wasn't like I got too many of them.

****

I had the four to midnight shift on Saturday. The place was dead: it was chilly and rained intermittently, like it had been doing all week, so Felicia had time to show me an adorable little purse that Tony had bought for her. It was shaped like a little jewelry box, and she said they came in a bunch of different colors. I just had to have one, so I asked her where she'd got it.

"A store called *Mythology*, at the Westside Pavilion."

I felt a little small town right then, because I wasn't sure exactly where the Westside Pavilion was located. But Felicia wasn't smug, just because she had a thoughtful fiancé that bought her pretty things whilst they visited someplace that wasn't here. "It's in LA," she said.

I reflected that maybe if my husband and I were all in love like Felicia and Tony, he might buy me presents, too. But even though the honeymoon was over – there had never been a honeymoon, ever – there was no reason why he couldn't stop by the Westside Pavilion and pick up one of the darling little purses for me, seeing as how he was in LA anyway.

Wes had never been what one would call thoughtful, nor overly demonstrative, and he'd been even more distant than usual all week. Maybe he was preoccupied about his job; maybe the rain was making things too wet at *Wandering Springs*. Whatever. But if I asked him, I was sure that he'd stop at the Westside Pavilion and buy me a purse, perhaps on his lunch break tomorrow, or after the conference concluded. All I'd have to do was send him a picture of Felicia's, and he could go over to this *Mythology* place, and take a few pictures of the ones they had left, so I could pick out the one I wanted. My husband might not be overly attentive, but he was adept at running errands.

I took a picture of Felicia's little bag, then texted Wes: *How far are you from the Westside Pavilion?*

I was returned a text immediately, so I knew he had his AutoResponder app running: *No cellphones allowed in conference. Will get back 2 u ASAP.* I shrugged, confident that he would indeed get back to me as soon as possible, and then I could instruct him as to what I wanted him to do.

Trade picked up a little bit – some people just want to drink on a Saturday night, the weather be damned. So I didn't think about the errand I had for Wes again until about nine o'clock, when there was a lull. I called, and when he didn't pick up, I sent the same text again: *How far are you from the Westside Pavilion?* Again I got the automatic message: *No cellphones allowed in conference. Will get back 2 u ASAP.*

No building conference was still going on at nine o'clock on a Saturday night. Obviously, stupid Wes had forgotten to turn the AutoResponder off. He wouldn't know I was texting him unless he actually looked at his phone. I frowned. I really wanted him to go over and buy that purse for me tomorrow – it wasn't often he got to LA, and I never got out of Riverside.

Wes and I also had this GPS locator app on our phones called Find My Friends. I usually used it at quitting time – I would send a request to see how close he was to being home after he got off of work, so I'd know when to start dinner. He used it the same way – if he was already home when I was working an early shift, he never failed to have a nice meal waiting for me. And it was never cold, because he could gauge how long it would be before I'd be home, based on where the app said I was along the freeway.

So I thought that I would just look to see where he was now, get the name of the bar or hotel, and call there, have him paged – since he wasn't answering his phone and he still had the AutoResponder on. I would tell him that I wanted him to go buy me that purse.

But a funny thing happened when I requested that my phone Find My Friend. When I asked it to Find My Husband. Instead of showing a map of downtown LA, where he was supposed to be, it didn't show a map of LA at all. It showed an aerial shot of Riverside. And there was Wes's picture. And there was Maddie's apartment building.

I blinked in confusion; I was not immediately disconcerted, not immediately suspicious. My first thought was that somehow, Wes had left his phone in Maddie's car, maybe after the gig last night. Why Wes would be in Maddie's car – but wait a minute. There was no gig last night. Wes had left for LA straight from work – he'd already packed a little suitcase earlier in the week.

Still, I was only confused. Maybe Wes had stopped by Maddie's place on his way to the conference, maybe he'd somehow left his phone at her house. Although that was pretty unlikely – Wes never left his phone anywhere. If I was tracking my sister, that would be a reasonable explanation. Maddie was always leaving her phone behind, in the car, at the office. She'd lose it in her own apartment. Her phone was just a modern convenience to Maddie, just the next technological step up from a landline. She didn't text on it very often, didn't have any cool apps, didn't even go on the internet with it.

But Wes's phone was a part of him. He played games, listened to music, asked Suri questions. It was his only line of communication from the jobsite, and while he sometimes let the charge run down, I had never known him to *leave it* anywhere.

A tiny spark of wrongness unsettled me. Besides, Wes had to have his phone with him, he had to be in LA, because how else would he have the AutoResponder telling me that there were no cellphones allowed in the conference?

Unless he was lying about all of it.

The phone rang in my hand and I jumped. It was Dad. I pushed the button and said hello.

"Are you working, Mary?"

Why would Wes tell me he was going to LA and then not be in LA? Why would he be at Maddie's house?

"Mary?"

"What, Dad?"

"I was wondering if you might want to take a ride out to the bridge and look at the river. It's been raining all week, and it should be good and high right now."

A thought struck me. "Did you call Maddie and ask her?"

"Maddie's not picking up. Come, on, Mary! Go with me! Look at the swollen river, marvel at Nature's fury! Like when you were a kid!"

"It's dark, Dad. And it's raining." *Why would Wes be at Maddie's house?*

"It stopped raining. You're right, it is dark, but they put in those streetlights, so I thought that we might be able to see the water, and—"

"I'm working, Dad. Maybe we can go out to the bridge tomorrow. Try Maddie again. I think she's home." *With my husband.*

"Okay, Mary. I'll talk to you tomor—"

I hung up. I didn't have time for Dad and his stupid bridge, didn't have time for the awesome forces of Mother Nature right at the moment. My husband was not where he said he was going to be.

I sent another Find My Friend request, and was amazed to see that Wes was no longer at Maddie's apartment. Instead, he was at the Chinese take-out around the corner. *He was fetching them a little late supper.*

I called Maddie; the phone rang and rang, but she didn't pick up. She would want to have her phone turned on, in case Wes wanted her to reiterate what she wanted for din-din, but she didn't want to talk to me.

A gang of frat boys came in, cold and wet and looking for four or five pitchers of liquid warmth. Waiting on them should've taken my mind off of the suspicion that was trying to take it over, trying to blot out all reasonable thought. But it didn't. The suspicion – that my husband, *my husband,* the one person in the world that belonged *to me,* was with my sister – that suspicion just grew and pulsed in my head like a black, oozing tumor.

Maybe Wes *came back early* from the conference, some logical part of my mind suggested, just like he'd done that day when we'd been picking out bridesmaids' dresses for my sister's wedding-to-the-pervert that had never occurred. Maybe he'd put his phone on AutoResponder this morning, forgotten about it, left LA, stopped in to see Maddie on his way home . . .

Why would he stop in to see Maddie on his way home? What did they have in common, except for his ridiculous band? Maybe he'd be leaving soon, maybe he'd soon be on his way home. Maybe it was all innocent . . .

I requested his location again. He was back at her apartment.

Maybe all those late nights they spent together at *The Beachcomber,* maybe the adoration that she'd always shown to him when he sang – oh, my God, he was so *ridiculous* when he sang! But maybe Wes had responded to it, maybe he'd remembered the old days, when Maddie had been his own personal adoring groupie . . . oh, my Christ! *How long had this been going on?*

I texted Maddie: *Why is my husband at your house?*

A pause. I could picture her, reading my message, realizing she'd been found out. Getting up from where they'd been all snuggled up on the couch, eating Chinese – *maybe they were snuggled up in bed!* She'd go out to the kitchen, so he couldn't see her typing her response. If he knew they'd been found out, the cowardly bitch might want to play it off, he might want to leave and come home where he belonged. And Maddie didn't want him to leave. She wanted to keep him. *She wanted to steal him!*

We have to talk, Mary.

That was answer enough for me. I set my phone down on the bar, and calmly poured myself a shot. I was amazed at my calm. My sister thought she could steal what belonged to me, and she wanted to talk about it. Oh, we would talk, all right. I threw back the shot, felt the liquor burn its path through my insides, just like the anger was burning a path through my brain.

It didn't have anything to do with sex. Had not my sister and I shared enough men, sat around and giggled and compared notes, once upon a time? Hell, she'd been with Wes long before I had – she had loved Wes, worshipped him. How could I possibly care if he was allowing her to do so again? How could he pass up such a thing? I certainly didn't worship him.

When we were kids, my mother used to drag out her forty-fives. She and Dad still had a record player – it was an anachronism, even then. That was the good old days, when they were still together, raising their twin daughters, all of us one big happy family, gleefully dancing around in the living room, listening to old tunes on their scratchy antique record player. A snippet of one of those old tunes came back to me, from a band called *Supertramp:*

Don't you look at my girlfriend
She's the only one I got
Not much of a girlfriend
Never seem to get a lot

My supertramp of a sister had always gotten a lot. She'd always gotten everything. The big house with Mom, the nice car, the great job. She'd gotten to fall in love and contemplate marriage, not once but twice.

And still she couldn't do anything right. Her first love was an immature child, her second some kind of pervert. Her first love had abandoned her, had chosen me, and while I didn't love him, that didn't erase the fact that he was mine.

He's the only one I got.

And Miss Maddie, who had always had all the good things in life handed to her on a silver platter, was not going to sidle up to the salad bar and plop my husband onto her tray, just because she suddenly had a whim to do so.

Not much of a girlfriend
Never seem to get a lot

Maddie had gotten everything she wanted in life, while I had to make my own way, work for what I wanted. And what had I wound up with? No true love, no happily ever after bliss for Mary! Just nights in a smelly old bar, and a husband that I could take or leave. But he was mine to take or leave, and he was good enough to keep me company. I would not leave him – not to her, someone who had gotten her every wish fulfilled in life, and still managed to mess everything up. I might leave him someday, but not to her. And by God, she wasn't going to take him. Not now, not ever.

Yeah, we need to talk all right, I texted back.

When?

Why don't you come over here right now? Leave my husband at your house and come on down. We'll talk.

I'm not coming out tonight. It's raining.

A thought struck me when she mentioned the rain. It was a dark, evil thought. But she wasn't gonna steal my husband.

A neutral place then? I texted.

What?

Meet me on Dad's bridge. North sidewalk. Half hour.

I'm not coming out tonight. It's raining, Maddie repeated.

Dad says the river's up. I cant believe you'd do this to me, Maddie. If you don't show, I'm gonna jump.

I turned my phone off.

MADELINE

"She's not gonna jump," Wes said. "It's just a ploy to get you out in the rain."

I sighed. It was just like Mary to be so childishly demanding, so my-way-or-the-highway. And so histrionic. The only outpost of civilization within walking distance was a Sizzler on the Jurupa Valley side, and it was still a long walk down from their parking lot to the north walkway of the bridge; it was dark, it was cold, it was raining. But a windswept vantage point, complete with raging torrent nearby – to my sister, it was the perfect setting for our confrontation over Wes. Not a little terse adult discussion over a latte at Starbucks. Not even a screaming argument at my place, beyond the ears of curious onlookers. No. It had to be theatrical, complete with threats of suicide, out on the lonely, dark bridge that had always meant so much to our dad. Seriously.

"Whatever," I said. "I have to talk to her sometime."

"But this is just silly, Maddie. What next, pistols at dawn at ten paces?" Wes grinned self-consciously, and I realized that he was embarrassed because all this melodrama was over him. It was all his fault, the result of his indecision, his flip-flopping back and forth between sisters. "Do you want me to go with you?"

"No," I said, and he looked relieved, just like I knew he would. Wes was *the one,* and I loved him completely. But he did have an undeniable yellow streak when it came to facing any kind of emotional confrontation, even ones that were a result of his avoidance of other emotional confrontations. "I'll handle it." I put on my coat and kissed him. "I'll play her silly, over-the-top game. If I'm not back soon, call out the gendarmerie, or whoever it is that's in charge of administrating duels."

"If you need me to come out there, just call."

"I need you, Wes," I said and hugged him. "But not for this."

MARY

I turned my phone back on and tapped another round of pitchers for the frat boys, then told Felicia and Debbie that something had come up. Concern marred the features of my pretty friends' faces. I smiled, realizing that they were the only friends I had – my thieving sister was certainly no friend of mine. "It's nothing," I assured them. "Just a little bump in the road. But I have to take care of it right now. I'll tell you guys all about it tomorrow."

"Jon's gonna be pissed about you leaving," Debbie said darkly.

"Fuck Jon," I said, and when she quaked fearfully at that, I added, "once I tell him what's going on, he'll understand."

"You can't tell us now?" Felicia asked.

"No, honey. But it'll all be settled soon."

They nodded, and I pulled my bag from beneath the bar. *Looks like I'm not going to get one of those cute jewelry box purses after all*, I thought, and frowned. I put on my coat and headed for the door. The rain had stopped, but it was still misty and cold. As I got into the car, my phone rang. It was Wes. "How's LA?" I asked.

"Just so you know," he began. Oh my God, how I hated that expression, and he used it all the time. *Just so you know, I'll be home late. Just so you know, we're out of coffee. Just so you know, I'm fucking your sister.* If he was telling me, then I would know, wouldn't I? Why add that stupid phrase?

"Just so you know," he said, "I've made up my mind. You can make Maddie go out in the rain and scream at her on the bridge, but it's not gonna make any difference. We're through, Mary. It was a mistake from the start. I've made up my mind."

I laughed then. The nerve of him. "Why do you think this has once single thing to do with you, Wes? Your decision means nothing. *You* mean nothing. This is between Maddie and me." I hung up before he had a chance to say another word.

****

The traffic was light on the bridge, people scurrying home to their loved ones in the misty darkness, headlights and tail lights. The Sizzler parking lot was practically empty – it was past nine-thirty, and I figured that they were no doubt closed, the only people left in there a few bus boys and dishwashers. I didn't see Maddie's brand new Kia, but I knew she would show up.

My threat of suicide – it didn't pack a lot of emotional power in text form, but I couldn't have said it out loud without laughing. What did I have to be suicidal about? I was the robbed party here, the victim. If anyone should be suicidal, it should be Maddie. She should be overcome with grief and guilt at what she'd done, for stealing from me the only thing that I had.

But the words, glaring accusingly at her from her phone would be enough: *I'm gonna jump*. She obviously didn't know me anymore, if she thought she could just so cavalierly steal from me. So how would she be able to gauge if I was serious or not? I was serious all right, deadly serious, but not suicidally so. But Maddie didn't know me anymore, so my threat would rouse her from my husband's arms and get her out to Dad's cold bridge, so we could finish this thing.

I walked down the gentle grade from the Sizzler and started across the bridge. I found the cold bracing, but refreshing. It placed a cool hand on the fever of my rage, enough to calm it into ordered thought, but not enough to dispel it. Nothing would ever dispel it. Maddie had never in our lives pissed me off like this. There was no explanation that would make me forgive her for this blatant theft. It attacked the very core of everything we were – sisters, family – what kind of a monster steals from family?

I thought Dad would be sad to see the state of the brand new bridge, already: there were snarls of graffiti on the wall; a horrific splash or bright red paint that looked like blood. A little past the center of the bridge, one of the streetlights was out. I pointed the flashlight from my phone at its base, and saw that the electrical plate had been pried open. It gaped like a surprised mouth, stubs of wire sticking out like spiky teeth. I'd heard Wes talk about thieves at the jobsite, busting open the streetlights for the copper wiring they contained. It wouldn't happen when the houses were built and occupied – even copper thieves were not bold enough to hit streetlights in a ritzy neighborhood. But while the site was under construction, the defenseless streetlights were easy prey. As were these, on the lonely bridge.

It was not as if the cops could see the 211s in progress as they whizzed over the bridge, pull over, hop the wall and apprehend the perps. I was surprised that only one of the lights was dark, based on how easy the theft must be.

I thought of my thieving sister again – stealing the copper from the street lights was a piece of cake for the determined thief, just like she supposed stealing my husband was going to be a cake walk for her.

But she would find that my vigilance was superior to that of the municipality responsible for keeping the lights burning on the bridge. My vigilance was absolute.

I put my phone in my jacket pocket, set my purse down at the base of the streetlight. A two barred guardrail was set in the concrete wall at about chest height. It would take a very strong man to push someone off of the bridge – he would have to push his victim backwards, then quickly reach down and grab their feet, then flip them over. It would take strength, stealth, deliberation, premeditation. And the design was safe enough that no staggering bums could accidentally stumble and fall in, either.

But the base of the street light had been no doubt inadvertently constructed as the most convenient of steps. One, two – and I was sitting on the rail. It was probably five inches wide, and the distance to the top of the wall was just as comfortable for putting one's feet there and sitting on the railing, as if it had been built especially for it. I imagined that kids would be jumping off all the time in the summer, if the water was as deep as it was now. Just the kind of thing for teenage boys to do on a dare. The drop wasn't enough to harm you, if there was water in the river. But when it was warm enough to consider swimming, the water would be just a trickle through hard, unforgiving sand.

And now, any obstacles to jumping off that might exist in the riverbed, boulders or logs, stray chunks of concrete with rebar sticking out of them, were invisible in the darkness. The water was cold and swift, and even if you managed to avoid the hidden rocks, the exposure couldn't possibly be good for you. I didn't think you'd die of hypothermia, but there was always the possibility, if you were swept downstream and had to wander around in the river bottom, wet and shivering, before you could find your way out again.

But I wasn't worried about falling off, and I certainly didn't intend on jumping. I sat on the railing with my back to the unseen, rushing river below, one hand lightly holding on. Had the streetlight been working, a concerned citizen speeding by on the bridge might have seen me sitting there, and called the authorities to report my unsafe behavior. But I was invisible to the motorists on the bridge, safe in my pool of darkness from the crippled streetlight.

MADELINE

I saw the battered old Ford that my sister drove these days, all alone in the darkened Sizzler parking lot. I pulled in next to it, turned off the car, and took a deep breath. So she really intended to go through with this melodramatic bullshit. Whatever.

"The time has come," the Walrus said,
"To talk of many things:
Of shoes and ships and sealing-wax
Of cabbages and kings
And why the sea is boiling hot –

And why my beloved twin sister would pull a horrendous practical joke on me, why she would allow it to destroy my relationship with the only man I'd ever loved. Why she'd never copped to it, why she'd never explained. And why she'd taken up with him, married him, when she didn't even like him.

"And whether pigs have wings."

I walked down the hill, grateful that at least it had finally stopped raining. I took one step onto the concrete of the north side walkway and hesitated. I discovered that I was afraid, although not about having it out with Mary. There was nothing to be afraid about on that score. It was just an unfortunate unpleasantness that we were going to have to get through before we could carry on with our lives. I no longer felt even a flutter of guilt about what had happened between Wes and me. Mary had played a joke on me and it had caused me to lose Wes. I had him back now. Whatever relationship Mary felt she had with him had been obtained under false pretenses – she was not entitled to it. It was not valid. He didn't want to continue it, and she would just have to get over that.

I wished that Wes was there with me – my mother had always said that the best way not to get raped and murdered after dark was not to be out gallivanting around by one's self after dark. And certainly not gallivanting around on some lonely deserted bridge, where not one single person could hear you scream. Underneath which were known to live all kinds of undesirables.

I took a deep breath. I had come this far, and it was time to finish it. I would appease Mary's melodrama. Hoping that the undesirables were all snug in their bushes below – then I remembered that their bushes were all underwater now, what with the swollen stream – I stopped wishing that Wes was there with me. Because in the final analysis, this really didn't concern Wes at all, now did it? This concerned something that Mary had done to me, and something that she perceived I had done to her. It was between us. Wes was peripheral, so it was just as well that he wasn't there.

I walked cautiously across the bridge, on the lookout for rapists and murderers hiding in the shadows. The toughest part was crossing in front of a blacked out streetlight – any manner of monsters could be crouching there. I hurried past, thinking that maybe I'd read Mary's text wrong – I was past the center of the bridge and she was nowhere to be seen – was she on the other side?

As I was about to enter the pool of light from the next streetlight, Mary called my name, and I practically jumped out of my skin. I spun around – how had I passed her? I saw that I'd missed her because she was sitting on the railing beside the dead streetlight. The idea streaked through my mind that maybe she was suicidal, sitting up there in the dark like that, nothing between her and the drop to the angry river below but the empty air and her hand lightly clutching the railing. But I felt no pity. She was the aggressor here, I the wronged party. Thinking of the disgusting nature of her prank, all the unnecessary heartbreak it had caused, the idea that she was suicidal passed from my mind. Mary was just mean. She had climbed up there so she could startle me when I passed.

"Come down from there," I said. "Dad would have a cow."

"Why don't you come up here by me?" she replied. "It's safe enough. The rail is nice and wide." She glanced behind her at the water, and even though I knew she couldn't see it, she said, "The view's great. Dad would love it." I stood beside her at the rail, looked over into the darkness. I shook my head.

"You always were a chicken, Maddie," my sister said, her voice dripping superior derision. "Always. This cowardly theft of yours proves it, so why should I be surprised that you're too afraid to climb up here and sit by me?"

I understood at once the make-up of her anger. I saw its color, its height and breadth and depth. She didn't love Wes, had never loved him. But for whatever reason, she had married him, and he was her possession now, just like Raggedy Andy had been. And no one, especially not her twin sister, was allowed to touch or even look at what belonged to her alone.

"All right," I said, and dropped my purse beside hers on the sidewalk. "Scootch over." Mary made room for me, and I climbed up from the base of the streetlight and sat beside her on the rail. I had to let her know that I was not afraid of her anger, her righteous indignation at my alleged *theft*. If anyone should be angry, if anyone should be righteously indignant, it should be me.

I looked at her. Waited. She was the one that had called for this dog and pony show at this ridiculous spot, so she could start it off. Finally she said, "So tell me, my only sister. How long have you been screwing my husband?"

I smiled, closed one eye, as if toting up a long period of time. "It's been a minute," I said at last.

"It only takes a minute," she replied immediately. "I never could understand what you found so glorious about all that."

Again I was struck by the idea that Mary wasn't furious that I was *screwing* her husband. The physical betrayal meant nothing to her. Hadn't we shared enough men in the past? No, Mary was angry because I was screwing *her husband,* her possession. It was not the sex, the betrayal, the adultery – it was the theft that she was so upset about. In her mind, she owned Wes, just like she'd owned Raggedy Andy, and he was hers to do with as she pleased. And it pleased her not a little bit to have me tramping all over her proprietorship.

"Did you think I wouldn't find out? I knew something was up with him, all week. Even while we were . . ." she trailed off, then added, "It still didn't last more than a minute, but I knew something was up with him."

She thought that I'd be outraged to discover that Wes had been playing us both, perhaps while he was making up his mind. If it was true, I wouldn't have been outraged. Her *physical* relationship with Wes had never been the problem. Wes's choice of her over me had been the problem, my love for him had been the problem, my inability to let him go. He had chosen her, and the fact that they had sex together was not a specific agony to me – the idea that he was lost to me forever, body and soul and laughter and company had been the agony. So if Mary wanted to intimate that she had been intimate with her husband since he'd again been intimate with me, it wouldn't have bothered me, even if it was true. I'd told him to go home and evaluate his marriage had I not?

But it was just a sad, cruel dig on Mary's part, and I laughed at her. Wes had not been intimate with her. He'd made up his mind before

211

he'd left my apartment last Sunday. He hadn't considered his marriage for two weeks like he promised he would; he hadn't considered it for even one day. He'd immediately started machinating to be with me again this weekend, first thing Monday morning. He was through with his wife, and had not gone back for one more *minute*. But I was not going to argue with her over this lie. We had other lies to argue about.

I said, "He was going to tell you tomorrow, actually. Come home, pack his shit and leave you. We just wanted one more weekend together before all this . . ." I gestured with one hand, keeping the other one firmly on the railing. "All this unpleasantness."

"You've never had to work for a single thing in your life, Maddie. Have you ever even realized that? You're a spoiled brat. Everything was always just given to you, and it's just like you to believe that you can just waltz up and take something that isn't yours. Wes, worthless as he is, is mine. I worked for him. Why do you think I'm just going to allow you to steal something that doesn't belong to you?"

Again I smiled at her. "Because I can, Mary. I already have."

She blinked dumbly at that, then changed her strategy. "How can you treat me like this, Maddie? How can you be so cruel? He's the only thing I've got."

If possessive anger wasn't going to wipe the smile off my face, then perhaps pity might. Poor Mary, lonely and destitute in a cruel world. Poor Mary, all alone with no one to call her own except the man I loved, who loved me. It was all bullshit. I realized all at once that my sister was like the dog in the manger, keeping the oxen from their hay – he wasn't going to eat it, but he wasn't going to let them eat it either. Mary didn't want Wes, didn't love him, had never loved him. But she was goddamned if she was going to let me have him.

"You ain't got shit, sister," I said and giggled. "Wes is no more yours now than he was before . . ." I pretended to reconsider, a little fake look of surprise on my face, like I had just recalled the reason that I had lost Wes in the first place. "That was a pretty childish thing he did, not believing me, running off."

"That's because he *is* childish. He's a coward. Worthless. I knew it all along."

"Yet you married him." Again my tone was as if I was reconsidering – maybe I would leave him to her. "He's your property now, your husband."

"That's right!"

I shook my head sadly. "But only for the moment. Come Monday morning, he's filing for divorce. Happy Thanksgiving, Mary, and Merry Christmas and Happy New Year. It takes six months for a divorce to be final in California. Just ask Mom." I looked over my shoulder at the unseen Santa Ana. "So when the water is gone again, when there's nothing down there but sand and weeds and a tiny little trickle, Wes is gonna be *my* husband. I've always liked the idea of a Fourth of July wedding. Red, white and blue. Fireworks."

I grinned at her expression of open-mouthed disbelief. She'd been falling for my seeming reevaluation. She'd actually thought I was relenting, that I would give Wes back to her, just because he was the only thing she had. She valued him the way she would again value Raggedy Andy if I suddenly snatched him from the memories of childhood and handed him to her, here on this cold bridge – only as a thing, an object, something she owned. She didn't deserve Wes, especially not after . . .

"I only have a couple of questions for you, Mary," I went on. "I've answered all of yours, but I will recap." I smiled happily. "How long have I been screwing your husband? Two weekends now. Why do I think I can get away with it? I don't think I can. I know I can. I already have." I winked at her. "Is he going to divorce you? Yes, and as soon as it is legally possible. Is he going to marry me, and are we going to live happily ever after? Yes, again as soon as it's legally possible."

Still she was speechless, so I went on. "So, seeing as all this is going to occur, I have a few questions for *you*, Mary. The curiosity is just killing me, so here goes: did you play that disgusting joke on me because you wanted Wes for yourself?"

She blinked rapidly. "I never wanted Wes, Maddie. Wes is a loser."

"Yet still you married him," I said conversationally. "Still you get me out in the middle of this stupid bridge to bitch me out for taking back what should've never been yours at all. Still you whine about how he's your property, how he's all you've got. So I have to assume that you did that horrible thing to you own sister, because you wanted the loser for yourself."

"What are you talking about? What horrible thing?"

"Remember Jason's movie, Mary? *Rolling Blackout's Hometown Debut?*" I took my hand off the railing long enough to make the director's gesture. "Remember how you hated him always filming in your bar?" She nodded slowly. "Well, you forgot that he installed cameras that ran all the time, to capture crowd reactions. We watched the raw footage, Mary, just last night, as a matter of fact. We saw you sitting at a table with that asshole with the smiley face tattoo. Wes started to freak out again, thinking it was me."

"He is such an idiot," she said.

I smiled. "But he is my idiot, and I'll thank you to refrain from insulting my fiancé." I paused, letting that little reminder settle on her. "We saw that guy come in, saw you give him free drinks. Was he some guy you were seeing, Mary? You don't even give your . . . soon to be ex-husband free drinks."

"He's a drug dealer. His name's Andre. He lives in Bakersfield now."

"That would explain the Roofies."

Mary blinked. "I don't know what you're talking about, Maddie. I might have sat down and had a drink with him once, but that was it. He was Benny-from-the-tobacco-lounge's buddy." She had obviously figured out that a camera that caught her and Andre at a table wouldn't have caught them at the bar. So I explained it to her.

"How do you think I know you gave him free drinks, Mary? There was a camera across from the taps, too. *I saw you.* I saw him give you the Roofies, saw him show you how to chop 'em up and put 'em into my drink." I smiled benevolently at her. "But just so you know, Mary, I forgive you. What have I got to be mad at you about now? Even if Wes and I hadn't already decided to get back together, after we witnessed your little series of rendezvous with the drug dealer, that would've sealed it." I laughed. "I had to stop him from coming up there and smacking you."

"Who?" she asked.

"Wes."

"Wes threatened to smack me?" Mary laughed then. "Right. Wes is gonna smack me. And I'm a Chinese jet pilot."

MARY

I considered my sister in her smugness, back on her I-get-everything-I-want high horse. She thought she was going to get away with taking what didn't belong to her.

I remembered overhearing the pawnshop owner from across the street once, when he was sitting in my bar talking to his buddy. "So I just smiled at the cop and said, 'I'm a businessman, Officer. I'm not here to investigate sad tales of failed engagements. She told me the ol' man had abandoned her at the altar, and she wanted to sell the ring he'd given her. How was I supposed to know it was stolen?'"

Maddie was the same way, smug in her crime. The pawnshop owner knew the ring was stolen, but he didn't care. He was out for a buck. He didn't care about the girl's theft and he knew he couldn't be prosecuted for his own crime. So he'd just smiled at the cop and shrugged. Maddie was the same way. She'd stolen what wasn't hers, and thought she'd gotten away with it scot-free, so she dared to smile at me. She thought she had her prize, was confident that I wasn't going to get him back.

But it wasn't the loss of the prize that had me so enraged, it was the nerve of the theft. *But just so you know, Mary, I forgive you.* Oh, my Christ, she even talked like him! I didn't want Wes back. She could have him. They deserved each other.

But regardless of a robbery victim's feelings about her stolen property, the thief must still be punished. Especially if she was a smug, superior, laughing-in-my-face thief like my sister.

"So I want you to tell me two things, Mary," Maddie was saying. "The first is how you pulled the whole thing off. The second is why you would do something so despicable to me over a man."

"What are you talking about?" I asked her again.

"It's obvious that you wanted Wes for yourself. That's why you did this. To make me look like a whore, so he'd leave me, so you could have him for yourself."

I threw my head back and laughed so hard, that if I hadn't had a firm grip on the railing, I would've gone over into the cold water. It was just like her to be so self-centered. Everything was about her. What I had done to *her*, what I wanted to take from *her*. She was the thief, not I.

People who have everything handed to them *expect* everything to be handed to them, so I guess I couldn't expect her to see what I'd done for her. I couldn't expect any gratitude. Gratitude was an unknown to people like her. They got what they had coming – they deserved it. There was no need to thank anybody for it. I was going to see that my smug, ungrateful, thieving sister got what she deserved, got what she had coming. But first, I would show her the error of her ways.

"I wanted Wes for myself? That's such a laugh. I never wanted Wes."

"Yet still you married–"

"Yeah, I know." Jesus, she was such a one trick pony. "But I didn't pull that prank on you because I wanted Wes. My God, how selfish you are! You're so selfish, you don't even realize when someone does you a favor."

"*A favor?* You need to start from the beginning, Mary. You know how much smarter you are than me. Even though I'm not the one that's about to be a divorcee."

Maddie grinned, and I thought, *That's right, yuk it up, you thieving bitch, just like the pawnbroker. Be smug in your crime, just like he was. But the pawnbroker eventually got shut down for receiving stolen goods, now didn't he? And your comeuppance is almost at hand.*

"I'm just not getting how what you did to me could be in any way construed as a favor," she said. "Please enlighten me."

"Okay. You send this childish man-boy brat into my bar to insult me. I can tell he's a bastard, through and through, just by the ease with which he batted those baby blues at me and propositioned me as if I was a whore. It came so easily, so naturally to him.

"Then you tell me that he's so wonderful, that you're in love with him. *Why can't she see?* I think to myself. *Why can't she see that he is nothing, that he's an immature coward, that he can't possibly love her?*"

Maddie shrugged. "He doesn't love you, I can see that."

You think you have it all figured out, don't you, you selfish, smug bitch? I thought. But I'd make her see that I was the one that loved her, that I was the only one looking out for her. I was the one that loved her, right up until the moment when she'd dared to steal from me. And I would make her pay for that, but before I did so, I'd show her that the idea of stealing her stupid boyfriend had been the farthest thing from my mind.

I ignored her remark and continued. "Then the next second, the next thing I know, you're planning to marry this asshole. I couldn't believe it – how could you think this idiot was *the one?* I could see his shallowness, his inherent, native vulgarity. *You're the kind of girl that likes to have fun. With guys just like me.* What kind of a man says something like that to a complete stranger?

216

"Certainly not the kind that had any business being with my sister. He was such an ass, and I knew that whatever he was calling love for you was just some kind of flimsy infatuation. Something that would never stand up to any kind of test."

"So you set out to test him. Did you set the fire at the jobsite, too?"

"Don't be ridiculous, Maddie. I'd planned to do something sometime when Wes wasn't around, then suddenly on New Year's Eve, Wes wasn't around. We were going to a party where there were going to be a lot of strangers, so I thought . . . why not do it tonight? I called Andre. He was already at Benny's party.

"I was afraid that I would give you too much, that I might hurt you, so I gave the pills back to him, and he slipped the right amount into your drink. After a few minutes, you started to get groggy and hang on me, so we took you to the back bedroom. I borrowed some guy's phone . . . it was just supposed to be Andre, but at the last second, Andre left and came back with some other dude. They never touched you, Maddie. They just . . . well, you know what they did. I took a few pictures. I sent them out to a bunch of people. I gave the phone back to the guy. He said it was a fucked up thing to do, but Andre and I thought it was hilarious."

"Hilarious," Maddie repeated.

"I was going to let you sleep it off at Benny's. When and if Wes showed up, I would've showed him where you were. You were safe back there. Nobody was going to mess with you. Just another drunk girl on New Year's Eve. But Felicia found you, and she insisted that we take you home."

"And the rest is history."

"It wasn't supposed to go the way it did, Maddie." Now I felt a little apologetic, because this was the truth. "I knew that Wes would act like the immature baby that he is. I knew that he'd get pissed off and start accusing you of being part of those pictures. I figured that you'd get so mad at him for being such an ass, that you'd realize your mistake. I thought you'd realize that he wasn't the one, that you were far too good for him. I figured that *you* would break up with *him*, Maddie.

"I figured that you'd tell him to kick rocks, and he would, and then you could find somebody better. Someone who deserved you. I never would've imagined in a million years that the cowardly bitch would have the balls to leave *you.*"

"But when he did leave, and you saw how broke up about it I was, why didn't you say something then?"

217

"To tell you the truth, Maddie, you didn't seem too broke up about it. You didn't run after him when he took off. You cried a little bit the first day, but when I tried to tell you not to go to that wedding with Drew, that Wes might not appreciate it, I seem to remember your exact words were, *Fuck him.*

"And I was in too deep then. The whole thing had kinda blown up in my face. I'd expected you to dump Wes, not the other way around. But still, the end result was the same. Wes was gone, out of your life, and the way was clear for you to find something better."

I paused. "And you did find something better, didn't you? Mom helped you, just like she always does. She provided you with an easy escape, and you took it, without a backward glance. You didn't even think about how much I'd miss you. And in another minute, you were all happy and in love again, with a better, richer, more sophisticated man. You had a little family. You were going to get married. Once again, you had it made."

"What happened when Wes came back?" Maddie asked flatly. I could tell that she wasn't seeing how I'd saved her, how I'd done her a favor.

"Wes is an idiot, Maddie, when are you ever going to see that? He's just an egotistical little boy. I opened the door. He thought I was you, and he started to apologize. He started to cry. So I forgave him." I grinned evilly. "I forgave him three times. Twice on the couch and once on the floor." She wanted to be smug? I could be a little smug myself.

"He didn't figure out that I wasn't you until the next morning, when he tossed me an orange and I caught it in my right hand. He got up to leave and I told him that you were gone, that you were getting married soon. You had your happy little life in San Diego, with your brilliant banker and your charming little girl.

"I was looking out for you yet again, Maddie. I didn't want Wes running down there and messing up your plans – I was sure Evan was not the type to appreciate your shaggy, hillbilly ex-boyfriend showing up on his doorstep. So I made it clear to Wes that you'd forgotten all about him. You'd forgotten all about me. You had moved on.

"But Wes stayed. One thing led to another, and we moved in together. We were lonely. We didn't have much, but we had each other. You were never coming back; not to him, not to me, so when he drunkenly asked me to marry him in Vegas, I drunkenly agreed.

"So, yeah, I played a mean practical joke on you. But my intention surely wasn't to take Wes away from you. My intention was to *save* you from Wes. And save you from Wes I did. It's not my fault that you couldn't find a good man if you were the only woman at a Goody-Two-Shoes Convention. It's not my fault that the one you thought was decent turned out to be a pervert. Wes wasn't any good for you before, Maddie, and he's not any good for you now, if for no other reason than he belongs to me now."

Then I heard his voice from down the bridge, calling her name.

"I'm here, Wes!" she cried, and I heard distant footsteps running towards us. He called again, and she answered again. Now he couldn't be more than a few yards away. Maddie said to me, "The only problem with all that is that, whether he's good for me or not, I want Wes back now, Mary. I have him back."

"That's what you think, sister," I said. I reached across and gave her shoulder a quick, hard little push.

WES

I was climbing the walls at Maddie's place. All this shit was going on because of my dumb-ass mistakes, and I decided that she shouldn't have to be out there in the cold and the dark by herself. So after about a half hour, I went out to the bridge.

I put my emergency flashers on and drove slowly, searching. People honked and sped around me. I saw them sitting up on the rail beneath a dead streetlight, only outlines in the darkness. That was just nuts. I sped across the bridge and pulled the car over as soon as it was possible to get out of the travel lane. I started running down the bridge, calling Maddie's name. I'd decided that she'd been out in the cold with her crazy bitch sister for long enough.

Then just as I came up to them, everything seemed to happen like one of those jerky, speeded-up clips from bad movies. Mary shoved Maddie, and she flailed backwards and to her left. She started to go over, but she also leaned into Mary, grabbed onto her. So Mary went right on over with her. I found myself with my chest against the rail, arms outstretched, grasping nothing but wet air.

I looked over but could see nothing but blackness. I screamed Maddie's name again and heard a faint cry of *Help!* I ran down the walkway toward Riverside, then up the shoulder of the road. Somehow, I managed to cross four lanes of Van Buren Boulevard without getting run over. The adrenaline must've helped me focus on the right moment to run – I heard a lot of honking horns, but somehow I didn't get hit.

I started down the wet, grassy hill on the other side, still screaming Maddie's name. I heard another faint cry of help, downstream in the blackness. I stopped at the river's edge and called 911.

When the dispatcher asked me what my emergency was, I said, "My name is Wes Thomerville. My wife has just jumped off the Van Buren Bridge, and she dragged her sister over with her."

"How many people did you say are in the water, sir?"

"Two. My wife and her sister. Now there's going to be three, because I'm going in after them."

I heard the dispatcher say, "Sir! Don't–" then I set my phone down on a boulder of riprap and dove into the river.

The water was icy and I came up gasping for air, and immediately sank again. My fist smacked into something hard and I pushed off to keep from hitting my head. I could hear the water rushing all around me but I could see nothing: the river ahead of me was in complete blackness. The lights from the bridge revealed nothing. I called Maddie's name again, and heard a faint answering cry. The water was deep and swift and I hoped that the fall hadn't broken her up too badly. She might still be okay, if I could just find her, if the water didn't sweep me past her.

It seemed like I was in the water for a lifetime, calling Maddie's name, hearing an answer. The voice seemed to be getting closer – I realized that she wasn't being dragged ahead of me anymore, but must've somehow made it to the bank or to some sandbar. But I couldn't see anything.

At last a voice sounded almost directly to my left. I swam toward the bank in the blackness, grabbed at the slimy vegetation, dragged myself out of the water. I tried to stand up, slipped, almost fell back in again. I called to Maddie – a voice said my name from several yards upstream. I crawled through the rank vegetation, unable to stand in the muck.

At last I found her, clinging to the side of a rock, whitewater rushing around her, trying to pull her off. I dragged her up into the weeds, and I collapsed backwards into the mud, holding her tightly to my chest.

Moments later, the helicopter showed up, and immediately found us with his Nightsun searchlights. I looked at Maddie, finally able to see her. Her coat was gone, and her shirt. She shivered uncontrollably against me in only her bra and her flayed jeans. Her shoes were gone. The white skin of her arms and chest was covered with abrasions. I said, "Are you hurt?"

She didn't answer. She had fainted.

****

The hospital treated and released me. I had a few scrapes, might've caught a cold from the icy water, but I was okay.

Maddie was still unconscious. She had abrasions and contusions over her whole body, had broken her left arm in two places, had broken her left ankle. They were treating her for hypothermia. The doctor told me that they would be taking her in to surgery as soon as she was stabilized. She was going to need pins in her arm, and maybe a plate in her ankle.

Mary hadn't been brought to the hospital. She was still missing.

The doctor told me there was nothing I could do, that I should go home and get out of my wet clothes. Somebody – the cops or the hospital – had called Maddie's parents, he told me. It would be best if I would go get into some dry clothes and then come back. He didn't expect any change in her condition for several hours.

I was standing in the lobby of the hospital, trying to decide what to do next. I felt damp and miserable and a little feverish. The doctor was right; I needed to get into some dry clothes. But my apartment was a million miles away on the other side of town – and that place had never been my apartment anyway. And I was on foot – the law had no doubt towed my truck off the shoulder by now.

But I didn't care about my truck, didn't care that I was cold and sick. I didn't care that they hadn't found my wife yet. I was worried about Maddie, the ordeal of falling off the bridge, the injuries she had suffered. Surgery, pins and plates. The ordeal she was going to suffer when she woke up. I didn't want to go back to my apartment, so I asked the lady at the front desk to call me a cab.

I'd go back to Maddie's. I had clothes there. I'd take a hot shower, maybe down something to handle my cold, and then I'd come back.

"Mr. Thomerville?"

I looked over my shoulder. A young patrol cop was standing there. "I'm Officer Evans." He offered his hand and I shook it. "We found your cellphone." He handed it to me, and I said thanks. It was nearly dead. He asked me what happened.

I told him tearfully that I'd witnessed my wife jump from the bridge. "Mary was up on the rail, and Maddie was there with her, trying to talk her down. I showed up just in time to see Mary stand up. Maddie grabbed her arm, tried to hug Mary to her. I lunged for them. But it was too late. Mary leaned forward, and dragged Maddie over with her."

I put my face in my hands and sobbed. My sorrow was real, but it wasn't for my wife. I thought about how close I'd come to losing Maddie, how I might *still* lose Maddie, and the tears just fell of their own accord. Evans put his hand on my shoulder and I wondered insanely how he'd drawn the short straw to have to be the one to go talk to the grieving husband. Maybe they always sent the rookie: he didn't look more than twenty-two.

I sobbed again and asked him, "Have you found my wife yet?"

Evans shook his head. "But they're combing the river bottom. They've got three helicopters out there." He took out a notebook, asked for my information. "We'll let you know as soon as there's any news." He handed me his card, looked kindly at me. "Is there anything that I can do for you?"

I shook my head. I told him that I'd left my truck on the shoulder – he agreed that it had no doubt been towed by now. He offered to drive me over to the impound to claim it, or anywhere else I needed to go. But then the cab pulled up outside the lobby doors. Evans told me that he'd keep me informed. I told him that I would be back at the hospital, waiting for his news, as soon as I got some dry clothes.

****

Even in the face of all this tragedy, I was at the mercy of technology. Maddie didn't have a house phone. Who has a house phone anymore? I plugged my phone in and took a hot shower, found some dry clothes. I sat on the corner of Maddie's bed, still tethered by the charger, and called *Mickey's*. I told Felicia that there'd been an accident on the bridge, that Mary was missing, that Maddie was in the hospital. After the stunned silence, she said, "Oh, my God, Wes! She was just here! She said she had something to take care of, then she took off . . . Oh, my God, Wes, I'm so sorry!" After another moment we hung up.

I called Drew, told him the whole story. There was no need to provide him with the fiction that there'd been an accident, or even that Mary had jumped from the bridge. I told him that we'd discovered the truth about the pictures, that Mary had discovered the truth about Maddie and me. I told him that Mary had pushed her sister off the bridge, that I had witnessed it. I told him that the only reason that Mary had gone over too was that Maddie was flailing for balance and had grabbed hold of Mary's arm . . .

"I'll be there as soon as I can," he told me and hung up.

When I got back to the hospital, I met Joanna in the hallway outside of the waiting room. Maddie was in pre-op, no visitors allowed, surely not someone as tenuously related to her as her brother-in-law.

Joanna hugged me and we cried together. She told me that there had been no word about Mary yet. I asked her if she knew how long Maddie was supposed to be in surgery.

"I don't know, Wes," she said and looked down at the floor. "Leslie's in there, and the doctor came in and talked to her and Larry. I didn't want to . . . ." Leslie was Maddie's mother. "I didn't want to be in the way."

I thought about the bitterness of blended families, especially at times like this. Joanna loved both of her husband's daughters, and she no doubt wanted to be in the waiting room with him, to comfort him, to hold his hand, to cry with him. But Maddie's mother was in there, too, and even though there had been hardly a word spoken between her and her ex-husband in years, Joanna felt that it was not her place to

223

be at her husband's side right then. Larry and Leslie were Maddie's parents at this painful time – Joanna was just an outsider. I thought that her decision to stand out in the hall and let them have their time was kind and generous of her, and I hugged her again.

I walked into the waiting room. Maddie's parents both stared at different places on the wall, each lost in their own worlds of fear and worry and sorrow. I could see that they were not capable of comforting each other. They both looked up at me. I thought I saw some kind of accusation in Leslie's eyes, as if she thought that all of this was somehow my fault. Or maybe it was just my guilty conscience I saw reflected there. She couldn't know about my reconciliation with her busted-up daughter, couldn't know that I'd told her missing daughter that I wanted a divorce. But I knew. It *was* all my fault.

Larry nodded at me and we went back out into the hall. He said a few words to Joanna. They hugged, then Joanna hugged me again. Then she left.

"What happened, Wes?"

I shook my head. "Mary jumped off the bridge. She dragged Maddie over with her."

I hadn't needed to specify which bridge. There was only one bridge in these parts to Larry. "Why, Wes? Why would Mary try to kill herself? I was just talking to her earlier tonight. I was just talking to her, about going out to the bridge . . ." A look of shock crossed his face. "Why would she do it, Wes?"

I thought it would all come out in the end, one way or another, whether they pulled Mary from the river alive or dead. As the minutes and hours wore on and we had no word, I was beginning to accept that Mary was gone. No one could survive out there in that cold, tumbling water this long.

Either way, Maddie and I were going to be together. We were going to get married, finally live the life that we'd once planned. So there was no use lying to Larry, conjuring up some mythical depression that had led his daughter to leap from his favorite bridge. If I was going to go ahead with the fiction that Mary had jumped, I might as well tell him the most logical reason why she might've done it.

"She thought I was sleeping with Maddie."

Without pause, without accusation – with just a little expression of surprise – he asked, "Are you?"

I shook my head. "It was just a misunderstanding, Larry. Maddie and I . . . we were once . . ."

Larry patted me on the shoulder. "I understand, Wes. Sometimes, women can just be so . . . ." He let the thought die.

224

I considered that perhaps no one would understand more than him. Larry and I were friends. We'd had drinks a couple times together, ogled the women at the bar. The fact that both of us were not single bothered him not at all. Women were there to be looked at, to Larry.

He hadn't blinked an eyelash when I'd showed up with Mary instead of Maddie last Thanksgiving. Larry, who had once changed women like socks, held no grudge against me for changing my mind about which one of his daughters I wanted to be with then, and he didn't now.

He would worry about Maddie's injuries, and if Mary was dead, her father would be devastated, as any father would be. But he wouldn't blame it on me, not like her mother did. Whatever had been going on between Maddie and me – and I could tell from the look on Larry's face that he didn't believe there had just been a misunderstanding. Just such a misunderstanding had led to his own divorce, once upon a time. But regardless if he thought I was two-timing my wife, Larry didn't blame any of it on me. We were all adults, these things happened, sometimes partners got switched. He would never understand Mary's tragic overreaction to it. But Larry Rearden understood that a man's changing his mind happened sometimes.

I wondered if I would ever tell him that Mary hadn't jumped, hadn't dragged Maddie over with her. I wondered if the stigma of suicide was better or worse than the tragedy of attempted murder and accidental death, if they didn't find Mary alive. I wondered if I would ever tell Larry that I'd seen Mary shove Maddie, and that Maddie had grabbed her sister, trying not to fall backwards, but in the end, they had both gone over. It hadn't been depression over the discovery of her sister's betrayal that had led Mary to jump. She hadn't jumped at all. It had been revenge and it had been a push.

I doubted if Larry would understand a vengeful Mary any more than he would a depressed one. All the strong emotions inherent when relationships ended badly were lost on him. None of his had ever ended badly, at least as far as he was concerned. They'd just ended, and he'd moved on.

We'd all been like Larry, once – me, Drew. Just drifting through relationships from woman to woman – meetings, hook-ups, break-ups, make-ups, final break-ups. Then I'd met Maddie, lost her, found her again. Drew had Connie. Even Larry wasn't like Larry too much anymore – he might still ogle the women, but I'd never known him to talk to a single one of them. He had Joanna now. But he would never blame Mary's suicide on me – if it turned out she really was dead – just because he thought I was indecisive about which sister I wanted.

Women's reaction to relationship problems – even his own daughter's – were not something that Larry considered too much.

Felicia came in, and Debbie, and Jon. They comforted Larry, gazed in through the large glass window at her mother, staring at the wall. They each went in and said a few words to her. They hugged me, looked searchingly at me. But none of them asked me why. Eventually they left.

Larry stood in the hall beside me silently as the time crawled by, waiting for his broken daughter to be out of surgery, wondering what had become of her twin. At dawn, Officer Evans walked through the double doors at the end of the hall. I could tell from the look on his face, and I felt the hot tears well up again. But again, my tears weren't for Mary. They were for Maddie, and for their parents, for Felicia and Debbie and Jon, for anyone who would mourn for Mary, who would feel her loss. My tears were for anyone who would hear the suicide story, and ask themselves if they could've stopped her.

Only Maddie and I knew what she really was: a conniving bitch. Jason's footage had proved it to me, not to mention her murderous rage, her attempt to kill her sister. I would not miss her.

Evans said softly, "Mr. Thomerville, we've found your wife." He looked at her father, then back at me again. "They pulled her from the river a little while ago. She's . . . deceased. I'm sorry." I nodded, sunk into one of the plastic chairs that lined the hall. I looked down, watched my tears hit the patterned linoleum floor. Larry walked slowly into the waiting room to break the news to her mother.

"If there's anything I can do," the young cop said. He looked even younger than he had earlier, and again I wondered why they made a kid deliver such devastating news. "If there's anything you need . . . you have my card."

I told him thanks, shook his hand. He looked at me helplessly. "I'm sorry for your loss," he said, then walked slowly back up the hall.

I watched Larry tell his ex-wife that their daughter was dead. I watched her sob, put her face in her hands. I watched her embrace her ex-husband, saw her glare hatefully over his shoulder at me. I was just a philandering son of a bitch to Leslie, cut from the same cloth as her ex-husband, as all men. I looked away, accepting her rebuke.

After a while, they came out of the waiting room. They didn't hold hands, didn't lean on each other for support, and I pitied Leslie then. All of us had somebody to comfort us, to hold us while we cried. Larry had Joanna, and I would have Maddie when she recovered. Everyone had someone but Leslie. She looked at me with hatred again and said,

"If it's all right with you, Wes, I'd like to . . . make the . . . arrangements."

It would certainly be all right with me – it was bad enough that I was gonna have to endure a funeral, the condolences of all Mary's friends. I was gonna have to play the disbelieving, grieving husband of a suicide – when all along I knew that Mary had tried to kill her sister. The only reason that Mary had gone in the river at all was because she'd been a little too close when she pushed Maddie.

So Leslie was more than welcome to make the arrangements.

I nodded silently, reached into my pocket and handed her Evans's card. He would know where they'd brought Mary. Leslie and Larry could shoulder the burden of that awfulness to come – they could go identify the body. They could handle the arrangements. My only concern was with the sister that was still alive, the one that I loved. I suddenly wished for them to just be gone, to follow Evans down the hall and out the doors. I wanted to go sit by myself and wait for Maddie to get out of surgery.

After another heartbeat, my wish was granted. Leslie just walked silently away – there was nothing left for her to say to me, now was there? The trifling man that had drove her daughter to suicide? What could she possibly have to say to me? Larry hugged me again, then followed her down the hall.

Hours passed. I sat in the waiting room and performed the necessary acts that had to be done, even in the face of death and tragedy. I called my boss – he offered condolences, told me to take as much time as I needed. I called the people that cared about Maddie – Gordy, the guys from the band. They rushed to the hospital, stood around helplessly for a while, eventually left.

Everyone that called themselves Mary's friends already knew.

The day passed, and still I sat in the waiting room. Other families came in, waiting for their loved ones to be out of surgery. Larry came back to have me sign some document – it said I was allowing Mary's body to be released into her parents' hands, allowing them to *make the arrangements*. We cried again together. Then Larry also left.

A doctor came in – Dr. Hawkins – he was young, just like the cop. He told me that Maddie was in post-op, and it would still be several hours before she would be awake, before she could have visitors.

"Since she's going to sleep for a while," he said gently, "why don't you go home and get some rest yourself?"

I took his advice. I went back to Maddie's apartment and collapsed on her bed. The exhaustion of the whole ordeal – the injury to the woman I loved, the death of her sister; the pain and grief of their friends and family – had taken it out of me more than I realized. I slept till five o'clock Sunday night, when Drew pounded on the door.

We embraced, and he said, "Maddie's out of surgery, but they wouldn't let me in to see her. Her mom was in there with her for a while, said she hadn't woke up yet. She told me to tell you that the service'll be on Tuesday."

I winced. "So soon?"

Drew shrugged. "I don't know what to say about that. I don't know anything about those kinds of things." Anyone else would've said they were sorry about Mary, but not Drew. He wasn't sorry any more than I was.

We went back to the hospital. Maddie was in a room with a large glass window, and we stood in the hallway, looking at her still form on the bed. She looked very young; almost as young as the poor cop that had been forced to deliver all the bad news, as young as the doctor I'd spoken with. There were scrapes on her forehead, braces and bandages on her arm and leg. Tubes, IVs.

Drew said softly, "What about Mary, Wes?"

I shrugged. "Her mom told you. The service is on Tuesday."

"I meant . . . did you . . . go? Did you see . . .?"

I shook my head.

Drew blanched. "Then how do you know . . . has Maddie been awake at all? Before the surgery? Has she said anything?"

I shook my head again. Drew looked through the window again, licked his lips nervously. He touched my arm so I'd look him in the eye. "How do you know that's Maddie, Wes?"

"What are you talking about? Of course it's Maddie!"

"How do you know, Wes?" Sorrow and a kind of fear creased his face. "You said half her clothes were gone . . . how do you know that's her? You said they went over together . . . maybe you saved the wrong–"

"I know that's Maddie in there, Drew!"

"But how do you know?" he insisted softly. "What if it's . . ." Drew couldn't finish the awful thought.

I realized that I didn't know. I'd only assumed, only wished. I'd saved the twin that I wanted to save. But what if I was wrong? I couldn't tell them apart when I was standing right next to them, talking to them, making love to them – I surely couldn't tell in the throes of an icy, black, river rescue.

They were identical. As it had been amply demonstrated to me, the only way to tell them apart for sure was to observe which hand they used. Maddie's left arm was broken in two places, there were pins and maybe a plate in it – she wouldn't be using her left hand for a while.

"I'll know when she wakes up. I'll know as soon as she says my name."

But would I, though? If the twin in the bed was Mary, she would wake up to find all the doctors and nurses calling her by her sister's name. They only thought she was Maddie because I'd told them that she was. What if she saw the hope in my eyes – what if she decided to pretend that she was Maddie? She'd done it to me before, when I first came back to town. She'd let me whine and cry and apologize and beg for forgiveness, then she'd let me make love to her. I hadn't had a clue – they looked so much alike – I hadn't even suspected that she wasn't Maddie.

It wasn't until I got up the next morning. I looked for a sheet to cover up my sleeping woman, the woman that had forgiven my so thoroughly for my dumb-ass mistake. I found one in the hall closet, but then I'd peeked in Maddie's room, found it empty. I'd suspected then, but I still didn't know – there was no way I could tell from just looking at the woman asleep on the couch. I didn't know it wasn't Maddie until I found out that the woman I'd just slept with was right-handed.

What if it was Mary in there? What if she woke up, discovered my error? What if she decided to pretend she was Maddie, to punish me? What is she let me take her back to Maddie's house, help her convalesce, talk about our plans for the future? What if she waited, bided her time, healed – what if she waited until things were back to normal again, what if she waited until after we'd had sex again – before revealing that she had duped me, that my Maddie was dead, and she was just conniving, bitch Mary?

If someone had walked by just then, they would've been shocked at the way Drew and I were staring into the room. Gone was the sorrow, the concern – Drew and I stared at the still figure on the bed like she was a monster, a zombie, a sleeping vampire risen from the dead.

"Fingerprints," Drew whispered at last.

"They're not going to fingerprint her, Drew! She just got out of surgery for Christ's sake! She's unconscious! What would her parents say?"

"Not her," Drew said, his voice still not above a whisper. "The other one. The . . . the body." I looked at him. "It's the only way, Wes." He nudged me, nodded down the hall. "Here comes the doctor. Ask him about it."

I cleared my throat. Feeling like some kind of ghoul, I asked Dr. Hawkins if I could have a word with him. He stopped, looked at me expectantly. When I didn't say anything, he looked at Drew.

"Here's the thing, Doc," Drew said. "That might not be Maddie Rearden in there."

Dr. Hawkins eyebrows went up in very unprofessional amazement. He looked at me, then back at Drew.

"They both went off that bridge, Doc. Maddie and her sister. They're twins. One of them is dead, and the other one . . ." he gestured through the window. "Wes thought he saved Maddie . . . but maybe he was wrong."

"When she wakes up, she'll tell us who she is."

"Well, we were kinda hopin', Doc . . ." Drew wheedled. "We don't want to wait until she wakes up. We thought you might be able to . . . have her sister . . . the body . . . fingerprinted."

Again the doctor's eyebrows shot up. "Are you out of your mind?"

"It would be a terrible mistake for the hospital to make," Drew suggested. "The grieving parents, the grieving friends, the grieving husband." He nodded at me. "All mourning the wrong sister, maybe even burying the wrong sister, all because the hospital failed to make a positive ID."

"I wasn't the attending–"

"But we've brought this to your attention now, so it would only be right if you looked into it, and–"

"I'll make a few phone calls," young Dr. Hawkins said. "Wait right here." He turned and strode off down the hall. I heard him mumble, "Fucking *twins,*" under his breath.

"Thanks, Doc!" Drew called after him. He grinned at me.

Dr. Hawkins waved over his shoulder and was gone out the double doors.

Drew's grin faded as he looked through the glass again at whichever Rearden sister lay still sedated in the hospital bed. "You're sure you can't tell them apart?"

I shrugged. "Not like this. When she wakes up . . . I guess I can interrogate her, ask her things only Maddie would know . . . but even then . . ."

"She could claim she hit her head, doesn't remember," Drew said darkly.

We stood there in silence for what seemed like a long time. When the double doors at the end of the hall banged open, we both jumped.

Dr. Hawkins said, "The body's already been taken to the funeral home. It's out of my hands, gentleman. If you want to clarify who that young woman really is, you're going to have to call her parents, get *them* to have her sister's body fingerprinted." He considered me with a look of mild disgust. "I wouldn't recommend it, though. Haven't the parents been through enough? Just be patient. She'll tell us who she is when she wakes up."

****

I was not alone with . . . with whoever it was when she awakened. The good doctor had also informed her parents that their daughter would soon be awake, and they sat on either side of her bed, peering at her. Leslie went out of her way to make it uncomfortable for me to be in there with them, with her silent, hateful stares, so I stood out in the hall with Drew and waited.

Dr. Hawkins passed us once, looked in the window, consulted his watch. "It won't be long now," he said, as if he was waiting for the ball to drop on New Year's Eve. He entered the room and told Larry to ring the nurse and have him paged the moment she opened her eyes.

And at last her eyes fluttered open. She looked at her mom, looked at her dad, looked down at the braces on her arm and leg. The very first thing she said was, "Where's Wes?"

Larry and Leslie looked through the window, but they only saw Drew standing there. I was already in the room. "I'm right here, Maddie," I said. I stood at the foot of her bed. I wanted to take her hand, wanted to tell her that I loved her, but her mom and dad were blocking my path to getting any closer to her.

She smiled weakly at me. It was Maddie. I was sure of it. Almost one hundred percent sure.

Leslie said, "The doctor's on his way, honey." She gestured at all the tubes and wires, braces and IVs. "He'll explain what's going on. Lie still till he gets here."

And then Dr. Hawkins was standing in the doorway, and there was just not enough room in there for all of us, so I came out into the hall again. He looked curiously at me as I passed him. I nodded, smiled.

"Ah, Maddie," he said. "I'm Dr. Hawkins. You took quite the little tumble! How are you feeling right now?"

In the hall, Drew looked expectantly, fearfully at me. "Is it Maddie?"

"The first thing she said was, 'Where's Wes?' Would Mary say that?"

231

Drew looked through the window, but the doctor was blocking his view. "So you don't know then?"

"It's her. I'm sure of it."

Drew looked doubtfully at me. "You don't sound sure."

"Wait till her parents and Dr. Feelgood leave. Then we'll go in there, talk to her. Mary doesn't really even know you. Between the two of us, I know we'll be able to tell for sure."

After what seemed like forever, the doctor emerged at last, followed by Leslie and Larry. "She seems like she's gonna be okay, Wes," Larry said. "The doctor said everything looks great. She's asking for you."

I thanked Larry and went into the room. Maddie was still dazed, and blinked expressionlessly at me. I sat in the chair next to the bed, took her undamaged right hand. We looked at each other silently for a long time. Drew came in and stood at the foot of the bed. Maddie glanced up at him, then back at me, still expressionless.

Finally, I said, "Tell me a story, Maddie." I smiled at her, and after a heartbeat, she smiled back. She glanced at Drew again, and I was sure I saw a blush rise up her neck and stain her pale cheek. She smiled shyly at him and he smiled back, then she looked at me again.

"What kind of a story do you want to hear, Wes?" she asked.

I was sure it was Maddie then – the blush confirmed it. She'd been embarrassed that I'd told Drew what she'd written about me – the blush confirmed that it was her. I turned and grinned at Drew.

"I'll come back in and see you in a little while, Maddie," he told her. "When you're done with this guy."

I stood up and kissed her carefully, gingerly on the mouth, told her I loved her.

"And I love you, Wes," she said softly. "I've always loved you."

I was sure it was Maddie then, because she'd said almost precisely these same words to me before.

Yes, I was sure it was Maddie, my own true love.

I was almost one hundred percent sure.

.

Also by LM Foster

A Passing Resemblance
Contrariwise – A Tale of Twins
Corvino
Crypsis
Duck Feet
Peter's Sisters

Two Green Keys:
Two Green Keys
Adapted for the Screen

One Wilde Ride Trilogy:
Part One: It Might Have Been
Part Two: An Exceptional Boy
Part Three: What Should Never Be

Stars and Guitars:
Talk To a Movie Star
Where The Guitars Play

Tom and Wiley:
This Carnival of Strange
Wiley Royce
Generally Recognized as Safe
Wiley Royce Versus The Martians

www.ingramcontent.com/pod-product-compliance
Lightning Source LLC
Chambersburg PA
CBHW070610130626
46556CB00001B/333